Jim Sutherland's hands tightened on Shalimar's reins. The buckskin snorted when Jim half-turned in the saddle to look at Mescal, his wife. Even the weeks since their quiet wedding hadn't fully convinced him that the child-turned-woman who had been adopted by his folks after her parents died could really be his. A quiver of pain ran through him. If only ...

Gary Dale spent his childhood reading the novels of Zane Grey and vowed one day to write westerns. *VOICES IN THE DESERT* and *ECHOES IN THE VALLEY* are the realization of that childhood vow.

PROUD HERITAGE SERIES ✦ 2

ECHOES In The VALLEY

GARY DALE

BARBOUR BOOKS
Westwood, New Jersey

Typesetting by
Typetronix, Inc., Cape Coral, FL

90 91 92 93 94 5 4 3 2 1

FOR
Lauraine Snelling,
devoted supporter
and friend

PROUD HERITAGE SERIES ✦ 2

ECHOES In The VALLEY

GARY DALE

PART I
Apache

1

The debt had been paid — in full.

Apache sagged in the gray stallion's saddle, touched King's flanks sharply with his heel, and ignored Carter's yell, "Come back. You're hurt. We'll . . ."

The disembodied voice dwindled. The little group of men who had willingly laid aside prejudice and ridden with a half-breed in search of justice vanished into the murky predawn. Agonizing miles later Apache slowed his mount and stopped. He had put enough distance between himself and the posse to risk a full examination of his wound.

He slid to the ground, dropped King's reins forward over his head. "Stand." The big gray snorted and obeyed.

Apache pulled his bloodstained buckskin shirt over his head, ignoring the early spring morning chill that struck his heated skin. Then he gritted his teeth, felt the small hole high in his chest, and grunted. No lump of lead remained under the skin, nor had he expected it.

"Coward Comstock's bullet went on through," he muttered. "Not straight, though, or it would have hit a lung. Must have angled." Probing fingers confirmed his suspicions and loosed a fresh rush of blood from a little below his shoulder blade and under his left arm.

"Lost a lot of blood." Apache pressed hard with his left hand and was rewarded with a lessening of the flow. Suddenly dizzy, sweat streaked his dark, high-boned face. "Maybe too much." He swayed and laughed, the hoarse sound shattered the quiet morning. "What's one more dead Apache?"

In the space of a heartbeat Jim Sutherland's face flared into memory, then Jon's. Warmth flowed through Apache's veins. He had been far more than that to the Sutherland Sons of Thunder.

His lips twisted. Standing there remembering didn't change things. Even though his lung hadn't been hit, this kind of bullet wound could become infected and send raging fever through a man until he gladly closed his eyes in death to escape the torment.

For a single moment he considered turning King back toward Daybreak and the Sutherland ranch — the only real home he had ever had. The next instant he revolted. "If I die, it will not be in the white man's way. But can we make it, King?"

1

Long, desolate miles stretched ahead of him, but the stronghold of refuge hidden behind the waterfall shimmered, tantalized. His saddlebags held food, blankets, bullets. Hours before he had secretly packed them, knowing that no matter what happened he could never return. No matter what kind of skunk Radford Comstock had been, he was white. And no matter how much the Daybreak posse backed Apache, his Indian blood would make it impossible for him to be found innocent if he killed the white skunk, as he expected he would. Jim must not have blood on his hands when he went home to Mescal.

Strange, after all the years of injustice and persecution, why couldn't he accept it? Why did the fires of hatred against the whites burn brighter with each new incident? Most of all, why did the God the Sutherlands talked about let a man be born into such a world?

Apache's strong right hand fumbled with the saddlebags and found what he sought: a clean shirt he could use to pad his wounds. He caught one side of it with his teeth and awkwardly tore a small strip to cover the small hole where the bullet had entered his chest. Next he ripped a much larger chunk of material and stuffed it against his side. Finally, he tore out the sleeves, tied them into a crude knot, and wrapped them over his chest and under his arm to hold the bandages in place. Later he would seek out the healing herbs and leaves known to all of his race and use them to fight infection. For now, he had done all he could.

Water from his canteen served to relieve his parched throat and soak his roughly bandaged body. Cupping his hands, Apache let King lap up a small amount. "It will be up to you," he told the powerful horse. "You're desert bred and trained. If anything can get us where we need to go, it's you."

He swung back into the saddle, reeled a bit, then breathed in great gulps of cool air that helped to clear his senses. "King," Apache's voice rang in the stillness. "I give you my word. If the fever comes, if I know I am dying, I will set you free. You can go home."

He lifted the reins, noted the daylight creeping through the heavily clouded sky, swerved from the traveled trail, and headed north and east, into the eternity of miles and pain that lay ahead.

Weary hours later they stopped near a small pool of water. King nickered and lipped his fill. Apache drank until he could hold no more, refilled his canteen, and unconsciously thanked whatever gods he had for the spring rain that had filled the depression.

His exposed body felt cold, yet already an inner heat warmed him. Even riding in the cool day had not prevented what he knew could destroy him. The leaves and herbs he had gathered and pressed against the wounds would take time, if they worked at all. Just washing out the stained bandages and whole shirt after he and King stopped drinking sapped Apache's magnificent strength.

Back in the saddle after forcing himself to eat a few bites of dried meat, the feverish man faced things squarely. King raised his head when Apache spoke, pricking his ears. Few who travel the desert remain totally silent in the face of the eternal silence that stretches on forever. Apache and King shared a comradeship common to men and beasts who struggle against the forces of nature, and Apache found it easier to talk to the big gray than to most humans.

Pine gave way to cedar as the lone rider slowly guided King on until evening shadows lengthened and darkness crouched, waiting to swallow them. Still they went on, more by instinct than by sight. At last, Apache's iron will melted to the fever, and he almost fell from the saddle. Dirt and blood and sweat mingled into stoic knowledge and bitter pride. He could go no farther this night, but they had reached the place he sought. A small dry cave long known to him in his solitary wanderings offered protection from the chilling night wind. Sparce grass provided graze for King.

It took Apache's last ounce of energy to build a small fire, make a broth from dried beef, force himself to eat it, then stumble to the cave and wrap himself in blankets while King contentedly munched outside. Yet sleep eluded him although his tortured body cried out for rest. Instead, a series of scenes in their entirety haunted his mind, drove spears of red-hot pain into him. When sleep at last claimed him, the scenes continued, starting with the moment Jim burst into the Daybreak saloon backed by his father, Carter, and the rest. No, even before then. At the moment when Jim turned to him in the velvet-black night and asked, "Can we keep it from being a slaughter?"

"Perhaps. It all depends on Comstock. Wait here!" Apache crept away from the others, swiftly ran to the sheriff's office. Empty. Back to the posse and the saloon. Only a few horses patiently waited by the low building. Good. The fewer present, the more chance of avoiding a massacre.

A second scouting, this time of the saloon itself. Through the dirty window Apache's keen eyes located those inside: Comstock, six of his outlaws, a bartender who might or might not interfere, and two town drunks who would be harmless to either side.

"Stay outside the window until your eyes can stand the light," Apache whispered to Jim. A few moments, then, "Now!"

A board creaked under Jim's heavy foot when he forged ahead and through the doors, a revolver in each hand. "Up with them!"

Apache shoved his way to Jim's side.

"Well, if it ain't the preacher!" Comstock said, an ugly smile on his face.

"Not the preacher." Jim flipped his revolver in the way only he could do.

The craven man stared at Jim and damned himself with, "I hung you!"

'You hung my brother — for a crime not even I was in on.'' Jim's accusation tried, convicted, and sentenced Comstock in one line.

"We could hang you right here . . . just as soon not have your dirty blood on this town's conscience . . . get out!"

Thundering hooves down an inky street. Jim's triumphant shout, "Not a shot fired," followed by a single explosion.

Poised for pursuit, reassured by Jim's, "I'm okay," Apache galloped after the fleeing outlaws, only dimly aware of shouts and the steady beat of the posse's horses close behind him.

Night had swallowed Comstock and the others. The few moments earned by the surprise attack on Jim gave the outlaws enough of a start to hamper the determined posse. Sheer fury at Comstock and at himself for not disarming the enemy spurred Apache on. Once King stumbled and Apache slid from the saddle to check on the grand animal's condition. After a snort, King paced without limping, and Apache leaped back into the saddle.

The pause had given Carter and his men time to overtake Apache, and Carter's voice grated in the dark. "Should have hanged them right there. We'll do it when we get them."

Apache's fierce anger leaped in anticipation. Then he said, "No. Jim doesn't want killing. We'll find who fired and take him back for trial. The others will never come back. Not after this."

Carter swore again but reluctantly admitted, "Guess you're right. It's Jim's game, the way I see it. But it ain't the way I'd play it."

"Neither would I." Apache's low whisper was cold. "Careful, I hear horses. Get down and follow me."

Single file, the little band of men bellied over the uneven ground, across needle-strewn forest floor until Apache gripped Carter's shoulder in warning. His barely perceptible whisper passed from man to man in equally quiet orders.

"Now!"

"Hands up," Carter yelled, and Apache burst into a tiny clearing where dark shapes still sat their winded horses, giving them a quick rest before heading out.

A volley of profanity split the predawn air.

"Enough," Carter ordered.

"Cover them. I'll check their guns." Apache glided from outlaw to outlaw, flipped open their gun chambers, and spilled bullets to the ground. He deliberately left Comstock for last, knowing what he'd find. "None of these has been fired," he told the posse just before he stepped toward Comstock.

"Vamoose." Carter waved the livid-faced men away. "If any of you ever come back, It will be shoot on sight."

Echoes of horses' hooves rose and died.

"Now, Mister Comstock," Carter said. The posse's guns steadied.

Apache turned to the rustler and approached him. Wild-eyed coward that he was, Comstock quivered, then reached for his gun. Hatred overcame his fear, and Comstock shot.

Apache staggered but jerked Comstock from his horse before Carter could fire. "Now you'll hang," he hissed between teeth clenched against pain and weakness. He pinned Comstock's gun arm against his side.

Carter flipped his rope over a limb.

With incredible strength, Comstock wrenched free from Apache, turned the gun, and shot — not Apache, but himself. His blood mingled with Apache's as he slid to the ground.

Panting, Apache stared at his enemy, then at the gaping posse. "I reckon Jim won't care if I take King." He forced himself to run the short distance to where the horses stood waiting, Carter and the others right behind him.

"Where do you think you're goin', you crazy Indian?" Carter bellowed as he followed.

Apache grinned, knowing it wasn't a curse. He gathered the reins, sprang to the saddle. "Take Comstock back."

"But what am I goin' to tell Jim?" Carter protested.

"Tell him . . ." Apache hesitated, conscious of growing pain and his need to get away. "Tell him the debt is paid."

Apache sagged in the gray stallion's saddle, touched King's flanks sharply with his heels, and rode into the murky predawn.

Apache jerked, sat up. His entire body felt on fire. The vivid nightmare slowly faded into reality — a cave, blood-stained bandages where his wounds had reopened from his tossing. He wet the bandages from the canteen, pulled them from the wounds without flinching, and applied pressure, then added more of the herbs and leaves that were his only hope. The cold canteen water in his feverish mouth and throat relieved him more. He stumbled to the cave's entrance and whistled for King, noticing how black the night had grown. Which night? He had no way to tell.

A soft nicker followed by the stamping of hooves preceded King's approach.

"Good." Apache kept his left arm close to his body and stroked King's tangled mane with his right hand, combing the coarse hair with his fingers. "I don't have to worry about you deserting, do I, King?"

King whinnied and stamped again.

Even his slight effort had cost Apache. Weakness forced him down, and he crawled back to his blankets, again adjusting his crude sling. As long as the fever forced his tormented body to sleep, the wounds must remain covered. Once he could stay awake, the clean high Kaibab plateau air would do more to heal him than all the measures he could take.

Time after time he fell into a stupor of sleep, only to rouse, repeating with cracked lips, "Must set King free if I can't make it. Must send him home."

Hard on the thought came the knowledge that he must not free King until every hope vanished. Once the big gray stallion swept into the yard of the Triple S, nothing on earth would keep Jim and Matthew Sutherland, even Mescal, from coming to find him.

"Never!" Fierce pride rose in him, temporarily drowning out his pain and fever. "Wounded animals find a hole, a cave, a shelter away from their kind and all others. They die alone or heal after a time. I will do the same. But if only I could get to the waterfall."

His delirious mind seized on the waterfall, that shimmering cascade hiding the long tunnel through a rocky mountain that opened into a valley of incredible beauty. Hour after miserable hour Apache forced his brain to picture the waterfall, the coolness and spray where he had stood with water cleansing his body of trail grime and sweat. It helped to picture it. There was lush grass and plentiful game, except in the hottest summer months when scorching winds blew and yellowed the grass, forcing the game to seek feed elsewhere. The sun in the smiling blue skies soaked into a man with its healing warmth, except when those skies burned brassy and tortured with relentless heat, intensified by the red rock walls.

Apache's body twitched. Sweat poured. Had he been mistaken? Had spring become summer? Was he trapped in the protean valley that offered friendship and betrayal, comfort and misery?

Yet, through all the suffering, the knowledge that he had been true and paid his debt — first to Jon, then to Jim — never left him. At times it was all that saved his sanity; that and the ever-present memory of his promise to free King.

Now and then Apache speculated in his lucid moments. Was the shot that hit Jim really harmless, or had he shouted that to release the posse? What if he lay dead, the way his beloved twin lay dead, both from Radford Comstock's hand?

Apache groaned at the thought. Visions of a broken Matthew Sutherland, a haunted Abigail, a Mescal whose face grew thin and bitter, whose shadowed eyes enlarged, all blended into a wavering dream. One by one they rose to accuse him. He could have saved them so much if he'd tracked and killed Radford Comstock months before. Why had he let Matthew, Jon, and Abigail hold him back? In spite of his hatred of all things white, had he — a despised half-breed Apache — weakened through the Gospel the Sutherlands lived rather than preached? Had he faltered in his determination for revenge because the white God of the Bible began to seem real to him?

Most of all, had an impossible hope been born when Jon gave his life for his brother — then nurtured when that same brother, who hated his captor,

Apache, refused to leave him to die in the valley? How many times had the story of the Jesus who died so others could live crept into Apache's disbelieving heart to seek lodging? Each time, it became harder to uproot.

What if it were true?

What if this Jesus hadn't just died for the whites, but for all? The Sutherlands should know. They read their Bibles daily. They opened their hearts and their home to all — even a fallen half-Apache."

"No one could care that much!" Apache writhed. Fresh pain attacked, leaving him senseless, prey to more nightmares, more reliving of the past, and to more questions, especially the turning question: What if it were true? It hammered into his brain until he felt pulled apart.

2

"Charley." The soft call echoed down the years.

Apache forced his eyes open. His body leaped to respond. Wrenching pain gripped him, and he fell back to the cave floor, unconsious of the present, forced to relive the past he had thrust from his mind a thousand times.

"Charley."

The young half-breed ran to his mother, noting the ever-present sadness in her eyes. "You called for me?"

Running Deer nodded. Her once beautiful dusky face still held traces of the loveliness that had attracted and won Charles Campbell's heart. Yet Charley's keen eyes, trained to follow the eagle until he vanished into the distance and to spot even the most motionless animal, saw more than beauty. Instead of growing fat like many women of the tribe, Running Deer's slender body and hollowed face became thinner all the time.

The beginning of fear touched Charley. One quick glance at the carefully placed food portions brought a quick protest. "I will not eat all that while you . . ." He pointed scornfully to the pitifully small amount of food before Running Deer. "While you do not eat enough to feed a small one."

His mother gently smiled. "It is all I want, my son. Now eat."

Something in her steady gaze made the rebellious boy eat, although it choked him.

When he finished, he demanded, "Why? Why must I eat when there is litte food and you go without?"

A wave of sadness marred the dark watching eyes. "A day will come when you must be strong."

"I *am* strong," Charley boasted. He lifted a wiry arm. "Do I not defend myself against our village boys well? Can I not run with the horses and leap like the deer?"

"Oh, yes, and I am proud." His mother's eyes brightened, then a strange hopelessness dulled them again. "And yet, you must become stronger, wiser, more cunning. Our runners bring word that the white enemies are near. They will come soon, and when they do . . ."

Charley leaped to his feet, his bare chest heaving. Hatred filled his face

8

and contorted it almost beyond recognition. "When they do, I will kill them and protect you."

Fear replaced Running Deer's sadness. "No! My son, you must promise. When the white soldiers come, you are to flee. You must hide and not be seen."

"Never!" It rang through the still twilight until those gathered around nearby small fires turned curious gazes their way.

"Sit down and be still," Running Deer ordered.

Trained to obedience yet despising himself for it, Charley sank to the ground. "Why must I listen to a woman?" He stared straight into his mother's face. "I am a warrior, not a child. What do women know of enemies and fighting?" He angrily scuffed the hard-packed earth with his heel, which was toughened by miles of desert races with the other boys.

"You must learn many things before you will become a man," his mother told him quietly. The tone of her voice prevented Charley from a quick answer.

"It is no good to fight the white soldiers. When one dies, a hundred more come." Running Deer's farseeing eyes gazed into the future. "Even our chiefs know this. The day will come when the Apache will live peacefully with the whites or be scattered as the desert sands in a storm, to be no more." She raised her hand when Charley opened his mouth to speak. "These things I know."

The finality of her words held her son back, but only for a moment. Then he tightened his lips into a straight line and hissed, "How do you know more than our medicine man, more than our chiefs, when you are only a woman? You say our chiefs believe this. Why, then, have they not told us?"

A gray shadow crossed her face. "They would rather die than surrender to the whites as other tribes have already done."

Charley sat up straight and crossed his arms in regal dignity. A parting ray of sunlight sneaked through the dusk and settled on his determined face. "Then I too will die."

"You must not." The words fell from Running Deer's lips, small stones into the boy's stream of revolt. "You are half white. You can make a life with them."

"As you did?" His face gleamed cruelly as the darkness fell.

For many minutes the woman's gaze pierced the shadows. Charley silently waited, half-glad, half-ashamed at his thrust.

"If I had been wiser, things might have been different."

The boy leaned forward, arms at his side in surprise. His mother seldom referred to the time she had spent away from the Apache village. Would the silence of years now be broken? Although he hated the whites, deep inside he had a longing to know of the man who had fathered him. Perhaps it lived there because of the taunts of the Apache boys.

"Charley, Charley. What kind of name is that?" Young Gray Wolf had thrown at him years before.

"A *white* name," Little Eagle had sneered.

"White, white, white. You are white." The circle of menacing boys had closed in on him.

"I am Apache," Charley had shrilled, fists and feet and butting head vanquished the others. His very fury changed him to a wild animal with all the strength needed to survive.

The boys had scattered, with Charley hard on their heels. Yet the taunting had never ended, although his blood-brother foes carefully kept out of reach.

Some good came from those early persecutions. Charley had forced his weary body on miles after others his age gave up on the trail. He ran and climbed and practiced with every ounce of sinew and muscle, until no boy in the tribe could come close to his ability in running and riding and shooting.

To balance the good, an abnormal hatred of the whites changed the boy's attitude from tribal enmity to a personal war against the whole white race. Only in these feelings could Charley vent his anger against Charles Campbell, who had deserted Running Deer and their son years before.

Now he waited — hesitantly, eagerly.

Blue dusk shrouded Running Deer. She pulled her worn blanket close around her body. Her face lay in shadow.

Time passed and she did not speak.

Charley could wait no more. "Tell me." He had no need to say more, nor could he have uttered what trembled on his sun-cracked lips.

"You know your father's name. Charles Campbell. He settled in a small valley where grass grew tall and springs gave water. After a time he built a trading post in a time of peace. He treated Indians and whites fairly." Running Deer's voice lowered until Charley strained to hear her.

"I saw him when I rode past the trading post. A rough man, bearded and ugly, called words I didn't understand, then followed me into the forest."

Charley's blood raced. Had his father been that ugly, bearded man? His hands clenched until his nails bit into his palms. He wanted to cry out for her to stop.

"The man's horse outran my pony. Under a huge pine he caught up with me and jerked me from the saddle. He tore my clothes, even though I fought. Drops of blood fell from his face where my fingernails drove deep, yet his hands gripped me and I knew I could not free myself." Running Deer's breath came in quick gasps, as if she fought all over again.

Charley's nerves screamed. A fresh wash of hatred turned the night as bloodred as the man's face had been.

"I fell. My enemy fell with me. Then a voice rang in the forest, a voice like thunder. 'Get up, Scoggins!' "

Relief left Charley dizzy. His mother's attacker hadn't been Charles Campbell.

"I will never forget," Running Deer whispered. "Scoggins released me. I fled to my pony and mounted. Yet I could not leave. Fear for the white man who had saved me was greater than my fear of Scoggins.

" 'Stay out of my business,' Scoggins yelled.

" 'Dirty business like this can inflame the whole area,' the other man said.

"Scoggins's eyes looked red. Couldn't my rescuer see his danger? Then Scoggins spat on the ground and said, 'Want her for yourself, do you, Campbell?' His face became even uglier. 'Wait 'til people around here find out you're an Injun-lover?'

"The other white man's face turned to lightning. *Crack!* Scoggins fell and lay still. Something inside me burst. I hoped he was dead, but I didn't think he was. I couldn't move, even when my pony snorted and backed away.

"The white man called Campbell looked up from the man on the ground. He spoke in my language. 'What are you called?' he asked.

"I could not speak at first. Then I thought of what he had done for me and said, 'I am Running Deer.'

"He told me his name was Charles Campbell. Something in his eyes told me much more."

Charley slowly uncurled his fingers, which had been clenched until the knuckles shone white. His voice sounded harsh in the night. "If I had been there, I would have killed Scoggins."

Running Deer shook her head. "It would have done no good. Scoggins only did what many others would have."

"But not Charles Campbell?" The boy held his breath.

"No." The clear, direct answer satisfied him, and he breathed hard, remembering the fight in the forest.

Again Running Deer stayed silent a long time. Then she softly said, "I knew I must not go where Scoggins might be." She sighed. "I could not help it. I longed to see Charles Campbell, so I hid my pony in the forest many times and crept to the trading post. I thought no one saw me, but one did. A long time later Charles Campbell told how he watched me come like a wild thing, curious but afraid." She fell quiet. "One day, my son, you will know how it was with me and why I risked danger just to see the man who had become everything to me.

"Charles began leaving small gifts for me, and I knew he had seen me. He left ribbons, a mirror, a brush. I hugged them to myself. And then one day when the trading post lay empty in the sunlight, he called to me.

" 'Running Deer.'

"Terrified at being discovered, I fled — only to return the next day, and the next. Each day he called to me. I didn't answer. He never called when others were at the trading post. But one day, when the leaves of the aspen danced in the air, he called, 'Running Deer, will you be my wife?'

"For many days I did not go to the trading post. I hid in my secret place, but I could not forget what he had said. I looked at the braves in the tribe, those I had known since childhood. My father said I must soon go to one of them. I could not. All I could see was the difference between them and the brown-haired white man with eyes that matched the summer sky.

"I knew my father would send me away forever if he knew my heart. At last I could wait no more. I slipped away to my secret place by the trading post. Many small gifts waited for me. I knew how disappointed Charles Campbell must have been when I did not come.

"I waited and waited and waited. White men came and went from the trading post. Would they never be gone? Evening set the sky on fire. The trading post lay empty, except for Charles Campbell. Suddenly he stood before me. His eyes sought me in the grayness after the sunset. "Running Deer, will you be my wife?'

"He held out his hand. I stepped from my secret place and put my hand into his strong one, the same hand that had once struck down my enemy."

Charley crouched in the darkness, huddled in the blanket he had reached for without knowing he did it. Never had he felt pulled two ways, as he did now — pulled the way Little Eagle had pulled the wings of a small bird until Charles struck him down and the bird fell to the ground, already dead. Something inside him yearned to know the white father with the summer-sky eyes. Yet bitterness over the way he was treated in the Indian village warred with desire.

Running Deer sounded tired. "Charles Campbell did not just take me, my son. You must always remember that. We stood before a white man who married us in the white man's way. Charles Campbell said I could not be his wife unless we were blessed by his God. He said he wanted everyone to know he loved me, and after a long time, when you came, he proudly showed you to all who came to the trading post. As soon as you were old enough, he taught you to sit a pony. While I taught you our language, he taught you his. He said someday you would need to know, for you would walk two paths."

Charles could be still no longer. "Then why did he leave us? Why didn't he stay at the trading post? Why did we come back here, where I am hated and you are not welcome?" All the years of persecution and shame burst into the single, eternal cry, "Why?"

"He had no choice."

Charley felt the way he had when a pony had turned and kicked him in the stomach.

"Charles Campbell kept us until he knew we were in more danger at the trading post than in the Indian village."

"Why?"

"Scoggins never forgot. He came again and again to the trading post when Charles Campbell made trips to bring supplies. I had a rifle and knew how to shoot, but Charles Campbell said if I killed Scoggins — even when he attacked me — the other white men would do terrible things."

"He should have stayed with you, taken care of you!" Charley felt sick at the picture in his mind: his mother, protecting herself, then dragged away for killing a snake.

"He begged me to go away with him. He said we'd go to a different place, to a place where we could be left alone. But I could not." Once more her words fell like stones. "All he had worked for lay in the trading post. No one else wanted to buy it. They were afraid of the Apache. Peace had gone. Terrible things would come."

The sadness in his mother's voice hurt Charley more than any other part of the long story. "What did you do?"

"I told him I could not leave the land of my people. Then I falsely said I would think on what he said while he went for supplies. An hour after he went down the trail, I slipped away with you. I didn't know if my father would let me come to the village, but I prayed and tried to plan what to do if he turned me away. I decided I could not be truthful. If I told him Charles Campbell no longer wanted me and that I had brought you back so you could be Apache instead of white, my father might allow us to stay.

"All the miles to the village I made myself practice the lies I would tell. I believed the only way to help Charles Campbell was to do this. So when I faced my father I said, 'I want no more of the whites. I have come back.'

"For a long time I thought he would drive me away. Then he saw you. Pride came into his face. He had no other children or grandsons. We stayed."

"And Charles Campbell. What of him?"

Running Deer's story fell to a whisper. "Runners told that he had been hurt on the trail. A long time later they brought word that the trading post had been burned. Nothing remained but ashes. I have thought Scoggins set the fire — and told Charles Campbell we were in the building."

Charley's flesh crawled. "Then this man does not know we live?"

"No." Running Deer timidly touched her son's hand in the darkness. "It is best."

With all the hot blood of his age, Charley jerked his hand free. "Yes, it is best. If Charles Campbell had no more wisdom than to believe Scoggins, let him think we are dead. I am Apache, not white. You have called me the white name, but no more. I will be called Apache, not Charley. And when the whites come, I will join my brothers and kill them. If I die, it will be as Apache, not as the son of Charles Campbell."-

Yet the next instant the thought that would echo in his heart through everything that lay ahead came: *Who would I be, what would I be, if Running Deer had gone with Charles Campbell, the brave man who rescued her and married her in the white way and proudly showed his son to all?*

And for the first time another question planted itself deep in his mind: *What did the white God who Charles Campbell said must bless his marriage with Running Deer have to do with a half-Apache boy despised by both Indians and whites?*

3

Even the depths of fever and unconsciousnes couldn't keep Apache's magnificently developed body from shuddering on the cave floor when the nightmarish dreams changed. A long period of blankness preceded memories that came alive until Apache groaned in his stuper and beat his fists on the bloodstained blankets beneath him.

The day he had desperately tried to forget with the passing years dawned sullen. Bloodred streaks heralded a morning filled with fear. Dogs snarled. Women gathered their children close while they hurriedly snatched belongings, for word had come that the white soldiers lay waiting for daylight to attack. The red rocks Apache and his companions had climbed a hundred times frowned down at them, no longer friendly.

"Why did our runners not bring us word sooner?" Apache whispered to Running Deer.

"All were killed but Lame Wolf." Her busy fingers tied strong knots in the deerskin bag that carried extra clothing and a little food. "You saw him when he came."

Yes, Apache had seen Lame Wolf, too old to fight but too proud to remain in camp with the women and children. When he crawled back to warn them, his moccasins left a blood trail across the dried earth. He collapsed and moaned, "Go! The soldiers come."

A feeble wave of his hand toward the entrance to the small clearing sheltered by red rocks brought foam to his lips. "Big Eagle betrayed us."

The next moment Lame Wolf lay dead. Only the red dust stirred by his falling disturbed the village. Then a high wailing began.

"Stop!" Running Deer leaped to face the others with all the grace that had earned her the name she carried. "We must do as he says and go. Pack only what you can easily carry."

"What of the horses?" Apache asked.

She shook her head. "The soldiers know where we are." Contempt for a tribesman who would betray his people twisted her face, and she spat. "The soldiers will come with horses. Our hope is to scatter into the caves and canyons."

"I will watch the trail." Young Gray Wolf left his dead grandfather and ran back the way the old man had come. Something in his face stopped Apache from following.

"Get water," Running Deer ordered. Her flying fingers made short work of her task and she turned to help the others.

Apache raced toward the spring, wishing he had been with the braves, shivering at the coming of the soldiers. Carefully balancing himself so he wouldn't spill even one drop of his precious burden, he started back to the village. Long before he reached it, he heard shots and screams. He dropped his burden and ran as if the devil wind chased him. He burst into the thicket that partially screened the camp.

The morning sky had fulfilled her promise. Everywhere he looked, from rocks to sky to the village itself, bloodred stains and reflections faced him. Young Gray Wolf lay in a seeping pool, his mouth still open in a warning scream, his wild eyes fixed on his dead grandfather. Bodies of women and children who had scattered from the onslaught formed heaps where they had fallen. Others valiantly fought with sticks and rocks and the few rifles left in camp.

One of these was Running Deer.

"No!" Apache's protest lost itself in the din of running horses, the clash of swords, the haze of gunsmoke. He clenched his fists and beat against a branch that had caught his flying hair.

Then he saw the rough, bearded, ugly man who grabbed his mother by her long, still-beautiful hair. He caught the terror in her eyes and heard her scream in recognition, "Scoggins!"

The single word stopped Apache the way a bullet felled a deer. In the heartbeat of hesitation, a knife flashed. Scoggins laughed, a terrible, gloating sound. A moment later a surprised look crossed his ugly face. He clutched at his chest and fell, victim of some deadly shot from a little behind Apache.

Apache whirled, but before he could discover who had fired, something smashed into his head and he fell heavily, his lifeblood mingling with the red earth he loved.

An eternity later, Apache opened his eyes and struggled to sit up. Dizzy from the loss of blood and his long lapse into unconsciousness, at first he could not stand. His eyes would not focus. When they finally did, the first thing he noticed was darkness.

How could this be? Not a glimmer of light showed. Had he lain here senseless until nightfall?

He struggled to his feet and collapsed, too weak to think, only able to drag himself to the shelter of the thicket.

When he woke again, he lay wondering why he looked into a roof of leaves. Then the awful realization of the massacre sank into his brain. He crawled out of his frail shelter, sick but determined. His faltering steps skirted the dead with their faces to the sky, many frozen in expressions of horror. "Running Deer?" he called, as he had called so many times before.

This time no quiet voice called back.

Apache forced his feet toward the spot where she had been struck down. Unlike the others, her still face showed little expression. Had the recognition of Scoggins wiped fear from her and replaced it with the mask so often worn to hide her feelings, even from the son she loved?

Scoggins lay dead at her feet. He wore no uniform. A quick glance around showed that if soldiers had died in the attack, their bodies had been taken away. Why not Scoggins? Was he so low even the whites hated him and left him to the circling buzzards that began their gruesome work?

Weak and sickened, Apache retched again and again. So this was the way of the white man — to attack women and children. To scalp and strip and leave the remains to the beasts and buzzards. He wiped his mouth, found a little water in an unbroken pot and rinsed his mouth, then washed his face. Would the soldiers return? Why had they not scalped him, too? And where had the shot come from that killed Scoggins?

Apache slowly walked back past the thicket. A little behind the place he had been the day before, he found another body.

Little Eagle's sightless eyes stared up at him. Did he only imagine shame on the stark, dead face, or had the treachery of his father imprinted itself on his son forever?

Trying hard to remember, Apache worked it out in his mind. Little Eagle must have seen him in the thicket. He must have heard Apache's cry when he saw Scoggins kill Running Deer, raised the rifle, and fired.

"Then how was I wounded?" Apache gently touched the swelling on the left side of his head. No bullet had done that. A slow suspicion grew, and he retraced his steps to where the branch had caught his hair and held him back. His keen eyes searched the scuffed dead leaves, the footprints, and the distance from there to where Little Eagle lay. Suspicion turned to belief. The moment Little Eagle fired, he must have leaped toward Apache, knocked him out with the rifle butt, and hurled himself back into the open, hoping to save the companion he had taunted.

The more Apache looked at the ground, the more convinced he became. Why else would the soldiers have missed a senseless Apache boy, even in the thicket?

Feelings he had never experienced except for Running Deer threatened to choke him. Had this been Little Eagle's way of repaying the terrible debt Big Eagle had made by his betrayal? How could Big Eagle do it? Had the white soldiers given him whiskey? If so, where would they have found Big Eagle? He must have known his own son would be in camp. Or had there been false promises by the white soldiers, promises to kill only the warriors and spare the women and children?

"We will never know, Little Eagle." Apache knelt by the dead boy who could easily have been him. "Good-bye." He closed the staring eyes and placed small stones on the lids to keep them shut.

Faint from all that had happened, Apache helplessly looked around the silent camp. Dozens of bodies. He could not bury them. If the soldiers returned and found the bodies gone, they would know that one lived to tell of the deeds of that bloody day.

"I cannot leave Running Deer to the buzzards." His defiant voice echoed strangely in the lifeless place. With the last of his strength, he managed to find a blanket that had escaped the bloodbath. He wrapped his mother's body in it and carried her out of camp, making sure his feet trod only bare rock, where he could not be tracked. He hesitated, then trudged back the way he had come. Little Eagle would share Running Deer's sleeping place.

Many hours later, Apache put the last huge red rock into place. He had concealed the bodies so the rocks over them looked as if they had been there forever. No beast or buzzard could mutilate Running Deer or Little Eagle.

The packed deerskin bag lay where his mother had left it, ready and waiting. Apache slung it over his shoulder, glad it had been far enough away from the slaughter so no blood stained it. He forced himself to eat a bit of dried meat; then, with a final look at all he remembered as home, he walked away from everything except the awful memories seared into his brain with a white-hot brand.

He never went back.

Weeks dragged into months, months fled into years. Apache communed only with the eagle, the sky, the red cliffs. He traveled north, west, south, east, to the mountains, into the valleys, deep inside canyons no white could ever penetrate without guidance. He was always alone, except for his hatred and the wild. Hundreds of sunrises greeted the lone figure atop a rock. Hundreds of sunsets and twilights nodded good-bye. He grew in stature, toughened into steel and fire by his fight to survive. His only joy came from fighting the elements and winning. Sandstorms, floods, fire, and cold had no stronger will than Apache.

But he never went back.

Neither did he contact others until his trail ran across a man as wild as himself. Yet a few times he heard news of the world outside the desert and mountain and canyon. His mouth twisted when he discovered the great Geronimo had surrendered. Running Deer had been right. The Apache must live under the white man's rule or be no more.

Time melted into time, and fall came again. Apache felt the restlessness always within him swell until he could hardly bear it. He needed the contact of others, even though they despised him and he hated the whites and wasn't accepted by Indians. Cut off from both races, he wandered until the gold of aspens and cottonwoods and the white-tipped peaks promised winter.

A longing for the beautiful Kaibab plateau filled him. There, miles of parklike meadows provided forage for deer, and wild turkey lay on the north side of the great canyon with the raging Colorado River far in the bottom. Apache's mouth watered. Wild turkey offered relief from his usual plain fare, mostly gathered from the land and supplemented with salt and sometimes with flour gained by infrequent stealthy midnight raids on trading posts.

When he reached Daybreak, riding a wild pony he had captured, his hunger for the sight of another human's face proved too much. He reined in at the edge of the small cluster of buildings that passed for a town and watched people come and go from a hiding place. Secure in his chosen spot, he saw the swaggering men, a few women, fewer children.

Bitterness raged in his heart. As Charles Campbell's son, he should be able to walk the dusty streets. Instead, he skulked in the shadows, knowing the war against the Apache had not ended for many. Some of the very men who lounged and laughed in the streets would shoot on sight if they saw him lurking in the trees.

Lips compressed, Apache glided away, leaving no trace of his presence. Once outside town, he followed a trail through the forest, drawing in great breaths of pine-scented air, letting the healing forces of the place do their work.

A few miles out, the pony went lame. Apache slid to the ground and examined its foot. "Too bad. I won't be riding you." He dug a sharp stone from beneath the hoof and the pony nickered, but still limped.

A warning chill swept through Apache. An answering shinny, cut off as with a rude hand, caused him to slap his pony's rump and yell, "Go!" before diving for shelter behind an enormous ponderosa pine trunk.

The warning chill had been too late. Crashing shots shattered the peaceful glade. Apache fell without a cry, aware of hearing only, "Got 'im, boys. Another good Apache!" Thundering hoofbeats dwindling into the distance. Then nothing.

A lifetime seemed to pass before Apache awakened in a strange place. A second lifetime passed before he found himself staring into the face of a white girl.

An involuntary movement betrayed his intentions. Incredibly strong hands held him against something softer than pine needles. Jarred pain tore through his back and chest, and sweat bathed his body like a waterfall.

"We are friends," a voice said in his own language.

Apache managed to turn his head. A tall, massive white man held him pinned. Piercing gray eyes reassured the captive more than the words. "You've been shot five times in the back. Rest."

Apache fell back into the bottomless pit.

Days later, Mathew Sutherland, his wife, Abigail, their son, Jon, and daughter, Mescal, gathered around Apache's bed. "It had to be Radford Comstock and his men," Matthew said frankly.

Apache's heart leaped at the words. Some of his feelings must have shown on his usually inscrutable face, for Jon put in, "Don't think about getting him. You'd be hung."

"I know." Apache said in the tongue his father had insisted he learn. "I am Apache." His face contorted. "Half."

If the Sutherlands were shocked, they didn't show it.

"Want to tell us about it?"

Apache shook his head. But when he learned that the slender, brown-eyed, dark-haired girl Mescal had found him bleeding to death along the trail and somehow lifted him onto her buckskin Shalimar, something stirred. Never had anyone done anything except raise a hand against him. "Why?"

It took Jon and the other Sutherlands the rest of Apache's healing time to explain. He couldn't understand their talk of a white God who not only let his son die but sent him into battle — not to defeat enemies but so they could live! Yet if the Sutherlands hadn't cared for him. . . . At this point, Apache always shrugged, even while he listened.

"Apache will pay his debt," he promised when the Sutherlands insisted he owed them nothing. Gradually he told them a few things from his early life: about Running Deer, Scoggins, and Charles Campbell. About Little Eagle. But one thing he did not tell was how Running Deer went back to the Indian village of her own choice. Instead, he said what he had come to believe over the years. "Charles Campbell deserted us." He felt he spoke the truth. If his father had wanted to know what happened to his Apache wife and half-breed son, he would not have listened to Scoggins's lies.

One day Matthew came to Apache. "You once said you wanted to pay this debt you've got in your head that you owe us."

Apache only nodded.

"Then would you stay for a time?"

Apache roused from his shock. "You ask me — Apache — to stay on the Triple S?"

"I do." The gray eyes never left the watching dark ones. "Jon's twin brother, Jim, is probably dead. He's been off fighting Indians."

"Apaches?"

"Yes." Matthew's steady gaze didn't even flicker. "I don't apologize, though I tried to get him not to go. He wasn't like Jon."

"No." Apache thought of the serious, blue-eyed, brown-haired man who had spent so much time talking with him, man-to-man, not white to Apache.

"Well, Jon's got it in his head he wants to preach."

Apache hid his amazement and merely said, "Both sons — you will lose."

Matthew forced a laugh. "Just about. Now," his hard-bitten manner returned, as if he regretted letting Apache see the real pain inside him. "I need another good hand. Some of my boys are loyal. Some aren't and can probably be bought off by my worst enemy."

As light dawned, Apache drew his lips back in a snarl. "Comstock."

"I'm more afraid of what he might do to Mescal than his stealing our cattle." Matthew dropped his guard and leaned forward. "She's good at riding and roping and shooting. Shalimar's the fastest horse around. How that buckskin can run! Still, Comstock's bragged he'll have Mescal even if he has to drag her off on the end of a rope. She hates him and slapped his face so hard it sounded like a pistol shot when he made a dirty remark at the dance in Daybreak." He paused, then deliberately added. "It was the morning after that dance that Mescal found you and brought you in."

Apache felt as though red-hod spears had been thrust into him.

Matthew continued, his face determined but gray. "I can't cage Mescal up. It'd be like caging a wild critter. She has to run and ride free or die. And Radford Comstock's the marshal of Daybreak, with a passel of kinfolk behind him. Jon and I have been kind of taking turns looking after Mescal, riding with her. If he leaves . . ."

A vivid thrust of memory claimed Apache — the story that fell from Running Deer's lips of another time, another man who pulled her from her horse and tore her clothing. He looked deep into the waiting gray eyes and saw there everything he had heard of the kindness of Charles Campbell. Once a white man had saved an Apache girl. Now an Apache would protect a white girl from one who followed Scoggins's rotten footsteps.

Three words bound him to the Sutherlands with all the honor of his forefathers. "I will stay."

4

The heavy nightmare lifted. Apache's bandages, clothing, and blankets were wet from the healing sweat that signaled a breaking fever. Once he turned to mumble, "King?" Through his agony, the big gray's soft whinny told him all was well.

Even that effort cost him. Now his visions brought relief, not torment. He could almost smell the freshness of the peeled logs that formed the Sutherland home, the sturdy flowers waving in the wind. If only he could taste the water from Haunting Spring, which never went dry! How it would ease him, as it had when he lay at the Sutherlands' mercy long ago. He remembered the good plain food Abigail and Mescal served in quantities, laughing and urging their menfolk — and Apache — to eat more.

In his dreams, the collie Gold Dust romped with Mescal, followed Jon, curled at Apache's feet. He heard laughter, something that had been denied him as a child. Although the Sutherlands faithfully studied the Bible and lived out what they found there, laughter had a special place in their home. Apache never laughed, not even at the antics of Mescal's multitude of pets: coons, squirrels, birds, and deer. Yet a certain contentment filled an emptiness he hadn't realized lay within him.

When he wasn't guarding Mescal under the pretense of teaching her woods lore known only to him, Apache spent time with Jon. After the initial grumbling of the hands, they gave him a wide berth and avoided him whenever possible. Matthew Sutherland had wisely decided not to give Apache tasks that would put him into contact with the others — at least not until they had learned to tolerate him. So as winter passed and Apache's wounds healed cleanly under the expert nursing care known to all frontiersmen and women, for the first time in his life, Apache felt at home.

A hundred times Jon spoke of his twin. The poignant blueness of his expressive eyes touched a tiny chord in Apache. Had he not felt the same thing Jon felt for his missing brother Jim when he knelt by Little Eagle's body?

"They called us Sons of Thunder, after James and John in the Bible," Jon said. "We were wild, eager for danger." He sighed, and a shadow grayed his face. "I wonder where he is now. Because Jim's part of me, I always felt I'd know if he died. Yet if he's alive, why doesn't he come back to the Triple S? Geronimo was taken, and the fighting's settled down."

"He left in anger?"

"Yes." Jon's eyes darkened. He hooked his thumbs in his belt and let out a long breath. Startled by the sound, one of Mescal's pet squirrels scolded and ran up a pine trunk. Jon didn't seem to hear. "We needed him here, but he laughed and said things were too tame. He wanted me to go with him. I could not." A great longing swept over his face. "When Jim called good-bye and rode off, part of me went with him."

Apache didn't answer, and Jon turned and walked away, his boot heels making sharp indentations in the ground.

Another time Jon and Apache got caught out in a bad storm. Too far from the ranch house to get home through the pounding snow and cold, they holed up in a rocky area Apache had spied in his wanderings. The closeness of their quarters and the raging fury outside gave them time to talk. Again, Jon spoke of Jim. "It's been more than five years now. He's probably dead." Jon poked at the fire Apache had built by using the inside of tree bark and carefully adding the dryest small branches he could find.

Apache remained silent, yet resentment flickered and caught fire, the way the bark had done. He could not hurt Jon by suggesting it would be best if his brother did not return. Yet wouldn't the same restlessness that had driven Jim to leave only bring trouble to his family? Apache shrugged. What was Jim Sutherland, killer of Indians, to him? He probably lay dead, just like Running Deer and Little Eagle and the others. If he lived and came back? Apache shrugged again. Jon could go about his preaching. Jim could guard Mescal. There would be no need for a half-breed, and Apache could vanish into the forest. The thought brought a pang he instantly subdued. Why should the idea of leaving make him feel hollow and empty?

Yet from that moment, a special hatred for the unknown Jim gnawed inside Mescal's silent protector. Not because he had hunted and killed Apaches. Not because all white men except the Sutherlands and Charles Campbell were enemies. Something deeper lay behind his growing feelings, although Apache didn't know what.

Spring roused from hiberation, shook itself, and stretched into warmer afternoons, with cold enough nights to serve as a reminder that it couldn't be trusted. Snow gradually melted. A few courageous flowers poked their heads through the ground and delighted Mescal. She confided to Apache one day, "I don't see how anyone who watches the seasons can help believing in God and His Son."

"Why?"

She rocked back on her heels from where she'd been using brown hands to unearth more flower shoots. "You know how in the fall everything dies? The cottonwood and aspen leaves change to yellow and gold then brown and finally drop to the ground dead."

"Everyone knows that." Yet Apache couldn't help feeling curious at her statement.

"Ugly, brown bulbs stay underground all winter. When spring comes, the sun and rain make them alive again. See?" She pointed to the uncovered tender sprouts just above ground level and didn't wait for him to answer. "After Jesus died, they buried Him, but it didn't do any good. He rose and lived again, just like the bulbs and the trees that look dead live again."

His gaze followed Mescal's to the tiny green life on the trees around them. "How can a man live after he is dead?"

"Don't you think a man is worth more than a bulb? Why shouldn't people be treated at least as well as the trees and flowers?" Mescal demanded, her face flushed, ready for battle.

Apache thought about it. "Perhaps the spirit lives as an eagle." He watched the silent predator's mighty wings case a shadow on the clearing.

"Not as an eagle. As a real person, only with a body that can't get sick or hurt or ever die again," Mescal insisted. Her brown hands stilled. 'But we have to believe in God and His Son, Apache."

He folded his hands majestically, turned, and stalked off. Such foolishness did not deserve a reply. Yet many times the absolute sureness of what Mescal believed swam in his mind and her echoing words disturbed him, and he cursed the white blood in him that allowed a moment's thought to such a story. When the white man's God showed enough strength to stop the killing and let all men walk free, Apache would listen.

Jon seldom spoke of Jim now. Neither did the others. Yet Apache overheard an enlightening conversation one early evening. Hidden by the shadows of the porch, strangely unwilling to join Matthew and Jon as he often did, his sharp ears caught Jon's question. "Dad, if Jim came home, would he be welcome?"

"Do you need to ask?"

"No."

A moment later Apache saw them clasp hands in the gloom before Matthew strode away. Apache moved.

"You there, Apache?" Jon called.

Apache silently glided across the space between them. Something made him ask, "Why would you welcome back one who left when you needed him?"

"He's my brother. I would die for him if he needed it." Jon's hoarse words sank into Apache's churning mind.

"The way the white God's son died."

"Yes."

Apache grunted and disappeared into the shadows. But later he heard Matthew Sutherland reading from the Bible, and the words froze the listening Apache to the place where he stood against the log wall.

Matthew's voice rang out the story of a son who went away as Jim had gone; how that son grew sick and hungry and at last dragged himself home, wondering if he would be welcome. A strange hunger filled Apache when the father in the story ran to his son, crying out that he who had been lost was found, he who had been dead was alive.

What if he, a wandering, outcase half-Apache, had had a father like that? He had a vision of massive, gray-haired Matthew Sutherland running out to a second Jon, bringing him inside, and rejoicing. This was quickly followed by a second vision, where a brown-haired white man with summer-sky eyes proudly carried his half-Indian son.

Before the prayer that always followed Bible readings in the Sutherland home, Apache fled as if a thousand devils chased him. Why should he stay here, chained in a hundred ways? He must break free and get back to the crags and canyons before his white blood betrayed him completely. Hours of solitude in the forest restored his sanity. At last he came back to the Triple S ranch house, strangely feeling that the story he had heard would one day be his undoing, yet powerless to leave before he paid his debt.

Again and again he wondered if Jim Sutherland had ever been worthy of the love his family held for him. Apache's lip curled, yet the thought persisted.

Filled with restlessness, Apache spent more time alone, waking long before the early rising settlers and sliding into the forest. The fresh coldness stirred his senses, promised he knew not what, forced him to run swiftly. One such morning a saddled, riderless horse stood not far from the ranch house. Apache started, then cautiously backtracked its hoofprints. He found Jon under a huge pine, coughing and retching. As Apache started forward, Jon stood, weaving as if drunk, staring at him.

The next instant Jon clawed for the Colt revolver that had slipped from his holster when he coughed!

Had Jon gone mad from fever? Apache headed for him at a dead run.

Jon found the revolver, cocked it, and aimed. The explosion nearly deafened Apache, who was almost next to Jon, but a terrible cough made the Colt waver, and the bullet went wild. Apache's hands closed onto Jon's shoulders like talons. The revolver fell. Apache kicked it away and yelled, "Jon!" His black eyes stared into blazing blue eyes.

Then, "No. You are the other one. The black horse is yours?"

Sick, weak, yet unbelievably like Jon, the twin brother — the Indian killer — had come home.

Apache struggled back to consciousness. "Tired. So tired." He thirstily sipped a little water, again called King, and relaxed when he heard the faithful horse's nicker. His head pounded, but the wounds had remained closed. Most of the fever had gone, but weakness kept Apache from doing little more than redressing the wounds and staying in the small cave.

This time he did not sleep, yet the memories demanded his attention. A whirl of events marched through his mind: catching Jim Sutherland's horse and getting Jim into the saddle, calmly ignoring the white man's curses. The homecoming, with Matthew, Jon, Mescal, and Abigail in the yard. Matthew's, "God in heaven, my son!" shattering the spring air. Jim's craven cry, "Mother, I've come home to die."

Apache saw again the scornful Mescal, goading, taunting, until Jim leaned against Jon and sweat stood out in great drops. He remembered the days and nights of fear and his own knowledge that he had been right. It would have been better if Jim had never returned.

Then he remembered the night Mescal sought him out, demanding repayment of his debt to the family. He must take Jim to the desert and either cure or bury him. Memories of the long march and longer healing time that followed gave way to the humiliation of Jim's about-face. Then came the months of survival after Apache's accident kept them in the valley behind the waterfall. Jim refused to save himself from summer's parching, and eventually the gripping of hands between half-breed and white sealed their strange, forced partnership.

Then there had been a homecoming such as the one Matthew Sutherland had read from the Bible — a homecoming that included Apache as a friend and savior.

Apache mentally leaped over the winter months that followed, the coming of spring, the terrible scene when Radford Comstock hung the wrong twin for a nonexistent crime.

"Let the past be forgotten," Apache stated. His voice echoed in the cave.

Now that he no longer had a fever, he must eat. He needed broth and bits of meat and bread. How long had he lingered in the cave? King still had sparce graze, but he must be moved soon. No longer did the promise to send the big gray home haunt Apache. Many days later, he swung easily to the horse's back and began his journey.

For a long moment he looked south and west. One by one, he bid farewell to those he left behind:

Carter and the posse, who would brag how they once rode with a half-breed Apache and had been proud to do it.

Matthew Sutherland, gray-haired patriarch of his family and follower of the white God he claimed loved godless half-breeds, too.

Abigail, always aproned, loving, motherly in a way Running Deer had never had the chance to be.

Jon, who lay quietly beneath a gravestone, yet whose bravery and sacrifice still puzzled the Apache who had loved him as a brother.

Jim, separate, yet part of Jon, the best part of him only showed itself when the worst happened.

Mescal . . .

But Apache would not think of Mescal, the slender girl who would marry

Jim. She had saved him, and he loved her. Not with the hope of ever possessing her, but with the love of a heathen for his idol. She was all the things Apache saw and held precious in nature: courage and fire, storm and calm.

Because of Mescal, he must turn north and east, away from the Triple S, back to his solitude. Lips pressed together in an unflinching, unswervable line, Apache touched King's flanks with his heels and headed back to the stronghold behind the shining waterfall.

Twice he had ridden this trail with Jim, once at Mescal's request, once because he knew Jon would have wanted him to stay with his twin. Now he rode alone, except for memories he wished would die and leave him in peace.

Haggard and weak, Apache and King came to the hiding place. The waterfall shimmered and splashed as beautifully as ever. The verdant valley spread green before him with its protection and abundant game. King rolled in tall grass and drank his fill of sparkling water after the rationed feed and drink on the trail.

Day after day Apache gained in strength. Pain gave way to twinges that stopped entirely after a few weeks. The same pure air and spring sunlight that healed Jim so long ago now did their work with Apache. He slept with his wounds open to the healing sun and air. He rose at dawn, tramped the valley, and rode King so he wouldn't get fat and lazy. He learned to love the big gray more than any horse he had ever ridden or owned. Sometimes his mouth twisted. Was his feeling for the grand horse all tied up with the fact that King offered his only unbroken link with the Sutherlands and with Mescal?

When his returning strength permitted, Apache climbed the red rocks and watched sunrises: sullen, glorious, angry, and clear. From the valley floor he observed sunsets: red, gold, purple. Majestic and timid. And always the peace of the valley did its part to heal his body and soul.

For a long time the sheer loveliness of his surroundings and the companionship of King gave him what he needed. April flounced into May. May hummed into June, with its blossoms and fragrances mingled into unmatchable perfume. Then each ever-warmer day whispered, "Time to go." Every night star twinkled a warning. "You cannot stay here in summer. The relentless sun once felt defeat at your hands, but not again. Go."

With the knowledge that he must leave came a bittersweet realization: Paying his debt to Jim and Mescal hadn't freed Apache. Every fibre of his being longed for the Triple S, the Kaibab plateau, the Sutherlands. The tiny spark lighted by them and perhaps fanned by their God had made a travesty of his self-sufficient aloneness. The challenge of desert and mountain and canyon, the glory of survival against the elements — where were they? Gone, along with his proud inner boast that he needed no one.

Apache lingered, loath to leave the valley, yet knowing that before long the lush grass would grow sere and yellowed. The singing waterfall would still to a murmur, perhap seven die if the summer suns refused to give way to storm clouds. At last he prepared to go — but where? Back to his lonely life?

Only then did Apache face the ultimate truth: He could no longer exist without other people, as he had done so long before. The next morning he packed his few remaining supplies, mounted King, and rode through the cave passageway. He halted by the waterfall only long enough to note the sadness of its music.

Hating his own weakness, he started back.

The whites had won, after all.

PART II
Charley Campbell

5

A wave of red and white cattle swept over the rise and down the rough valley floor.

Faint shouts from cowboys, who rode as if part of their horses, reached the motionless three watching from a pine-covered bench above.

"There's Dusty!" Mescal Ames Sutherland's still-new gold wedding band flashed in the spring sunlight when she waved toward the moving figures below. "And Dave and Shorty and Slim." She quieted Patches, her dancing pinto pony, and her tanned face gleamed against the dusky frame of her dark hair. Deep brown eyes lit with joy. "It's so good to have new stock coming in. The Triple S without cattle's like . . . like . . ."

Jim Sutherland's hands tightened on Shalimar's reins. The buckskin snorted when Jim half-turned in the saddle to look at Mescal. His wife. Even the weeks since their quiet wedding hadn't fully convinced him that the child-turned-woman who had been adopted by his folks after her parents died could really be his. A quiver of pain ran through him. If only Jon . . .

Jim shook himself. Regretting the past wouldn't change anything. Yet the raw spot inside him, which had begun when his twin, Jon, gave his life to save Jim's, hadn't healed but pulsed fresh whenever Jim remembered.

"Well, the show's about over." Silver-haired, massive Matthew Sutherland swung Dark Star toward the ranch house. "Coming, Mescal? Son?"

"I wish I could have gone with them."

"I know." Steady blue eyes met matching eager ones. "Give yourself time. Doc said a gunshot hand wouldn't be much good bringing in a herd of cattle."

"That little scratch?" Jim flexed his left arm and carefully hid the twinge in his shoulder blade from showing in his face. "Doesn't bother at all."

"It did when the boys left," his father reminded him. Suddenly he grinned. "Seems to me a time or two when you hugged Mescal that shoulder acted up."

Jim laughed. Sunlight set little motes dancing in his light-brown hair. "It was worth it!"

With a loud "Haw, haw," Matthew sent Dark Star down the trail home.

Soft red streaks tinged Mescal's smooth skin the way northern Arizona dawns tinge the sky. Jim never tired of her moods. Sometimes she was pensive and thoughtful; other times, shadowed but resolutely looking toward the future; now and then shy as the fawns who bounded away but later came and ate from her hand.

The cattle below wearily trudged on until the riders halted them. Then they stood or lay, obviously glad their journey had ended. Jim and Mescal rode down to meet the four faithful riders halfway.

"Any trouble?" he called as soon as they were within hearing distance.

Bowlegged Dusty doffed his sombrero and mopped his sweaty face with a lurid bandanna. "Naw. Quieter than Daybreak on Sunday night since you signed on as sheriff!"

The other three riders laughed appreciatively. Encouraged, Dusty continued. "'Sides, we heard that what's left of the Comstock clan up and headed for another part of Arizona." He pulled his mouth into a droll shape, and his eyes twinkled.

"Yeah," Slim put in. "They said they were goin' for their health."

Another roar of laughter.

Dave and Shorty weren't about to let their pardners get ahead of them. "Funny," Dave said, "I never thought this part of Arizona was unhealthy."

"Me neither," Shorty solemnly added. "'Cept for skunks 'n' critters like that."

Still laughing, the four headed for the bunkhouse and corrals near the big log ranch house, leaving Jim and Mescal to follow, but not without Dusty's parting shot. "Someday I'm goin' to get me a spread and be the boss and get to stay home with a purty gal while my pore old cowhands do all the work." He disappeared around a bend of the trail.

"I'd rather have just those four than a dozen other hands," Jim confessed. He stared up the trail where joshing and singing could still be heard. "Now my shoulder's healed, I can't wait to get back out with them, working the cattle."

"I'm just glad things have quieted down around here," Mescal said. "It's good to have peace and not . . ." she broke off.

Always sensitive to her feelings, Jim soberly finished, ". . . not having to be home waiting with Mother while your menfolk are off doing what they have to do."

"Yes." Mescal's voice sounded muffled.

In the space of a single hoofbeat, Jim understood more than ever before the extent of suffering she had experienced. First her father, next her mother, then Jon. At last, the terrible waiting, helpless to do anything, tortured by imagination that mocked even the most faithful prayers and pleas for God's strength and help when Matthew and Jim rode into Daybreak along with Apache and the posse.

Of one accord they swerved their horses when they came to the well-trampled trail that led to a silent spot nestling in a small clearing. New grass and tiny flowers had sprung up on the mound of earth by its split-aspen marker.

JON SUTHERLAND
GREATER LOVE HATH NO MAN THAN THIS . . .

A sturdy brown hand covered his own. Mescal whispered, "The marker reminds us of his life and how good can come from evil."

Jim turned his hand palm up and squeezed hers. "If it weren't for that, I couldn't go on."

The gentle breeze carried freshness and a hint of late afternoon chill as it swayed the guarding trees in a spring benediction. Jim and Mescal turned back toward the ranch house, passing Haunting Spring, which never went dry. A few moments later, the dusty corral with tired horses, the barns, rambling bunkhouse, and the peeled-log ranch house loomed before them.

"Want me to rub down Patches?" Jim offered, just to see Mescal's eyes flash.

"Never! No good hand lets someone else care for her horse." She looked indignantly at him. The long braid she wore when riding had slipped from beneath her hat, and the loose ends curled.

"You're no hand. You're my wife." Jim couldn't help grinning when he said it, even though his hands rapidly loosed Shalimar's saddle and swung it over his shoulder. He slapped the buckskin's rump and sent him flying into the corral, then carried the saddle into the barn and hung it on the wall.

He didn't beat Mescal by a minute. She had Patches in the corral and the saddle in the barn before he could go back and help her.

"Come 'n' get it before I throw it out!" Curley, the cook who presided over the bunkhouse and refused help even when extra hands hired on for roundup, bellowed from the open window.

"You eatin' with us, boss?" Dusty smirked from the bunkhouse porch. Washed, their clothes changed, the quartette who lounged against the porch posts hardly resembled the sweaty four who had brought in the cattle.

"Naw." Shorty stuck his nose in the air and held out one hand with his fingers extended, palm down. "You dumb cowpuncher. Would you be eatin' Curly's cookin' if you had a wife?"

Dusty rolled his eyes. "I sure wouldn't be sittin' at the table with you."

"Shhhh." Dave put a hand over his mouth in mock warning but didn't lower his voice. "You'll hurt Curly's feelin's and Slim'll have to cook."

Slim didn't act perturbed. He shrugged and ominously asked, "Remember the last time I cooked?"

Jim bent double, laughing along with the hands, but when another grizzly-bear roar came from inside the bunkhouse, the men disappeared and Jim and Mescal headed for the ranch house.

"What did he mean?" Mescal pattered alongside Jim's longer steps.

"You mean you missed something on the Triple S?" Jim couldn't resist taunting. "I thought you knew everything that went on."

Her chin raised. "Are you telling me or not?"

"Sure." Jim chuckled. "Remember when Curly got laid up a few weeks back and couldn't handle cooking?" He waited for her nod, hugely enjoying himself. Not often did he have a range joke she hadn't heard — at least one fit to repeat.

"Well, seems that the four of them made a deal. They'd draw straws to see who took Curly's place until he got back on the job. Slim lost. But he said he'd cook on one condition: Anyone who complained got the job.

"Dusty and Shorty and Dave — even Curly — agreed. It was the worst thing they could have done. Slim can't cook mash for the pigs, let alone anything people would eat, and he hates kitchen work worse than poison. The first time he made stew, it stuck. He tried rice pudding and had enough rice to feed Daybreak." Jim couldn't hold in his glee.

"Anyway, the others knew they couldn't complain, but the night they came in tired and hungry and Slim had dumped three times too much salt in the potatoes, Dusty had enough. He called Slim several choice names I hope you've never heard, then he said, 'This stuff's so salty no one can . . .' About that time he remembered the deal, especially when he saw Slim's eyes gleam and a stupid grin start all over his face. The only thing worse than Slim's food would be having to cook. Fast as a bullet, Dusty swallowed the mess in his mouth and added, '. . . but it's just the way we like it!' "

"What happened then?"

"They all howled, and Curly allowed as how he was feeling a whole lot better and Slim could get back where he belonged, punching cows. But ever since, you better not ask Dusty to pass the salt or you're liable to get it dumped over your head."

Supper over, twilight shadows making purple patches in the yard, the Sutherlands settled down for a short time before their early bedtime. A great log in the enormous fireplace drove back the evening chill. Jim's mother, Abigail, and Mescal finished the kitchen work while Matthew and his son tallied up the cattle the hands had brought in.

"In a couple of years there's no reason why the Triple S can't be back on its feet," Matthew predicted. "We've stayed alive even with our cattle being run off. With the Comstocks gone, I doubt if there'll be more than petty thieving — cowpokes branding mavericks or steeling a steer for beef."

"Carter told Dusty and the boys he hadn't lost a single head since we rode into Daybreak." Jim stared into the fire, remembering a hundred other fires he'd shared with soldier comrades, with Dad and Jon and the boys, even with Comstock's gang. And with Apache.

A great longing inside him rose and demanded attention. "Dad, do you think Apache made it?"

His father's eyes retreated into caverns under his bushy brows. "I don't know."

Jim felt the keen scrutiny and laughed mirthlessly. "Funny, it wasn't that long ago I rode and killed every Apache I could see." His fingers clenched until the knuckles showed white. "Never women or kids, though. I hung back on the camp raids. Couldn't stomach what went on." In the brooding silence Mescal came up behind him and stood with her hands on his slumped shoulders, ever mindful of the left one that involuntarily flinched if her fingers rested too heavily.

"Even when Apache brought you in, I didn't see signs that you'd changed," Matthew said dryly.

"I hadn't. I hated his guts, hated my weakness, and almost hated you all for having him here." The confession released the guilt Jim had carried for a long time.'

"What really made you change?"

Jim considered his father's question. Honesty warred with his natural Sutherland reserve. "I guess when I found out I couldn't leave him to die in the waterfall valley. Or when I knew we probably wouldn't make it until the rains came."

"No two men can be forced to depend on each other for survival and come out anything except bitter enemies or brothers." Matthew tapped his fingers on the arm of his chair.

"When it ended, I knew Apache had used my very hatred to keep me alive," Jim admitted with a pang. How clear the memories remained!

"I think he's alive."

Jim had forgotten Mescal's presence until she stepped into the firelight. He made room for her next to him on the blanket-covered couch. The sureness of her statement sent a thrill of hope through him. All the peace and joy of the Triple S couldn't override the shadow of Apache's absence, especially when Carter had described his wounds.

"Why do you think so?" Matthew inquired, his fingers now still.

"Apache knows how to survive. He couldn't have been hurt any worse than Jim was when he came back." Mescal stubbornly looked at each of them. "If he could care for Jim and bring him back, then . . ." Her voice died.

The grain of hope expanded in Jim to a shaky belief that she could be right. "If he'd only come back! Once he told me, after Jon died, 'I will eat and sleep and stay with you day and night until the debt is paid. Then I will never see you again. And give thanks for that!' "

Jim's impassioned words hung in the air until Mescal asked, "Don't you think he changed his mind?"

"Perhaps." But Jim's hope withered. "Even if he does heal, won't Apache go back to his Indian ways, to the eagle and wild things? What place has he with others?" Jim clenched his hands and slowly released them.

"Now that I know what God has done for me, I wish I could make Apache believe, too." Would he ever have a chance to let Apache see how much the truth had changed a bloodstained Indian fighter?

"He heard the message of Jesus when he lived here," Matthew reminded Jim. "Jon talked to him, too. Whether it did any good or not, we don't know."

Jim tried hard to remember, bringing snatches of conversation from that endless scorching summer to mind. What was it Apache had said? Slowly, the comfortable room changed to desert night. The flour had run out. In their red-walled prison, Apache had caught and roasted small lizards. Jim gagged at the memory, but he had eaten them to survive.

Even the night stars seemed hot, and the wind that should have cooled them blew from hell itself. In their forced comradeship, Apache had opened his heart. With little chance of ever leaving the valley, the tragic blend of red and white had said, "I am like the mule — not horse, not ass. A breed between, who belongs nowhere. White men curse me. Red men despise me. I am nothing."

Jim felt as helpless now to find an answer as he had when Apache went on.

"Your brother preaches a God who loves all. If it is true, why must I walk alone? I can never marry an Indian or a white woman. I will die and be buried in a nameless grave, forgotten. There will be no son to carry my name. I cannot bring another into this world to bear what I suffer. One day the Apache will be gone forever. One day the Apache will be free, and that is the day we are all dead."

Did Apache now lie in the hidden greenness, wound open to the healing air, as Jim had once lain? Did he thirst as Jim had thirsted, face death in every shadow, and watch it sit, grinning and waiting?

Beads of sweat sprang to Jim's face. No one who hadn't gone through it could know the cost or the voices that mocked, taunted, and enticed — day and night — until the canyon walls turned to blood and the pitiless sky to brass.

With an inarticulate cry, Jim leaped from the couch and bolted through the front door into the darkness. He felt Mescal's understanding movement, heard his father say, "It will take time. Perhaps a lifetime."

Then he closed the door behind him and stumbled across the wide porch. His faithful collie, Gold Dust, a little older and slower now, silently brushed against him and trotted near.

After the initial adjustment, Jim's keen eyes accepted the yellow glow from a bunkhouse window, the night-white moon scouting the ranch from a hilltop, the scudding clouds that played tag with a breeze and painted sky pictures.

Despite his turmoil, the familiar scene quieted him. He turned again to the clearing and his twin brother's grave.

Voices from the past mingled with the growing wind.

His own, deriding: "Jesus, a sissy."

Jon's: "Suppose saving my life meant taking my place and dying yourself so I could live?"

Jim's own admission: "Not many men would do that."

"One did." The eternal plan of salvation in two words.

"Not just one, God," Jim burst out to the night. "Three. First Your Son. Then Jon. Then Apache." Desire grew within him, stronger than any force that had ever laid hands on his spirit. He could do no more for Jon than to keep the memory of his life alive by following the pattern that he — no, that Jesus — had set.

But somewhere out in the vast awfulness of northern Arizona or southern Utah lay a half-Apache, a soul created and loved by God, who had saved Jim's life and paid his debt as he promised. Living or dead, he represented every lost soul who had ever wandered desert, plain, or mountain, always seeking, seldom finding the one Comrade who could bring healing and peace and who could triumph over even a lonely, unmarked grave.

6

Jim Sutherland marked the night the new cattle came as still another turning point in his life. Once he bared his heart and shared how he longed for Apache to know and love Jesus, nothing could ever be the same. Matthew and Abigail wisely refrained from probing; Mescal did the same. Yet as the days passed and grew warmer, Jim did two things that showed his inner turmoil. First, he carried Jon's worn Bible, even when he rode. It lay inside his shirt beside his heart, a reminder of the responsibility he must face since the world had been deprived of his brother's life.

The other thing he did was more unconscious than conscious. No matter where he rode, walked, or worked, a dozen times a day he turned his gaze north and east, toward the direction Apache must surely come from. He didn't even realize how often he did this until one day he and Mescal rode to a promontory that overlooked a far distance.

"You miss him more all the time." Not a question, a statement.

Jim nodded and looked into her understanding face. "Yes."

Silenced by the pain in her husband's voice, Mescal simply rode on, leaving him statuelike on the rocky bluff, looking north and east.

The unendurable waiting abruptly shattered into restlessness. Not since the nightmares after he fell in battle had Jim tossed, turned, and cried out in his sleep, to wake at dawn unable to remember what tormented him, heavy-eyed and dull. Night after night they went on, until in desperation Mescal pleaded with him to see the Daybreak doctor.

Matthew shook his head when Jim refused, his wise gaze never leaving his son's face. No doctor could cure a hurting heart or still a troubled mind.

More and more Jim studied Jon's Bible. Short periods of peace followed, but the nightmares never stopped.

One night Jim didn't come home. All night Mescal lay wide-eyed and fearful. Had the Comstocks returned? Had Shalimar thrown his rider? She scoffed at the idea, and yet the wild country in which they lived offered a hundred types of peril. Before daylight she climbed into her buckskin riding clothes and ran lightly toward the corral.

A large dark shape loomed in front of her, and she muffled a scream. "Jim?"

"Yes." The first rays of dawn showed him, haggard but steady-eyed, more at peace that she'd seen him for weeks.

Mescal clutched his jacket. "You're going after Apache."

"I have to, even if he hates me for it. I keep thinking, and if he were all Apache, it would be different. He isn't. He's half white." He drew in a ragged breath. "At least I'll know if he's dead. It will be easier than wondering."

"He isn't dead." Again, Mescal's flat statement fanned the coal of hope in Jim's breast to a tiny, flickering flame.

"I don't think so, either. I don't care how badly Apache got hurt or how sick he might be, he'd never let himself get so slow he wouldn't send King back." An image of the big gray stallion raised from a colt danced in Jim's brain.

"That's right." Mescal clutched his arm. "He always loved King. He would never let King die in the desert, and King's smart enough to get home from wherever Apache may have taken him."

A lamp flared in the window, signaling that Matthew and Abigail had risen to begin their long day's tasks. Jim held Mescal close. "We have to tell them, then I'll pack." Before she could reply, he headed her toward the front door. Stopping only to kick the sand off his boots, Jim strode into the kitchen with Mescal in front of him.

"Dad. Mom. I'm going to find out about Apache."

The looks on their faces shocked him. Neither looked surprised, and Matthew said, "It figures. When?"

"Today. The boys — and Mescal — and you can handle things, can't you?"

Matthew Sutherland snorted like a war horse whose ability was being questioned. "I handled things a long time before you came along. I guess I can still totter around enough to boss the boys — and Mescal."

"Not Mescal!" The girl planted both feet firmly, her hands on her hips. "Mescal won't be here for you to boss, Dad."

Jim burst out, "What do you mean you won't be here?"

A confident smile trembled on her lips as she cocked her head to one side. "I'm going with you."

A vision of the long, hard ride, the twisted trails, and what he might find along the way or behind the waterfall brought Jim's loud protest. 'No!"

"Oh, yes,' she told him. "You can call it our honeymoon, if you like." A smile curved her mouth even more. "Remember when I married you? You promised someday to take me on a honeymoon when your shoulder got better and we could be spared from the Triple S." She shrugged. "I'm calling in that promise, Jim Sutherland!"

"Some honeymoon," he jeered. "Dust and heat and hard riding and . . ."

"Just when have I shied away from dust and heat and hard riding?" she demanded, every trace of her smile gone. "I can outride and outrope and outshoot most of the hands that ever stepped foot on the Triple S or into Daybreak, including you!''

"You're loco to even *want* to go," he accused. "Think this is going to be a vacation or something? A little camping trip? It's going to be miserable — and fast. Once summer starts . . .''

Mescal just crossed her arms over her breast and stared at him.

"Dad. Mom. Tell her she can't go.'' Jim turned to his parents for support.

Matthew raised his hands in surrender. "Not me! Mescal's old enough to know what she's doing.''

"Mother?'' Jim grabbed at straws.

A soft look highlighted her worn face as Abigail looked at Mescal, then at Jim. "Mescal must follow her man.''

Even as he threw his own hands into the air and muttered, "Can't fight all of you,'' Jim heard in his mother's words the story of her life — the following of her husband wherever he led. God grant that he and Mescal could experience the love and companionship that had dwelt in the Sutherland home for over thirty years.

The next instant he barked, "If you're going with me, get packed.''

"I already am.''

"How could you be packed when I didn't know until now I'd be going?''

Mescal gently took his hand. "When we married, we became one, even as you and Jon once were one. I knew.''

With a muttered exclamation, Jim wrenched his gaze from Mescal and looked at Matthew. "How do you handle a girl like this?'' he complained, then dropped one arm over Mescal's shoulders and turned her toward their bedroom. "Since you're ready, how about tossing some extra clothes into a saddlebag for me while I see about food, water, and feed?''

She hesitated, stood on tiptoe, and kissed his cheek, then hurried away. Jim went out to the corral with his father.

"Sure you won't rest up a day since you stayed out all night?'' Matthew asked.

"No.''

"Shalimar needs the rest, even if you don't,'' Matthew warned. He opened his eyes in surprise as Shalimar, Patches, and Dark Star raced across the corral to them. "Why, he isn't even winded! You must not have done much riding last night.''

"I didn't,'' Jim confessed. He gathered nosebags and feed, then filled canteens. "I took Shalimar, thinking I'd ride until I got tired enough to come back and sleep without having nightmares, but when I got to Jon's grave, something made me toss the reins over Shalimar's head and let him stand. I spent the rest of the night leaning against a big pine, thinking.''

"I'm glad Mescal's going with you, even though it surprised me when she stuck to her guns the way she did!'' Matthew slapped his leg and laughed heartily. "Never saw the beat. Her standing there never moving a muscle and determined as all get out to go. She reminded me of the spunky way your mother had when we first got married."

Jim spun on one boot heel, amazed. "Mother? Spunky?"

"That's right." Matthew grinned. "She set me down hard a whole lot when you and Jon were little. She could still do it, if she had to. I've mellowed a lot." His direct gaze held Jim's. "God knows how hard it's been for me to keep control of myself at times. If it hadn't been for Him and for your mother, I just don't know." Matthew shrugged his massive shoulders.

"Then Jon and I came by our nickname, Sons of Thunder, honestly," Jim couldn't help saying.

Matthew just laughed again and slapped his son's shoulder with a heavy hand. "I'll rustle some grub for you while Abigail's getting breakfast. Might as well get an early start if you're bound to go today."

Jim's voice stopped him short. "You know I have to go, Dad."

The shaggy head nodded, but Matthew strode to the house without answering, leaving Jim strangely comforted and prepared for what lay ahead.

They made short work of breakfast and packing. "Mescal, you'll ride Dark Star," Matthew ordered. "Patches is a good pony, but not up to this kind of trip. We'll give him a rest while you're gone."

Jim agreed. Dark Star and Shalimar's stamina would be needed long before they returned.

Matthew had more advice. "You won't need another horse on a leadline. King can pack Apache out — no matter what."

Jim forced himself not to show how that "no matter what" twisted his guts into a knot.

A glorious sun had just fully awakened and begun its day's shining when Jim and Mescal waved good-bye and rode down the long trail. In perfect accord, they stopped at Jon's grave, knelt, and asked God to bless their search. Silently rising and mounting, they rode on, knowing that whatever lurked waiting for them could be faced with the strength of faith born and bred into them by Christian pioneers whose only security lay in trusting God.

Once he accepted the fact that Mescal intended to go, Jim found himself continually torn. Joy over her presence was tempered with unease about the trip's outcome. Never did he see an ugly, dark-winged buzzard cast its shadow on the ground before them without examining whatever grisly remains lay exposed. A fallen deer, a jackrabbit — nothing escaped Jim's scrutiny.

It had been so long since Apache rode away wounded that Jim told Mescal, "No use trying to pick up his trail now. Spring rains will have washed it away long ago. We'll head straight for the waterfall."

"And if he isn't there?"

"We'll go back home."

Inevitably the conversation turned to the other times Jim had ridden this trail. "I remember nothing of the first ride except pain and jolting and knowing Apache had captured me for some terrible punishment of his own," he told her. "I saw nothing except Apache and King. It seemed impossible that he could simply sneak into my room and take me away without rousing the family."

A spasm of pain crossed and distorted Mescal's features. "You'll never know how hard I prayed before asking Apache to kidnap you. I knew little hope remained, in any event. I had to take the one chance available." Her hands tightened on the reins until Dark Star tossed his head in protest. "I also took the risk that if you died, the Sutherlands would cast me off. Jon almost did, when he learned what I had done."

"Poor Mescal." Jim felt his chest constrict and breathed in the clean evergreen and sage scented air. "Thank God you had the courage and faith in Apache to take the chance." He rode closer and patted her clenched hands. "No one ever had a better wife."

The soft color that stained her cheeks matched the red rocks and dirt that were beginning to appear.

Jim went on. "When we dragged home and got here in that snowstorm, I didn't see much, either." He relived their hopelessness just before they reached the Triple S.

"If the first trip into the canyons was bad, the second was pure torture. Not physically, but mentally." He bit his lip as he thought of riding away from his dead twin, filled with grief, remorse, and guilt.

"It's over," Mescal sharply reminded. "Jon wouldn't want it to be otherwise."

"I know." Jim fixed his gaze on the distance and quickly added, "Even coming back not knowing how things were didn't give me time to pay much attention to all this." His wave included the plateau from which they'd descended, the distant sands and rocks and limitless sky. "All the way home I wondered if Mom and Dad would even let me in."

"Jim." Mescal sounded hesitant, and he turned to her immediately. Was the trip proving too painful for her, as it was for him?

"Do you think that maybe someday you will preach?"

Glad for the change of subject, Jim considered before answering. Only the click of the horses' hooves on the firm trail broke the silence. "I've thought about it a lot," Jim admitted.

"And?" Mescal inexorably asked.

"Never — unless I know I am called of God, the way Jon knew he was called."

"Do you think you ever will be?" Mescal, his beloved tormentor, pushed him to the utmost. Her face showed the importance of her probing.

After a long time Jim said, "I don't think so. I think I can do more good by living what we believe the way Dad and Mom do, and speaking out when

I can." His anxious eyes sought her understanding. "If I spent the rest of my life studying and praying and trying to live the way Jesus and Jon lived, I still couldn't repay the debt I owe them. But if I could show Apache the way to salvation, my life would be worth something, and I'd know Jon would be proud of me."

He saw mist rise to Mescal's brown eyes, felt the love she had for him, and knew more than ever how committed he had grown, not only to finding Apache, but to helping save him.

Deeper and deeper they rode into the brakes. Sunny Mescal quieted, awed by the tortuous turns, the canyons crossed and recrossed. Even Jim's sharpest warnings hadn't prepared her for this.

Finally they found the familiar bend. The seemingly inaccessible box canyon lay as Jim remembered it. The crumbling ledge that Apache had once ridden into the gushing waterfall beckoned.

"Stay close," Jim warned, then paused and slid from the saddle. "Here. Shalimar knows it better than Dark Star." They changed mounts. At first Dark Star shied, refused to step along the narrow path, but at Jim's urging, he finally snorted and gingerly went forward with Shalimar right behind, Mescal staring and still.

They rode through the waterfall, into the dim cave and passageway, and out into sunlight bright on the crimson cliffs. It took a moment for Jim's eyes to adjust from gloom to the mile-long hidden valley and its clear, lazy stream winding between cottonwood banks.

Yet even before his eyes could examine the valley that Apache had once called paradise, an awful feeling of emptiness overwhelmed Jim. Deer raised startled heads at the intruders. Small animals scurried to cover. Sage and wild flowers nodded, but that was all.

7

"Apache? King?"

Apache . . . King . . . the bleeding cliffs echoed.

Jim cupped his hands around his mouth and shouted again, "Apache! King!"

Once more the echoes mocked the two who had ridden so far with dwindling hope. *Apache . . . King . . .*

Jim slowly slid from Dark Star's sturdy back. He mechanically loosened and threw down the saddle while Mescal did the same for Shalimar. The weary horses stood knee-deep in grass already yellowing in places, nose deep in the welcome stream.

Jim despairingly turned to Mescal. "I thought they'd be here." He surveyed the valley, unwilling to believe gray King wouldn't come at his call and that Apache, no matter how much he still suffered, wouldn't run swiftly toward them on moccasined feet, gliding over the ground in his incomparable and matchless run.

Too caught up in his disappointment to look nearer, he whirled when Mescal exclaimed, "They have been here!" She eagerly pointed to the remains of a campfire, its ashes barely scattered.

Jim hesitated between elation and reality. "It could be from before." He stooped to the telltale gray pile of ashes.

Mescal's scornful voice interrupted his examination. "You think ashes lie still for months when the wind sweeps through?" She walked a little way toward the horses. Her keen eyes spotted something, and she pounced on it with a little cry. "Horsehair, Gray horsehair." She held up a few strands.

Jim stared, the blood draining from his face. "King." Then his doubting mind added, "But when?"

Mescal walked on and stopped immediately. "Come here, Jim." She stared at the ground.

In two strides he reached her and looked down. Unquenchable hope burst into his body with a triumphant sweep. "Horse droppings. And they aren't very old."

He grabbed Mescal, lifted her against his chest, and swung her around in a mad dance. "They're alive! Apache and King are alive." He swung her again, then a sobering thought clutched at him and he slowly put Mescal

41

down. "At least King is."

"Don't be stupid," Mescal flared. "If Apache isn't alive, just how do you think King got out of the valley? He obviously isn't here, and no one else knows about this place. Even King isn't smart enough to go back through the cave and passageway and along that narrow trail!" Her anger raised Jim's flagging spirits. "Besides, King's too smart to leave a valley when there's grass and water like this." She indicated the contented Shalimar and Dark Star with a pointing finger.

Jim scarcely heard her. His eyes sharp with joy, he scanned every foot of the area where they stood, finding what he sought — moccasin prints. Yet his stubborn refusal to believe the best made him examine the entire valley that day. Everywhere lay evidence that Apache had been there, but how long ago? Jim found it impossible to tell.

"He may have gone for supplies," Mescal suggested that evening when they watched their campfire flames burn toward the star-sprinkled sky. "We can stay, can't we?"

"Only for a short time," Jim told her. "We don't dare let summer trap us." He leaned against a saddle, still barely able to believe what must be the truth. When Mescal lay asleep in the curve of his arm, Jim silently thanked God that the first part of his desire had been granted. Somewhere, perhaps known only to God, a half-breed Apache and a gray stallion named King slept or watched the same friendly stars that guarded Mescal and Jim.

For three days Jim, Mescal, and their horses stayed in the valley, hoping for Apache and King to return. Yet every hour that passed made that less likely. Even those three days saw changes too clear to be denied. The stream slowed its babble to a murmur. Shalimar and Dark Star browsed for food, nosing aside the ever-increasing dry, yellow grass to munch what green still remained.

On the third night Jim admitted defeat. "We leave tomorrow." Sadness stared from his eyes.

Mescal shivered but said, "At least we can be glad they're alive."

"Yes." Jim poked at the fire's dying embers, no warmer than the wind that had swept the length of the valley that afternoon. "Maybe someday . . ." His voice died along with the fire, and long after Mescal slept, he stared into the moonlit night and thought of things too deep to share with his beloved wife. When he slept, he returned to the day he first walked this entire valley, then returned to throw himself facedown into the shrinking stream to cool his hot arms and face — that moment of truth when he had leaped to his feet, torn open his shirt, and seen how his wounds had healed.

Most of all, he saw the rare smile that had transformed Apache's features when he screamed, "I'm well!"

Apache had replied, "I know."

Jim came awake clinging to the memory. Why, the very girl who slept beside him was a gift from Apache! How could he bear it if the silent-footed half-breed vanished back into the lairs he knew so well? What if Jim never saw him again?

From the innermost of his heart, Jim prayed, "Please, God. Take care of him, wherever he is. And someday bring him back."

Mescal stirred, and Jim forced his body to relax and sleep. They would need strength for the long ride home.

In the time it took to ride from the secluded valley to the Triple S, summer attacked with full force. Time after time, clouds scrambled across the sky, but they never gained enough force to drop their healing rain to the parched land. After the first day, Jim and Mescal reverted to Apache's way of travel. They slept the long, hot afternoons away in whatever scrubby or rocky shelter they could find and traveled in the cooler evenings and nights. Once away from the snakelike canyons, Jim knew the way well enough to use the moonlight and starlight and guide himself by the North Star.

Their first whiff of pine when they reached the Kaibab plateau smelled of home. Long before they reached the Triple S, Shalimar and Dark Star pricked their ears and picked up speed. Gold Dust met the dusty four at the edge of the clearing, a bundle of barking excitement that brought Matthew and Abigail to the porch.

For a long moment they faced Jim and Mescal, then Matthew demanded, "Well?"

"They'd been there — Apache and King — but were gone by the time we reached the valley."

Matthew let out his breath in a great explosion. His craggy face beamed. Abigail's mouth trembled into a smile. "Thank God!"

"Looks like it was a pretty hard trip." Matthew's quick glance reminded Jim how worn they must look. He slid from the saddle, dropped Shalimar's reins, and turned to Mescal, who had already dismounted and started toward the corral with Dark Star close behind her. "Want me to rub him down?" Jim called.

Before she could refuse as usual, Matthew intervened. He clumped down the steps and gruffly ordered. "You two get cleaned up while Abigail fixes you something. I imagine by now you're out of supplies. "I'll take care of the horses." He seized Shalimar's reins, caught up with Mescal, and whistled to Dark Star.

"Sounds good to me." Jim hadn't realized how tired he was until he made short work of washing up and dropped into a chair by the homemade table that held steaming plates of bacon, eggs, and fried potatoes. "Are you as hungry as I am?" he asked Mescal.

Laughter chased away her weary look. "As if you need to ask." She forked a mouthful of potatoes and beamed at Abigail. "We stayed three days extra, and that meant short rations. I'm starved!"

Three platefuls later, Jim sighed. "Guess I can't hold any more." He looked regretfully at the almost empty bowls.

"That will keep you until supper," his mother predicted.

"Maybe me, but probably not Mescal."

Her proud chin raised. "If I ate the way you do, I could go all day . . ." she yawned in the middle of her threat.

Matthew came in from tending to the horses and asked, "Before you fall asleep, how about telling us what happened?"

"Not much." Mescal's contagious yawn brought Jim's mouth open, too. "I couldn't tell just how old the signs were, but I'd guess not more than a week, maybe less. Mescal thought Apache might have gone for supplies, so we stuck around. Then it got hotter and hotter. Shalimar and Dark Star had to hunt for feed, and we couldn't stay any longer." This time his yawn threatened to dislocate his jaw. "Sorry." He stumbled to his feet and held out a hand to Mescal. "We'll talk later."

Hours afterward Jim awakened, refreshed and alert. Mescal had disappeared from their room, and he heard her soft laugh from the kitchen. Late evening rays found a chink between the logs and sent a final beam into the shadowy room. Jim stretched. A bed felt good after all the nights out. He rose to full height and stretched again, wishing Apache and King had been in the valley and wondering when or if he'd see them again.

All through the hot July days, dampened only rarely with brief periods of rain, Jim thought of the missing two. August scorched its way into early September before enough rain came to do much good. Abigail's flowers drooped in the afternoons, then perked up at night when she watered them. Dusty, Slim, Shorty, and Dave rode side by side with Jim, Matthew, and usually Mescal. Ranch work went on, no matter how the weather treated them. Those months would always be remembered as a time of peace. As Dusty said, "Nary a rattlesnake around, 'specially the two-legged kind."

Jim marveled and rejoiced. At least so far, another cattle thief gang hadn't discovered Daybreak was no longer Comstock territory. Mescal rode alone when he couldn't go with her, with no need of a guardian. Abigail again sang hymns when she worked, and Matthew teased Mescal unmercifully, asking when a new Sutherland could be expected to come along. Jim knew his father did it just to see the brown eyes flash and the haughty look come into her face when she retorted, "You'll probably have him on a horse before he can walk. Why should I have a boy just so you can spoil him?"

"You could have a girl," Matthew reminded with a twinkle in his eyes. "I like girls, too."

"Me, too. Especially this one," Jim always put in and hugged her. "You just go right ahead and have that new Sutherland whenever you get good and ready, and I'll see that Dad doesn't take over!"

One of the things Jim had feared when he accepted the job as sheriff of Daybreak was that his ranching might suffer. Until now, there had been no problem. Petty thievery and quarrels between neighbors were handled quickly, apparently to the town's satisfaction. Yet the afternoon Jim rode into town and met Carter, he expressed what had been on his mind.

"I'm not sure keeping me as sheriff's the best thing," he told the older man.

"How come?" Carter never minced his words.

"First of all, I'm not in town. By the time someone comes and gets me, the trouble's usually over."

"Are you complainin' or just statin' facts?" Carter grinned.

"Not complaining!" Jim put up both hands. "It's just that . . ." he hesitated.

Carter's keen eyes swept over him. "You want to be free in case somethin's heard about that half-Apache friend of yours."

Jim started. "How'd you know?"

Carter spit a stream of tobacco juice at a nearby clump of weeds, hitting it dead center. "I got eyes in my head, don't I?" He spit again. "That ain't all. You're also wonderin' what Daybreak thinks if you take off like you did a few months ago, leavin' the town kinda unprotected."

"That's it," Jim admitted. "If I'm sheriff, I should be around whether I'm needed or not."

Carter didn't even crack a smile. Instead he said quietly, "The way I hear tell, folks are thankful enough for what you and your Apache did, they're willin' to make do with what time you can give." He held up a range-cured hand when Jim started to answer. "All us boys who acted as your posse and came for the Comstocks still consider ourselves dep'tized. Any trouble happens along when you ain't around, we'll handle."

Jim couldn't speak. His hand shot out and gripped Carter's powerful one.

"I reckon that settles it." Carter grinned a tobacco-stained grin and walked away with the humping gait of a man who spends most of his time in the saddle.

Exactly a week later Jim came in from the range to find a strange horse in the corral. His heart thudded. Had Apache lost King, found a new horse, and come back?

He burst into the house.

Carter sat at the table drinking coffee from a mug.

Jim's heart slowed to its normal beat. He managed to hide his disappointment and shake hands with Carter. "What brought you out this way?"

Carter's eyes sparkled. "Got news you might wanta hear." He deliberately took another sip of coffee.

"Someone steal your best horse? I notice that nag in the corral isn't the one you usually ride," Jim taunted.

Carter sputtered and swallowed what Jim knew would have been some choice cuss words if Abigail and Mescal hadn't been there. "Fine thanks I get for ridin' out here. Naw, no one stole my horse, an' the one in the corral ain't a nag. He's good enough to ride out to see you, though!''

Even gentle Agibail chuckled at Carter's vehemence, but the next minute Carter dropped his taunting and leaned forward. "Wasn't your half-breed Apache's other name Charley somethin'?''

The tick of the clock sounded loud in the sudden silence. Jim stared as Matthew boomed out, "That's right. Charley Campbell.''

Carter sat down his mug with a solid thump. His eyes gleamed the way they had done when he told Jim he and the boys would handle things when needed. Excitement and satisfaction oozed from him. "I knowed it! Charley Campbell. He's the same one.''

"The same who?'' Jim demanded, shaken to his dusty boots, dimly aware of Mescal gaping at Carter.

"The same Indian who's turnin' the Kanab area upside down.'' This time Carter didn't stall but rushed on. "I sent one of my boys up north to see about a horse that's s'posed to be the fastest horse in these parts. While he was there, he heard stories about this Apache who showed up from God knows where. Rumor says he just came ridin' into the Circle Q and asked for a job.''

"When?'' Jim dug his nails into his palms until they ached.

"Long about early June or the middle of June.''

"It's him.'' Mescal's lovely face glowed. "It has to be him.''

"What happened?'' Jim's hoarse voice made it out of his tight throat.

Carter scratched his head. "Owner of the Circle Q asked what he could do. This Apache put on a show like they'd never seen before: ridin', ropin', shootin'. He got hired on the spot.'' Carter shook his head. "Didn't last, though.''

"Why?'' Yet Jim knew the answer long before Carter spoke.

"You know how 'tis. Some folks round about are still fightin' the Indian wars. The feller who talked to my hand said most of the men kept their distance but let Charley alone.'' He regretfully shook his head. "One loud mouth got smart an' tried to pick a fight.''

"What happened?'' Dear God, if Apache had killed a white, even a loud-mouthed white who asked for it, he'd be tracked and killed. It wouldn't matter that he acted in self-defense. Not in these times, when some still fought the wars that had ended long ago.

"Funny thing, First Apache — or Charley, as he calls himself now —just stared at Mr. Big Mouth until all the brag went out of him and he backed down. Then Charley quit his job and rode off on the big gray horse every hand on the Circle Q wanted to straddle.''

Tick. Tick. Tick. The clock kept time with Jim's churning thoughts. Why hadn't Apache beaten down his enemy, the way folks would expect? Did he remember some of the teachings overheard at the Triple S? Or did he simply consider his tormentor not worth destroying?

Matthew's solemn question broke into Jim's turmoil. "Did your hand hear where he went?"

Carter shook his head. "Not exactly. I guess Charley told the Circle Q boss he'd try for a job on another ranch. 'Fraid he won't do much better. There'll always be another big mouth lookin' for trouble." He hoisted himself from his chair. "Jim," Carter's gaze never left the younger man's face, "reckon you'll be needin' the boys an' me to look after Daybreak for a while."

Once more Jim clasped the weatherbeaten hand that offered strength and understanding. Then Carter headed out the door and back to his waiting horse, leaving the Sutherlands to deal with the news he had brought.

8

The next morning Jim left for Kanab. Mescal remained at the Triple S.

"I wonder why she didn't holler about coming?" he mused when he passed Haunting Spring, noting how the aspens had already begun putting on their yellow and gold fall garb. He laughed, and Shalimar's ears pricked. "I thought I'd have one fight on my hands." Jim hunched his shoulders inside the fleece-lined coat. It felt good on this nippy morning when crisp, clean air warned that in spite of the brilliant sun's beat, winter lurked in the woods, waiting to pounce.

His thoughts outran him and boggled up the miles he and Shalimar must cover between the Triple S and the Circle Q. It seemed a lifetime since that spring morning when Apache rode away. Hard to believe only about six months had passed. What had those months brought to Apache? At what moment had he decided to become Charley Campbell and try living with the whites?

"I just bet the red rocks of that valley closed in on him until he couldn't stand it," Jim surmised. He involuntarily pressed his legs closer against Shalimar's sides. The buckskin picked up speed, but Jim slowed him. Weary miles beckoned, and even Shalimar's superb strength mustn't be wasted.

The weather continued warm in the afternoons, cold at night. At the higher elevations Jim awakened to frost, then a skim of ice on the water he'd left in a pan. That morning he blew on his hands to get out enough numbness so he could build his fire, glad for the heavy gloves Mescal had thoughtfully packed. He also told Shalimar, "Old boy, we've got more than distance to beat. "We've got to find Apache — Charley — and get back before winter comes."

Once he crossed into Utah, his heartbeat kept time with Shalimar's steady cadence. Every step brought him closer, closer. But to what?

Jim refused to answer his own question. "If Apache — Charley — is going to work for a white outfit, there's no reason it can't be the Triple S."

The big buckskin tossed his head as if in agreement and kept his nose pointed due north.

Jim located the Circle Q with little trouble. His keen gaze swept the well-cared-for buildings in the red rock rimmed valley, then the cattle, horses, and cowhands mingled in the distance. Alert and ready, Jim slowed Shalimar and rode up the short lane that led to the main house. Before he could dismount, the front door flung open. A booted, spurred giant filled the doorway. "Light, stranger."

Jim slid from the saddle and tossed Shalimar's reins down so he would stand.

"What can I do for you? Looking for a job?" Gray eyes bored into Jim.

He shook his head. "No. I'm looking for someone."

The eyes turned to flint. "We don't want trouble around here. You a lawman?"

"Not me." Jim's quick laugh cleared the air. "A friend of mine hired on awhile back. Half-breed."

"Charley!" The instant smile on the weathered face turned to a scowl. "Best hand I ever had. Too bad he wouldn't stay." The scowl deepened. "I offered to fire the next man who made it hot, but Charley just shook his head and said he'd stayed long enough anyway."

Then the rancher added, "Grand horse, that gray he rode. Looked like a king and lived up to his name, all right. Not a piece of horseflesh around that could match him." He strode down the steps to Jim. His searching eyes took in Shalimar, who showed little fatigue in spite of the long ride. "Hmmm. Your buckskin looks like he could give King a run."

"He can. They've run together many times."

The rancher turned a curious look on Jim. "How come you're out chasing a half-breed Apache?"

"He saved my life." Jim clamped his lips tight.

A low whistle escaped the giant's lips. A brawny arm and gnarled hand shot out and gripped Jim's. "Good luck. Anyone lucky enough to have Charley Campbell for a friend's one fortunate hombre." He dropped Jim's hand and gruffly invited, "Come eat before you go. Or stay the night and talk to the boys."

Jim hesitated. If Mr. Big Mouth, as Carter called him, still rode for the Circle Q, there could be trouble.

"The boys got so used to Charley doing more than his share of the work that when he left, they up and made it clear Simpson wasn't welcome around here."

"Simpson's the hand who tried to pick a fight with Charley?"

Again the gray eyes gleamed like polished pewter. "Yeah. Wish I'd been there. According to the boys, Charley just crossed his arms over his chest and stood there staring the way he'd do at a snake that crossed his path. Except he didn't have to strike." The Circle Q owner scratched his head. "I have to admit, if Charley stared like that at me, I'da probably backed down, too."

Only too well did Jim know that inscrutable, haughty stare! Now he laughed. "Most of us would."

The ranch hands clustered around Jim when they got in from the range, eager to find out who he was and what news he carried. Jim decided to leave a good word for his friend and told them how Apache had been rescued by Mescal then paid his debt again and again. He finished with, "I wouldn't be here now if it hadn't been for him."

"That's what I call a real pard," a young-old cowboy muttered, and a little murmur of assent rippled through the bunkhouse.

"Try the other ranches around here," the gray-eyed giant advised when Jim mounted Shalimar the next morning. "I heard Charley was at the Lazy J, at least for a time."

"Thanks." Jim shook hands again and headed Shalimar down the lane. When he reached the end he called back, "If you hear anything, send word to the Triple S out of Daybreak, will you?"

"Sure will!" The stentorian yell echoed in the still air and warmed Jim's heart, even though his face felt cold from the early morning chill.

Day after day limped by. Jim and Shalimar visited ranch after ranch, some squalid and huddling, barely existing, others prosperous and busy: the Lazy J, the Rocking R, the Triangle Dot, the Half Moon. The days grew colder, and Jim grew more discouraged. How could one man, even Apache, stay just over the next hill, or maybe on the next ranch? How many times would Jim hear the same story with little variation except the names — one rotten apple in a barrel of hands, most of whom might avoid Charley while still respecting him. Always that speckled one who had to prove himself against a half-breed, and who inevitably found his courage slip away when faced by the strange stare only Apache possessed.

More troublesome than not finding the man he sought were the rumors. Apache had grown to be almost a living legend. Sooner or later some foolhardy cowboy would get drunk, find bravery in a bottle, and decide to become a legend himself by killing Charley. Jim shivered at the thought. He must find Apache first. But where?

His search led far north of Kanab, then west. Never had he seen country such as this. Shalimar picked his way over black lava rock where white-trunked, gold-leaved aspens quivered and whispered the coming of winter and other secrets. A rumor that someone fitting Charley Campbell's description had ridden that way led Jim doggedly on — only to find a stranger.

Tired and saddle sore, Jim turned back to Kanab. He had left messages all along the way. He doubted if he'd missed a ranch in the entire southern Utah area, except perhaps the one hidden spread where Apache worked and silently waited for the day he would ride on. A hundred prayers shot upwards. Still his quest remained fruitless.

Shalimar needed new shoes, and Jim had to restock supplies. A few miles before they reached Kanab again, he told his faithful horse. "We can't do any more. Every trail's run out. We'll get outfitted and go home."

A few stinging white flakes hit his thin face. "None too soon, either."

They pulled into Kanab during the first storm of the season. It wasn't a vicious attack, but soft snow that crunched under Shalimar's hooves. By the next morning the sky was cleared. The blacksmith obligingly put aside other work and shoed Shalimar when Jim told him how far they had to travel.

"Get going as soon as I finish." The big man cast an experienced glance at the sky. "It looks good now. Could have a real Indian summer, but you never can tell, and like you said, it's a long way to Daybreak." His hammer rang. "I'll have him ready by the time you get breakfast."

Jim strolled down the wide street and into a small restaurant. Ham and eggs, buckwheats, fried potatoes, and a quart of coffee later, he paid for his meal and started for the blacksmith shop. A shout stopped him in the street.

"Hey, are you Sutherland?"

Jim whipped around. "Yes. Why?" He waited while the short, heavy man who had called came out into the street.

"You the feller who's been askin' around about someone named Campbell?"

Jim felt the blood drain from his head. "Who wants to know?"

The panting man blurted out, "He's here. Campbell, I mean. Rode in a few days after you headed north."

"Where is he?" Jim grabbed the man's arm.

"At the hotel."

Jim didn't even wait to say thanks. Apache, in the hotel where he himself had spent the night? Impossible! Yet the man seemed so sure. Jim ran off, leaving the other man rubbing his arm and muttering something indecipherable.

In his eagerness, Jim nearly tore the hotel door from its hinges. "Campbell," he gasped to the proprietor. "Which room?"

"Ten, but you can't . . ." His protest faded. Jim had already disappeared up the short flight of stairs.

Seven. Eight. Nine.

Jim paused and took a deep breath. *Ten.*

The door swung open. Someone stepped out. Jim reeled in disappointment. The cadaverous man who softly closed the door behind him bore no relation to Apache.

"Can I help you?" he asked.

"Campbell. Isn't this Campbell's room?"

"Yes, but who are you?"

"Jim Sutherland. I've been looking for him."

The searching eyes raked him. "Well, you've found him — what's left of him."

Jim couldn't speak.

"I'm Dr. Clark. Your friend — or enemy — has about one chance in ten of living past Christmas."

Horror shrouded Jim. "What's wrong with him?"

"Lung fever."

"What?" Dr. Clark's death sentence couldn't be true. How could Apache have . . . Hadn't the wounds healed . . . The Circle Q hands and other ranchers and cowboys Jim had questioned never said anything about Charley Campbell being sick.

The watching eyes suddenly came alive. "You say you're Sutherland?"

Jim nodded, his head still whirling.

"Then I guess this is yours." Dr. Clarkly slowly pulled a creased letter from his pocket. "I told him how bad he was and that he might die any time. He gave me this, said to find the man who was looking for Campbell."

Jim paid little attention to the letter stuffing it in his coat pocket. "Can I go in?"

"Why not?" Dr. Clark shrugged. "Can't do any harm." He swung the door open and stepped inside. When Jim crossed the threshold, he heard the click of the door closing behind him.

In the shaded room a blanketed figure occupied an iron bed, motionless, breathing heavily. The sight sent nausea through the visitor. *Why, God? If Apache has to die, why here, among those who have no real interest in him? Was I wrong to pray that his bullet wounds would heal? Apache would rather have fallen in the desert or mountain or valley.*

He had come too late. if only he had taken Mescal home in June and followed Apache then! Why had he waited too long?

A slight movement of the covered figure snapped Jim out of his self-reproach. He clenched his hands at his side and crossed the small, cheerless room as his eyes adjusted to the dimness.

He reached the bed and looked down.

He froze.

The matted hair on the thin pillow showed dark from sweat. The eyes that slowly opened in an unspoken question were deep blue.

Jim's legs gave way and he dropped to a chair Dr. Clark must have placed next to the bed.

"Who are you?" The terrible whisper rang in his ears.

"Jim Sutherland. You are Campbell?"

Crimson spots showed beneath the skin that was drawn tightly over high cheekbones. Luster and something Jim couldn't identify leaped to the sick man's eyes. "Yes." Pleading erased some of the shock in those blue eyes. "You seek me?"

"Not you." Relief released Jim from his amazement. He uncurled his stiff fingers. "I seek Charley Campbell, the half-Apache who saved my life."

"My God!" It was not a curse, but an anguished prayer that winged into Jim's very soul. The half-spent man raised himself to one elbow. "Don't you understand?" the weakening man cried. "I am Charles Campbell, and the man you seek is my only son!''

Stupefied, Jim watched the red stain form on the man's shaking lips. Then Charles Campbell fell back, senseless.

"Clark!" Jim tore open the door, praying the doctor had stayed in the hall.

"Here." Flying fingers checked Campbell's pulse, lifted his eyelids. Dr. Clark shook his head. "What happened?"

Jim tried to explain. "The man I've been looking for. This is his father. He thought his son was dead."

"Never mind all that. Put three drops from the smallest bottle in my bag into the glass with it. Go fill it with water. He's still alive, but I don't see how."

Something deep inside Jim stirred. He hurried to obey Dr. Clark, and a few minutes later they were rewarded by seeing Campbell shift from stupor to a natural sleep.

"You'll stay with him?"

Jim solemnly nodded.

"Good." The doctor set the life-restoring bottle on a small table, the third and last piece of furniture in the barren room. "Every three hours, just like we gave him now. Day and night, or you'll have a funeral on your hands." He straightened from the bed and gave Jim one more level glance.

"I also suggest you read that letter. If it's important enough for him to order me to see you got it, just maybe you'll learn something you need to know." He consulted a round watch on the chain he pulled from his watch pocket. "I have other patients to visit. I'll check in again this evening. Anything you need in the meantime?"

Jim steadied his mind. "If you'd tell the blacksmith to take Shalimar to the livery stable." He pulled money from his pocket and handed it to Dr. Carter. "And tell the proprietor I'll be staying on."

Approval lightened Dr. Clark's face. "Good." He snapped his bag shut. "You must think a lot of Campbell's son."

Jim only nodded, and Dr. Clark went out, leaving him along with the father Apache believed had deserted him.

For a long time he couldn't force himself to read the crumpled, dirty letter. Instead, he watched the sleeping man's face. He remembered the blueness of the eyes that had filled with an indescribable expression. Once Charles Campbell must have been handsome. Jim examined every inch of his face and found, under the ravages of illness, deep furrows that showed suffering. Yet those lines showed no viciousness or hatred, only an uneasy peace. This man had a source of inner strength. Jim's heart leaped. Could Apache's father be a Christian?

At last Jim opened the letter. How many years had the man carried it? How many miles had it traveled? His whole body shook when he read the words.

Dear son,

For more years than I care to remember, I have thought you were dead, along with Running Deer, the only woman I ever loved or married. Now, one of the men who rode in the attack on the Indian village called me to his deathbed and confessed the terrible hoax he and Scoggins and a few others carried out. I had no reason to disbelieve the men when I returned from getting supplies to stock the trading post. I found it in ashes. Scoggins swore you and your mother had been trapped inside. The others backed him up.

I thought I would go mad. My wife. My only son. For weeks and months and years I wandered. Yet the time came when I could neither outrun the past nor keep from coming back where I had once been so happy.

I came back just a few months ago and camped where the trading post once stood. Then the dying man sent for me and I learned everything — how Running Deer died — everything. The man swore he hadn't seen you during the attack, so with every heartbeat I pray that you somehow escaped the massacre by those of my race.

My son, I will spend the rest of my life searching for you. God's love has allowed me to keep my sanity. Perhaps His love will also one day lead me to you. Word has come of a man named Sutherland who also seeks you.

I know I am doomed to die, perhaps soon. When I get near to that, I will give this letter to someone who can send it to this Jim Sutherland. I send it as a sacred trust that he must accept so you will receive this letter.

Do not let the way the whites have distorted the message of Jesus Christ keep you in bonds of hatred. My great desire is that you might know and accept Him so we will meet — sometime.

Your father,
Charles Campbell

PART III
Whispering Sage

9

Apache had halted by the singing waterfall that June day when he knew he must leave the valley. Already its dying source had muted the water's song to sadness similar to the hush autumn brought with its dying leaves. Nothing could withstand the summer heat in this torn and jagged land, not even the waterfall that hid Apache's stronghold.

For a moment, Apache stood transfixed. He had entered and left the cave and tunnel entrance before. Why should this time feel so different?

King nickered and Apache absently stroked the big gray stallion's neck. "Shall we go home, boy?"

Did the intelligent animal understand? Did the toss of the magnificent head, the quick snort, and the deep dark eyes that had witnessed life and death, summer, winter, spring, and harvest see across the trudging miles to the Triple S? to Shalimar and Dark Star and the Sutherlands? to plateaus and draws, promontories and Haunting Spring and the ponderosa studded land where dusty cowboys and red and white cattle mingled?

Nostalgia filled Apache. For most of his life he had walked alone. Now the white blood in him clamored for the sight and sound and smell of men.

Hating his own weakness, yet powerless to fight any longer, he started back.

Fate decreed differently. Before King had gone two miles, his right foreleg slipped on loose shale and he slid. Apache leaped from the saddle in one fluid movement and hauled on the reins. King scrambled back to the trail but gingerly touched down his foot, as if testing it.

"Let's see, old boy." Apache examined the injured leg and relief colored his words. "No swelling." He dug a small, sharp stone from the hoof.

King whinnied, but still limped a bit.

Apache never wasted time with indecision. "Its' too far and hard, going back to the Triple S," he told his companion. "We'll head for Kanab as soon as you're able." Rather than force King the short distance back to the hidden valley, Apache made camp where they were. By the next afternoon King barely limped.

"I won't ride you until you're all right," Apache promised. He looped the reins over his right arm and they started out again. When they came to the trail crossing that led to the Triple S, both King and Apache looked

55

south and west for a long time. Then Apache firmly headed the big gray
west and a little north, toward Kanab. The next day he rode for short time
periods, interspersing them with rest or leading King. Time after time he
gazed at the fantastic formations, the stunted sage, and the omniscient buzzards overhead waiting, always waiting.

A wry smile crossed his carved features, bringing light to his dead-black
eyes and dark skin. "I wonder if the hell the Sutherlands believe in is worse
than this?"

King only rolled his eyes, and Apache chuckled low in his throat. The
sound startled him. When had he ever laughed? The next instant he reverted
to his usual taciturn self. What lay ahead perhaps held no more laughter
than he had experienced until now.

Sometimes as he rode and walked and rested, Apache talked over with
King the incredible idea that had fastened itself clawlike into his brain. With
out arrogance, he knew he could outrope, outride, and outshoot any man in
Utah or Arizona — and Mescal! Instead of provisioning at Kanab and beginning the long journey to Daybreak, why not give himself a try at living
the white way for a time? There must be ranchers who would hire him, once
they saw his skills.

Apache grunted. He'd have to prove those skills, maybe many times.

"Suppose I can't stand being tied to a ranch?" he asked King, wishing
the farseeing horse could answer. "What if I go back to the Triple S and
only my solitary crags and ravines can satisfy me?" A vision of the fresh
sadness the Sutherlands would experience on losing him again haunted
Apache. Day and night he wrestled with his problem, finally telling King,
"It's best to try it somewhere else first. Then . . ." his eloquent shrug left his
fate to the gods.

Once the decision had been made, Apache eagerly rode toward the
future. He arrived in Kanab, inquired about ranches needing hands, noted
how storekeepers' eyes bulged when a half-breed Apache spoke English and
asked about work!

One excowboy whose wrinkled face resembled a parched, cracked creek
bed advised, "Me, if I wanted work . . ." he cackled, but Apache caught the
regret in his eyes, "I'd hit up the Circle Q. They're the biggest an' best outfit
around."

Heart beating an unaccustomed excitement, Apache followed the old
man's directions. Long before he reached the well-cared-for buildings in the
red rock rimmed valley and the short lane that led to the main house,
Apache felt hundreds of eyes fixed on him. Cattle and horses and cowhands
alike started. Some of the cowboys spurred their mounts and fell in behind
Apache, keeping their distance but alert to his every move.

For the first time since the death of Running Deer and his tribe, Apache
wanted to laugh. Armed escort, that's what he had. One muscle in his cheek
involuntarily twitched.

"What's all this?" A powerful yell halted the trail-stained Apache, King, and the band of cowboys riding in behind him as Apache got opposite the log corral. A booted, spurred giant strode out of the barn. Gray-steel eyes bored into Apache. "Well, I'll be . . ." The intense gaze shifted to King, impressive even through his coat of dust. The gray eyes gleamed. "Mighty nice piece of horseflesh you got there," the man said. "You want to sell him?" He repeated the question in Apache's own tongue.

"No. I am looking for work," Apache said in English.

A ripple of surprise stirred the watching cowboys

Not a muscle of the man's face moved. "Who are you? What can you do?"

The moment Apache had anticipated, feared, and prepared for had come. "I am A . . . Charley Campbell, half-breed."

The cowboys rode forward in a bunch. Apache could hear them shifting in their saddles, tensed and ready.

"I can ride and rope and shoot." Black and gray glances met. Neither wavered.

"Prove it."

Apache had expected this. "King is worn out. Do you have a horse I can borrow?"

A loud guffaw came from someone behind Apache. He whirled, but the weathered-faced giant's voice turned him back around.

"How do I know this ain't a trick? You ride in here wantin' a fresh horse. Maybe there's a posse after you." The man scratched his head, and his men pressed closer and formed a half-circle behind Apache and King.

Inscrutable as always, Apache carelessly waved from King to the corralled horses. Disdain underscored every word. "Think I'd ride out of here on one of those and leave King here?"

The silence told him he had won. With a final look at King, the ranch owner barked, "Banty, cut out Lucifer."

"Yessir!" Banty's gleeful yodel warned Apache. He slipped from King's back, tossed down the reins, and followed the mass movement to the corral. Banty had already opened the gate and headed toward the bunched horses on the far side. To Apache's surprise, the bowlegged little man expertly roped and hauled out a screaming horse black as chuck wagon coffee. Admiration licked through Apache's veins at the skilled way Banty kept the furious horse's nose down so he couldn't buck.

"Has he been ridden?" Apache asked.

This time the guffaws echoed up and down the valley. The man's wintry smile and quiet, "Naw" roused the survival spirit in Apache that had kept him alive for years.

"Good." He glided across the corral, sizing up Lucifer with every step he took.

"I'll hold him. You saddle him," Banty panted, muscles tense from the strain.

"No saddle." Apache vaulted to the horse's back, twined his fingers in Lucifer's long, coarse main, gripped his long, sinewy legs against the horse's quivering sides, and wound them under the black's belly. "Let him go!"

Banty slipped his lariat loose and with surprising agility ran to the fence and climbed to the top rail. Apache let out a war whoop that froze the on-lookers and set Lucifer in motion. One warning, convulsive shudder, then the aptly named beast went into action. Never had he sunfished, leaped, whirled, and tried to rid himself of the clinging burr the way he did now. He did a series of leaps high in the air, coming down in jolting, stiff-legged bucks that delighted the cowhands. Apache only gripped tighter. Miles of bareback riding from childhood had turned Apache into an immovable object.

Lucifer screamed with hatred, and Apache yanked his mane harder.

"Ride 'em cowboy!"

Lucifer's next tactic included trying to scrape his rider off against the log corral, scattering the watchers from the top log. Another dizzying round of bucking followed his failure to dislodge the strange brown man who bedeviled him.

"Open the gate," Apache hollered. Sweat drenched him, and the slight tug of his long-healed wounds told him the rest of the battle had to be fought with different weapons.

Banty swung back the gate. Apache leaned forward and screamed into Lucifer's ear, "Go, you big devil. *Go!*" A mighty leap and they were free, flashing past the open-mouthed men, past King, down the short lane, and onto the hard-packed road.

Through the wind rushing in his ears, Apache heard two voices.

"Come back, you stinkin' half-breed horse thief!" one yelled.

"He'll be back." Apache knew the final bellow came from the ranch owner. He allowed Lucifer to stretch out and run the way he needed. Miles flew by. Lucifer didn't slacken his pace. Apache made no attempt to control him until, spent and trembling, the black broke gait, slowed, and stopped. Only then did Apache take the short lead rope attached to the hackamore and turn back toward the Circle Q corrals.

A group of silent men waited in the same spot he had left them. They watched while Apache led the defeated horse into the corral, slid off, and asked, "Shall I rub him down?"

"I reckon so." A broad grin lighted the Circle Q owner's craggy face. "Never saw such ridin'." His gray eyes almost twinkled. "What else can you do, Charley?"

A mighty roar went up from the cowboys, but Apache decided to get everything over with immediately. Before he could reply, a drawling voice said.

"Not bad — fer an Injun."

Apache recognized the voice that had called him a stinking half-breed. He slowly turned to a bigmouthed, redfaced lout at one side of the whispering group, then said, "Banty, how about using your rope?"

"Yessir!" Banty yodeled in the same tone he'd used when told to cut out Lucifer. He handed the coiled lariat to Apache.

After a few practice swings to put his audience off guard, Apache suddenly whirled a practiced loop, dropped it over his heckler's head and shoulders, and pinioned the man's arms to his side. "Not bad — fer an Injun," he mimicked before snapping up the tension until his captive couldn't move.

With all the fickleness and humor of the range, the boys led by Banty, howled in glee and rolled on the ground. Apache loosened the loop and flipped the lariat off the struggling man as easily as it had gone on. Banty obviously wasn't in any condition to want the lariat, so Apache neatly coiled it and hung it on a fence post. Then before the little group could recover from his performances, he played the third. He whipped out the Colt he had worn for years and neatly placed six shots into the trunk of a huge cottonwood across the lane so accurately they formed the letter C.

"Not bad — fer an Injun," Banty commented as he ambled across the lane to stick his fingers in the bullet holes.

"Do I have a job?" Apache demanded of the stupefied ranch owner.

"You shore do. Any gang around these parts who hears we've got a man who can do what you can will steal someone else's cattle and horses — not ours!"

Apache noted the roar of approval didn't include the redfaced man's voice. Instead, he sullenly mounted his horse and muttered something about getting back to the cattle.

"Funny." Banty's innocent air didn't match his shrewd blue eyes. "Never before knew Simpson so anxious to work."

He reminded Apache so much of Dusty on the Triple S that a rare smile momentarily softened the tired traveler's sweaty face.

"Hey, you ain't so ugly when you grin," Banty told him. "C'mom, I'll show you the bunkhouse." His voice died in the gravelike stillness and his face turned grim.

Apache caught the sidelong glances of the men, their unnatural stances. Admiring a half-breed's riding and roping and shooting skills was one thing. Sleeping in the same bunkhouse with that man was a whole different story.

"I'm used to bunking outside, especially in good weather," Apache said, catching the relief in some of the men's eyes. His lips tightened. So Charley Campbell would still be a loner. Well, he had been alone on mountains, in valleys, canyons, and the desert. Being alone in the midst of a busy ranch couldn't be that much different. He turned to King, who patiently rested and waited. "Shall I turn him in with the others?"

"No." The Circle Q owner came out of his private thoughts. "I don't know how well you broke Lucifer. Turn your horse — King, you said? — out with the free ones."

"He'll like that." But first Apache spent a long time talking to King and rubbing him down. Then he cared for the still-weary Lucifer, who relented to his ministrations without more than a token protest.

Within a few weeks, Apache had become Charley Campell. Hearing the stentorian yells, "Charley, time fer chuck," and "C'mom, Charley, there'll be brandin' an' ridin' left tomorrow" from the cowboys made it easier to adjust to his new name than he would ever have thought possible. The ranch work matched any ranch work, with long days broken by Sundays off. Some of the boys rode into Kanab on Saturday nights, but not Apache. The Circle Q had to some degree accepted him. The town of Kanab only heard the rumors.

For the same reason, Apache didn't go to church services, although sometimes he actually missed the Bible reading and the prayers he had heard from the Sutherlands. *A strange thing to miss,* he taunted himself bitterly. yet with each Sunday when he had time to think, questions echoed through his mind. Most of them had to do with the Grand Canyon sized gulf between him and the other hands.

One lazy afternoon when he and King had a good run down the valley and slowly made their way back to the ranch, Apache told his faithful friend, "I'm glad you're all rested up, old boy. Somehow I can't help feeling we'll be moving on, maybe soon." A pang reminded him how far he had traveled since his days of satisfied aloneness.

"It's all Simpson's fault," he burst out. His eyebrows met in a fearful scowl. "I can't prove anything, but he's stirring the others up. Not Banty." He thought of the curious but uneasy acquaintance that was becoming close to friendship between them

The runt of the outfit had frankly admitted, "Until you came, I got all the tricks an' horse laughs. Appears to me we'd better stick together." His blue eyes and solemn face showed he meant everything he said.

The rest of the outfit either ignored Apache or weaseled out of the dirtiest jobs and left them for him. Apache found himself being humiliated by Simpson and a few of his cronies time after time by sly remarks that could easily be passed off as jokes if Banty repeated them to the owner, the way he wanted to, penetrated even Apache's tough skin. He had expected the usual range tricks for the newest hand. He had even anticipated them. The most unmerciful teasing meant a little acceptance. So despite his fierce and almost unconquerable desire for revenge, he handled finding his bedroll wet by moving his sleeping place everynight and hugely enjoy the furtive glances and secret excursions to where the boys thought he'd be. He also controlled himself when he discovered the new saddle blanket he'd bought with his first paycheck cut to pieces and crudely fashioned into a covering for one of the pack burroes.

"Don't let them go too far," Banty privately warned. "Some of the boys are just about ready to give in an' make you welcome 'cause you don't squeal and you don't show you're mad." He sighed and shook his head. "Simpson's been braggin' he's up to somethin' big. Watch him."

"Thanks." Apache said, and from that moment on he unobtrusively kept Simpson in sight during the daytime and spied on him at night. His reward came two nights later when, concealed in the darkness between the bunkhouse and the corral, he saw three dark figures steal out catlike and melt into the shadows. Faint sounds of saddling told Apache something more than a special night watch lay ahead. For the past several days the boys had been in off the range. A special town holiday loomed ahead, and the hands were free to go.

Apache stole closer to the corral. He heard a low voice protest, "I don't like it, Simpson. Tricks are one thing. What you're goin' to do is just plain mean."

"Aw, shut up, will you?" Simpson snarled. "Once the half-breed gets the idea he ain't wanted around here, we'll all be better off." A coarse laugh followed, then the creak of leather and quiet hoofbeats as Simpson and his follower rode away.

Apache pondered. Where would they go in the middle of the night, and how could it affect him? They'd finally given up trying to locate his sleeping places. He bet they knew he had been on to them all along.

He didn't have anything worth stealing except his well-hidden clothes, his gun, and . . .

King!

The thought exploded in his brain, calling out all the hatred and urge to retaliate that lay within. Charley Campbell or not, if they touched King he'd kill them and take whatever punishment came. He raced for the barn, found an old lariat that needed mending. *God, let it hold.* His unconscious prayer escaped unnoticed.

Apache rapidly found the unfrayed end, swung a loop, and headed back into the corral. His eyes found Lucifer. *Zing.* The rope sang, faltered, noosed the black.

Seconds later Apache led Lucifer through the gate and onto the trail those two dark shadows had taken, straight for the range where the horses grazed by starlight.

10

Utah stars that looked close enough to pick faithfully lighted the earth. Apache had no trouble following Simpson and his comrade. The deep anger that had engulfed him when he realized King had to be the object of the two men's midnight ride settled into cold, determined hate — and something more. Even Simpson wouldn't kill such a magnificent stallion as King, would he? Could any man sink so low, even in response to gut-wrenching prejudice?

Apache's tuned ears caught every night sound, including the creak of leather and the ceasing of the soft pad-pad that showed how cautiously his enemies had proceeded.

"King."

Apache started at the low call. He tensed, ready to call out the exact minute Simpson moved.

A soft whinny, followed by the restless movement of other nearby horses, answered.

Apache slipped from Lucifer and clamped his hands tightly around the black's nose and lower jaw in one movement. Lucifer pranced in protest but could not fight that grip.

Night-trained eyes fastened their gaze on the two men, who had also dismounted. Again Simpson's partner protested, "This is a dirty trick. I don't like it one bit. An' that big half-breed ain't goin' to like it, either!"

So? Shut up unless you want me to tell what I know about you."

The starlight showed Simpson's crouched figure. When he reached into his pocket and brought out something, a silver glint reflected.

"King."

Now they were away from the ranch itself, Simpson made little effort to keep his voice down. Unholy glee showed when he bragged, "C'mom, King. I'll just give you a little haircut, and . . ."

In a flash Apache knew the glinting tool in Simpson's hand wasn't a gun or knife, but wire cutters. Relief warred with a fresh spurt of loathing. No wonder the other cowboy had protested. Cutting King's waving mane and tail would mark the horse forever.

A third time Simpson called, "King."

Shuffling feet answered. On the Triple S, every horse came when called.

Yet some instinct, some inner awareness must be warning the big gray. King stopped a good ten feet short of the waiting cowboys. He raised his head. Sniffed. Then with a show of heels he danced back when Simpson lunged toward him and sped toward the poised Apache.

Another minute and Apache would be discovered. Without warning, he leaped onto Lucifer and charged the two statutelike cowboys. Just before he hit them, he swerved the black, turned, and saw how the men scattered from Lucifer's wicked hooves before he raced into the darkness.

"What spooked that horse?" Simpson's furious demand splintered the quiet night.

"What!" The voices carried through the clear air. "Better be askin' who, not what."

Lying flat on Lucifer's back so he couldn't be seen, even if the others followed, Apache stifled a desire to laugh. A broad grin erased some of his anger but none of his contempt. But he had no time to linger. Quietly yet rapidly he headed Lucifer toward the ranch. He must get the black back in the corral before his enemies returned. The rest of the horses had scattered, and Simpson had little chance of finding King again.

Apache barely made it. With a quick apology to Lucifer for not rubbing him down, he freed the black and rolled under the bottom log of the corral to hide in the shadows. Seconds later the other two sneaked their horses in, did what had to be the worst job ever of caring for their mounts, and freed them. Apache waited long after Simpson and his cohort tiptoed into the bunkhouse, then quickly cut Lucifer out and removed all traces of his midnight escapade.

The rest of the night Apache lay watching the stars and remembering the Sutherlands and the Triple S. They seemed farther away and more remote than the friendly stars that shone and twinkled down on him. Perhaps he should give up all attempts at being Charley Campbell. The whites had never accepted him and never would. In the meantime, what about Simpson?

The question rode with him all the next day and the day following. *What about Simpson?* Apache knew that if he stayed on the Circle Q, trouble lay ahead. That first day Simpson avoided him, but Apache never looked up without seeing the man's baleful eye on him.

The second day Simpson resumed his taunts, remarking in a loud voice how unusually stinking the Circle Q was these days.

"Could be some cowpokes don't know enough to wash," he complained at the top of his voice. "Then, it could be . . . other things." He looked straight at Apache.

Banty roared to Apache's defense. "If you don't want to wind up with an Apache haircut, you'd better learn to keep your big mouth shut, Simpson."

At the word *haircut,* Simpson turned mottled purple, sent a sidewise glance at Apache, and slunk off when Apache folded his arms and stared into his eyes.

The next morning Apache packed his sparse gear, saddled King, and rode up the lane to the main house. "I'm moving on."

The steel-eyed giant of a ranch owner tried to protest. "Why? If it's Simpson — an' it's bound to be — he can get off the Circle Q, far as I'm concerned." Fire blazed in the cold eyes. "So can any other man who feels the same."

Emotion gripped Apache, but he shook his head. "I've been here long enough. It's time for me to mosey on." Only the softening of his midnight black eyes showed his appreciation of the giant's offer.

"Sorry to see you go." His boss counted out money. "Ten dollars bonus for breakin' Lucifer." He grinned and eyed King. "Still won't sell?"

"No." Apache stuffed the money in his saddlebag.

"Where will you go? There's a lot of ranches around here, an' you've got the reputation to get on at most of them."

Apache merely nodded, wheeled King, and rode off. He didn't look back. But once out of sight of the ranch house and the valley with its horses, cattle, and cowboys, he stopped, turned, and raised one hand in silent farewell.

"Boss likes us," he told King. "Banty, too." An unrecognizable feeling touched him. "I bet Jon Sutherland would be surprised if he knew we rode away from a sure fight. Jim, too, and the rest of the Triple S." He shrugged. Range talk always spread worse than wildfire. What stories had already been carried and grown bigger since he came to the Circle Q?

Apache found out soon enough. The boss of the Lazy J almost fell over himself in his eagerness to hire Charley Campbell. So did owners of the Rocking R, the Triangle Dot, and the Half Moon. Summer deserted the Kanab area. Fall descended. Nights turned chilly, mornings frosty. Yet Apache moved on. Each time he began to feel at home on a ranch after proving his skill with horse, rope, and gun, one rotten apple cowhand managed to spoil at least a few others. For the most part, the hands left Apache alone, except for those fateful few destined to change Apache's future.

At the Half Moon, a new problem arose. The rancher's daughter took a fancy to the new hand and made no secret of it. Apache despised her ruses for showing up where he worked and the hundred pretenses she made to gain his company. Deep in his heart Apache carried protection against such girls and against the women who haunted saloons and attempted to lure him. Mescal Ames, now Mescal Sutherland, represented everything a woman should be. Except for his mother, Mescal had been the only girl or woman to touch Apache's life and rouse both love and dedication. He had buried his mother. He had also buried in the unseen depths of his heart a love that asked nothing except the right to protect and some way repay Mescal for saving his life.

Unfortunately, his very aloofness spurred on the Half Moon girl's advances until the pack of cowboys she had turned down in hopes of someone better grew sullen and resentful of her obvious pursuit of Charley, who ignored her.

This time Apache simply rode out at night rather than risking meeting the shallow, vain girl again. The one thing he carried away with him was precious — knowledge that her father knew his daughter well and would believe no wild tales the spoiled and frustrated girl might choose to tell.

Where should he ride now? How many more ranches would welcome him, only to prove impossible? Should he turn and go south and west, back to Daybreak, where at least he was known if not accepted by many?

Should he hole up in the warmth of canyon bottoms that seldom held snow and always offered graze for King?

Solitude or slavery?

"By all the gods of earth and sky," he burst out to King, who faithfully plodded through the first warning snowfall, "have I no other choice? Why should the color of my skin forever keep me apart? Why are there barriers that can neither be crossed nor torn down? Am I a wild thing to either be caged or driven far from all people?"

Yet in his bitterest moments Apache could not deny the unconquerable hope he secretly denied and scorned but could not quite kill. Surely, the next ranch would be better. The spread over that next rise or around the bend in the trail would offer a place where Charley Campbell could work and forget the past.

He often remembered how the Sutherlands believed the white God's son Jesus came to earth for all — whites, Indians, even half-breed Apaches.

"If it's true, not many people around here seem to know it," he scoffed to the only companion he could fully trust. "Most of these ranchers claim to follow the white God. What good is it? Except for the Sutherlands, not one of them acts like *all* means for me, any more than for you, old man."

King tossed his head as if in agreement and Apache called out to the leaden sky, "If you exist, white God, you are a God of many faces — and none of them shines on the Apache."

Only the increasing snowflakes replied. Empty-hearted, dissatisfied, hating the Sutherlands for awakening in him this terrible and unquenchable gnawing, Apache turned his face toward the canyon country. No more would he try to live among the whites. If he must suffer, let it be as an Apache.

His chiseled lips set. Somewhere, some time, the desert sun would gleefully watch the buzzards pick clean his bones. Until then, what did it matter how a "stinkin' Injun" lived?

Apache's journey from the Half Moon back toward Kanab became a bittersweet trek. In spite of his determination to forsake Charley Campbell, his moments of friendship with Banty and the owner of the Circle Q perched on his saddle horn and mocked him. He shut his mouth tighter than ever and rode on. The fickle season warned him how short a time he had to reach his destination before snow blanketed the land and hid its imperfections with a mantle of deceptive softness that masked winter's cruelty. To be caught in a blizzard without shelter offered certain death.

With the impending winter came a slight lessening of Apache's morbid thoughts and a return of his survival spirit. He had fought cold and storms before. He would again, unless he died in the canyons.

Did the snow gods sense his challenge? Long before he reached Kanab, Apache knew he needed shelter. The wind's whine had grown into a scream in the last hour. Flakes changed to hard, hurting ice pellets that attacked man and beast. Apache cared less for himself than for King. If he had been near one of the ranches, he would have unhesitatingly sought and received at least a surly welcome according to the law of the range.

Instead, he traversed a faint trail rapidly filling with snow. "Must be someone living around here. This is no deer trail," he surmised and urged the reluctant King forward.

The trail grew dimmer. The day changed from gray to white. Snow deepened and clogged King's hooves. Again and again Apache cleared them. He could no longer see into the driving snow. With a quick loosening of reins, he leaned forward and shouted into King's ear, "It's up to you," then stayed slumped forward to avoid some of the force of the blizzard.

King snorted once and moved on. This time when his hooves clogged, his half-senseless rider, buffeted by the storm, didn't stop him. Step by careful step, King continued.

Suddenly he stopped. The cessation of the movement that had lulled Apache now brought him fully alert. "What is it, boy?"

King whinnied.

Apache stiffened in the saddle.

King whinnied again.

This time Apache's straining ears caught the distant but unmistakable sound of a horse neighing in response. He wearily freed King's feet, his exposed hands and face stinging from the beating the storm had given him.

"Go on, King," he ordered when he remounted.

Minutes, hours, or years later, they brushed past a snow-laden tree branch that all but obscured a tiny clearing. Apache peered through the gloom. Had the sun broken through? He shook his head to clear his thoughts. His heart pounded when he saw the dim outline of a building just ahead. Another neigh proved the dark shape wasn't just a mirage. Flickering light shone feebly through a tiny window. Firelight? A candle?

It didn't matter. Apache's mouth set in a grim smile. This godforsaken place could be a hideout for robbers or a meeting place for so-called respectable cattlemen not above building up their herds by hiring crooked cowboys. When he walked across that tumbledown porch and opened the door, would it be a trap?

He led King along the dark wall to a roofed extension of the building itself. Animal heat and a welcoming nicker greeted him, and he stabled King next to the bony horse already there. King immediately began munching the sparse hay that had been sprinkled on the hard-packed earth.

"Hands up!" Something hard poked him in the back.

Apache considered whirling and attempting to catch his captor off guard. He gave up the idea immediately. Even if it worked, he couldn't ride King off into this storm.

Instead, he obediently held his hands high, grimly amused that the storm had done what no one had ever done before — caught him unprepared and allowed someone to get the drop on him.

Another prod and a low, "Take one step at a time and don't turn around" set Apache walking to the porch.

"Shall I go in?" he asked when the pressure on his back wavered for a heartbeat.

"Yes." Now the voice only whispered. Another sharp jab into Apache's spine warned him that whoever walked behind him meant business. He carefully opened the door, swept a glance around the interior of the small, warm room, and stepped inside. Even that quick look showed the room barren and empty. Good! One person to contend with meant that much less danger.

The next thought relaxed him, and his arms involuntarily started to relax.

"Keep them up!"

Apache winced when another jab caught him in the healed bullet wound under his left shoulder blade.

"Who are you, and what do you want?"The man whispered.

Why didn't he speak up? Apache wondered. He answered, "I'm called Campbell. I'm on my way to Kanab from the Half Moon." No point in saying he no longer worked on the Half Moon.

"How did you get here, to the cabin?"

The relentless pressure never let up.

"Can I put my hands down?" Apache asked.

"No!" The single word hissed in the silence that was broken only by the snapping of a log in the fireplace.

Apache sighed. "Look, mister, I'm not looking for trouble. King and I got caught in the storm and he followed the trail in here."

A short gasp and a terrified, "You found the trail?" spoke for itself. Whoever lived here or had taken refuge here didn't want to be found.

Apache frowned, then admitted, "I wouldn't have, except I'm half-Apache." His muscles tensed. Would the next sound be a shot? The silence was so long Apache's nerves screamed.

"You said your name was Campbell. Not *Charley* Campbell."

So his reputation had preceded him to this hidden cabin. At least it didn't sound like his captor planned to shoot him right off. Should he take a chance and dive to one side, then roll and grapple with him?

He didn't have to.

A little sigh that could be relief ended with the last words Apache ever expected to hear just then.

"Thank God!" the whisperer said, and something slithered to the floor.

Freed from the persuader in his back, Apache whipped around and stared into the dimness. A slender, dark-haired, dark-eyed girl in buckskins had dropped to a rude chair and sat with her face buried in her hands. A stick lay at her feet.

"But . . ." Apache rubbed his eyes. Had he gone snow-blind? His blood ran cold, the way it had done on that long-ago day when he saw his mother killed.

"Mescal! What are you doing here?"

11

In the eternity before she dropped her hands, Apache's heart pounded with fear. Had Jim been killed? Or the whole Sutherland family? Had Mescal come looking for him with winter lying in wait? What terrible thing had happened to send her to this place? How had she ever found it? Or had the bony horse in the lean-to brought her here the way King had done for him? Where were Shalimar and Dark Star?

Trembling hands fell from the tragic, convulsed face. Apache took one step forward, snatched a log, threw it on the fire, and stared at the girl.

She was slender and disheveled, her raven hair in two thick braids, her velvet eyes bright with tears. She gazed up at him.

But she was not Mescal.

"Who are you?" he demanded hoarsely, disbelieving his own eyes, even while he noted the dusky skin that no amount of sun could cause.

"I am Whispering Sage," the girl so like Mescal said. She no longer whispered, and her musical voice filled the humble room. I am Navaho."

Now that the flames in the fireplace brightened the room, Apache saw both similarities and differences between this girl and Mescal, yet when Mescal rode in her buckskins with her hair in a braid, the two looked enough alike to be related.

"What are you doing here alone?" Apache folded his arms across his chest and demanded. His quick survey of the thin-blanketed cot, the pitiful store of food on the broken-legged table, and the havoc in Whispering Sage's face spoke for itself.

Her words confirmed it. "I had no other choice." A long sigh escaped her lips. Had she been holding it in for days, weeks, perhaps years?

Stirred first by her resemblance to Mescal then by the kindred feeling of loneliness recognizing loneliness, Apache deliberately turned from the girl and fed the fire until it roared up the chimney. He silently removed his coat and laid it on the hard-packed earthen floor that showed signs of sweeping. He knew she watched him, and he swung around to ask, "How is it that you speak English?"

"First we must eat." She roused from the lethargy she'd slipped into from sheer relief. "I haven't much, but you're welcome to what there is."

"No need for that," he told he gruffly. He shrugged back into his coat

69

and struggled the white distance between porch and lean-to, glad for the good supply of dried beef, salt, jerky, dried apples, parched corn, and flour he carried. When he glided back into the cabin, he tossed the knapsack to her without speaking, then stood steaming by the fire until its heat warmed body and soul.

Still, he couldn't help but wonder what kind of story he would hear, and when the slender girl ate as if famished, he felt the strange kindship he had felt earlier.

Deft hands made short work of cleaning their heavy plates and forks, then Whispering Sage settled herself on the edge of the cot. The room held no chairs, so Apache sat cross-legged on the floor.

Whispering Sage's story began the same way many desert stories did. A well-meaning tenderfoot white missionary and his wife visited her Navaho village and were impressed with the young girl's beauty and intelligence. Convinced that she could rise above her surrounding, they pleaded with her to let them give her a home. They would teach her white ways and the white religion.

Both of Whispering Sage's parents had died years before. She often longed for more than the village life offered, without even understanding what those longings were. She loved the missionary and his wife immediately, and after many months they succeeded in winning the consent of the Navaho chief to provide a home for the thirteen-year-old girl.

"For five years I lived with them," Whispering Sage said sadly. "They taught me so much!" Her deep eyes glowed. "All about the white Father and His Son Jesus. I knew Jesus took my place and died so I could live always." If she heard Apache's disbelieving grunt, she ignored it. "Everything changed this last spring. The missionary and his wife took fever. I cared for them, but they both died." One diamond tear hung on her downcast lashes.

"Why didn't you go back to your people?" Apache asked harshly, knowing the answer before it came.

"I tried." The drooping head sank lower. "They no longer welcomed me. I no longer could accept their way of life. I had become a different person because of the white missionary and his wife."

Rage exploded inside Apache. "Why should they make Indians into people who will never be accepted? Why don't they leave the Indians in what little peace there is after all the long fighting has ended?"

The dark eyes opened wide. "Oh, but if it hadn't been for them, I would not know of Jesus!"

Apache grunted again. His lip curled. "So where is this Jesus when you need Him?" He cruelly examined every inch of the rude cabin. "He lets you almost starve and live in fear."

Whispering Sage shook her head until her fat braids swung. "I thank the white Father that I escaped when I did." Her sturdy chin lifted. "I have not starved."

"But why are you here at all?" Apache persisted. "Weren't there other whites who wanted to care for you?"

"Oh, yes." Venom replaced the shine of her eyes. "Many. Especially the whiskey-guzzling storekeeper at Kanab. And Simpson."

Apache's lithe body landed on both feet in a single spring. "You mean Simpson of the Circle Q?" He clenched his fists in memory of the humiliation and a certain night among the horses.

Whispering Sage only nodded and kept her steady gaze fixed on the crouching Apache. "He waylaid me when I was sixteen, told me someday I'd be his woman." Contempt twisted her beautiful mouth. "Not his wife, of course, just his woman. I told the missionary and his wife, and they protected me. I could not ride free or walk in the valleys without them."

"What about the storekeeper? Did he want to marry you?" Apache's hands curled into talons.

A bitter laugh that could have sprung from Apache's own heart echoed in the quiet room. Again Whispering Sage's lips twisted. "Marry a Navaho? Never! Besides, he already has a wife, if you can call the drab woman who has borne his children a wife."

"And still you believe in the white God of many faces!" he burst out, angered and scornful.

"Such men have nothing to do with the white God," she told him. The ringing clarity of her voice stilled Apache's protest. Her lovely face gradually lost its contempt and became more beautiful than the delicate Sego lily. "Does the braying of a mule change the song of a meadowlark? Both are what they are."

Unable to answer her reasoning, Apache asked, "How did you find this place?"

She looked pale beneath her rich brown skin. Her lips drooped at the corners, and faint shadows discolored the delicate skin beneath her eyes. "All summer the hotel keeper let me stay in a small room and have meals. I cleaned the rooms and helped in every way I could." Her thin shoulders raised and slumped. "With winter coming and few visitors, he could no longer keep me. No one else wanted me to help with cleaning and cooking — except the storekeeper.

She bit her lip and a tiny bright stain of blood marred the smooth surface. "I heard that the Half Moon ranch needed a cook, so I crept away in the night. It was no longer safe for me to stay in Kanab."

"Where did you get that bag-of-bones horse?"

Color rushed back to her face. "I didn't steal him. When I left the Indian village, the chief gave me a present of a silver and turquoise bracelet. I traded it for the horse."

"You know you were cheated."

Her winged eyebrows rose in surprise. "Of course! I expected no more. But what could I do?" She forestalled his next remark by rushing on. "The poor old horse went so slowly I knew he needed rest. Three times I heard hoofbeats behind me and hid." Her figure grew rigid. "I peeped from under the bushes and saw Simpson ride by." Genuine fear shone in every muscle. "I didn't know how he knew. Perhaps the hotel keeper told him, or the man who sold me the horse. When he had gone, I found this old trail. Even this . . ." she gestured around the cheerless cabin, ". . . is better than what lies behind." She bravely looked up at Apache, who loomed over her like the shadow of a soaring eagle. "I thank God for it."

He could not answer her defiance. Here sat another like the Sutherlands, someone who held to her faith in the white God, no matter what happened. Strange. Just when he had determined to bury himself away from the white world and their changeable God, he had come face-to-face with both again.

"Charley Campbell, do you wish to speak of yourself?"

Apache's face relaxed into almost a smile at the quaint way she had of expressing herself, even though she spoke good English. He pondered for a time, fighting his natural reticence and weighing it against the desire to tell this courageous girl everything. The desire won. Prodded by gentle but undemanding questions, Apache opened his heart while snow pelted the roof, the fire grew low, and the room chill.

"You have suffered much," Whispering Sage said when at last he finished. "One day . . ."

He shook his head. "There is no day for a half-breed Apache." He abruptly stood. "Cover yourself and sleep." He caught the half-smothered little gasp. "Have no fear. I am not like Simpson of the Circle Q." He banked the fire with more logs, lay down on his saddle blanket, pulled another blanket abound him, and faced away from the girl who so resembled Mescal.

With the capriciousness of autumn, the snow lingered for a second day, then the weather changed. The third morning Apache woke to sun-strewn red cliffs that glistened more white than red. Whispering Sage's cot lay empty, the blankets still rumpled. Something bubbled in a pot hung in the fireplace and sent out an enticing aroma.

Apache glided to the door, glad for the clearing day but perplexed. What was he going to do with Whispering Sage? To leave her here was unthinkable. To allow her to go on to the Half Moon meant possible trouble. The owner would treat her well, but the foolish daughter couldn't help but be jealous of the Indian girl's beauty.

A little voice deep inside advised, *take her to the Triple S.* Apache shook himself impatiently. He had set his course, and it didn't include going back. Coils of circumstance bound him. What other choice was there? If Whispering Sage stayed in the Kanab area, sooner or later either the storekeeper or Simpson would get her.

An echo from the past sprang to Apache's mind, one of the things he had carried since childhood. His mother's voice, admonishing, "Charles Campbell did not just take me, my son. You must always remember that. We stood before a white man who married us in the white man's way. Charles Campbell said I could not be his wife unless we were blessed by his God."

What a world lay between the honorable man who had fathered him and the whites who took Indian girls at their pleasure! But all the remembering in the world didn't solve Apache's problem of what to do with Whispering Sage — unless he took her home to the Sutherlands. They would welcome her, he knew, for her own sake, as well as for his, and for the sake of the white God they worshiped.

Apache stared into the snowy world and saw visions of Mescal and Whispering Sage running with the collie, Gold Dust; of them mounted on Shalimar and Dark Star; of them sitting at the end of day with needles and cloth, mending or stitching. He also saw himself in the big ranch house living room, standing in the shadows, listening and watching.

"We haven't much food left." Whispering Sage stepped inside, eyes sparkling from the cold day.

"I know." Apache stared at her and made the decision. "Can you stand a long, hard trip?"

Her eyes opened wide. "Of course. Why do you ask?"

"I will take you to the Triple S. If the weather remains clear, we will have no trouble. If not . . ." his expressive shrug covered that possibility.

Whispering Sage hesitated, then said, "Will . . . will I be welcome?"

"Yes." A world of assurance underlined the one word.

Light crept into her face, but she only asked, "When do we start?" Slim, brown fingers clenched and unclenched.

"I must get a better horse than yours, and supplies," Apache told her. "You should stay here until I do. Kanab is not the place for you — or for me. To buy a horse there would be stupid." He considered for a moment. "The owner of the Circle Q likes me and asked me to stay. He will sell me a good horse and not ask questions. He also keeps a storehouse of supplies and will give me what I need."

"I . . . I have no money."

Apache looked at the buckskin-clad girl facing him without shame. "It doesn't matter. I have what I earned on the ranches." He planned more out loud. "When we start, we will not go through Kanab but make a wide circle. We will stay away from all who might wonder. King is well-known. We cannot pass as just two Indians traveling. There is food enough for you to last through tomorrow, and I will return the next morning."

He found it hard to resist her pleading eyes when she said, "I wish I could go with you."

"You can't. If we were seen, there would be trouble." His numble fingers knotted a small pouch with a few pieces of jerky that would hold him until he reached the Circle Q.

"Will you see Simpson?"

The question hung between them.

Apache chose to treat it lightly. "No white man sees an Apache unless the Apache wills it." He could sense her relief. "Don't leave here until I get back. If I'm delayed, it won't be for long. Remember, stay here." The unspoken words *where you're safe* rang in his heart, and he knew she understood.

"I will pray for you."

Apache didn't scoff as he would have done three days earlier. If it comforted her, fine. Prayers to a white God of many faces might be of little use, but they could hurt nothing.

A few minutes later he and King backtracked the trail. Apache frowned. Broken branches from their struggles through the blizzard clearly marked their path. No one should be out after the storm, yet when Apache reached the trail's entrance, he brushed the snow smooth and erased all sign.

Uneasy, Apache pushed on toward the Circle Q and reached it unobserved in the growing dusk. The horse buying transaction and provisioning went as smoothly as he'd predicted. The gray-eyed rancher said. "You're welcome to Lucifer. None of the other boys can ride him. Simpson tried 'for he left. He got chucked off, and the boys about split. Oh, your Arizona pard drifted in lookin' for you."

Apache's eyes glittered. "Jim Sutherland?"

"Ahuh. Said he'd heard you were here. I told him to check out some of the other ranches. He can't be far behind you."

Apache thanked him and rode away. So Jim had come after him! Should he scout around and see if he could find him? No. Whispering Sage wouldn't be safe until he got her to the Triple S. With Lucifer and King, they could outrun any horses he'd ever seen except Shalimar.

The trip back to the lonely cabin where Whispering Sage waited took longer. Lucifer wasn't to be led, and he didn't like leading King. Finally Apache mounted Lucifer, whistled to King to follow, and got the nervous black settled down. Even when the warning little voice that had served its master well in the past cried, *faster, faster,* Apache held to a steady pace. He kept on by moonlight and only rested when the moon gave up its uneven contest with rolling black clouds and vanished into their murky depths. He snatched a little sleep and rode on as soon as night moved into gray dawn.

When he arrived at the turnoff to the cabin, Apache froze. The carefully concealed entrance lay exposed and crisscrossed with horse tracks! The same tracks wound and twisted over the crooked trail, into the clearing, and ended in front of the ramshackle porch. A magnificent bay munched the last of the hay in the lean-to; a curl of smoke rose from the chimney.

Apache halted Lucifer and tied him to a nearby cedar. He did the same with King and saw the reproach in the big gray's eyes at this unaccustomed procedure. Then on fleet and silent feet, Apache weaved in and out of brush, to the lean-to, keeping downwind of the bay.

"Ahh." The horse wore a Circle Q brand, as Apache had expected. Simpson must be inside.

Every ounce of hatred for Simpson and admiration of the courageous Navaho girl who trusted in an unseen power for protection joined in a mighty catapult toward the house. Through the dirty window Apache saw a scene often repeated in range gossip, usually in whispers.

Whispering Sage stood backed against the fireplce, eyes wide, a sturdy log in one hand.

Simpson stood poised in front of her, his back to the cabin door. The menacing figure almost dwarfed the slender girl who showed no sign of fear.

Noiselessly, carefully, Apache stole to the open door.

"Think you can run from me, you wildcat?" Simpson's grating voice sent strength through Apache. "I swore I'd get you, and now I have." He laughed suggestively. "Thanks to the smoke from your fire."

The next instant the impassioned Simpson lay face down on the floor, straddled by Apache, whose full weight had hit him from behind.

"Charley! Thank God!"

If he lived to be older than the canyons, Apache would never forget Whispering Sage's voice which mingled with the dull thud of her frail defense slipping from nerveless hands to the floor.

12

Red rage engulfed Apache. Knees like steel pinned the writhing Simpson fast. Hands made strong from years of wilderness living closed around the cowboy's throat and tightened until only a choking sound could come out. A panorama of Whispering Sage's face and Scoggins attacking Running Deer changed Simpson into every white man who had ever wronged an Indian girl.

Yet through the roar in his ears Apache heard a crying voice he could not ignore.

"Charley, for the love of God, no!"

The red haze receded. Apache looked into Whispering Sage's terrified face and at the small hands that tried to pry his fingers from their awful task.

"Don't do it," she sobbed. "He isn't worth killing."

Had someone else long ago said that? Apache couldn't recall. His knees remained taut, but his fingers loosened from the senseless hulk beneath them.

"Is he dead?" Stark fear etched Whispering Sage's face and made her old.

Apache's knees held firm, but he lifted his hands and shook his head. "No. Just unconscious. But why did you stop me?"

Her gaze never left his face. "I could not let you kill — even him." Contempt chased some of the horror from her face.

"It would have been the first time," Apache admitted, then he averted his eyes from the blaze of radiance in her face. "I had no chance when my village fell. Later I walked alone." He proudly raised his head. "The Sutherlands kept me from killing Comstock on sight, but I would have helped hang him if he hadn't turned his gun to himself."

A moan from Simpson rippled the silence that followed his words. Apache involuntarily tensed. He gazed helplessly at Whispering Sage. "If I don't kill him, what would you have me do with him? You'll never be safe anywhere, as long as this snake is around."

"Make him swear to leave and never come back to Utah or Arizona," she pleaded.

"You think he would keep such a vow?"

"I believe he will be afraid not to," she whispered. Her slim brown fingers clenched and unclenched.

Apache only grunted, unconvinced and unwilling to take a chance. "If there were a way he could be . . ." His heart pounded. The beginnings of a cruel smile settled on his lips. "Get my lariat off King," he ordered.

Whispering Sage hurried to obey. When she returned Apache bound Simpson's hands behind his back, then lifted him to the cot. Simpson opened his eyes and recoiled. Apache stood in front of him, knife in hand. The keen blade that had once opened Jim Sutherland's wounds to the clean healing air flamed molten silver in the desolate cabin.

"Campbell!" It burst from suddenly pallid lips and echoed in the room. Simpson's eyes rolled wildly. "What are you going to do? Ahhh . . ." He tried to move back from his approaching enemy but only succeeded in huddling against the wall. Sheer terror stamped itself on his face, and his gaze never left that flickering, menacing blade.

"The only thing to do to skunks is to kill them." Apache heard Whispering Sage gasp behind him but took a step closer to his victim.

"I . . . I was just goin' to . . ."

"I know what you were going to do, white man!" Apache's denunciation cut short the fumbling lie. "Even a 'stinkin' Injun' knows what kind of man you are, and Utah will be a lot better place without you." He raised the knife.

The whimpering sound behind him and the dirty yellow of Simpson's skin encouraged Apache to get on with his task. "Remember a certain moonlight night in a horse pasture?" he taunted. "Remember a big, dark horse plowing between you and your sidekick and the dirty business you were up to?"

"So it was you!" Simpson's mouth foamed. "On Lucifer." He frantically struggled against his bonds. Apache sickened at the sniveling coward before him, a far cry from the bold rider who swaggered and terrified an Indian girl.

"I'll do anything. I've got some money. Take it. Just don't kill me," Simpson babbled.

"If I let you off this time, will you promise to leave Utah and Arizona and never come back?"

A cunning gleam crept into Simpson's eyes. Before he could agree, Apache told him, "If you're ever seen in these parts again, I'll hunt you down the way I do mad coyotes."

"I'll go and not come back."

"You swear?"

"I swear." But the gleam grew brighter.

Completely in charge of the situation, Apache sneered and raised his knife. "I'll just give you a little more reason to keep your word."

The knife flashed.

Whispering Sage screamed. So did Simpson.

Apache fixed his hand in Simpson's tangled hair and jerked the man's contorted face forward. The knife descended. Apache hissed, "You'd have marked King forever by cutting his mane and tail. Well, you won't want to be seen around here any more than King would if you'd ruined him."

In a single slashing motion he sliced off a great hank of hair not more than a quarter of an inch from Simpson's scalp and threw it on the earthen floor. "Don't move. It would be too bad if the knife slipped and whacked off an ear." Savage enjoyment of his task raced through Apache. Again and again he cut, until a great pile of coarse hair covered the floor where he stood and Simpson's scalp shone dirty through the stubble that remained.

"There!" Apache spat on the hair and stood back to admire his work. Stripped of both hair and dignity, Simpson cowered on the cot. His face worked, and his bulging eyes stared at the pile of hair.

Apache turned when a sigh like aspen leaves in the wind escaped Whispering Sage's lips. She stood frozen, gazing at the shorn Simpson. The next moment a wild ripple of laughter slipped through the hands she had clamped over her mouth. Then another.

Simpson's head whipped up at the sound. He tried to free himself, but the sturdy knots held.

Whispering Sage laughed until all the held-back tears of many months flowed down her smooth brown face. She finally managed to say, "I . . . I don't th . . . think Simpson will s . . . stay."

Apache inclined his head toward the struggling man. "Remember, if you ever come back . . ."

Simpson didn't answer. Neither did he speak when Apache calmly took his gun. Apache untied his lariat and hustled the beaten cowboy out to his horse. "Don't get any ideas about hanging around," he warned, although he had little fear of that happening. Except for a last fearful glance, Simpson did nothing except spur his horse down the trail toward freedom.

"Where do you think he will go?" Whispering Sage asked. The shadow that had been in her eyes ever since Apache first saw her had vanished — he hoped forever — along with her tormentor.

"Not to any of the ranches." Apache watched the disturbed foliage quiver, then still. "He may head for Texas or Colorado." He shrugged. "His kind don't last long, wherever they go." With a finality that placed the incident in the past, he said, "We'll go now, if you're ready."

She nodded, slipped into the cabin for her few belongings, and trotted after him to get the horses. She mounted King with all the ease of long hours in the saddle and followed Apache and Lucifer away from the clearing. She didn't look back, Apache noted with understanding. The cabin held horror for her.

His heart swelled. Wouldn't the Sutherlands be glad he hadn't killed, even with good reason?

"Thank you."

Had Whispering Sage's thoughts traveled the same road as his? Apache caught the poignant look and didn't pretend to misunderstand. Her gratitude lay more in his not killing Simpson than in saving her. He chose to ignore it and said, "Once we get to the main road, we'll turn your bag of bones loose and let him go where he wishes. He'd only slow us down."

The tired old horse appeared only too willing. When freed, he merely walked to the nearest patch of grass and began to graze.

Their strange journey home to the Triple S found the two riders in a multitude of situations. For a short time Indian summer prevailed and Apache rejoiced. Although Whispering Sage rode well and never complained, his keen intuition knew that her stamina lagged by day's end. He never asked, but he suspected she had grown frail from lack of good food. Those suspicions became certainty when he watched her eat. He supplemented their stores by killing rabbits and roasting them. In a few days his efforts paid off, and the girl no longer drooped low in the saddle when she thought he wasn't looking.

Apache had long ago decided to avoid main trails. Although it meant traveling longer, they would be safer. Bands of outlaws often roamed the range and could be counted on to kill him just for his two magnificent horses. He shuddered to think what would happen to Whispering Sage in that event, so he continued to watch every track while keeping a sharp eye on the weather.

Shortly before they reached the turnoff to the waterfall valley, they woke to a scowling sky and rising wind. Apache hesitated. If they continued on toward Daybreak, they faced miles of open space as well as the canyons. It seemed strange to discuss plans with another, but he told Whispering Sage, "Perhaps we should hole up in the valley for a few days. There will be good feed for the horses. The game will have come back with the fall rains." His black eyes penetrated the growing gloom. "If terrible storms come we can make camp in the cave or tunnel."

Her eyes brightened. "Can we go there? A few days rest would be good. For the horses," she quickly added.

A new emotion disturbed Apache. Tenderness for the grave girl who unquestioningly followed where he led made him say, "Yes. It will be good — for the horses." He didn't look at her to see if she found anything unusual in his remark.

The waterfall that had dwindled when Apache last saw it now foamed and spilled over the rocks below. Whispering Sage's mouth made a little round "o" when she saw it, but she didn't falter. "You'll get wet," Apache warned. "But once we're through, I'll build a fire and we can dry. Lucifer's not going to want to go through, so don't come across the ledge until I get through the waterfall."

She nodded, eyes big at the narrow tricky ledge.

"King's been in and out. He won't balk," Apache promised. He tightened his knees against Lucifer's sides, pulled the reins taut, and after some struggle, got the snorting, protesting beast through. A few moments later King and Whispering Sage came into the cave and tunnel.

Apache rode ahead, then turned, eager to see the girl's expression when she first saw the hidden valley. She didn't disappoint him. Her first all-encompassing glance at the narrow red-rimmed valley, with its sparkling stream, green grass, and blowing cottonwoods, reflected the same inner delight Apache knew each time he returned.

The threat of storm hung over them for several days. Apache's trained eye told him it would pass and Indian summer would continue. Even the deserting leaves that yellowed and fell failed to disturb him. Once he remembered Mescal talking about how dry, brown bulbs and barren trees lived again. Her question, "Don't you think a man is worth more than a bulb?" came to mind, and in the long talks he had with Whispering Sage, he found her demanding much the same. The days they spent in the valley brought them together the same way those parched summer days with Jim Sutherland had changed them to brothers.

Long before the threat of storm abated, Apache climbed the highest pinnacle and faced a far greater storm: He loved Whispering Sage. Not with the love he still remembered having for his mother, Running Deer. Not the love for Mescal that asked nothing but the right to serve. His love for the Navaho girl matched the love of eagle for eagle, buck for doe — the crying out of body and soul for his mate in a way he thought had been conquered years before by its very impossibility.

Did she sense his feelings? Did she know the gladness that leaped in his savage nature when she lightly ran through the cottonwoods or bent above the cooking fire or brought a bit of colored stone for him to see? If not, why did she talk about how the white God created woman so man need not be alone?

One evening Apache said, "Will you marry — someday?" and hoped she would not hear the bitterness in his question.

Too honest to lie or evade, Whispering Sage raised her head and looked deep into his troubled eyes. "That is for you to say."

All the enemies he had ever faced had not shaken Apache as much as her unexpected answer. "You mean because of Simpson?" he harshly asked.

"No." The glossy head drooped. Apache leaped to his feet and into the darkness, cursing the gods that had forced him to meet her when he had vowed to walk alone. Yet the next morning he couldn't help returning to the subject. They had walked the length of the valley and climbed to a high place where they could watch the sun rise.

"We'll be leaving soon."

"Yes." A world of sadness gathered in her voice.

Apache observed the pinkening sky. "I cannot marry. I cannot see my sons suffer as I have done." He waited, wondering why he had opened his heart to her more than he had ever done before.

For a long while Whispering Sage sat with folded hands. Rose and saffron streaks faintly touched with violet curled above them and cast a glow. Far below, the stream showed silver, the horses tiny. Around, above, and across lay what Jon Sutherland had named "the bleeding cliffs." They ran the gamut of pinks, reds, and oranges, capturing forever the sky's reflections in stone.

Whispering Sage spoke. Apache strained to hear her low voice. "Would you deny your sons all this because life also brings suffering?" She slowly moved her hand north, east, south, and west.

Nailed to his rocky perch by her question, Apache let the morning sink deep into him, as he had done countless times before. The word *hope* sprang to his mind. Only after the sun bounded over the tallest cliff and devoured the morning coloring did Apache say, "We must pack." He stood, yet lingered with his gaze turned to Whispering Sage. Abruptly he said, "Do you really believe the son of the white God came for Indians? For half-breeds?"

The girl's serene face and confident, "I know it," struck like a blow.

"How?"

"How does a bird know to sing? How does an eagle know to fly? When the missionary taught me about the white God and His Son Jesus, I knew in here." She pressed her hand to her heart. "The empty hole became filled."

Apache winced, but quickly hid it. How well he knew the empty hole inside she referred to! Especially since knowing and leaving the Sutherlands.

"What has the Son of God — if the white God really is — to do with an outcast thrown aside by two races?"

Compassion filled her face, and something more. "Jesus knows what it is like to be scorned. He was Jewish. Not half-Gentile and half-Jewish, but all Jewish — the descendant of Jewish kings. Yet His own people crucified Him!"

Apache felt the blood drain from his face.

"They nailed Him to a cross and put a crown of long thorns on His head. Then they spit on Him and mocked Him and told Him if He were really the Son of God, to call on His Father to save Him."

All the old doubt warred with the truth of her story. "Why didn't He, then? I would have done anything to save my mother!" Apache felt himself tremble. "Was the white God so weak He had no warriors who would come?"

Whispering Sage didn't waver. "The white God was so strong He let it happen."

"And you worship such a God?" Apache could not accept such a thing. "How can anyone respect a God who stood by and let His Son be put to death in such a way?"

The glory of the morning sky couldn't compare with the glory in Whispering Sage's face. "Someone had to pay the price. Someone had to be sacrificed for all the sins of the world. Because Jesus died, we can claim His sacrifice and we will be pardoned and forgiven and live forever." Her last words rose until the canyon walls echoed, *forever . . . ever.*

"If a man could believe that . . ." Apache found it hard to get anything past the crowded feeling in his throat. "If even a half-breed could believe it, life might be worth living."

The look on Whispering Sage's face gradually changed. Apache could not help seeing the love that shone from her eyes. She quietly said, "It's the only thing that makes life worth living, Charley. Not just for a Navaho or a half-Apache, but for anyone." She rose and quietly laid one hand over his clenched fist, and for one heart-stopping moment, Charley came very close to believing.

13

A few hardy purple asters and some late goldenrod nodded to Apache and Whispering Sage as they rode by. The change in terrain from red rock canyons to high plateau exhilarated the man. Every hoofbeat brought them nearer home. He could picture their welcome. The Sutherlands would be overjoyed, and Whispering Sage welcomed. Apache could barely keep his eyes from the lovely girl whose expressive dark eyes mirrored her love for the land they traveled — and for him. He dared not speak of the fragile growing feeling between them, and he still fought against it. Could he marry, as he had vowed never to do? Could he father sons and daughters who would not belong to either the Indian or white world?

Suppose Mescal and Jim and Whispering Sage and others who believed in the white God were right? Wouldn't it mean there was no white world, no Indian world, but one world offered salvation by a brown Son of God from a faraway country?

Long hours Apache pondered, until he faced his own heart. *He wanted it to be true.* His lips curled and his nostrils flared. The whole story sounded impossible. Still he could not forget the steadily growing vision of what his world could be with Whispering Sage by his side. Her spirited riding, her gentle laughter, and her flashing eyes settled deeper and deeper into his heart. No wonder Simpson and the storekeeper had coveted her!

Late one evening just before dusk, Apache slipped away while Whispering Sage knelt by their campfire kneading biscuit dough. An overpowering urge to be alone and away from her filled him with the need to think more clearly than he could when with her.

On silent feet he stole to a rise of ground from which he could see the flicker of the fire and still be apart. The love he had fought and jealously guarded surged through him. "I am happier than I have been since I walked away from the grave of Running Deer and Little Eagle," he murmured. Wind-rustled leaves agreed.

Apache sat on. How clearly and separately the segments of his life stood out. Childhood ending in tragedy. Young manhood ending on the Triple S. The past months ending with — what?

"White God, if You are there, give me a sign," he suddenly called, keeping his voice low enough not to disturb Whispering Sage.

83

Only the wind answered, and it held no prophecies.

Apache sighed. Had he expected mighty thunderclaps or voices shouting in his ear? He grunted in disgust at his own weakness and slowly walked toward Whispering Sage's call.

"Charley. Supper."

His insides twisted. If only he could answer that call every night for the rest of his life! Did he dare flaunt the gods of desert and mountain and canyon and sky? Wouldn't they laugh in his face, snatch away what he held more dear, and triumphantly destroy him?

Or was the white God more powerful than all other gods, as Whispering Sage and the Sutherlands insisted?

"Which of you would send your only son to die for the sins of the people?" he challenged. "You, wind? You, sky? You, earth or fire or water? Speak to me."

Still no answer came, and Apache shrugged and refused to consider the matter any longer. There would be time for that when they reached the Triple S.

Ragged, dirty, and tired, they at last rode down the trail that led to the ranch house. When they passed the bunkhouse the hands had just come in. A little snow lay in sheltered areas, but the ground lay needle-covered and bare for the most part.

"Hi-yi! Lookit who's here!" Dusty's wild yell created pandemonium. Slim, Dave, and Shorty stampeded behind the awkwardly running cowboy.

"Apache!" "Where yu been?" "Hey, who's that?"

Their sweaty, grinning faces warmed Apache's heart. The rare, faint smile they had seldom seen lighted his dark countenance. "This is Whispering Sage." He waved at each cowboy in turn, indicating, "Slim, Dave, Shorty. Curly's the cook on the porch."

He got no further. The ranch house door burst open while the men doffed their dusty hats to the tired girl.

"Praises be — it's Apache!" Big Matthew Sutherland's face wreathed in smiles. "Abigail, Mescal, just see who's here." Moments later they crowded around. Matthew's eyes gleamed when he got a good look at Lucifer. "Boy, I'd almost go back on King an' Shalimar an' Dark Star for that one!"

Mescal pushed foreward, eyes on Apache. Something stirred deep in their darkness. "But where's Jim?"

"The Circle Q said he was looking for me, but I couldn't hunt him up."

"He left weeks ago to find you. He heard you had been in the Kanab area." She laughed tremulously, then looked at Whispering Sage, who had wearily slid from King's saddle. "You poor thing!" Welcoming hands reached out. "Come inside and I'll help you. What's your name?"

"Whispering Sage. Charley found me and brought me here."

Apache saw her body tense. He caught the uncertainty in her face that disappeared immediately when Mescal put an arm around her and turned toward the house.

"You'll want to care for the horses," she flung back over her shoulder. "I'll take care of Sage."

The shortened use of Whispering Sage's name startled Apache. He had never called her anything except her full name, but he liked Sage. It stood for sturdiness, determination to survive even the harshest weather, and it bloomed year after year, no matter how little rain came, spilling its own desert fragrance on its companion, the wind.

Dusty hobbled forward, crowded close by the others. "You mean you didn't see Jim at all?"

Apache shook his head. "I worked from ranch to ranch, then got caught in a snowstorm." He briefly sketched in his trek to the tumbledown cabin and how Whispering Sage held him up. The guffaws of the hands and Matthew and Abigail's smiles quickly turned to anger when he told how Simpson and the storekeeper had hounded the girl after her missionary friends died.

Matthew's eyes bored into him. "So what happened to this Simpson?"

Apache gathered Lucifer's reins and whistled for King to follow before carelessly saying, "He decided to leave Utah and Arizona — for good." He didn't miss the significant look between Dusty and the boys, but refused to say more.

"The boys can look after your horses," Matthew offered.

Apache shook his head. "King's better than a brother, and Lucifer's just learning to behave." He permitted himself a little grin. "I'm not sure what he will do to anyone except me, though." Lucifer's quick toss of his head and flailing hooves backed up Apache's statement. Even the long trip hadn't taken the chili pepper out of him.

"Your cabin's ready and waiting," Matthew said when Apache had hung the gear in the barn and rubbed down both horses.

All this time? Had they been so sure he'd come back? Yet it felt good to step into the small home and wash off his trail grime before supper. He changed into a clean buckskin outfit and realized how starved he was when Matthew tapped at his door and said, "Supper's on the table."

"I wish Jim had found you." Mescal longingly glanced out the window.

"Funny he never caught up with you." Matthew laid his heavy fork on the table. "I guess you stayed one holler ahead of him. Here, have some more grub. You two look half-starved."

Apache accepted second helpings of the venison and gravy, mashed potatoes, and hot biscuits. When had he eaten like this? He stole a look at Whispering Sage, who had discarded her dirty trail clothes and wore a blue and white checked dress Mescal must have provided. Her well-stocked plate of food had rapidly disappeared, and the look of quiet peace on her face made all the hardships they'd faced worthwhile.

The evening sped past, what with the Sutherlands telling of the new cattle they'd purchased and run in and Mescal trying to draw out a few shy comments from Whispering Sage. Once when Matthew's curiosity got the better of him and he hinted around as to why Simpson suddenly decided to leave the country, Apache caught Mescal's sly look when she demurely said, "The way I hear it, he didn't like the last haircut he got."

Apache hid a grin and glanced at Whispering Sage, who bit her lip and stared at her fingers.

"That happens sometimes," he responded to Mescal, glad to see the old mischievous look back in her eyes. Then his eyes glittered. "Jim didn't go after me because there's trouble on the range, did he?"

"Naw." Matthew put aside the bridle he had been mending. His shaggy silver head raised, and the piercing eyes softened. "He — we all just wanted you back home."

The strange tightness that occasionally banded Apache's chest returned. It stayed all the time Matthew took down the big old Bible and read the story of the lost son and the glad father. His poignant voice carried Apache back to the first time he had heard the story, read in the same way so many months ago. Matthew's prayer that followed thanked God that "Apache has come home" and asked blessings on "our new daughter Sage," making it clear how they felt about the travelers.

Misty-eyed, the two girls, so like yet unlike, stood as Mescal announced, "Sage's room is all ready. Tomorrow we'll get her buckskins washed and see what else she needs."

"Good idea." Abigail smiled at them both. Her face showed traces of the beauty that had captured Matthew's heart forever years before. "We have plenty of wool and calico to sew, but she'll want those buckskins for riding."

Sage trotted after Mescal the same way she had followed Apache across the miles. A little pang for those days filled him, but when she turned at the doorway and said, "Good night, everyone — and Charley," the look in her eyes reassured him. She had changed dress, but no more. Her unspoken love, only hinted by a few words in the valley, shone clearer than the North Star in December.

Once Apache had sneeringly called the valley behind the waterfall paradise. Now he knew a kind of paradise of his own. How many times did he look up from his range and ranch chores and see Whispering Sage mounted on King? Matthew had suggested she use the big gray while Mescal stuck to her pinto, Patches, and Matthew rode Dark Star. That suited Apache well. He had tamed and begun to love Lucifer second only to King and Shalimar, the buckskin Jim rode away on to find Apache. After a few more initial fights, the black had learned to come to Apache's call and accept carrots from his hand. A few sharp cuffs turned the greedy, snatching mouth gentle, although Lucifer never let anyone else near him. A few times Mescal called him but the racy black kicked up his heels and tore to the far corner of the corral.

Every evening Apache listened to the Bible verses and the head of the house of Sutherland's prayers. He saw the earnest attention Sage gave when she drank in learning to increase what she already knew. He noticed how she lost part of her shyness and answered readily when spoken to. He watched streaks of red creep into her smooth brown cheeks when Matthew roughly but kindly teased her the way he did Mescal. It all went deep, and Apache trembled on the brink. If all whites who claimed to believe in God, the Father of Jesus, lived the way the Sutherlands did, how simple it would be to accept that way!

The only flaw in the late fall paradise was Jim's continuing absence. Indian summer alternated with snow flurries. Thanksgiving came and went. The cattle drifted down into the draws where it stayed warmer, safe until the spring roundup. The hands had time to hunt deer and wild turkey, loaf and quarrel good-naturedly, and think. Still Jim did not come. If it hadn't been for a brief and curious letter, the Triple S would have been forced to believe Jim had vanished into the north. A passing rider dropped it off at Daybreak, and Carter brought it to the Triple S. His big grin and firm handshake for Apache, plus his goggle-eyed but respectful stare at Sage, showed how glad he was to see them. He stayed to hear the letter, too, and shook his head in bewilderment along with the rest of them.

It read,

Dear Mescal, Dad, and Mother,

I've run up against something interesting here in Kanab. I'll be heading home as soon as I can, but not just yet.

Don't worry. I'm well, staying out of trouble, and still have enough money.

I aim to be home no later than Christmas, but tell Carter that if he and the boys don't want to keep being deputies I'll understand. They may want to name a new sheriff. Don't bother writing; I may not be here.

See you soon. I miss you all.

Mescal broke off and blushed. "The rest is personal." She hugged the letter to her breast.

Carter scratched his head. "I don't get it. What in tarnation's keepin' him? It ain't Apache. He's here."

"We're as mystified as you are," Matthew admitted. The others agreed.

Mescal reread the note. "At least he says he'll be here by Christmas." Her eyes softened. Apache's keen eyes caught the dewy look in her face when she added, "He can't miss us as much s I . . . we do him."

That afternoon Apache swiftly walked to Haunting Spring, then to the glade where Jon Sutherland had been buried. Why should a sense of foreboding fill him? Jim said in the note that he was well and not in trouble. Why then did a shadow dim the sun of life on the Triple S in the fallow season?

He shook himself but couldn't dislodge the gray wings of doubt. As day fled into night and night burst into day, Apache waited and wondered. he spent more time alone, unwilling to dampen the spirits of the boys, the family, or Whispering Sage. Once he beckoned Mescal aside and asked, "Shall I go for him?"

He saw longing battle with common sense before she shook her head, sighed, and said, "No. We know he's all right." A pearly glow had replaced much of her summer tan. "I just hope he comes soon."

Apache considered going anyway in response to the unease that remained in spite of hard riding, hours with Whispering Sage, and the growing conviction he could never escape either the beautiful Indian girl or the white God. Still, he tarried, bound by invisible and ever-tightening webs to the ranch. At last he decided. No matter what weather came, if Jim wasn't home by Christmas as he'd promised, Apache and King would take the trail.

Now the world changed rapidly. The snow in the sheltered areas mingled with fresh falls. The temperature dropped. At such a high altitude, freshly dressed meat could be hung up in the trees and freeze solid while safe from marauding animals. Apache hunted tirelessly, enjoying the company of the cowboys who gladly followed his lead to the best places for game. No day proved too cold for him, and usually at least one of the boys or Matthew accompanied him. Often Sage bundled herself into the warm clothing Abigail and Mescal had helped her make. Her clear eyes and rich coloring contrasted well with the scarlet wool hood she wore. Her native instinct made her the best of companions, and while she didn't care to shoot, no squeamishness kept her from helping pack home part of the meat.

Apache marveled at how quickly she had become part of the Triple S. Fondness for her showed in every move the Sutherlands made. She and Mescal giggled like children over secrets for Christmas, which rushed toward them. The cowboys adored her from afar and tumbled over themselves in offering gifts gathered or made from the land. Apache knew Dusty had almost finished the deerskin moccasins lined with soft rabbit fur from animals he had killed. Slim and Dave sawed and hammered on a bookcase in which to keep the cones and rocks she loved. Shorty quit smoking so he could buy her a comb, brush, and mirror like Mescal's. Curly, the cook, taught her how to make dishes from recipes he'd jealously guarded from Mescal and Abigail!

One day Mescal braced the whole outfit. Her eyes flashed in mock indignation. "I'm getting mad," she told the nonchalant five who innocently listened wide-eyed. "Until Sage came, I got the attention around here. How come not now?''

Sage blushed, but Dusty raised his apparently astonished face. "Why, Mescal, you're still our gurl, but now that Jim up and married you, we gotta find us another one!"

Sage fled, but Mescal retorted, "What chance have you got with Apache around?" She darted a quick look at him.

"Not much," Dusty admitted. His eyes brightened with devilment. "If he don't hurry up, though, I might just shine up to Sage. She's shore a good gurl and deserves a dee-voted husband."

Everyone roared at the redfaced, bowlegged cowboy's remark, but Mescal warned Apache, "Our boys won't be the only ones with that idea. Soon as spring comes and word gets out that the prettiest girl around is out here, we'll have hands from every ranch for a hundred miles riding in on Sunday afternoon."

Apache held his face rigid, but her warning brought a flash of pain. Long ago another white man had fallen in love with an Indian girl and married her. Would Sage follow that trail? Remembrance of her trusting face quieted his racing pulse. At least for now Sage had nothing but friendship for all except her rescuer, although the boys chose to hope otherwise.

PART IV
Echoes

14

So close, yet so cursedly far.

Jim Sutherland disconsolately stared through the hotel window at the dusty Kanab street slowly changing to mud. Gray drizzle matched his mood. How could he have missed Apache by such a small margin? He turned to the steel-eyed Circle Q owner who had hailed him in the street a few minutes before.

"Did he say why he wanted to buy another horse or where he planned to go?" Slim hope folded defeated wings when the rancher shook his head.

"Naw. I'd say it must be quite a journey, though. He took enough provisions to last a spell. I meant to send word to the Triple S, like you asked. Had no idea you were back in Kanab."

"I found his father here, probably dying."

Amazement lightened the rancher's face. "Of all the .. . How'd he happen to be here?"

Jim shrugged. "I guess he got word of Apache, or Charley as he's known here, and his skills. Charles Campbell about did himself in getting here." A vision of the tall, still figure lying upstairs floated in front of him.

"What do you aim to do?"

The question Jim had asked himself night and day sounded loud in his ears. Again he shook his head. "I don't know."

His informant stood and slapped his hat against his thigh. "Well, I have to get back. If — when you see Charley, tell him there's always a job for him on the Circle Q."

Jim retorted, "There's always a job for him on the Triple S, too."

"Reckon you've got a prior claim." The harsh lines in the other's weather-seasoned face relaxed. "By the way, my boys ran across somethin' funny a few weeks back." A seamy grin spread and showed strong, white teeth. "They took a shortcut between draws to check out some driftin' cattle. Hoofbeats suddenlike made them wonder, and a moment later a rider swept across in front of them." He scratched his cheek and fixed an unwavering stare on Jim.

"Funny, Banty and the boys swear it was Simpson, lyin' low over his horse's neck."

"Simpson!" A powerful thrill shot through Jim.

"Yeah, but that ain't all. When the rider jerked his head around to see who the boys were, his horse broke stride and reared. The man's hat flew off."

"So?" Every nerve in Jim's body screamed.

"So that man had been purty near scalped. Banty said it looked like his hair had been whacked off 'til there wasn't much more than fuzz left." The rancher cocked his head. "It wouldn't surprise me if Charley up and taught Simpson a lesson." He leisurely strode toward the lobby door.

"Wait." Jim followed, clenching his hands. "Did Simpson & or whoever it was — look hurt or anything?"

"Naw, more's the pity. The boys said nothin' much could be wrong with a jasper who hightailed it out of there as fast as that rider did. Guess he didn't like his haircut." A whoop of laughter carried the rancher through the door and into the rain and left Jim relieved.

"Wonder how come Apache chose to cut his hair?" Jim pondered, then sighed. "I just wish he'd told the Circle Q where he planned to go. What would he need that second horse for? King's more horse than anyone needs."

The unanswered questions played tag in his brain for days. So did his dilemma. Should he head back to the Triple S? How could he leave Charles Campbell, who clung to life by sheer willpower, spurred on by Jim's stories of Apache's life since Mescal brought him home from the glade after Comstock's cowardly attempt at murder.

"I'd like to thank that little girl," Charles said wistfully. His thin hand plucked at the sheet, but his blue eyes shone as clear and bright as Jim's own.

He never tired of the stories, asking Jim again and again to tell every detail. Sometimes memory of his own anguish made Jim cringe. Yet the man before him had suffered even greater agonies than he, if that were possible.

"I have to let Mescal and the folks know I'm all right," Jim muttered one afternoon while Charles slept. He borrowed pencil and paper from the hotel proprietor, who frankly admitted he was glad for two steady roomers in a usually slack season.

Although he detested writing letters, Jim filled several pages with his long trip, his discoveries at the Circle Q, the journey north, the reputation Apache had earned with his skills. He licked the end of the pencil and went on to tell how his heart almost stopped when Dr. Clark told him Charles Campbell lay dying — and the overwhelming relief when he found Apache's father instead of Charley. He told of the letter Dr. Clark gave him that showed how innocent Charles had been of wrongdoing toward either Running Deer or his son, and the man's anguish until he learned the truth.

When he finished, he reread the letter and slowly tore it to bits. Suppose Apache hadn't vanished into the canyons? What if he had decided to go home to the Triple S? How would he act if a letter came saying Jim had found his father — the man who kept alive his hatred of the white race?

"He might bolt before I could get home and tell him the truth," Jim admitted under his breath. He bowed his head for a long time. Then he grabbed a fresh page and scribbled a few words to explain his long absence, yet told nothing more. He closed with special personal messages to Mescal and stuffed the single page in an envelope. It would have to do.

To Dr. Clark's amazement, Charles Campbell continued to not only hang on, but even improve slightly.

"Don't go getting up any fancy hopes," The doctor glared at Jim as if he were responsible. "I've seen this happen before, a kind of rallying. It probably won't mean a thing or make any difference." His beetling brows almost met above his eyes.

"But don't you think he's a little better?" Jim persisted.

Dr. Clark snorted. "Don't you listen, young feller?" He snapped his bag closed, carefully keeping his voice too low for the listening patient to hear. "If it ain't patients hounding me about their condition, it's families and friends and whatever you are. Just take it one day at a time." He disappeared into the hall.

"The doctor doesn't give me much chance, does he?" The blue eyes demanded the truth. "I wouldn't care, if I could just see my son one time."

Jim's gaze fell before that poignant blue light. "Uh, doctors don't always know it all."

"Sutherland. Jim, have you heard any more about Charley?"

Jim took a deep breath. Charles had a right to know. "I found out a while back that he bought a horse from the Circle Q and a lot of provisions."

"What does that mean?"

Jim grimaced and stared around the barren room. "Who knows? Probably that Apache decided to forget whites and go back to the desert and valleys."

Charles refused to accept the pessimistic outlook. "Or that he might be riding back to the Triple S?"

"I thought of that," Jim agreed. "I hope he did, but I just don't understand why he needed a second horse. He'd never leave King. Besides, he rode into the Circle Q on the gray. The horse he bought is a black named Lucifer — the one he rode the first day he signed on at the Circle Q. I guess no one else can get near him and he's one of the fastest horses in southern Utah."

"Do you think he's found a friend, maybe another outcast?"

The words *like him* hung unsaid in the air, but Jim quickly dispelled them. "No. I can't see Apache getting close enough to anyone to make him ride with them, unless on a ranch where they worked. The only reason he ever took me on was because he got stuck in the valley that summer."

Time after time Charles Campbell returned to the idea that his son had gone back to the Triple S, the same way a deer goes back to a salt lick. Every time his eyes grew brighter, and one evening he said, "Jim, can you get a wagon through to your ranch?"

Shock at what he saw in the other's eyes froze Jim, but he answered, "It's possible. But it's a long, tough trip."

"How soon can we leave?"

The quiet voice lifted a protesting Jim from his seat by the bed. "Hold it, Campbell. Think I'm going to head out for the Triple S this time of year in a wagon with a dy . . . sick man? There'll be snow and God alone knows what."

"Does it matter?" Charles raised himself on one elbow. Twin red spots sprang to his thin cheeks. "Jim Sutherland, if you knew you were dying, would you lie here in bed? Or would you take a chance on making it home, knowing that if you didn't, you'd die under Arizona skies? What difference is there? We know our souls go back to God. Why should we care about the passing?"

A mighty torrent of words filled the room. "I love Arizona, and there's always a chance Charley's at the ranch. I'd give my life to see him and tell him . . ." he choked. "I ask you again: If it were you, *what would you do*?"

For a brief moment Jim felt he had exchanged places with the other man. Every emotion known to mankind flashed through him, ending with the eternal hope that refused to quit.

Jim gripped the thin hand that still held surprising strength. "I'll dicker for a wagon. We'll go soon." He stumbled out, glad to escape the look in Charles Campbell's eyes and feeling he had seen into a naked heart.

Dr. Clark had plenty to say, all of it explosive. "You are both insane," he told them flatly when Jim took him to see Charles later that night. Yet respect showed in his eyes, and the next instant he admitted, "Yes, you're loco. But I'd do the same." Quickly he reverted to his usual, brusque self. "Now, what you want, Sutherland, is a wagon that can have layers of cedar boughs laced so the tips are uppermost. Cover them with blankets. This will help soften the bouncing.

"Once we get Campbell on the wagon, he needs more blankets piled on and a sheepskin lined coat and heavy underwear. Just lying there he's going to get cold, otherwise. Don't forget a heavy, waterproof tarp and you . . ." he glared at Campbell. "Don't get any ideas about proving yourself tough. At the first hint of rain, you pull that tarp over you, head included, and keep it there, do you hear?"

"Sure, Doc." But the blue eyes showed no submissiveness.

Two days later they started home. Jim secretly called himself the fool Dr. Clark pronounced him to be. Yet his admiration for Apache's father grew with every creaking mile. If the man suffered, it didn't show, except for an occasional drop of blood on his lip where he must have bitten it to keep from hollering.

By nightfall, exhaustion showed in the corded face, even when Charles forced himself to eat what Jim prepared and joke about how slow and ornery the two workhorses were that pulled the wagon. The third night the joking stopped and Charles asked, "What are you holding back?"

Jim started and knew a guilty flush betrayed him in the firelight. Did he dare tell Charles the one fact he had held back, fearing it would destroy the indomitable will that kept his companion going beyond reason?

"What is it, Jim?"

The cowboy awkwardly poked the fire, then abandoned all pretense and threw another small stick on. "I don't know how Apache will act when he sees you." An explanation spilled out. "Somehow he's built it up in his heart that if you really cared, you'd never have believed Scoggins."

It sounded raw and hurtful in the night air.

"I see." Campbell lay quietly for a long time before saying, "Then I just pray that God will give me the time to redeem myself. If He doesn't, will you . . .?"

"Of course." Jim couldn't bear to have the sentence finished. "Sometime, somewhere, even if Apache isn't on the ranch, I'm bound to find him." His throat felt like he'd swallowed a tumbleweed that stuck halfway down. The strong brown hand clasped the thin pale one.

Jim's prediction came true: Snow, sleet, hail, rain, and wind attacked them. Several times they had to hole up in whatever shelter they could find. Jim anxiously scanned the skies. How long could they withstand the elements? Indian summer had long ago succumbed to winter's icy hand. Even the warmer days in the canyons offered little comfort. The Kaibab plateau's higher elevation encouraged early winters.

No longer on a trip but now in a marathon, they doggedly went on. Shalimar's stamina stayed high. The ornery workhorses settled into harness and pulled from daylight to dusk. Even Jim's range-hardened muscles strained from sawing on the reins and wishing he could be astride Shalimar. Only the patient endurance he saw in Charles Campbell kept Jim's lips clamped shut when he wanted to shriek.

The night inevitably came when Jim said through cracked lips, "Campbell, I hand it to you. If you could make it this far, there's no reason you can't make it the rest of the way. "We've just one more hard day."

"So close!" The whisper accused Jim.

"I wouldn't tell you before, in case we got held up again." His now-practiced eyes noted the fatigue that almost blotted out Campbell's gladness. "Just hold on." He took a deep breath of winter air. "Mother and Mescal can make you into a new man. There's eggs and chicken and milk and . . ." he broke off and hastily turned his head.

For the first time, he saw Charles Campbell cry.

Darkness had swallowed the land before the groaning wagon with its precious cargo reached the Triple S. Jim debated stopping at Daybreak and quickly discarded the idea. His longing for home surpassed everything else. To see Mescal and Dad and Mother and share with them the responsibility for Apache's father overrode all else. The last few miles required the last of his superb skill guiding the horses unfamiliar with the terrain over the dim track to the Triple S with only the light of a few determined stars that had penetrated the cloud cover.

Thank God they were almost there. If he knew anything at all about weather, another storm lay ready and waiting.

Campbell hadn't spoken for miles. Jim could hear slight movements and knew his passenger still lived, but deep inside he wondered. Had he been right in promising a possible healing at the Triple S? If Apache hadn't been seen or heard of, would his father lose the tremendous will that had brought him so far? Would he lie beside Jon without seeing the son he had loved as a boy and sought as a man?

Jim felt a mighty war within himself. Suppose Apache were there? Could he keep him long enough to give Campbell a chance?

"I'll do it," Jim vowed. "God, give the strength and wisdom to meet whatever happens." With a last jolt, the long journey home ended. "Whoa."

Before Jim could clamber from the wagon, they surrounded him: Dad, Mother, Mescal . . .

"Apache, thank God!"

Heedless of everything except the surging joy inside him, Jim bounded from the wagon and wrung the half-breed's hand. He vaguely noticed a girl who looked a bit like Mescal hovering in the doorway back of the others, but only Apache's mighty grip seemed real, Apache's slow smile shining in the light of the lantern Matthew Sutherland held high.

A small tornado attacked him. Jim dropped Apache's hand and lifted Mescal off her feet. She cried and kissed him and whispered, "You were gone so long," and Jim knew he really was home.

A low sound from the wagon brought Jim to his senses even before Matthew boomed out, "What have you got there? Why'd you bring a wagon through this time of year? Shalimar looks fine."

Jim tore free of Mescal's encircling arms and stepped to the wagon bed. He carefully removed the tarp from the prone figure and whispered, "Follow my lead."

If Campbell answered, it was too low for Jim to hear.

"Dad, Apache, help me here." He removed the top layer of blankets and clutched the side of the wagon, suddenly worn out. "Carry him in, will you?"

Apache raised the unconscious man in his mighty arms and crossed the porch. A low cry from the girl in the background roused Jim from the lethargy that had crept over him, born of strain and toil and sleepless nights. "Dad, he . . . I . . ."

"You can explain tomorrow." Matthew's voice rolled out. The next moment Jim found himself caught up in arms as strong as those that bore Campbell and carried past familiar rooms to his and Mescal's bedroom.

"Just let me sleep." A boot hit the floor, then another. Good old Dad. The next minute, oblivion.

Jim slowly opened his eyes. Strange. He smelled frying bacon. Impossible. Campbell couldn't be making breakfast. Besides, walls surrounded him where there should be emptiness dotted with gigantic pines. Reality struck. Home. They'd made it home!

Sudden fear sponged out the leap of joy in his heart. He slid his feet out of bed and into boots far cleaner than the ones Dad pulled off. What of Charles Campbell? Had he roused and told them who he was? What about Apache?

His aching muscles slowed his progress as he limped into the living room. Apache and the shadowy girl who now stood out in startling beauty watched him come.

"Apache, I am glad you are here." The simple words covered it all except the girl's presence.

"Jim," the sonorous voice reflected Jim's happiness. "This is Whispering Sage."

Even without explanation Jim knew why Apache had brought Lucifer and all the provisions from the Circle Q. He took the girl's hand, seeing her shyness and something more when she quickly glanced up at Apache. "It is good to be home."

"We have waited for you." Her low voice reminded him of a hushed brook in shady places.

The opening of a door whipped Jim around. Without considering the effect, he demanded of Matthew, "How's Campbell?"

"Campbell!"

Jim turned back to Apache. His stomach churned. Why had he blurted it out that way, when he had planned to carefully identify their visitor?

Apache's dark face looked curiously drained. Every trace of welcome and friendship fled, replaced with a molten mask that hid whatever burned within him.

"Did you say Campbell?" Apache took a step toward Jim.

An eternity later Jim got out through a mountain of despair and self-loathing, "Yes, Apache. Your father, Charles Campbell."

Apache didn't utter a single word. He merely turned and walked into the bedroom where he had gently deposited the unconscious man the night before — and just as gently closed the door, leaving Jim with his unspoken explanations.

15

Apache noiselessly glided to the bed and gazed down at his father. This, then, had been the meaning of the foreboding that began when Jim's letter came from Kanab. A terrible wrenching rose mingled with the premonition and whisper, "Flee while there is yet time."

He half-turned.

No. He must see and measure this white man who married Running Deer according to the God of the Sutherlands yet listened to Scoggins instead of seeking out the truth. He forced himself to consider the sleeping man, noticing how unconsciousness had given way to natural, healing rest. In vain he looked for signs of weakness. Even the emaciation that had carved its mark could not hide the strength and peace in Charles Campbell's face.

A long-ago memory stirred of Running Deer's pride when she related how the now-wasted man once carried his little son and showed him to the world. Apache felt the shackles of his hatred loosen and fall away. He passionately thought how differrent life might have been, if only . . .

His father moved, turned his head, and opened his eyes. Even though they were clouded with sleep, their intense blueness struck Apache. He gazed and saw them change, unaware that his sinewy body stood poised for the unknown. Puzzlement gave way to a question, replaced by a look no man on earth had ever bestowed on Apache.

"Charley?"

The man who had stood on pinnacles and watched the sun rise in radiance a thousand times trembled. Never had the glory of those moments equalled the radiance that dawned in Charles Campbell's eyes, and when he reached out a thin hand cried, "My son, my son!" Apache could stand no more.

"Father." It sounded strange on his lips — unaccustomed. He pressed his father's hand. "I am here. Sleep."

A curtain of weakness pulled the man's eyelids down over his shining eyes. For a moment Apache wondered if his father had recognized him and died. He laid his father's hand on the colorful handmade quilt, bent low, and grunted approval. The steady heartbeat and quiet breathing belonged to the living.

A long time later, Apache left the room as silently as he had entered.

Matthew and Abigail, Jim and Mescal, and Whispering Sage waited.

"Well?" Jim's direct question could not be ignored. Apache folded his arms across his chest in his familiar pose. "It is well. Now he sleeps." Heart bursting, Apache crossed the room and opened the outside door.

He knew the rustle behind him came from Sage, but it stopped when Matthew said, "Let him go. He needs to be alone."

Grateful beyond expression, Apache made his way to his own cabin. Once inside he threw himself to his bunk and stared at the well-chinked ceiling. All these years he had hated and despised his father. Now that same father had come to him, and no hatred on earth could withstand the look in his face. Canyons Apache had considered uncrossable did not exist between them. A few words, a blue-eyed look meeting night-black eyes, and the years between might never have been.

"I've been so wrong," Apache confessed to the empty room. Something crackled beneath his head and he saw a letter that had slid from the pillow when he lay down to think.

Apache curiously turned it in his hands. Over the years he had taught himself to read and write, knowing if he ever entered the white world he must not be cheated because of ignorance. His heart raced. Crumpled, dirty from carrying, the message sounded in his ears as clearly as if the father who had searched for and found him, perhaps at the cost of his own life, spoke:

Dear son,

For more years than I care to remember, I have thought you were dead, along with Running Deer, the only woman I ever loved or married.

Now, one of the men who rode in the attack on the Indian village called me to his deathbed and confessed the terrible hoax he and Scoggins and a few others carried out. I had no reason to disbelieve the men when I returned from getting supplies to stock the trading post. I found it in ashes. Scoggins swore you and your mother had been trapped inside. The others backed him up.

I thought I would go mad. My wife. My only son. For weeks and months and years I wandered. Yet the time came when I could neither outrun the past nor keep from coming back to where I had once been so happy.

I came back just a few months ago and camped where the trading post once stood. Then the dying man sent for me and I learned everything, how Running Deer died, everything. The man swore he hadn't seen you during the attack, so with every heartbeat I pray that you somehow escaped the massacre by those of my race.

My son, I will spend the rest of my life searching for you. God's love has allowed me to keep my sanity. Perhaps His love will also one day lead me to you. Word has come of a man named Sutherland who also seeks you.

"I know I am doomed to die, perhaps soon. When I get near to that, I will give this letter to someone who can send it to this Jim Sutherland, and I send it as a sacred trust that he must accept so you will receive this letter.

Do not let the way the whites have distorted the message of Jesus Christ keep you in bonds of hatred. My great desire is that you might know and accept Him so we will meet — sometime.

Your father,
Charles Campbell

Apache slowly folded the letter and slipped it inside his shirt. It settled near the scars from Comstock's bullet. An involuntary cry rang out. "What a man!"

He is your father, echoed his heart. From the first time Apache realized why Running Deer had been drawn back again and again to the white man. His very goodness reached out and invited with an irresistible force. The same pride that once caused Charles Campbell to proudly carry his son and teach him the white language now rose in the son. Regret for the wasted years of hate and determination to fight death iself for at least a time of learning to know his father roused and shook itself into stubborn resolution.

Days later Apache stood at his cabin window watching the snow. Jim had just left, after telling him everything that transpired since Apache rode away the previous spring. It had been the first time they had to talk. Charles Campbell's mighty willpower had been tested almost beyond endurance in the wagon ride to the Triple S. Matthew Sutherland nightly petitioned God in prayers that raised the hair on Apache's head higher than the wildest war whoops ever had. Power and total assurance that, if it be His will, Campbell would live, left the women with tear-filled eyes, Jim and Apache and the cowboys who sometimes joined them strangely silent.

Christmas crept near. Charles insisted on being carried into the big room and laid on the couch by the fire. He refused to consider himself anything except on the mend. He ordered Mescal and Whispering Sage to bring in pine boughs and decorate the room and directed Jim and Apache to get the finest Christmas tree they could find. By nightfall he showed the strain, but day after day he held whispered conferences with various family members that resulted in frequent rides into Daybreak between storms.

Now Jim's words rang in his ears. "Dr. Clark in Kanab said he had one chance in ten of making it to Christmas. Seems to me there's no reason he won't get that chance. Apache, no matter what happens," Jim had stopped to clear his throat, "we want you and Sage to stay here. We'll throw up a cabin any spot you choose. A third of the ranch is yours. Dad and Mother and Mescal and I talked it over. It's . . . it's Jon's share." Jim hurried out before the speechless Apache could regain his senses and answer.

One-third of the Triple S. Whispering Sage, riding and running beside him. Children — black-haired boys and girls growing up in this beautiful land, never knowing the fear of hiding out or seeing their parents pursued. Perhaps even climbing on their blue-eyed grandfather's knees and learning of his great love for Running Deer.

Apache's blood ran hot at the vision. What man could ask for more than he had been offered? The look in Jim's — and Sage's — eyes told him it could happen.

Yet in his happiest moment, cold slid into his bones, a nameless dread of some further test by fire.

He laughed at the idea. What could the future hold by comparison with past sufferings, except a brighter lift? It must be dark superstition fostered by his tribe and even his mother that insidiously refused to let him accept joy and hope.

One day Carter rode out from Daybreak and brought the doctor with him, the same one who patched up Jim after the big fight. While the doctor examined Charles, Carter chewed the rag with the family and frankly said, "If I wasn't already married to the best woman I ever met, and if I wasn't too old 'cept to be your daddy, Sage, I'd sure hotfoot it out here callin'."

"You'd be welcome," she surprised them all by saying, then fled laughing, but hesitated in the kitchen doorway when the doctor came out from his examination with a grin on his face.

"Well, I'd never prescribe long wagon trips just before winter for patients with lung fever, but that — or something — looks like it's done the trick. Far as I can see, if Campbell keeps on getting plenty of rest and good food, by summer he'll be able to fork a horse and help round up strays."

A chorus of, "Praise God," and a growing knowledge that the "or something" had a lot to do with prayer gave Apache something else to consider. Had God really restored his father's health? If so, wasn't he, Apache, more in debt than ever? The eternal question came and went, depending on what he did. When he was cutting wood for the hungry fireplace, it receded, only to reappear in quiet moments.

Never had there been a Christmas like this one. The girls sang at their work. Jim whistled. Apache smiled more often. Oddly shaped packages appeared under the Christmas tree, and the kitchen smells almost drove everyone crazy. On Christmas Eve, just the Sutherlands, Sage, and Apache gathered after supper. The next day Dusty, Slim, Dave, Shorty, and Curly would join them for an enormous dinner and the giving and receiving of gifts.

All day Mescal drifted in what Apache thought was a daze. His piercing eyes tried to pin her down, but she just laughed and evaded him as well as Jim. After prayers she said in a shaky voice, "There's one present I won't wait until tomorrow to give. Jim," she turned to her tall husband. "Remember in September when I didn't beg to go to Kanab with you?"

Apache saw the surprise in his friend's eyes as well as in the others. Whispering Sage's face glowed.

"Sure. I wondered at the time how come."

A rich blush mantled Mescal's smooth face. "I suspected something, and it's true and . . ." a wide smile spread. "I kept it secret so I could tell you at Christmastime. "I . . . you . . . we're going to have a baby."

Jim just stared. Then he mumbled, "So that's why you didn't pester me." Realization finally came. "Whoopee! Hear that? I'm going to be a father!"

Apache's gaze sought his own father's. Had the white man yelled like that when he, too learned he would have a child? The steady blue look and slight nod told him yes. Apache's heart burned within him, and he said, "You will call him Jon."

Blank silence greeted his statement. Then Jim turned, his face on fire. "He will be Jon Charles, after my two brothers."

In the emotion-charged silence Mescal plaintively suggested, "It might be a girl."

Everyone laughed, and the moment vanished, except in Apache's heart.

Perhaps the Christmas mood completed what the patient witness of the Sutherlands and Sage and Charles had begun. When the others went to bed, Apache asked Whispering Sage to linger. He ignored Jim's knowing glance and lift of his eyebrows and waited until he stood alone with the Navaho girl.

"I have thought of all you said. I have remembered your wisdom. I do not wish to deny my sons and daughters life because of fear. Whispering Sage, will you marry me as Charles Campbell married Running Deer?"

He expected joy. He expected delight. Or shyness when she agreed. Instead she raised tear-dimmed eyes to his and said, "Charley, I do not know."

Apache's lips tightened into a straight, unbending line. "I thought you cared, as I do."

"I care so much I would follow you anywhere," Sage cried. Her face worked pitifully, and she appeared more broken than any time since he had known her.

"Then what is it?" He placed his hands on her shoulders but made no attempt to draw her close. A sudden thought turned his hands into vises. "Is it because I am neither white nor Indian? Or that the Apache and the Navaho do not dwell together?"

She shook her head. Firelight glistened in her dark braids and sprinkled golden motes through them. "Those things do not matter." She took a deep breath. "It is because I am a Christian."

Apache stared without understanding. "I know. I have many times thought of this. You will teach our children the way of the white God the Sutherlands and my father worship."

"It isn't enough, Charley. How can two become one when they do not agree?" Tears spilled. "You have heard the teachings of Jesus. Have you not thought of them and learned they are true?"

His hands fell to his sides, and he stepped back. "I have thought until my head felt the same way it does when too much sun falls on me and there is no shade."

He saw hope leap into her face when she said, "We could have so much joy if only you believed. There is no real happiness without the white God and His Son. There is no hope to live forever without them, and without hope, what is life?"

"Do you think I haven't considered this a hundred — no, a thousand times? Do you think I am wood and stone that I do not feel something I cannot explain when Matthew Sutherland prays and reads from the Bible? Whispering Sage, I would give everything I possess to believe in your Jesus. Sometimes I think I do. If the story of the white God and His Son is really true, it would change the world!"

"Only for those who accept it," she reminded. Her clasped hands flew to her breast. "Such as your father. God has given him life when no one thought it would happen."

"I know. But he is white."

"You think God or Jesus cares for color?" Sage sounded incredulous. "If God loves only whites, why didn't He make Jesus white? Why did God send His Son to be born of a Jewish girl, one of a despised race, perhaps with brown skin like ours?"

"I don't know."

"Our persecutions are nothing compared with His," she said softly. The dying firelight shrouded her until her features no longer showed clearly.

"What would you have me do? Bow myself to the ground? Do great things?" Apache demanded.

"It is not what I would have you do, but what God requires." Awe highlighted her simple explanation. "You must recognize that we are all sinners. You must ask forgiveness and be sincerely sorry for anything you have done that is wrong."

"Is that all?" A tumult rose in Apache's breast. "How can a god expect so little!"

"There is more." Whispering Sage's shadowy voice broke. "You must confess that Jesus is God's only Son and claim the pardon He won by paying the price of our freedom by His death on the cross."

"So I would again be in debt."

"Yes, Charley, We will be in debt to Jesus for what He did every second of our lives. If He had not come, death would be the end for all." She hesitated, then stepped so close he could see her face upturned to his. "The only way we can pay even part of our debt is to live as Jesus lived."

"You mean the way the Sutherlands do?" Apache turned it over in his mind. "Caring for strangers, dealing honestly with all?"

Sage nodded. "Yes." She clutched his arm. "And by forgiving . . ."

A blanket of ice dropped over Apache. So the white God of many faces had planned all this by bringing his father here and showing him the sweetness of Whispering Sage. The harsh laugh tore into the room like a desert sandstorm, filling it with stinging, hurting particles. Now he knew the truth. It had been a cruel joke to show a half-breed who dared reach for a new life how insignificant he was. More insignificant than a single grain of desert sand, twisted and tortured by every passing wind. Yes, it was a white torture worse than that Running Deer had suffered.

A moment more and Apache would have fallen before that same treacherous white God and asked forgiveness through His brown Son. Instead he hurled his hatred at Whispering Sage, "I will have nothing to do with a God who promises life and when a man is humbled, tells him he must forgive the snake who bites him!"

16

Christmas came and went, subdued by Apache's withdrawal into himself. All the joshing of the boys, the delight when Whispering Sage unwrapped the new buckskins he had asked Abigail to make from soft deer hides he brought and cured, even Jim's newly awakened happiness did little to reach the suffering man. His rare smile all but disappeared, and when he overheard Dusty asking, "What's eatin' Apache? He's crankier than a sore-footed bear," his mouth twisted.

He avoided the others as much as possible, and the weather tempered enough to permit long walks and some riding. Night after night he paced the length and width of his cabin, longing for spring and freedom. In his pacing he set his course. At the first sign of spring he'd go back to his solitary life and try to forget that for a short time he had known something better.

If the Sutherlands suspected his problem, they never let on. Apache tried to be himself when he visited his father. The one good that remained came from Charles Campbell's improvement. Every day he grew a little stronger. Apache told himself that by spring he would be able to face the second loss of his son.

A week of extra hard weather that kept even the indomitable Apache inside left him like dynamite that only needed a spark to set it off. Nerves he hadn't suspected existed stretched to the snapping point, and when his father quietly said, "Charley, you need to talk about it," he exploded. It poured out from the broken dam of feelings until the room echoed with his hatred, feelings of betrayal by the white God, and disappointment.

He ended by demanding, "How can your God ask so much of a man?" then crouched and waited for the answer.

His father's blue eyes never wavered. "He asks no more than He Himself did. How do you think God felt, standing by and doing nothing when the people Jesus came to save crucified Him?"

"I know no father who would do such a thing." Apache drew himself proudly to full height.

"That is why He is God."

Only half-hearing, Apache said, "Yet the Bible says Jesus died to save all. Tell me." His eyes turned terrible. "If Scoggins and Comstock had called on God for forgiveness, what then?"

A poignant light filled the summer-sky gaze. "Only God would know their hearts, and if they sincerely repented or only cried out of fear."

One last question trembled on Apache's lips — the question his entire future depended on. "Father . . ." It still sounded strange on his lips. He swallowed, hard. "Have you forgiven Scoggins?"

The blue light died. Apache expected the same anger that raged in his heart and devoured his mind to flare in his father. Instead, the greatest look of pity he had ever seen filled Charles's face.

"How can I carry hatred when I know his condition?" Both hands spread out in wordless pleading. "Can you even begin to imagine the awfulness of being in eternal darkness, away from any ray of light? Think of the blackest night you have ever known. Even then, always the knowledge of a new day ahead lightened the night. For Scoggins and Comstock and those who choose evil, there is no more light — ever."

For a single moment Apache traveled back an eternity to the black night after the massacre. Velvet dark threatened to smother him as it had then, and morning brought little relief — except that in daylight he could fight off some of his horror. He involuntarily shuddered. How could anyone exist without light?

And yet — his jaw set. Part of him wanted to believe his father, the Sutherlands, and Sage. The other part whispered and taunted that such things were false and that his rediscovered father must be mad to lay aside his black memories. Apache backed away from the reaching hand and silent plea in Charles's eyes. Unseeing, he walked past Whispering Sage and, like one who walks in his sleep, made his way back to his cabin.

Peace eluded him even there. The walls closed in on him until he felt crushed. Fragments of sentences new and long-forgotten shrieked at him until he dropped into the stupor of sleep simply because he could stand no more.

Little changed in the following weeks. No storm outside compared with the storm inside Apache, and before the first brave flower dared poke its curious head above ground, Apache had packed his saddlebags. In the still, gray gloom just before dawn on an early spring morning, he stole from his cabin clad for the trail. The night before he had secreted his stores in the barn. Long before rising time he gathered them and headed for the pastured horses.

He whistled, too low for any but the horses to hear. King nickered and trotted to him. So did Lucifer.

Apache laid his hand on the faithful gray he loved and took a long breath. "Good-bye, old man." Then he swiftly saddled Lucifer, bitterly thinking how fitting it was to ride away on the devil-named and natured black.

He swung to the saddle — and froze.

"God go with you, Apache."

Jim Sutherland's strong hand reached out. Apache blindly gripped it. "You knew."

"Yes. The same way Jon and I always knew." Jim freed his hand and took a small, wrapped bundle from his shirtfront. "Take this." His voice shook. "Once you gave it to me and I found sanity and salvation. Now, I beg you as a brother, take it."

Apache could not refuse, though he recoiled when Jim pressed the package into his saddlebag. Something akin to a dull acceptance that he could no more escape the white God than he could Jon's worn Bible colored his voice when he said, "Good-bye. You will care for Whispering Sage?"

"Until you return," Jim's voice rang in the dimness. "Apache. Where will you go?"

Visions of a red-rimmed valley danced between them.

Apache's pain burst its bonds. He dug his heels into Lucifer's sides. The black snorted, leaped, and came down running. Only then did Apache call back over his shoulder, "Maybe to hell."

If Jim replied, the sound was lost in the drum of Lucifer's hooves. His surge to freedom rang in Apache's body and fired his blood. How long it had been since he'd raced this way. The way lay smooth and inviting, and Lucifer ran like a magnificent machine, wearing off the weeks of little activity. By the time the watery spring sun reluctantly rose, miles lay behind them and Apache had reined Lucifer to a walk. A pang of regret over leaving King mingled with the deeper sacrifice of the Triple S. When he came to a vantage point, he stopped and surveyed the ranch he might never see again. He forced down every vague dream of part ownership, home, children, and Sage. Such things had no place in the course he had chosen.

He looked back no more. To do so would be to open the door he had deliberately slammed and allow memories to weaken him.

Each time Apache reached into the saddlebags on his journey to the valley behind the waterfall, he touched the brown-paper-wrapped Bible. Every time this happened, he jerked his fingers away. His lips curved in an ugly smile. No book could turn a wronged Apache weak.

Your father is not weak, a little voice in his brain reminded. *Neither are the Sutherlands or Mescal or Whispering Sage.*

He ignored the voiced and rode on. This time Lucifer didn't balk at the waterfall but slipped through and shook the water drops off when they entered the blazing valley.

Nothing had changed. The eternal cliffs encircled the green valley; deer grazed, squirrels scolded, and birds sang. The puny sun promised flowers soon. The stream brimmed to its banks, and new cottonwood leaves fluttered and whispered.

But everything had changed. Apache had shown Whispering Sage every inch of the valley. Now he could not live there without a hundred memories of her laughing, wistful face. Here she had first let love creep into her dark eyes. There she had prepared a meal they ate sitting cross-legged on the ground across from each other.

"Must I be driven from even this place?" Apache's mighty protest rolled in valley and echoed from the cliffs, but brought no answer.

"Each day will be better," he told Lucifer.

The horse stamped and tossed his head. Apache gladly noticed how Lucifer responded now. Once he had been tamed, Apache showed the black some of the love he had for King. He talked to him, petted him, and in a few weeks Lucifer trotted after Apache the way Gold Dust the collie followed Mescal and Jim.

Through the horse, Apache learned something that gnawed at his own turmoil. Before Lucifer could accept his master, he had to be tamed and broken. Once he was, the rest followed.

"What has this to do with me?" Apache snarled. "Am I an animal to be tamed?"

Somehow he couldn't get away from the thought, and others crowded in to reinforce it. He thought of a mighty river freed from the captivity of winter that had dammed it with ice. The water rushed down and spread into a hundred streams that satisfied the thirsty land and gave life. Until the dam broke, the pent-up water stayed huddled in itself instead of running free.

At last sheer desperation drove Apache to remove the brown-paper package from his saddlebag. He cursed his weakness when his fingers trembled over breaking the string. Once the familiar book lay in his hands, he merely laid it aside where unexpected showers could not touch it. A few days later the memory of Jim's hoarse voice, saying, "I found sanity and salvation," caused Apache to open the cover. Jon's name in Abigail's faded writing brought back the love he knew for Jon Sutherland.

"I will read it for him — and for Jim," he told the listening valley. Rustling cottonwoods went on sharing their own secrets as Apache began reading — a slow process to the outdoorsman who had only learned to read to keep from being cheated by the whites.

He didn't know where to find some of the verses he had heard Matthew Sutherland read in his rich voice. He turned pages, reading a word here and there, and flung the Bible aside. What good could it do?

The Bible remained unopened while Apache sought relief in a dozen ways. He shot a deer at the far end of the valley and packed it in, glorying in his strength but panting at the effort. He climbed the pennacles, almost hoping he might fall into oblivion and become part of the earth. No. If that happened, Lucifer would die when summer came and the valley parched.

Perhaps that thought sobered him. "I cannot go on like this," he shouted, hating the echoing walls, yet loath to go elsewhere. What mattered where, as long as he carried this burden? If the beauty of his surroundings did not bring help, neither would other places.

A touch of fever turned Lucifer into a phantom demon who mocked in the night, "There is no light, ever." Apache awakened in a cold sweat, staring into total blackness. Not one star showed through. Were Scoggins and Comstock even now in such a condition? Apache shuddered, remembering how his father said that on the darkest night knowledge that a new day lay ahead lightened a man's spirits.

The next day Apache again took up Jon's worn Bible. He turned to the beginning and began to read.

Now and then he found familiar stories. Much of the time he struggled to understand. So many wars, just like those between the whites and the Indians, except with a difference: The white God helped the Israelites, or at least they thought He did.

Apache turned quickly over pages that just had names, and read here and there until he found stories that amazed him. He had never seen the sea, but he had seen enough sweeping rivers to marvel that human beings could walk through one as if it were dry land! No desert or mountain or sky god he knew could do such things. He read on, again scanning prayers of praise and songs of joy, meeting for the first time many who lived and loved, fought, died, and worshiped long ago.

Days grew longer, and Apache rejoiced. His few chores left him time to roam and think. Yet more and more he returned to the Bible. Often he started and stared at the page. Sometimes he read something out loud so he would remember it better.

He came to the end of what the Bible said was the Old Testament. For many days he read no more. Everything he had learned so far swelled and mingled in a mighty upheavel of feeling. He found it hard to believe the powerful God described in the stories could want a man to forgive his enemies! Were the Sutherlands and Sage wrong, after all?

His troubled dreams reflected his struggles. Whispering Sage's earnest upturned face came again and again, the same way it had on Christmas Eve. The pressure of her fingers on his arm and her voice saying, "And by forgiving . . ." haunted him, along with the look of great pity for his enemy that had burned in Charles Campbell's face.

April capered into May and rare loveliness. Bees dizzy and drunken with pollen droned in the warm afternoons. Apache returned to his reading. It had grown far more than reading for Jon or Jim. Now a tremendous force compelled him as he had never been compelled before. A wellspring of desire to settle forever the clamor inside him kept his searching eyes on the pages until night fell and he could see no more.

At times he paced the valley and considered what he read. "Why?" became his constant companion.

Why hadn't Jesus become chief of His people and saved them from persecution?

Why had He refused to call down fire from heaven when He was ill-treated?

Why had Peter become a sniveling coward?

Why hadn't Jesus' friends sprang to His defense instead of creeping into the night and saving their own skins?

Why? Why? Why?

Sometimes Apache felt the little valley recede. Stone walls and city gates replaced them, or hills from a land he only knew from his reading. Soldiers — not like the ones he had seen but dressed in strange garments and carrying spears — searched the countryside, and lines of crosses with their gruesome burden rose before him.

Still he read on — through the giving of the thirty pieces of silver, while his contempt for the man Judas leaped. Through the same kind of trial a half-Apache could expect before white men. Through the uphill struggle beside a man whose blood oozed from a crown of thorns sharp as the cholla that bit through heavy boots and into horses' legs. And at last to Golgotha, as forbidding as the massacre Apache once beheld.

His breath came in torturous gasps. His understanding stretched to the breaking point. In death, as in life, the man Jesus surpassed anyone Apache had ever known, even the Sutherlands or his father. Nailed to a cross, He turned to the thief beside Him who cried for mercy and promised that thief he would be in paradise!

What if the man on that cross who asked forgiveness had been Scoggins? or Comstock?

Apache raised his gaze from the Bible story. Had someone spoken? Or did the words rise from his own questioning heart?

"Only God would know their hearts, and if they sincerely repented or only cried out in fear," Charles Campbell had said.

With a loud cry Apache dropped the Bible and ran at full speed up the valley, a thousand devils prodding him with doubt and indecision.

Or were the devils not devils at all, but echoes in the valley brought here in his mind?

Jon: "Greater love has no man than this, that he lay down his life for his brother."

Charles: "Do not let the way the whites have distorted the message of Jesus Christ keep you in bonds of hatred. My great desire is that you might know and accept Him . . ."

The Daybreak doctor: ". . . long wagon trips — or something — has done the trick . . . Campbell be able to fork a horse . . ."

Jim: "He will be Jon Charles, after my two brothers."

Whispering Sage: "There is no real happiness without the white God and His Son. There is no hope to live forever without them, and without hope, what is life?" "If God loves only white, why did He send His Son to be born of a Jewish girl, one of a despised race?"

Apache stopped, turned, and pelted back to camp. He snatched the Bible and read on. The tamed Lucifer grazed nearby, useful once he had been broken. Apache vaguely heard the horse's gentle movement, then lost it in the spell of the age-old story.

Once more an image of the crucifixion rose in Apache's mind, and this time he quivered when he read Jesus' words, "Father, forgive them; for they know not what they do." He felt the truth of the centurion's cry, "Truly, this man was the Son of God!" and the quivering changed to a wild exultance that spread until he felt it would consume him when he rapidly went on through the story of the resurrection to the message, "Go your way, tell His disciples and Peter . . ."

The Bible fell unheeded. For an incredible second he felt the message could have been, "Tell His disciples — *and Apache* . . ."

Peter, the coward who had denied his Master.

Peter, the one who wept bitterly when the cock crowed.

Peter, sent a special message that conveyed forgiveness and love.

God, who sent His only Son to die for the world, and for Apache, standing by and watching His Son die — as a young half-Indian boy watched his mother die.

"I know of no father who would do such a thing." Apache's voice, ringing in his ears, and his own father's reply, "That is why He is God."

A few times in his life Apache had bowed before the might of creation, dimly recognizing forces in gale and storm he could neither comprehend or define. Now the proud spirit fell in submission not to force, but to the love of the Lord Jesus Christ. What were such as Scoggins and Comstock and Simpson, compared with the majesty of God? How insignificant the past when the future opened gloriously ahead.

Apache did not bow or fall to the ground. instead, he raised his tear-wet face to the sky and conquered the last obstacle — himself. "God, I forgive." It came as a whisper. He opened both arms wide and shouted with every fiber of his being. "I forgive, as You have forgiven me!"

This time the crimson cliffs echoed back, *forgive me, me, me.*

A cannon of joy burst in Apache's heart. A silent eagle cast the shadow of its mighty wings, and he watched it fly out of sight, experiencing its freedom. Lucifer trotted up and nudged him. He turned and looked deep into the intelligent animal's eyes. "You are no longer Lucifer, but Peter, the forgiven."

The newly named black patiently followed his master while Apache broke camp. The smiling sky, murmuring cottonwoods, and laughing stream kept their counsel when the mounted rider paused, knowing he would be back someday.

Then Charley Campbell, the man who had found his God, started his long journey home. His debt had been paid — in full.

Jim slid forward, taking care not to rustle. It might be a trap. For minutes he lay still, watching the firelit area. At last he was satisfied it was empty. The gang had gone. Then why did this chill grip him in claws of suspense? Why was he wearing Jon's coat?

Gary Dale spent his childhood reading the novels of Zane Grey and vowed one day to write westerns. *VOICES IN THE DESERT* and *ECHOES IN THE VALLEY* are the realization of that childhood vow.

PROUD HERITAGE SERIES ◆ 1

VOICES In The DESERT

GARY DALE

BARBOUR BOOKS
Westwood, New Jersey

Typesetting by
Typetronix, Inc., Cape Coral, FL

90 91 92 93 94 5 4 3 2 1

To Alan,
who likes westerns

PROUD HERITAGE SERIES ✦ 1

VOICES In The DESERT

GARY DALE

PART I
Jim

1

Jim Sutherland reined in his winded horse at the top of the rise and cursed him, ending with, "No-good crowbait. Should be left for the buzzards!"

Blackie snorted, breathing as heavily as the man he carried. It had been a long, hard climb up the overgrown trail. Both man and beast showed signs of strain.

Jim shivered and stared at the lopsided moon low in the sky. He grabbed his sides with his arms, as if to protect his body from the cold, spring night. Seven thousand feet. No wonder he panted.

"Fool!" he spat, knowing he lied to himself when he blamed the northern Arizona altitude for his weakness. Only too well did he recognize the signs that preceded the dreaded coughing spells he could not control. They started in the pit of his stomach, moved upwards, spread and spread until his body was racked with pain. All the fighting in the world could not stop them.

It couldn't be far now. He had passed Daybreak hours ago. If he could hold on another hour he'd make the Triple S. He never should have chosen the shortcut. It looked as if it hadn't been used since he rode out five years before. Strange that Jon — he checked his thought as it started. The racking cough threatened to defeat him just a few miles from the ranch.

"Not now!" His gasp was lost in tremors that shook his entire body and left him reeling in the saddle. He could taste the salty wetness of blood on his lips. His heart turned to ice. He could not stop now.

Blackie turned his head, peered at Jim, and took charge. So long as there was a trail ahead, even a dim trail, it was better to move than stand heaving while the man who had spurred him so cruelly on their long ride from Lee's Ferry shattered the peacefulness of the forest glade. Great white stars made ghostly shadows of frosty limbs and bushes. Blackie snorted again and headed down the trail. There must be something better ahead than this lonely trail and the cursing, coughing creature on his back.

Jim was dimly aware of when Blackie reached an open stretch and lengthened into a run. The coughing gradually subsided but with it went his remaining strength. He should pull Blackie in. He ineffectually yanked the reins but could not stop the now-terrified animal. Blackie swerved with the trail, rounded a bend, and rushed on. Jim saw the low-hanging branch too

late, just as it neatly swept him out of the saddle and into a crumpled heap of agony. Was this the end? He tried to think. He'd come so far, couldn't he make it the rest of the way? Despair rode his shoulder as he tried to sit up and failed. He had to see Jon and Dad and Mother. He had to tell them . . . but he wasn't going to be able to let them know he'd been wrong. The oldest "Son of Thunder" was done for — and he wasn't even twenty-five years old.

Like cannon fire bursting around him, scenes Jim had forced himself to forget rushed over him, taking devilish advantage of his weakness. He could feel foam rising to his mouth and stuffed his kerchief over it. It was useless to struggle. He could not escape the past. He gave a mighty burst of effort, almost made it to a sitting position, then fell back on the needle-covered ground with an inarticulate cry. . . .

"We've got him!" Jim yelled exultantly. "Geronimo's trapped!"

"Just like a dozen times before," the soldier next to Jim sourly put in. "These Sierra Madres have more hiding places than a bee's got honeycomb."

"Not this time." Jim's sweat-streaked light-brown hair shone in the hot August sunlight, his brilliant-blue eyes lit with fanatic fire. "I tell you, he can't get away!" He gripped his rifle.

"That's enough of that!" The order crackled from their commanding officer. Unshaven, dirty, he reflected the state of his men after a long march. "We're to capture, not kill."

"Tell that to Geronimo," Jim muttered but the sharp ears of the C.O. heard him.

"You'll obey orders, Sutherland!" he snapped.

"Yes, sir." Jim Sutherland's lips curved in a snarl, but he turned away. In the months he'd been in the army he'd learned to curb his violent temper, at least in the presence of officers. The good old army way had to be observed at all costs.

Those costs had been great. Even now Jim's best friend Lester Thorne lay in a post hospital, dying from lung-shot. Jim shuddered. The lines of hatred deepened in his face. As far as he was concerned, dead Apaches were the only ones to be trusted. If he were in command he'd make short work of Geronimo and his followers. Their history of raiding settlers, escaping captivity, and raiding again was legend. Even after making a truce with General Crook this past March, Geronimo had escaped on the way to Fort Bowie, where he was being taken to prison.

Jim shook his head. The year 1886 would live forever in Arizona history as a bloody battlefield. How he hated Indians! He dropped against his pack and munched a piece of dried meat. Where had the hatred come from? Not from Dad. Matthew Sutherland always claimed Indians gave back just what they got. If you were square with them, you were treated the same. He'd

proved it, too, back home. Jim shrugged. Navajos such as those in northern Arizona were a different story from Apaches. Kit Carson had rounded up most of the Navajos back in 1863, just after the Sutherlands came to Arizona. They'd been moved to Fort Sumner, in New Mexico. Four years later they were freed on condition they'd never fight again. They hadn't.

Their relatives the Apaches observed no such conditions. Tales of their burning and killing ran rampant. Sometimes Jim wondered — did they think scalping and raiding would keep out the hordes of settlers who were bound to come? Now that Utah was being populated, primarily by Mormons, other settlers would spill over into Arizona, the same way his parents had done years before. They had left the wagon train at Salt Lake City and headed south, never stopping until they reached the beautiful Kaibab Plateau, miles below the border. There they had literally carved their ranch out of the forest, using its trees and springs and grass for survival.

Jim bit into a hard biscuit — not much like those Mother made. A wave of homesickness left him angry. After five years, he should be able to forget that day he'd left home.

He couldn't. He could close his eyes and see Dad, forbidding and stern as he roared, "No son of mine is going to run off and fight Indians when the Triple S needs every hour of our lives! The Comstocks are lying ready to grab off our cattle in any way they can." His big fist shook the table. "And you," the accusing finger jabbed Jim in the chest, "you want to run off and join the army so you can fight Indians. There's going to be plenty of excitement right here, and you'll stay here, where you're needed!"

Jim's hair-trigger temper flared. "I'm leaving — now. And I won't be back." He wheeled toward his twin brother Jon. "You understand, don't you? I want more than riding and hunting and herding cattle and being ordered what to do!"

The face so like his own shadowed. "You think you won't be under orders in the army?"

"At least I'll be my own man." All the love he felt for the twin who'd been part of him forever spilled into his voice. "Come with me, Jon. We'll show everyone. James and Jonathan Sutherland, 'Sons of Thunder,' like they called us when we were small."

"How dare you blaspheme in this house?" The Sutherland patriarch raised his shaggy gray head. His gray-steel eyes drilled through Jim. "You were named and nicknamed from the Holy Bible."

Jim's pleading eyes never left Jon's face. "Well?"

Regret darkened the matching blueness. "My place is here."

Aware of keen disappointment, Jim turned toward the door. "Goodbye, Mother, Dad." He hesitated but there was no word from his father, and his weeping mother was beyond speech. "Someday I'll be back." Five minutes later he pelted down the path leading to freedom as fast as his horse could run.

He had missed them more than he had thought possible. And Mescal — he could still see the skinny, pigtailed, openmouthed thirteen-year-old standing by the spring as he swept his sombrero in a low bow and called mockingly, "Grow up pretty, Mescal. I'll come back and marry you someday."

Her brown eyes had spit fire, and her black pigtails had bounced as she scooped up a large pine cone and hurled it with unerring aim. It glanced harmlessly off his arm, and he waved again before rounding the bend that hid her from sight. He and Jon had been six when Mrs. Ames stumbled to the Triple S from a nearby homestead. Her husband had been hurt while clearing land. By the time Matthew got there, he was dead.

The shock of it was too much for his frail wife, scarcely more than a girl. Just before sunset, she died, after giving birth to her not-yet-due baby girl. She smiled, whispered, "Mescal. After the blooming cactus," and closed her eyes, leaving the tiny baby to become daughter and sister to complete the Sutherland family.

"Move out!" The order jerked Jim back to the present, with a grin still on his face as he thought how Mescal had been well named. Frail as the mother had been, the daughter thrived, until she was sturdy as the plant and sometimes as prickly when teased.

Jim clutched his rifle, scrambling to his feet. When the C.O. gave an order, it meant *now*.

"Look out!" The shouted warning came as Jim stretched cramped muscles — and too late. A rifle cracked, answered by a volley, and a "got him!" Jim was lifted from the saddle as if by a giant hand. At first there was no pain, just the sensation of having had his chest cave in. He glanced down. A neat hole in his shirt was rapidly reddening.

"Here!" The strong hands of the man next to him ripped open the shirt. Blood poured from the bullet hole.

"Did it go clear through?" Jim demanded.

"Yes." The soldier ran his hand under Jim's back, snatched the scarf from his throat and stuffed it over the wound, then did the same in front. "It's clean."

Jim coughed and tasted the sickish-sweet taste of blood. "Must have nicked the lung."

"Sure." The soldier's white face belied his hearty tone and the look in his face, and Jim closed his eyes against them, remembering Thorne, who'd been shot the same way. Somewhere there was more shooting, but he didn't care. He was so hot, and it was hard to breathe. When they came to put him in the hospital wagon, he fell mercifully unconscious.

He awoke in a cot next to Thorne.

"Hey, old man, glad you're awake."

Jim stared at his comrade's too-bright eyes, too-red cheeks. Was Thorne a living image of what he himself would become? He turned away, strangely apathetic. All he wanted to do was rest.

Time became meaningless, swimming by until Jim neither knew nor cared what day, week, or month it was. Even when word came in that Geronimo had surrendered in Skeleton Canyon and the war was over, Jim lay in a stupor. He and Thorne had been moved to Phoenix, where they were supposed to get better care. Yet when Jim tried to pin down over-worked doctors, he was brusquely told, "Rest. It's all you can do." He alternated between despair and hope as his fever rose and fell. Sometimes he laughed bitterly. This was the freedom he'd craved? He was strong, muscular, trained for endurance since childhood and hardened by army life. Could one redskin bullet fell him? Impossible!

The following weeks brought little change. The fever came and went, the coughing spells continued, and he accepted the truth: He was going to die in this stinking hospital. The same way Thorne died the day before. They hadn't wanted him to know. The doctors mumbled something about moving him to another room for special care, but Jim knew better. During the long afternoon, Jim stared out the small window in his new room. There was a mescal plant outside. It accused him the way the child Mescal had done when Jim impatiently threw down his fishing pole because he wasn't catching anything.

"Quitter," she taunted. He'd stalked off, and Mescal had grabbed the pole, sitting hour after hour in one spot — and triumphantly bringing home a mess of mouth-watering speckled trout.

The suffering man groaned. Why should he feel her eyes staring from the past, haunting him with the assurance *she* wouldn't quit, no matter what the odds were against her? What choice did he have? He was going to die.

It burst in his brain the way he'd seen overheated cans burst over a camp-fire — nothing said he had to die here. He could go home, back to juniper and pine and sweet cedar, to welcome springs and rugged mountains and canyons filled with game.

His elation gave way to defeat. They would never let him go.

"So what?" he grimly demanded of the innocent mescal plant. "So I'm going, and no one's going to stop me. They won't drag a deserter back to die when he's practically dead anyway."

Twin spots of red crept into his cheeks, and his eyes glittered. He stifled a cough, plotting and conniving how he could get away. He must not waste strength arguing or getting permission. He would need every ounce of what little remaining grit he had to get to the home that had grown infinitely precious, now that he knew it might be lost to him forever.

All winter Jim lay in his bed when others were around and forced himself to get up and move until his coughing spells stopped him when alone. He stuffed down all the food they gave him. He closed his eyes a dozen times a day and conjured pictures of himself riding home. He feigned even more sullenness than he felt, and the hospital staff was glad enough to let him alone. His outer wounds had healed. Unless he overdid, they would stay

healed. It was just that terrible sloughing away and harsh grip on his lungs that prevented him from springing from the bed and rushing off.

Spring came early. With it came cold knowledge — if he was to go, it must be now. He had fooled himself over the winter, fed by the hope of home. No longer. He was at his peak.

He left that same night, at 4:00 A.M., the hour when men's bodies are at their lowest ebb. He stole past sleeping men, hearing their snores and low groans, carrying boots in one hand, sombrero in the other. No uniform for him, to be discovered. Jim had seen them bring in a patient about his size days ago. When they had undressed him and hurried him off, Jim had silently slipped to the discarded clothing and hid it under his mattress. He had laughed when he heard them wondering where the dusty clothes had gone and finally decided someone had discarded them as worthless.

It felt good to be back in rough clothing instead of army issue. Jim felt his way, hoping no one would waken. The greatest danger was by the front door, where a dozing doctor sat. Jim crouched in a corner, then with an unaccustomed prayer that he would not cough, he crept forward — one cautious step after another, the way he had crept past enemies so many times when he knew he was outnumbered and his only hope of safety was to escape undetected. Now that doctor was his enemy, to be outwitted by skill and stealth.

The doctor stirred.

Jim froze.

The next moment the doctor's tired head dropped back over his reports, and Jim was free to slip out the partially open door. He didn't dare breathe too freely for fear of the cough, but odors that had been dulled by hospital smells called him: a pungent bit of crushed sagebrush; the sharp tang of a hard-ridden horse; the coolness of a night wind, born in some faraway mountain, sweeping across the desert.

The clank of arms sent him hurrying behind a twisted tree. "Sir, a patient is missing." The doctor's low call turned the night unfriendly, and Jim shivered in the shadows. How could they have discovered him so soon?

"Which patient?" The speakers were so close Jim could see the tired lines on the doctor's face, the glint of metal on the officer's uniform. His heart pounded until it seemed incredible they didn't hear it.

"Sutherland."

The officer sighed, looked out across the desert, back to the doctor. "What chance has he?"

"None, sir."

"Poor devil. Don't bother reporting him."

"Sir?" The doctor echoed Jim's surprise.

"I've seen him look across the desert as if he heard voices. If he has to die, let it be where he chooses." He saluted smartly and walked away.

Jim smiled, but his eyes stung. He had just heard his death sentence

spoken aloud for the first time and with no more feeling than someone passing the time of day. There were far greater things to consider than what he already knew. He had planned carefully. He would somehow get a little way out of town and hail the Prescott and Phoenix Stage. It took thirty hours to Prescott. From there he could get a ride with someone going north to Flagstaff, a mail or freight wagon, then another to Lee's Ferry. That would put him about seventy-odd miles from home. Could he ride that far?

He set his lips in a thin line. He had to. Lee's Ferry would be the only place he could borrow a horse. Those miles were going to be long. There were the Vermilion Cliffs and House Rock Valley in between.

He started his long walk to where he planned to catch the stage. Time enough to worry later about the ride home.

Every jolt of the stagecoach ride was hell. Jim kept his eyes closed and concentrated to keep from groaning aloud in front of the other passengers. He staggered off at Prescott and barely managed to get to a hotel, where he holed up two days before going on.

The wagon ride on to Lee's Ferry was worse. But as his strength waned, his determination waxed. He borrowed the best of a bad lot of horses and started home, stopping only when he knew to go on would be to fall senseless. He pushed and strained, seated drunkenly at times, swaying at others, laughing foolishly when the fever came. Until the tree branch caught him. . . .

Jim opened his eyes. Blackie was nowhere in sight. The silly moon and oversize stars had been replaced by streaks of early dawn. He flexed his muscles, gingerly sat up, and felt the familiar tearing in his chest.

"To be so near and yet so far!" He coughed until he retched. Spent, trembling, he fell back against the pine that had unseated him. He lay until his body stilled; then with superhuman strength, born of the iron will that had entered his very soul, he stood. His vision blurred from sheer weakness. Something moved, and he shut his eyes hard before reopening them and focusing on the clearing ahead.

A buckskin-clad Apache stood not fifty feet away.

Jim flung himself to the ground, clawing for the Colt revolver that had slipped from his holster when he writhed with coughing. His hands found it, cocked, aimed. The Apache was almost on him, coming at a dead run.

Jim pulled the trigger, but another seizure wracked him, and the bullet went wild. He was clutched by talon hands whose fingers bit into his shoulders. His Colt fell to the ground, and the Apache kicked it away.

"Jon!" The black eyes stared into his own and their expression slowly changed to something unreadable. "No. You are the other one." The Indian's gaze roved over Jim's sorry appearance. "The black horse is yours?"

"Who are you?" Jim tore free. "What are you doing here?"

Incredible scorn swept over the formerly impassive face. "I am Apache."

He rose and towered over Jim.

Even through Jim's anger and pain he could not help noticing the perfect English and the statuesqueness of the bronzed man above him. Apache stood close to Jim's own six-foot height but was more muscular. Long black hair fell past his shoulders and was caught back with a band. His buckskins and knee-high moccasins fit as if molded to him.

"You called me Jon." Jim's brain whirled. Apache made no move to harm him. What was he doing this far north? He must know the Sutherlands — he had changed *Jon* to "the other one."

"Come." Apache reached down a strong hand.

Hating himself for accepting an Indian's help, but powerless to get up alone, Jim grudgingly stood to his feet and brushed the hand aside.

Apache gave him a contemptuous glance and ordered, "Wait here," before disappearing into the trees.

Jim slumped against the mighty pine's lightning-scarred trunk, glad of the rest. His struggle and exertion had just about finished him. His face contorted. A spurt of hatred brought his tired body erect. He would obey no Indian! He would get home on his own, if he had to crawl. It was too ironic to be dragged home half-dead by an Apache. He would tell them what another Apache had done to their son and watch their revulsion against this savage who gave orders like General Crook.

He took a single step forward and was stopped by the sound of hoofbeats. Apache crossed the clearing, with Blackie trotting behind him. The big Indian ignored Jim's curses and swept him into the saddle the way he would still a protesting child.

Jim was nearer fainting than he'd ever been in his life, but the ignominy of being dumped into the saddle gave him strength to blaze out, "I don't know who you are or what you're doing here, but you're still nothing but a stinking Apache, and I hate your guts!"

The Indian's control was superb. "The feeling is returned."

If the stagecoach and wagon rides had been hell, that last mile was damnation. It was all Jim could do to remain seated. His anger had taken a terrible toll on his fading stamina. Only pride kept him on the horse. He suffered tortures, although Apache carefully led Blackie at a walk. Jim would not sprawl at the feet of his arrogant captor. Neither would he cry out. The blood on his lips, when they rounded the last bend, was not from his lungs, but from biting his lips to hold back screams as knives tore through him, bringing anguish.

"Stop here," he commanded.

He was rewarded with an eagle-swift look from Apache and a curt order to Blackie. Jim made no attempt to explain. Yet he knew when he crossed the threshold of the log house fifty yards ahead, it would be for the last time. He would fall into a bed, die, and emerge in a pine box, to be buried somewhere on the Triple S. So when he stepped inside, he must carry a sharp

enough memory of the home he had ridden away from so eagerly and had now sought to die in, to last the minutes and hours until it happened.

A great gasp of relief belched from his throat. Nothing had changed. The peeled logs were a little darker, and the trees and flowers were taller, but everything else was the same: Haunting Spring, which never went dry, was swollen now with its burden of melted snow-water; the dusty corral held a dozen horses; the barns; the rambling bunkhouse, where he'd played cards with the hands. A patina of early morning sunlight lay over it all, dappling through billowing white clouds that promised rain.

And the smell! Nothing on earth smelled like the resinous Ponderosa pines guarding the ranch like standing sentinels.

A curl of smoke lazily crawled from the rock chimney, and the smell of frying ham and wood smoke assailed Jim's nostrils, stinging his throat. What an utter fool he had been. Could any man ask for more than this? Yet he had chosen to go — now all that was left of him had come back, when it was too late.

A golden avalanche of frenzied barking shattered his bitter reflections. The collie raced around the corral and across the yard, straighter than a speeding, whining bullet on its path.

Jim's mind refused to accept what he saw. For a moment he was a boy again, beating Jon in races, but never their dog.

"Gold Dust?" Jim shouted incredulously.

The collie was closer now, leaping and bounding.

Jim tumbled from Blackie and met Gold Dust in a mighty embrace on the pine-needle ground, as they had done so many times before. Wounds, impending death, even the hated Apache above him were nothing to Jim Sutherland. His only reality was the ecstatic collie, the pet he had long thought dead.

2

"What's wrong with that animal?" The stentorian yell came from the open doorway.

Jim raised his head and gazed across the yard at his father, scarcely daring to look. Another wave of relief hit him. Dad had not changed. Tall, massive, he filled the wide door then stepped lightly off the board porch, piercing gray eyes and light step proclaiming him as the woodsman he was.

Before Apache could answer, a strong voice called, "Gold Dust hasn't acted that way since Jim left! You don't suppose. . . ." A replica of what Jim had been before the last battle ran from the barn and outdistanced his father. Immediately behind him was a full-bosomed, black-haired young woman, lissome, but with the same brown eyes that had haunted Jim in his hospital room. Mescal!

But his attention strayed. A slender woman appeared in the doorway. "What is it, Matthew?"

Pain that had nothing to do with lung-shot flooded Jim as he crouched by his dog. The figure in the brown linsey-woolsey dress must be Mother, but how could it be? Mother's hair had been brown as fallen leaves after rain; this woman's was snow white. Yet as she came closer he saw the brilliant blue eyes her sons had inherited. It was she.

Jon reached the cringing, huddling figure, stricken with shame over what he had done to his mother, bitterly regretting the stubbornness that had prevented him from even writing. Gall and wormwood threatened to finish in Jim Sutherland what the bullet had started.

"It's —" Jon let out a whoop, reached for his twin, wild gladness in every line of his body. "Mother, Jim has come home!"

"Wait," Jim breathed, wanting them to warn Mother before she saw what a wreck he was. He desperately struggled to get up. He must be on his feet and meet her like a man.

It was too late.

"God in heaven, my son!"

Her white face matched her hair and gleamed in the sunlight as she ran to fall on her knees before her prodigal Son of Thunder. Joyous welcome turned to horror at sight of his hollow cheeks, bright eyes, and bloody shirt and kerchief. *"Jim!"* She seized his hands with a grip that would never

again let him go. *"What have they done to you?"*

He buried his face in her calico-aproned lap as he had done so many times in the past when confessing a childish wrong and asking for forgiveness. Years fell away. He felt her hand move to his shock of roughened hair and remembered the gesture had always signified all was well.

He no longer had to pretend. Mortally wounded man dissolved into small boy as he clutched the wind-dried apron that carried the smell of comfort. He raised his head. A terrible cry of remorse tore from his innermost soul. "Mother — I've come home to die."

Silence pounded in Jim's ears. His body burned with shame like the Painted Desert in August. He could not lift his head to face Jon and his father after that cowardly cry. In all the battles he had never showed yellow. Now he curled into his misery, made worse by his own craven cry.

A contemptuous drawl cut the heavy air. "So you're still a quitter."

"Mescal!" Matthew Sutherland's roar as he whipped toward the sneering girl brought Jim to his senses. He threw back his head. Hatred shot from his eyes. *What did you say?"*

Her lips curled. She opened her mouth.

"Be silent, girl," Dad thundered, raising one mighty arm.

"Dad, no!" Jon sprang forward. "You'd not strike Mescal!"

Jim fought the red haze filming his murderous eyes. "Let her speak," he panted. Heart raw from his own cowardice, he felt even his lips turn white beneath her steady gaze. "If she knew the hell I went through even to get home, she wouldn't stand there like that." Memory of his agony roughened his voice.

"So it wasn't easy." Mescal didn't give an inch. "You made it, didn't you? Now are you going to lie there and die or get up and fight like a man? God help your regiment if you were no braver then than now."

Dad struggled for words that wouldn't come, but Mescal stepped closer. Jim could see tiny golden flecks in the depths of her challenging eyes.

"When you rode off, you told me to grow up pretty, and someday you'd come back and marry me." She swept him a slow glance, from worn, dusty boots to tossed brown hair. "You cut a mighty fine figure for a bridegroom, don't you?" Every deadly word struck like a bullet. In a pool of disbelief, she turned on her heel and ran into the woods.

"Don't pay her any attention." Jon's hoarse voice ended the ugly scene and he helped Jim stand. "She didn't mean it."

"She meant every word." Jim leaned on his twin, sweat standing on his forehead in great drops. He glared at the path Mescal had taken, then at the silent, watching Apache. The spleen he hadn't been able to muster to blast Mescal erupted. "You agree with her, don't you?" Foam coated his lips. "You think she's right about me."

A sardonic smile flickered across the set face. "I am only an Apache. What right have I to think or feel?" The swaying aspens parted, and Apache

disappeared between them.

"Why is he here?" Jim ranted. "I come home shot to pieces by Apaches and find one in my front yard!"

"He's our friend." Jon picked up his brother and headed for the log house, ignoring Jim's protests. Jim was vaguely aware of being laid on a cool bed, stripped, and bathed. He turned away from the broth Mother brought, but gulped the icy water he'd dreamed of in the five years of desert and mountain fighting, too tired to care for any of them, even Apache.

He never knew how long his semiconscious state lasted. At times he was red-hot, hearing shouts of Indians on the warpath. That was followed by trembling, cold shudders that even woolen blankets couldn't stop. Once he knew it was all over. Then a girl's voice rang in his ears, "Quitter . . ., quitter . . ., quitter." He gave a great heave of his body, and the murky depths drowning him receded.

One day he opened his eyes, too listless to move. The log walls of his old room smiled with sunlight from the open window.

"Decided to wake up, old man?" Jim saw in Jon's clear eyes the strain of what had passed. "Don't talk. Rest."

Jim's lips twisted. That's what the army doctors had told him. He stretched, aware of his terrible weakness. "How long?"

"Three weeks." Jon's blinding-white smile lit his whole face. He turned to the open doorway. "Mescal, bring broth."

"Don't let her in here." Jim shrank from his tormentor's presence. He might as well have saved his breath. Mescal seated herself in a chair hewn from a great tree and forced him to take the broth. He could see a faintly scornful twist to her drooping lips and faint blue shadows under her eyes. Aloof, silent, she slipped from the room as quietly as she had come.

"She hasn't been in here, has she?"

Jon's answer was succinct and betraying. "Day and night."

"Why? To see me crawl again?"

"You didn't crawl. No more talk now." Jon pressed Jim back against the pillow and followed Mescal.

Well, at least he wasn't dead, even if he was dog tired. Maybe there'd be a better time before it got him. He hoped so. He'd give anything just to go fishing once more. Jim sighed. That long trip home had taken a heavy toll. His thin hands plucked the patchwork quilt nervously, and when he heard Apache's low voice outside the window, his fingers curled into balls of hate.

One sunny morning Jon insisted on getting him into a chair. Panting with the unaccustomed exertion, Jim fell against the blanketed back. "What a miserable wretch I am!" He glanced through the open window and froze at sight of Apache. "Why's that snake hanging around?"

"Because of Mescal."

Jim's lips curled in disgust. "In love with her?"

The old fire Jim used to try to strike from gentler Jon blazed into a forest

inferno. "Don't be a fool! Of course Apache isn't in love with her." The fire died to smouldering. "I'm the one who's in love with Mescal."

"You?" Jim felt jolted. "Since when?"

"Since always." Jon measured Jim with narrowed eyes that still held ignited sparks. "I used to think you'd be my competition."

"Not for that wildcat!"

"She isn't a wildcat all the time." Jon's eyes glowed like twin mountain lakes. "She's wild and sweet and true. Every animal on the place comes at her call. She's made pets of coons and crows and deer. She can't pass a wounded creature. That's how we got Apache."

Jim's breath quickened.

"Last fall Mescal visited in Daybreak." A shadow crossed Jon's usually sunny face, and his big hands lay curiously clenched. "She doesn't often get away from the ranch, but Alice Johnson asked Mescal in for a dance and over Sunday, and Dad finally said she could go. I was going to take her, but she laughed at the idea. Said she could take care of herself." Jon broke off with a rousing laugh that brought a smile to Jim's lips, in spite of himself.

"She can, too." Jon laughed again. "She can outride and outshoot Dad and me. In a contest between you, I'd be hard put to know where to lay my bet."

"That's pretty easy now," Jim threw in sourly.

"I mean when you get well."

Jim thrust back a pang at Jon's confidence. Even though he was undeniably better, he hadn't told his family of the continuing night sweats and spasms of coughing he muffled in his pillow. Good thing Jon was sleeping in the attic, instead of his own bed that stood across the room from Jim's as it had done for over twenty years.

"Go on." He couldn't keep the curtness back.

Jon's face shone with admiration. "Mescal left Daybreak early. She got halfway home and noticed a flock of circling buzzards off to her right. She's rescued fallen fawns many times, so she swung Shalimar toward the flock."

Jim could see her swinging off the main trail, as much a part of the big buckskin as if she'd grown there.

"If she'd been another girl, she probably would have run screaming from the spot. Apache had been dry-gulched and left to die."

Similar scenes rose in Jim's brain: blood-spattered golden leaves, isolated forest glades. Now he added a slender figure, bent over a fallen Apache.

"He'd been shot in the back five times. He'd lost so much blood he was nearly dead. Mescal didn't dare leave him and ride on home for us. Don't ask me how a slender girl like Mescal got Apache on Shalimar. I asked her once, and her face gleamed. 'I had no choice. I did what I had to do.' Anyway, she got him here. We took care of him and learned his story. He's only half Apache. His father was a white settler who fell in love with an Indian

girl and actually married her."

"So that's why he speaks good English."

Jon nodded. "His real name's Charlie Campbell, but he won't use it. He says the whites have treated him even worse than the Apaches, who despise him for his mixed blood. He saw his mother killed in a surprise attack by the army. After Campbell deserted them, they were living in an Indian village." Jim's face darkened. "All the atrocities aren't on the Indians' side. Apache lay as if dead the whole time the massacre went on. He's been roaming Arizona alone ever since."

Jim brushed the story aside impatiently. "So Mescal saved his life. That was months ago. What's he doing here now?"

"It's a good thing he was here, or you might not be."

Jim had the grace to look ashamed. "Yeah." He turned restlessly toward the window. Early spring had given way to warmer days, although nights were still cold. "Things look just the same, but they aren't. Here you are in love with Mescal. An Apache acts as if he owns the place. Mother's hair is white. Anything else I need to know? I'd just as soon not stumble on much more without some warning."

Jon rose to lounge in the doorway, straight and strong as Jim had once been. When he turned toward Jim, a softened, strange look mingled with the sunlight in which he stood. "When you get well, I'll be leaving the Triple S."

"I don't believe it!" Jim was aghast. "You've never wanted anything but the ranch! Why, after we were born, Dad changed the name from Circle S to Triple S to show the three of us were partners." His voice dropped. "After I left, I used to wonder if he'd change it to the Double S."

"He wouldn't and won't. Not even when I leave to become a minister."

Jim stared, then bent double, laughing until it made him cough. "You fooled me that time! For a second I thought you might be serious."

"I am." Jon's lips smiled, but his eyes remained grave.

"Never! We're the original Sons of Thunder, remember? James and Jon." Jim laughed again. "Although you never were the big noise I was."

"Not the original Sons of Thunder, just imitations. The original James and John were disciples — too." The last word was almost a whisper. Jon reached out a sturdy hand, pleading for understanding.

"But why?" Visions of tired, overworked, lonely men riding sagging horses as weary as themselves danced before Jim's eyes. "You'll give up all this you've worked for, to be a preacher? Why?"

"I've asked myself that a thousand times." Jon's brooding look witnessed how true it was. "Maybe it started in childhood, when Dad used to read to us." He picked up a worn Bible. "Remember Moses and Daniel and all those heroes? I always had to have a hero. The whole time we were growing up, you were my hero, leading while I followed, even though we were twins."

The controlled voice brought stinging hotness to Jim's eyelids. He had never known Jon idolized him.

"Then you were gone." Endless sadness filled Jon's voice, giving a hint as to how much he had missed his twin. "I had to find another hero. I did — in here. Someone to look up to and follow."

"Someone to replace me." Jealousy crept into Jim. "If you had to have another hero, why'd you pick someone out of the Bible? Why not Dad? Who is it? Peter? I remember him, always losing his temper."

"No, Jim. I picked Christ."

"Impossible!" Jim fixed a stony stare on Jon. "Jesus? That sissy who didn't have the guts to fight back when they killed him? You have to be loco."

"He was no sissy. Those hills in his country were no easier to climb than some around here." Jon's penetrating gaze never shifted. "What's the greatest thing you could do for me?"

"Why," caught off guard, Jim hesitated, blue eyes darkening to twilight purple. "Save your life, I guess."

"Suppose saving my life meant taking my place and dying yourself, so I could go on living?"

Jim squirmed. "Not many men would do that."

"One did." Jon laid the Bible back on the table.

"So now you think the only way to pay your debt is to be a preacher!" Jim's sense of loss harshened his accusation. A chasm deeper than the Grand Canyon of the Colorado had opened between them.

"There are many ways to pay a debt. Apache's way is to be here when Mescal needs him."

Jim's lightning-swift response was enough to change the subject. "Why should Mescal need a stinking half-breed? She's got you and Dad and —" his face went gray. He had almost added "and me."

"We can't be with her every minute."

"I would hope not. Much of her company would send a man screaming into the desert." Jim's curiosity mounted. "Why does someone who can ride and shoot the way you say she can need a bodyguard?"

"Do you remember Radford Comstock?"

Liquid fire ran through Jim's veins. "I'm not likely to forget that slick rustler and his thieving family."

"He's sworn to have Mescal. Been crazy over her since she turned fifteen. She hates him like poison. At the dance in Daybreak she cut him dead and, when he made a dirty remark, slapped his face so hard it sounded like a pistol shot."

"Good for her!" Blood sang in Jim's ears, despite his dislike for Mescal as she had been since he came back.

"Gossip has it Comstock's laid bets he'll have her if he has to drag her off behind a rope, the way he would any wild thing."

Contempt flared. "What have you done about it? Why haven't you and Dad ridden over and wiped out the whole bunch of them?"

"Dad doesn't know, and I hope he never finds out. That's just what the Comstocks are waiting for. If we ride over shooting, it will give them an excuse to pick us off — and you know what would happen to Mescal."

"Why doesn't the Daybreak marshal step in?"

Jon's eyes turned to molten metal. "He isn't likely to do that when his name's Radford Comstock and he's been put in office by his swarm of relatives."

"So that's how it is." Jim's mouth curved in a slow, unpleasant smile. "Maybe having Apache around isn't so bad after all, with Dad not knowing and you wanting to be a minister. Apache might just come in handy."

"Especially when it was the Comstocks who shot him, even though he could never prove it." Jon sighed. "I won't be going away until things settle down." Longing crept into his face.

"If it means that much to you, guess I'll have to put off dying for a while." Jim was rewarded by a smile like sunlight through fog. "What's Mescal think of becoming a preacher's wife?"

"I haven't told her how I feel." Jon confessed with a grin.

"Why?" Jim could feel the muscles of his neck cord. "Think she's too good for you?"

"No. I believe down past all the prickles she may love you, Jim." At Jim's speechless look, Jon added, "I think she took what you said five years ago a lot more seriously than you meant it."

"Now you're the fool," Jim snorted.

"Any other girl in your life? Besides Alice Johnson when you both were kids?"

Jim was tired of the conversation. "I've had a lot of time to think about girls where I've been, now haven't I?"

Jim's message seemed to get through. Jon stretched. "I've got work to do. Now that you're getting better, Dad's on me about letting things slack." He strode to the door again and hesitated. "Jim, if ever you and Mescal care for each other, don't let me stand in your way." His spurs clinked as he finished and was gone.

"Mescal!" Jim spat in disgust. Yet an hour later, when he saw her cross the yard, he measured her with new eyes — not as the childhood companion or the haughty stranger who flayed him with her tongue, but simply as a girl-turning-woman.

Sunlight caressed her curly dark hair and stained her smooth skin as she knelt to tussle Gold Dust. Her rounded body without an ounce of fat was in perfect, symmetrical proportion to her straight shoulders. The prickly attitude she maintained around Jim was strangely missing. In its place was the joy of youth and living that had characterized her since babyhood.

Her naturally red lips parted in a perfect smile. Even from that distance

Jim caught the low gurgle of laughter in her slim, tanned throat as Gold Dust capered. Streaks of red colored her cheeks, and her pinned-up hair fell wildly about her like a black, cascading waterfall.

Jim caught his breath, and his sluggish blood stirred. She was beautiful. No wonder Jon loved her and Radford Comstock vowed to have her! Vaguely remembered feelings crept through him — feelings like those that died years before when Alice Johnson snootily turned him down for another escort. They struggled to be reborn, the way he watched butterflies kicking free.

On impulse Jim leaned through the open window. "Good morning, Mescal."

Her gaiety died. The flush of fun receded, along with her careless abandon in playing with Gold Dust. In vain the collie leaped and pawed and barked. Mescal straightened her simple cotton dress; the disdainful look Jim had learned to associate with her settled like a mask. "Good morning." She turned to smile at Apache, who had noiselessly stepped from the aspens.

Jim ground his teeth, unreasoning gall rising at the Indian whose presence he had barely begun to tolerate. Mescal must have said something to Apache, for he glanced at the window and Jim. For the first time a faint semblance of what might be called a smile touched his impassive face.

"By all that's holy, he'll pay for that!" Jim hissed through set teeth. "So will she."

All the long afternoon he sat in the chair by the window, seething with resentment at the girl who had once been like a sister, but who chose to befriend an Apache rather than be civil to her own kind. The longer he simmered, the more corroding became his hatred of Apache. By night he was trembling — and it ended in spasms of coughing worse than anything he'd had since his first week at home. This time there was no muffling it in a pillow. The fear in his parents' eyes was as real as the paroxysms that shook him. When they ended, most of his hard-won strength had been wrested from him, taking with it even the undying hope Jon had steadfastly clung to and cherished.

3

Why had he ever come home? Regret mingled with shame as Jim subsided from the coughing spell into familiar blackness. He had laid his plans well and carried them out, selfishly crawling home to die. Why hadn't he thought of what it would do to his family, having to watch his useless struggles? Mother, Dad, Jon, Mescal — her scornful face floated above him. She'd probably be glad enough to rid herself of his presence, since she thought he was a coward. Little snatches of memory: Mescal with Gold Dust; Mescal whispering with Apache; Mescal watching him with golden-flecked, contemptuous eyes — all combined in a whirl of frustrating helplessness shot through with pain.

Once he opened his eyes. Jon knelt by his bed. Jim struggled against the lump in his throat and weakly held out a wasted hand. It was instantly grasped by a hard, callused hand, and through the dimness of the turned-down-lamp lit room, Jon whispered, "Hold on, old man." The next time Jim surfaced from the drowning pool of misery, Jon was gone. The room was still. He must have quieted down — even the lamp was out. Jon never would have left him unless he thought Jim had dropped into natural sleep.

Something slid in the shadows, and Jim's illness gave way to caution. It couldn't be Jon. He never moved furtively, as the indiscernible shadow did.

"Who's there?" Jim forced himself to a half-sitting position and strained his eyes.

There was no reply, just a curious movement that made Jim's blood ice and his skin crawl.

"I said, who's there?" But his demand dwindled to a whisper. Something about that black shadow was terrifying. Fear such as he'd never known before clutched Jim's throat. Was it death lurking in that corner, waiting, just waiting?

How ironic! Moments ago he'd been wishing he hadn't come home. Now he wished the entire family was with him. He sank back on his pillow in exhaustion, biting his lip until it bled. He would not show craven again. His fingers picked at the quilt. If death wanted him, let it step forward boldly.

"Come on, you —" He couldn't get the curse out.

This time there was an answer — no more than a current of air as a tall figure loomed over him. For a moment Jim braced himself, then

18

automatically opened his mouth in a last cry for mercy. He was rewarded with a cloth roughly stuffed in his mouth.

Death wouldn't gag a man, would it? Jim fought strong arms lifting him from the bed and the cough that could go nowhere tearing inside him. His wildly flailing hands were stilled, but not before they contacted buckskin.

Apache!

But what was he doing — and why?

Jim struggled silently, furiously. He was overpowered as easily as Mescal might overpower an outraged kitten. The muscled arms lifted him, and Jim felt himself being carried. Red-hot anger burned inside, and again he fought, tearing out and striking blindly. Once he heard an involuntary grunt, quickly smothered.

Then they were outside.

It was starlight, and Jim's suspicions were confirmed. Apache carelessly tossed him into the saddle of a waiting, saddled and bridled horse. Shalimar! Jim heard the big black snort as ruthless hands tied him securely in the saddle.

If only he could get his hands free, get the gag from his mouth. Blue murder shot from his heart. Just one chance to sink his fingers into the treacherous throat of the Indian snake his family had saved, and he would die happy.

There was no chance. Apache crammed a sombrero on Jim's head, silently mounted King, Jim's gray stallion raised from a colt, and goaded him into a slow walk. Jim saw the long lead line between the two horses, noting how heavily packed King was.

What kind of evil scheme did Apache have in his half-white brain? Was he to carry Jim off somewhere and torture him even more than what Jim had already endured? What might happen while he remained in Apache's power? The thought brought great drops of sweat to the suffering man's forehead, despite the coldness of the night, and he strained against his bonds. He only succeeded in wearing himself into semiconsciousness. He slumped over, held in the saddle by ropes rather than will.

In the jumbled nightmare that followed their entrance into the aspen grove near Haunting Spring, voices screamed in Jim's ears. They must be part of what couldn't really be happening, he knew. Apache wouldn't dare creep in and abduct him! Once he thought he heard Mescal's voice in a low undertone. It was enough to rouse him from his stupor. Only the rustling of aspen leaves greening and whispering filled the air.

It was his last lucid thought. A heavy fog fell over him like a scratchy army blanket, and he knew no more.

Hours or days or centuries later, Jim opened his eyes. He lay on a carpet of pine needles, saddle propped behind him for a pillow. He could smell some strange, resinous odor that filled his nostrils with repugnance.

"Drink." The voice of his hated enemy mingled with the unwelcome

smell, and Jim turned his head to see Apache bending over him with a battered cup.

With every ounce of strength he could muster, Jim struck out at his captor's hand. His puny blow didn't even spill the contents of the cup. It did bring a blaze to the usually imperturbable eyes. Apache deliberately knelt against Jim, pressing the defending arm into the ground. He tipped Jim's head back and lifted the cup to his lips. Jim obstinately closed his mouth.

Apache's hard lips curled, and he immediately pinched Jim's nostrils together tight.

Gasping for air, Jim opened his mouth, was met by a deluge of bitter herbs, and automatically swallowed again and again, until the cup was empty and Jim choking from the acrid, unpleasant taste.

"You see," Apache told him, "There is no use fighting. You will do what I say."

"I'll see you in hell first!" Jim panted, hands clutching the ground in an effort to keep from screaming.

"Probably. Just remember —" He paused as if to allow the significance to sink in. "Wherever I am, you'll be with me."

Jim spat at Apache's moccasins. The next instant his left cheek glowed from the hard slap Apache administered much as he would cuff a dog.

"You rotten, filthy Indian!" Jim tried to spring to his feet but only succeeded in starting another coughing spell in his rage. When it dwindled, he glared at Apache through red-rimmed, tear-streaked eyes. "Hit a dying man!" He couldn't spill out his venom.

"I do what is necessary." The bronzed face didn't move a muscle, and he sounded almost bored.

Hatred a thousand times greater than anything he'd ever felt exploded in Jim. "I'll kill you for that someday."

Apache sneered, his face turning cruel. "If you live long enough, which I doubt." For a single moment his eyes bored into Jim with a fanatic light. The sunlit glade darkened, although the sun still bravely pierced through the trees. "James Sutherland, the mighty, crawling on his belly, making threats! Don't you know you are yellow clear through?"

His accusation was like pouring vinegar on an open wound, irritating the already-guilty feeling Jim carried over his cowardice. He opened his mouth to scorch the devil before him but never got the chance. Apache seized him by the front of his coat and half dragged him to Shalimar. "You'll do what you're told and like it, *white man!*"

It was futile to protest, better to save what energy he had. Deep inside Jim, determination was born. He would watch and wait, and if the God Jon was planning to follow let him live long enough, Apache would have an unguarded second, and Jim would strike. He would think no more of killing the man retying him into the saddle than crushing a snake beneath his boot heel. Strength that had faded in spite of love for family was born anew

by sheer hatred. There had to be a time. There would be. Jim would stay alive until there was.

Evening shadows deepened as they began their trek.

"Aren't you going to gag me?" Jim taunted.

"Why bother?" Apache's raised brows gave him an even more evil look. "You can scream yourself hoarse, and no one will hear you."

For the first time, Jim looked at his surroundings. Nothing to distinguish them from any other part of the Kaibab Plateau, except the change in trees from pine to cedar.

"Where are you taking me?"

This time a definite smile lit up the cruel bronzed face. "You said it earlier. To hell."

Jim cursed and turned away from the obvious enjoyment on Apache's face. The scrape of whiskers against his coat as he hunched lower in the saddle prompted a final question. "How long have we been gone?"

"Three days. For reasons I'm sure even a white man can understand, we are traveling nights only — and only part of them. It isn't my plan to push you into dying — yet."

Even Jim's anger couldn't ignore the sinister way Apache had stressed the word *yet*. He closed his lips and concentrated on staying conscious. At times he clenched his fists and chewed his lip to keep from pleading for rest. He was spared the final ignominy. At the exact time Jim knew he could go no farther, even tied as he was, Apache called a halt. There were more bitter herbs to be forced down him. Jim would not submit, and each time the same struggle occurred.

"Seems like you'd be smart enough to learn to give in," Apache settled back after still another tussle. He eyed Jim. "The sooner you learn who's boss, the easier it will be."

"Never! I'd rather be dead than give in to you, Indian."

"That isn't an alternative just now. If I'd told you back at the Triple S you could even come this far, you'd have thought I was lying." Apache's inscrutable eyes pierced to the weakest chink in Jim's armor. "Remarkable what one can do when he has to."

"I'm only staying alive to get a chance at you." Jim couldn't keep it back; all the hatred and anger spilled out in a rush.

"That's as good a reason as any." Apache wasn't even disturbed. He merely threw more brush on the tiny, controlled fire and stretched to his full, superb height.

Yet even hatred and anger couldn't keep up forever. Jim got to the point where he no longer knew or cared what day it was. They had left the plateau. Cool forests had been traded for red rock canyons. Northern travel took an eastern turn. Where in God's name was Apache taking him? Never had he seen land so desolate. Arizona Territory couldn't hold such places, could it, except deep inside the bowels of the Grand

Canyon of the Colorado? The day came when they no longer traveled by night. Jim had long since given up wondering why Jon hadn't followed. Even if he'd tracked them at first, now that they painstakingly traveled over sheer red rock, no tracks could be left. There wasn't a soft spot for miles.

One day Apache disappeared. By late afternoon Jim had to admit there were worse things than being captive. Apache had been careful to drive off Shalimar, and Jim had no strength to find him. He lay on a blanket beneath a shelving of red rock, looking across a sluggish stream toward red buttes and cliffs and crags hundreds of feet high. Apache hadn't lied. Hell itself couldn't be worse. There wasn't a blade of green grass in sight. The only sign of life was a group of small lizards sunning themselves on the rocks.

Was this Apache's revenge? To pack him up here and leave him to starve? What a diabolical plot! All the fiends of hell couldn't have planned it better.

Bitterness eroded Jim's insides, and as the second day passed, he grew feverish. The water in the canteen was low. He had no taste for food. Why eat and prolong the agony? If there was a God, let Him send death quickly.

Jim's prayer, if it could be called such, was interrupted by a soft footfall.

Was it gladness that he wasn't alone that brought the strange cry to Jim's throat? Apache stood before him.

"Did you miss me, white man?"

The gladness was short-lived. Jim forced himself to respond. "Were you gone?"

Dark eyes, keen as a hawk's, swept over him. Apache deliberately laid one hand over Jim's breast and pressed. Nausea threatened to overwhelm Jim.

"It's time to move on." Apache drove forward two pack burros, heavily laden with supplies, whistled, and Shalimar and King appeared. Jim's eyes widened. Evidently their strange journey wasn't over. He submitted to being tied in the saddle again, sagging against his pinnings for support.

Deeper and deeper they went. Once Jim shuddered, thinking even a well man could never ride back out without Apache's guidance. There would be no escape that way. Too many tortuous turns, and canyons crossed and recrossed. Part of the time they rode up stony ways. At other times they were in a stream or river. Hard as he tried, Jim could not place where they could be. It must be somewhere in Utah. He'd watched the North Star enough to know they had left Arizona days before. Travel was slow, exhausting, draining Jim of all he had except his hatred and relief over not being alone.

When he was ready to give up, Apache's taunts kept him going. When he knew he was dying, Apache's bitter herbs lessened his cough but did not cure it. His beard had grown until it bothered him. He was used to being clean shaven.

The night Jim knew was his last followed a bad spell. Red rocks ranging

from scarlet to crimson, which looked like spilled blood, swam together, and Apache had to carry him from Shalimar to a small cave. Jim finally asked, "Aren't you afraid of what Jon will do?"

For a tense moment Apache searched him, as if holding back a last, terrible blow.

"Well?" Froth rimmed Jim's lips, making his blue eyes terrible in his wasted face.

"He will do nothing."

"You mean because he's going to be a preacher and is supposed to love enemies and all that rot?" Jim's cracked lips opened wide in a hoarse laugh. "Don't count on that protecting you!"

"I'm not." Apache had never been more impassive. "He thinks you didn't want to have them see you die, so I took you away."

"What?" The word cracked like a rifle shot. What new torture was this? Jim stared at Apache, who never moved a muscle.

"You are slow of understanding, weak one. They know you are brave, all except Mescal," Apache's mouth twisted, and Jim wanted to slam his fist into its mocking curves. "Isn't it what they'd expect of their Son of Thunder?" He laughed aloud, a harsh, grating sound that echoed and reechoed between the cliffs frowning down at them.

Jim snatched at his words like a starving man at a crust. "All except Mescal?" He glared at his tormentor, whose face was even redder than usual, as the sun reflected from a vermilion cliff.

For the second time, Apache hesitated. Then he softly said, "Who do you think is behind all this?"

Incredulity, amazement, disbelief, and fear blended into a single word cry. "Mescal?"

Truth that could not be denied etched itself on the watching face. "Yes. Do you think I would choose to spend my time with you in this place?" His casually waved hand indicated the gloomy canyon walls and lack of life. "Mescal saved my life. I am repaying her."

"I don't believe you."

"Don't you, white man?" In one bound Apache was on his feet. "Then believe this. I do not lie. She planned it all. She begged me to take you away so they wouldn't have to see you die." Other words seemed to tremble on his carved lips, but they did not spill over. "Even I, Apache, would hardly have dared steal Shalimar and King, the choicest horses on the Triple S."

The blow left Jim reeling. "But why?"

"Who am I to know the secrets of white women's brains?" Apache shrugged and busied himself with making a fire. "Perhaps she knew it was too hard for your family. Perhaps she was tired of caring for you. Or perhaps she felt out here you would die like a man, not a sniveling coward."

"So you will bury me and carry word back," Jim jeered. "All about how Jim Sutherland gave up and died. Well, you —" He cursed softly and

horribly. "It's not going to happen. Do you hear me? I'll lick you and this cursed place and this sickness. I'll go back and tell them you turned traitor, tortured me, and that I finally killed you in self-defense and buried you here!"

The sun had dropped behind the high cliff, and shadows covered the camp. From their depths came Apache's voice, "You have spoken. Now we will see if white man lies."

Spent by the revelation, brain revolving, Jim fell senseless to his blanket. It was the last clear thinking he did for a seemingly endless time period. He was vaguely conscious of being cared for, of food being given him, and at last, of being put back on Shalimar. During the ride, his mind cleared. Vegetation had begun to appear, growing out of the rock walls. He dimly noted the start of surprise Apache showed over something on the trail and forced heavy eyelids up long enough to note hoofprints. So they weren't the only ones left in this yawning, gaping, wounded world. It didn't seem to matter.

Since the last confrontation with Apache, Jim's hatred had been split. If Mescal could do this to him, what might she do to Jon? Even when the extreme coughing and demanding fever spells came, one thought burned and beat in his brain: He must save Jon. He must get well, tell Jon what Mescal was — and warn him about Apache.

After the telltale marks in the trail, Apache moved with caution. He drove them both until they were ready to drop. Even the hardy burros and horses showed fatigue. Only Apache himself gave no signs of weariness. If he ever slept, Jim didn't know when. Any time he awakened, the grim reminder of his captivity was there with watching eyes, like a vulture hovering over a dying animal.

The next day it suddenly ended. They rounded a bend and were confronted by the end of a box canyon. Narrowed to a few feet at one end, the only way out was the way they'd come in. In one of his conscious moments, Jim could laugh. "Not so smart after all, huh, redskin?"

Apache didn't slow his speed. He kept riding along the crumbling ledge that narrowed, narrowed, until it disappeared into a gushing waterfall. Jim's jaw dropped as Apache rode directly *into the waterfall,* motioning Jim to follow. Not believing what he was doing, Jim let Shalimar pick his way after King and the burros. He blinked and tried to adjust his eyes from the glare of red canyons to the dim cave and passageway behind the still-rushing waterfall. His sluggish blood stirred. Step by step Shalimar found his way along the ledge above what seemed a large pool of water. Far ahead Jim saw a dim light that widened as they drew near. It must be the opening or entrance of the deep cave, hewn into the mountains of tortured rock.

At the opening he hesitated, unwilling to see what lay ahead. Perhaps this was just one more way Apache would make sure no one ever found his grave. The morbid thought brought a snarl to Jim's lips. He started to turn

Shalimar and was stopped by an iron grip on the reins. Apache, on foot now, led the snorting black out the opening into the sunlight.

Jim could only stare.

Rimmed in by the bleeding rocks, as he mentally called them, lay a verdant fertile valley, perhaps a mile long and a little wider. A lazy stream wound its way through cottonwoods, showing the elevation was lower than where they'd been before. At the far end, King was already knee-deep in green grass, and the burros were standing, waiting to be unpacked so they could roll. Sage smell melted into pungency as Shalimar trod through it and wildflowers, after Apache.

"Welcome to paradise," Apache told him, inscrutable face turned toward the far side of the stream, where deer grazed unhurriedly.

"Where are we?" Jim demanded, turning a fierce glare on Apache. "One of us will be buried here. I hope you. It won't hurt for me to know now where you've brought me, will it?"

"Not at all." Apache was already engaged in throwing the packs from the burros. "We are in the Utah brakes and have followed the Paria River the last few miles. Before that it was Cottonwood Creek, which cuts the canyon through the Paria Plateau from northeast area of Kanab, in the Vermilion Cliffs. That's why some of the valley floor is two thousand feet below the rim." His strong hands stilled. "You are only the second person I know who has been here."

"And you were the first." Jim tore his gaze free from the boxed-in valley surrounded by violent red cliffs. "Were you here before? You must have been, to find it!"

"No. My grandfather told about it. He learned of the hidden canyon and waterfall and valley from his father."

"You mean you brought me through all that twisting, turning trail without knowing where we were going?" Jim shook his fist at Apache.

"I knew."

His calmness enraged Jim. "You — you —" Words wouldn't come.

"Save your strength. You're going to need it for what we must do now."

"What do you mean by that?" Jim managed to slide from Shalimar, after Apache untied him. Menace hung in the peaceful valley where no fear should have been. Even the deer raised their heads, as if uncertain, then bounded a few feet away and resumed grazing.

Apache's closed face showed no emotion. He drew a razor-sharp knife from his belt and laid it on the ground. "I am going to open your wounds."

Thunderstruck, Jim couldn't move, but seconds later he threw himself to the ground and clawed for the knife. "You aren't carving on me, you red devil!" His nerveless fingers closed on the hilt but loosened as Apache's bone-crushing grip caught his wrist.

"I will do what I have to do." The cliffs above were no more feelingless than Apache's face.

"And let me bleed to death?" Jim choked out.

A faint smile touched the other's features as if a shadow had crossed the sun. "What's the difference? Bleed to death or cough to death?" He sighed and explained the way he would explain to a small, naughty child. "The wounds are healed on the outside but not the inside. By opening them up and letting the air in, they may heal inside. Of course, they may not. Either way, you don't have much to lose."

"You are not cutting me." Jim forced himself to stare directly into his Nemesis' face. "I won't give you the satisfaction of working me over and making me suffer more, then sitting there taunting me while I die."

Ice crystals tinkling against a window were no colder than Apache's words. They fell like heavy rocks into Jim's fear. "I thought by now you knew who was master. I was wrong."

Jim flinched in spite of himself. Raw reality faced him. He forced himself to keep his gaze steady, even when Apache drew back his mighty fist. He would not beg.

He felt a battering ram hit his jaw.

Then all went black.

4

Once, in childhood, Jim had heard someone speak of the seven devils. Now he knew it had been wrong. Those seven devils were multiplied into seventy thousand, all with the gloating face of Apache. They carried spears of glowing, red-hot, searing pain and thrust them into his body, leaving him writhing. Yet beaten into his brain was the cry, "No mercy. I will not cry for mercy." It shut his parched lips and sent blood into his throat, as he bit his cheeks to keep from screaming.

The sought-for periods of blessed unconsciousness in the abyss of darkness grew less. He was vaguely aware of the bitter herb drink forced into him and soft pads of wool pressed against the wounds Apache refused to let heal. During the day, unless they bled, Apache left them uncovered to the fresh air. Jim slept on a tarpaulin, face to the sky, his only covering against early summer storms the frail canvas Apache drew over his face when it rained.

By the time Jim could sit up without knives tearing at his chest, weeks had been consumed. "What date is it?" he croaked against his will.

"Sometime in July."

Jim closed his eyes and slid back to the ground. He found it impossible to believe, but after a few days of watching the sun's path and noting how early its streams sought him out, he had to accept that Apache had spoken the truth.

He gritted his teeth. Apache! The cursed machine who never made a mistake. Not once had Apache slipped enough to leave a gun where Jim could seize it. If he had — Jim smiled grimly. Would he shoot Apache or himself? The morbidness of the question bored into him.

Apache broke his thought by stepping nearer. He had discarded his shirt and wore only buckskin breeches and moccasins. Sweat glistened on the copper skin, and a film of moisture obscured his set face. For the first time Jim saw telltale signs of the long vigil and its toll on his guard.

"Tomorrow you walk, white man."

Jim didn't answer. Caught up in his discovery, he paid little heed. Let him think he'd won. It would throw him off his vigilance and give Jim the opportunity he'd prayed for. "Whatever you say." He caught the quickly hidden flash of surprise in Apache's face and turned away to hide his elation.

When Apache got Jim to his feet, it was like teaching a newborn colt to stand, then take a few unsteady steps. Great drops burst forth on Jim's forehead, and he would have collapsed if it had not been for the rocklike support of Apache.

Jim fell to his tarp and blankets, wondering if he'd ever get up from them again. The next day he walked farther. Within a week he had stumbled as far as the stream, noticing it was down since they arrived. It was hot, boiling, miserably hot, and every step was misery. Only Apache's goading, "Is the little boy tired?" gave enough impetus for Jim to crawl back to his nest. Disheveled, filled with anger, he held his tongue and inwardly gloated about how he would pay that sneering devil.

The day came when Jim walked the length of the valley. When he returned, he threw himself facedown into the shrinking stream, reveling in its coolness. The water laved his hot face and arms and whispered the message, "You're well."

Startled, Jim could not believe the truth of it. The next moment he leaped up, tore free his shirt, and gazed at the healed wounds. He had known for days he was better. Now it was time for the final test. He deliberately gulped in great breaths of air, waiting for the too-familiar rending that always preceded coughing spells.

It didn't come.

He gulped again.

Again.

Only the hot, sage-scented air moved in and out of his lungs.

"Apache!" he screamed, forgetting all else but his miraculous news. "I'm well!" He flung his arms wide, raced across the valley, shouting, leaping into the air, a madman running wild in his ecstasy.

Apache rose from the fire beneath two neatly spitted rabbits. A rare smile lit his face for a fleeting moment. "I know."

The words stopped Jim in his tracks.

Apache gave the rabbits a slight turn. "In a few days we will go home." His farseeing eyes turned southwest, as they had so often. His perfectly modeled hand indicated the stream. "Soon we cannot find water. The deer have gone elsewhere. We have used the rabbits. We must go while there is still time."

"Time! Who cares about time?" Why did an icy finger seem to count Jim's ribs? He met his foe's eyes squarely. "I haven't forgotten why you dragged me here, Apache."

His meaning was clear. Apache's smile twisted into contempt. "If you ever knew." He threw his ax across the small clearing, until it imbedded itself in a nearby cottonwood, and stalked off.

Jim glared, his joy melting into the old hatred. So he was cured. It didn't change the ruthless way Apache had kidnapped him or that Mescal planned it. He'd been too tough for them.

A twinge of shame sent red into his face, clean-shaven now with materials Apache had fetched along. Memory of long nights with the red man near forced him to admit that without Apache — he shut that door tight. Apache felt he had a debt to Mescal. What would she say when he rode back in, instead of Apache reporting his death? He closed his eyes and pictured her shock. It soothed his anger. When he got through telling Jon of the little plot, Mescal would pay for her treachery, and so would Apache. His teeth flashed white in anticipation, giving him the look of a snarling wolf.

The next day Apache busied himself with packing. Jim roused from his excitement and helped. Their supplies were dangerously low and as Apache had said, game scarce. They were leaving none too soon.

"Where did the deer go?" Jim raised his eyes to the end of the valley.

Apache shook his head. "They have ways." His deft fingers never missed a stroke of their work. "They are not helpless — like white men."

Jim was silenced, but the roar of vengeance in his head rivaled the diminished roar of the waterfall exit to the valley. He had decided to wait until he was closer to home to jump Apache. It was doubtful if he could get out of this hellhole without guidance. "I won't kill him," he whispered into Shalimar's mane. "But I'll make him crawl. Maybe I'll wait until we get home, so Mescal can see it."

At last they started: Jim first, the two lightly burdened burros, Apache last, on King. Jim turned back for a final glance. His face contorted. The sunlit valley had been the scene of agony and ecstasy, despair and hope. A faint haze from their last campfire still rose and hovered in the still air, the mute evidence dying before his eyes. It was as untrodden as when they came, except for lack of game. In the bowels of the earth it had been and would be an undisturbed pocket, hidden from people by its protecting cascade of water.

"Come."

Apache's reminder set Jim's face the other way. He slowly entered the cave that gave entrance to the valley, riding its dark depths this time in full knowledge, not half dead to his surroundings. Shalimar daintily picked his way and gained access to the crumbling ledge outside the waterfall. The burros started across, then hesitated.

"Keep them moving!" Apache ordered. "Tighten that lead line!"

All Jim's resentment bubbled into a great sore. He jerked the line. Shalimar jumped ahead. An instant later the line was torn from Jim's palm with a force that left it raw and bleeding. He whipped around. Froze.

"Look out!" he shrieked as a boulder bounded from somewhere above.

Apache pushed King forward, but the second burro brayed in fear and backed into the gray. King reared just as Apache reached for the lead line and crashed into the burro. Off balance, Apache grabbed for the reins. He was too late. King snorted and scrambled out of the pounding boulder's way, but not before the red giant neatly swept Apache from the saddle into

a huddled heap next to the waterfall.

Jim had all he could do to quiet the animals. He managed to get them up the trail a hundred yards and find a place wide enough to tie them. Then he slipped and slid back to Apache, leaping the missing spot in the path in a jump that left him breathless.

Frantically, he clawed aside smaller rocks, straining to lift the boulder. He uncovered Apache's face. There was pain in the dark eyes, but he was alive.

A thrill of something indescribable sprayed through Jim, and he redoubled his efforts.

It was no use.

"Go, white man." Apache's voice rang weirdly in Jim's ears. "You have your wish. Apache is buried."

Jim recoiled. He could feel the blood receding from his face as he stared at the pinned-down victim, helpless but unbowed.

"Go." Apache's voice was stronger now. Was it a final spurt of energy before death? "Follow the water. Turn right at all major canyon crossings. There is enough food. Kill the burros, if you must. Use the water sparingly." He licked his lips. "Tell Mescal —" He heaved upwards and fell back.

It was the hour he had dreamed of, the chance he had prayed for. To make Apache suffer the way he had suffered! He would die, but a horrible death. Buzzards would come while he lived and pick out his eyes. If he was fortunate, he'd remain unconscious. If not. . . . Jim's heart leaped. He had his revenge. All he had to do was get on Shalimar and go.

He sprang to his feet, face dark with passion. "Die, redskin!"

Apache's eyelids fluttered but remained closed.

Jim gave an exultant yell, reminiscent of his Indian-fighting days. One more dead Indian for the record. He backed away, keeping his eyes on his enemy, feeling his way across the broken trail, poising himself for the leap that would separate them forever.

Apache opened his eyes. The old contemptuous smile settled across his face. "Good-bye, white man." His eyes closed. The one free hand fell limply to the rocks and hung against them, blood making dark paths down the fingers and dripping into the water.

For an eternity Jim hovered on the edge of two worlds. Suspended in time, unable to move, he fought — and lost. Unwilling steps carried him back to the fallen man. Even more reluctant steps brought Shalimar as close as he could get the big horse to Apache. Five, ten, thirty minutes he struggled to get a rope from the saddle horn around the boulder, failing each try, until, "Now!"

Shalimar sprang. Jim tugged. Apache lay free, bloodstained and broken.

In spite of his newfound strength, it was no easy task to carry Apache even to a spot where he could be lifted to Shalimar's back. It was even harder getting Shalimar to jump the gap, but at last Jim had Apache hoisted

aboard the black. He led Shalimar through the waterfall and cave, hating the very thing he was doing, cursing himself for a fool.

Apache was limp, apparently lifeless. Yet Jim found a faint heartbeat and rejoiced. He stripped the Indian, checked him from raven hair to calloused soles. "Broken ribs, maybe three. Broken ankle. Smashed foot." He enumerated as he worked. "If an end of a rib or splinter doesn't hit the lung, he might make it." His laugh was gall. But his hands were gentle as he bound the ribs tightly, heated water and bathed the foot and tugged the broken ankle until it snapped back into place. Last, he made crude splints from sticks of cottonwood limbs. It was all he could do.

"More than I should do," he said harshly.

Apache moaned once but mercifully remained unconscious. It wasn't until Jim sank back on his heels that he felt himself watched and saw Apache's eyes were open.

"Now it's my turn." Jim deliberately looked deep into the black pits of pain. He held out a cup with a mixture of the herbs he'd found in Apache's saddlebags.

Apache grimaced, swallowed, and reclosed his eyes. It was the beginning of a curiously reversed but well-known time period. Jim used the same tactics on Apache that had been used on him.

The third day Apache motioned Jim to listen. "You must go." The urgency in his command was underlined by his fever-bright eyes.

"Not until you can travel." It was a relief to say it aloud, the decision that had cost Jim sleepless, troubled nights.

"Fool!"

Jim shrank from the blaze in Apache's face. "You can't call me anything I haven't already called myself." He thrust his hard-set jaw nearer. "Don't ask me why I didn't just ride off. I don't know."

Apache brushed it off as unimportant. "If you don't go now, you will die here."

A chill tickled Jim's spine.

"The stream will disappear. Even though we can get water from the waterfall, much of our way there will be none. It is already late July. No man, even a red man, can live through August here if the rains do not come. We will scorch like lizards in a frying pan."

"Then we'll scorch together. Remember what you said?" Jim's intensity made claws of his curled fingers. "I told you I'd see you in hell. You answered I'd be there with you. Now that's just where we are — together. Either we both get out, or we die here — together."

Apache's eyes turned to molten metal, reflecting the burning sun. "I was never going to tell you. You didn't deserve it!" Some of the color drained from beneath his skin, until for the first time, Jim saw resemblance to the way his white father must have looked. "Mescal sent me here with you, not to see you die, but to live."

"That's a cheap, conniving trick to get me to leave." But Jim's twisted lips had gone white.

"I do not lie, white man." Apache's sonorous tones rolled into the quiet valley. "She said, 'Bring him back well — for me.' "

There was no mistaking the truth.

Jim reeled, caught in a fury of crashing walls of hatred, understanding, and regret. With an inarticulate cry, he turned and ran as if pursued by a hundred howling wolves.

Hours later, he returned. Something in his face warned Apache not to reopen the subject. Jim had faced his crossroads and chosen. Even for the love Mescal had for him — and there was no denying it when Apache spoke as he had — Jim could not, would not leave. He had been forced to admit his entire stance about the fallen Indian had been wrong. Every indignity he had suffered had not been Indian revenge, but the necessary ingredients of saving his life! At last he knew what Apache had said when he flung out, "If you ever knew." Beyond the bitterness of past months something was born inside the oldest Son of Thunder, and that was gratitude for the half-breed who had done what he must.

Jim silently prepared a small meal, conscious of their rapidly dwindling supplies. It would be days and weeks before Apache could travel. Lips thinned with concentration, he apportioned the food then eyed the two burros. As Apache had said, if worst came to worst. . . .

Days later Jim stood on a small mound near their campsite, straining his eyes toward a small white cloud sailing overhead, fervently wishing it would join forces with the few other clouds. The earth had grown parched. The sun set nights in hazy, menacing purple streaks of heat. The little stream had vanished before the sun's demanding rays. For the past three days Jim had carried water from the waterfall.

A soft footstep behind him announced Apache's presence. He had hobbled the short distance, with the aid of a cottonwood limb. "Jim," he didn't seem to notice Jim's involuntary start. It was always "white man," or "Son of Thunder." Apache lifted one hand. "Tomorrow you go. If you wait longer, we will be trapped here until the fall rains. If they do not come," his shrug eloquently completed the sentence.

"You aren't ready to ride."

"No."

It hung in the air between them, until Jim roughly said, "I told you we'd go or stay together."

Apache searched the face grown strong and hard, then said, "You would give up home, love, life, for a stinking redskin?"

"No. For a — friend." For the first time, Jim held out his hand.

Apache stared at it, more emotion in his face than Jim had ever seen before, but he did not take Jim's hand.

"Jon asked once what the greatest thing was a man could do for another.

I said save his life. He asked what if that meant dying in another man's place, and I told him —" Memory choked off the words for a second. "I said not many men would do that." Jim turned squarely toward Apache. Blue eyes clashed with brown. "You took a chance on that. You knew I'd kill you if I could get a chance." His face worked. "Still you brought me here — and I'm alive."

Apache gripped his hand. "It was for Mescal." His look never wavered.

"I know. But I still owe you." He forced a hoarse laugh and turned toward camp. "The best way you can help me is to get well so we can both go home."

That night Jim dropped into uneasy, troubled sleep. He awakened to find it was still dark, except for the light of the uncaring white stars. What had he heard? Tuned to catch Apache's movements when he lay helpless, now Jim could feel more than hear some foreign sound.

He slowly turned his head.

Apache was creeping toward him, catlike in the dimness.

Jim lay inert, the old dread crawling through his pores. *What is the Indian doing?* His fingers felt for the butt of his gun, even while he remembered he'd tossed it aside earlier.

Intent on his task, Apache didn't notice when Jim cautiously changed position so he could observe better. The starshine glinted on a gun barrel. Through the clear night air came a faint whisper, "Good-by, white man."

Nausea rose in Jim at the treachery of the bronzed man who had taken his hand only hours earlier. He stared through the gloom at the impassive face that turned toward him. Indescribable sadness etched deep hollows in a face gone grotesque.

A flash of understanding brought Jim to his feet even as Apache turned the gun to his own head. The shot went wild, lost in the clusters of stars above. Jim's launching of his body, like a bullet, had struck the gun in time.

Apache fought, to no avail. His former superb strength had been drained. Minutes later he lay panting on his tarp, with Jim astride his midriff. "Why did you stop me?" The terrible accusation echoed in the valley. "You could have saved yourself." His struggles ceased, but his face shone, contorted in the pale light of the watching stars.

"We stay together." Jim shook his fist in Apache's face. The gun lay in the red dust. "Do you think I'll go back and tell Jon and Mescal you killed yourself to save my hide?"

Apache winced, and Jim pressed his point. "I swear to you that if you try again and succeed, I'll stay here with your body until both of us are buzzard bait!" He climbed off Apache and towered above him. "Before Almighty God, that is my vow to you."

Apache lay motionless, eyes glittering. Then he rolled over, awkwardly got to his feet, and held out his hand.

Day after weary day succeeded one another. After that one night, neither

mentioned leaving. Apache healed, was ready to ride — but too late. The streams needed for them to make the arduous journey were bound to be dry. Everything depended on if it rained, or when. They killed one burro and choked down the tough meat. Then the second. When it was gone, their supplies had dwindled to a little flour and salt. Apache fried "dough gobs" on rocks heated in the fire, tasteless pieces of bread made from flour and water with salt.

When the flour ran out, Apache came into his own. Jim tramped the valley, vainly watching for anything that moved. He would even have killed and eaten a buzzard, but ironically, none came. He returned to camp empty-handed, to find Apache roasting small pieces of meat on pronged sticks over the fire.

"Eat." Apache held out a morsel.

Jim obeyed, chewed the rather tough meat but glad to get something inside his always-hungry stomach. "What is it?"

"Lizard."

The meat came back up. Jim choked. But at the look in Apache's eyes, he forced himself to swallow, take more. "If anyone'd ever told me I'd eat lizard I'd have —" He shook his head.

"Men will do what they must to survive." Apache chewed thoughtfully. He was thin to the point of emaciation, as was Jim. "At least some men." He paused and Jim held his breath. In the comradeship of necessity Apache had begun to talk more, open up. Was it because there was little chance they would ever escape their red-walled prison?

"I am like the mule, Jim. Not horse. Not ass. A breed between, who belongs nowhere. White men curse and hate me. Red men despise me. I am nothing."

Jim searched for words. None came. There were no words to meet the exquisite suffering.

"My mother was beautiful, but an Indian. My father was respected, until he married her. Better for me if I had died in the massacre." Apache raised a hand to still Jim's protest. "Your brother preaches a God who loves all. If it is true, then why must I walk alone? I can never marry an Indian. I am too much white. I can never marry a white woman. The ones who would have me are as rotting leaves." His gloomy face darkened a shade. "I will die, be buried in a nameless grave, forgotten. There will be no son to carry on my name. I cannot bring another into this world to bear what I suffer. One day the Apache will be gone forever, tamed and herded by the white man, the same way other tribes have gone.

"But one day the Apache will be free. And that is the day we are all dead." He sprang to his feet and paced beside the fire. "The white man will build houses and schools. He will destroy the game and despoil the streams. Then he will remember the Apache — and know he has killed part of this land."

Jim sat stunned, blood racing through his veins. The truth of what Apache had said hit him like a cannonball. He watched the tall, haggard figure limp away into the cave entrance and was aware of cataclysmic revelations he could never let Apache know he had been given.

Apache loved Mescal. His eyes, constantly turned toward the southwest, betrayed him to the man who had been forced to spend weeks and months in this dying place with him. It was not the love Jim found had grown within his own heart since that day he learned she cared — a love that looked forward to possession, sharing, and happiness. Apache's love transcended human feelings. His greatest joy would be serving her, never letting her know he loved, and at last dying to save for her the unworthy, sniveling coward who had crawled home to die.

Jim set his jaw, watching the same southwestward direction Apache sought, seeing beyond canyons and red rocks, valleys and mountaintops and plateaus to the Triple S basking in the summer sunlight. Was Mescal even at this moment facing northeast, keeping her secret, praying and hoping and passionately longing to see them return? She would know they were long overdue. Did she watch every cloud, cursing it when it lazily drifted on, willing it to spill its blessed contents on the earth?

"If it doesn't rain soon, it will be too late." Apache's voice roused Jim. He glanced away to keep from betraying knowledge of Apache's carefully hidden secret. "What date is it?"

"Somewhere near the first of September." Apache's grim voice did little to reassure. "Now all we can do is wait. . . ."

PART II
Jon

5

Jon Sutherland stumbled down the attic stairs, self-reproach in every step. How could he have slept when Jim needed him so much? It had seemed like good sense when Mescal ordered him to get some rest after Jim's spell subsided, and he dropped into unconsciousness, but the sun streaming in through his window this morning accused Jon. The long strain must have been too much even for his toughened body — he'd gone out like stars before a sullen sky.

The room to Jim's door was closed when Jon got to it. He put one hand on the knob, intending to slip in as he had so many times before while his twin lay sleeping. It turned under his hand, then opened wide. Mescal stood in the doorway, a strange exalted look on her face. Jon could see rumpled sheets and blankets on the bed in back of her. "Why, what on earth —?" He stared. "Where's Jim?" Fear seized him. Had last night's spasms been the last? He grabbed Mescal's shoulders, shook her roughly. "He isn't. . . ."

"No." It hung in the air.

"Then where is he?" Jon demanded.

"Gone."

Jon's fingers tightened. He saw Mescal wince and hastily let her go. "I'm sorry, Mescal. It's just that I don't understand. Where has he gone and how?"

Something flickered in her eyes, steadied. A tiny pulse beat in her throat. Her arms hung motionless at her sides. "Apache took him away."

Blood leaped to Jon's brain. "Apache dared?" Jon whirled, his high-heeled boots clicking on the board floor. "And all this time we thought he was our friend!" Jon couldn't remember ever having been so enraged. "How much of a head start do they have?" He snatched his sombrero from the rack near the door and ran to the porch.

"*Wait!*"

Jon heard the sound of her moccasined feet behind him and turned back. "Don't try to stop me. Tell Dad and Mother I'll bring him back, and as for that Judas Indian —"

"Stop it!" Mescal caught his shirtfront in great handfuls, pulling him toward her. "Apache isn't going to harm him. Jim has gone away for our

36

sake, so we won't have to see him die. Can't you understand? Would you stay here and see us suffer, if it were you?''

His anger fled, replaced with illumination. "You mean Jim came all the way home to be with his family and now has turned around and gone off somewhere with an Apache to die?" He shook his head to clear the mist swimming in his brain. "It doesn't make sense."

Golden motes struggled to overcome misery in her dark eyes. "It's killing your folks and you, seeing Jim as he is."

"And you, Mescal?"

She sagged, and he was sorry he'd added the question. He put both arms around her, something he hadn't done since she'd grown up. He could feel the hard beating of her heart, but he had to lean close to catch her whisper, "And me." His hold tightened. Somehow he had always known it was Jim, even in the years and years his brother had been gone. Life was funny. It would be logical for Mescal to turn to the brother who had stayed home. Instead her heart had gone with the prodigal.

"Well! Never thought I'd catch you two spoonin' right outside Jim's window." Matthew Sutherland's hearty voice separated them, and his big grin spread across his face. "What's Jim to say about this?"

"Jim's gone. Gone somewhere with Apache to die in peace," Jon hastily added, when the smile faded in his father's eyes.

"No more than I'd have expected. Mother will take it hard, but I don't know but what that's best." Matthew smoothed the heavy gray forelock back out of his eyes. "The Indian'll take good care of Jim and let us know after it's over." He wheeled and strode into the house. "I'll tell Mother." A low cry a few minutes later split the silence, and Jon bolted to the corral. Dad could care for Mother better than he could until he overcame his own heartache.

Weeks later, Jon reined in the black he'd taken for his special horse since Apache and Jim rode away on King and Shalimar. "You're a grand horse, Dark Star," he told the stallion. "It isn't your fault you aren't gray and fleet as the wind." Regret filled him. "I never even got to tell him good-bye." But he knew he wasn't talking about the animal. Doubts assailed him. Why hadn't Apache returned? In the shape Jim was in, he couldn't have lasted. If something had gone wrong, and Apache'd been attacked, somehow he would have set King and Shalimar free. Jon would bet his life on it.

It had been such a strange summer: first Jim's homecoming, then his leaving. Sometimes Jon caught a look in Mescal's eyes that made him wonder. Was she hiding something? If so, what? She never lied. Still she acted strange. Dozens of times he had caught her looking north and east. Once he said, "Did they go that way?"

"Yes."

He prodded no more. Mescal had never been heavy, but she thinned to aspenlike straightness as summer lay its scorching blanket over the rim. Day

after day they waited for rain, and none came. Stillness settled over the family, each waiting, watching, perhaps praying for Apache's return. "Waiting kills," Dad remarked once, out of Mother's hearing. "She'll feel better once she knows it's over."

Jon caught sight of Mescal's face as she turned and slipped away into the woods. Suspicion crystallized. Mescal knew something the rest of them did not. He followed her, but she outdistanced him, and when she came back hours later, avoided him.

Now Dark Star whinnied and tossed his head for attention. Jon sighed. Dad was right — the waiting was killing them all. He slid from the saddle and tossed Dark Star's reins over his head. All the Triple S horses were trained to stand that way. A rocky promontory ahead lured him, and Jon dropped to the outcropping. What was he to do about his own life? Deep inside was the desire to become a minister, to bring hope and healing to those around him. Yet how could he leave now? He shook his head. His plans and dreams had to wait.

What if Apache never came back? Why hadn't he followed them that morning long ago, insisted he be part of Jim's death, the same way he'd been part of his life? Some minister he would make, when he couldn't even reach his own twin!

Dark Star nickered, and Jon raised his head. Fifty feet away, Mescal, on Patches, stood gravely surveying him. Girl and pinto seemed of one piece in the green surroundings. Jon had been so engrossed he hadn't heard them coming. He stood and started toward them.

"I'll come to you." Mescal expertly dismounted. The boy's pants she wore for riding, over the protest of Mrs. Sutherland, didn't hamper her the way the girl's long skirts did. She left Patches to graze near Dark Star and glided to Jon's perch. Disquiet rested in her eyes, and Jon could feel tension in the slim body, when they seated themselves again.

"What were you thinking? You looked so grim when we rode up." Mescal sifted a handful of pine needles and let the dirt slide through.

"I was wishing I'd followed Jim."

She started. A deep flush faded into alarming whiteness, but she only said, "It wouldn't have done any good."

Suddenly Jon could stand it no more. "Mescal," he measured every line of her face and nervous hands. "You know more than you're telling, and I'm going to find out what it is."

Instantly she was on guard. It showed in the way she leaned back from him and in the mocking light that rose to change her face completely. "Oh? And just what is it I'm supposed to be hiding? What guilty secret are you accusing me of?" Her quickly assumed mask wasn't good enough to cover the flash of fright in her eyes, just before she glanced away.

"If I knew, I wouldn't have to ask, would I? You've been keeping out of my way ever since Jim and Apache disappeared. This is the first time we've

been alone together." He dropped a hard hand over her small, shapely brown one on the ground between them. "Mescal, dear, what's come between us? Even if you love Jim, I'm your brother who loves you."

His tenderness hit a soft spot. He knew it reached the mark through the quick clutching of his hand by her strong fingers. A rock crystal sparkled in her dark lashes, and she shook her head to get rid of it. "It's just the waiting. If you only knew how hard it is!"

"Don't you think I do?" Gruffness replaced Jon's understanding. Anger at his own helplessness washed through him again and again. "There should have been more I could do. Instead, Jim went off into the desert or mountains or valleys somewhere. I can almost hear his voice calling me to come, the way he called me to follow his lead all the time we were growing up. But I don't even know where to start! Mescal, tell me where they went. I have to find my brother's grave and at least mark it. I can't stand thinking he's lying in an unmarked hole under a sand dune or a pile of rocks." He'd never meant it to pour out like that. Once started, the dam of anguish smashed before his tongue could stop it.

Mescal turned to stone. Each feature seemed chiseled by the harsh land in which they lived, where danger lurked beneath even the most beautiful day.

"Tell me, Mescal. Where is my brother's body?"

For a long moment she didn't answer. At last she turned to him. Her eyes were hollow as the brassy sun already poured out on them. "I don't know."

He recoiled. "But you said Apache took him, that they'd gone north and east." He was almost incoherent from the desolation in her confession.

"It's all true. Apache took him. I told him to."

For an instant Jon thought the hot breeze that had whipped by played tricks on his ears. He closed his eyes and reopened them. No, it wasn't a dream. He was still on the rocky promontory. He could see every direction, most of all the direction she'd said Apache and Jim had gone.

Mescal fixed her eyes on a distant tree and said in a monotone voice, "Apache said, if he could take Jim away, there was one chance in a thousand he could save his life."

Jon leaped to his feet, blood hot in his face. "You believed him?"

"What choice was there? We all knew he was dying. Even your father said it was better this way." Her lips set in a stubborn line. "I did what I thought was right. I still think it was, even now that —"

"That what?" he thundered. "Do you realize what you've done? You sent my brother into the wilderness to die with no one but an Indian. You knew how he felt about them. How did you persuade Jim to go?"

Her drooping head was answer enough. Jon clenched his hands until the nails broke the skin of his tough palms. "You didn't persuade him. You ordered Apache to abduct him, didn't you?"

"*Yes!*" Her cry rang from rock to rock, bounced off into a million shattered echoes, the way Jon's faith in her broke.

"Why? Why did you do such a terrible thing?" Jon panted for breath after the blow. "You knew how we all loved him. Yet you chose to —" he strangled on the words. "Is this the way you repay all our family has done for you?" He knew the taunt was caustic and rejoiced.

"I'm part of this family." Her eyes glowed like twin coals. "I wasn't born into it — Mother and Dad chose me to be in it. You talk about love — there are many kinds of love. Mine was strong enough to take a chance, that's all." She stood her ground, magnificent in her denunciation. "You smothered him. You would never have agreed to let him have that one long chance. I did."

The quivering aspens grew still at her defiance. The world held its breath. Even the cloud lazily strolling by paused.

She wasn't finished. "Don't you know I've asked myself the same questions a million times in the past few weeks? Don't you know that along with the sorrow we all share I've had to fight guilt? But in spite of the way it has turned out, if I had the choice to make again, this very minute, I'd do the exact same thing! I believe in fighting for life, not placidly accepting that the chips are down and hanging on to a rotten hand. At least I had the courage to give him that one chance."

Jon's brain reeled the way a small rock broke loose and merrily skipped down the cliff. "Then since Apache hasn't come back — Jim could still be alive." A sentence blazed in red-hot letters. "What do you mean, in spite of the way it's turned out?" Incredible hope turned to blackness.

Every ounce of fight drained from the girl before him, leaving her stark and spiritless. "If Apache had been able to make Jim live, they would have been back."

"Maybe not." Once she had instilled the possibility of life, Jon refused to let it die. "Maybe it took longer than Apache expected. Maybe they will ride in any day!" He spun around, lifted both hands to the sky. "As you said, Apache hasn't come back. Neither have Shalimar nor King. If Jim were dead, one of the three should have come!"

"Not from where they were going."

Mescal's words plowed into him like bullets. Jon could feel hope slipping, in spite of his frantic clutch at straws. "Where was it?"

"The Utah brakes."

"Then I'll go after them!" Jon could feel his heart glow. He dropped to one knee beside Mescal. "I'll find them, if it's the last thing I do on this earth."

"You can't. Even Apache wasn't sure he could find the place he wanted. His grandfather told him of a strange country through the Paria Plateau. There's a hidden valley, back of a waterfall. But if Apache didn't find it, he'd go somewhere else." Her dark head swung back and forth. Defeat slouched her shoulders. "There's been no rain. Even if they got there, and Jim got well, they couldn't recross the desert and get home."

A death knell drummed in Jon's ears. Everything she said was true. The hot summer had taken its toll even here. What would it be in a place such as she'd described?

"Do you think I should tell Dad and Mother the whole truth? I never lied. I just held back part of what really happened." Mescal's searching eyes insisted on an answer.

Jon felt weak from the rainbow of emotions he'd experienced: rage, relief, hope, despair, and gradual acceptance. He sank back to the ground beside her. Jim really was dead. There could be no doubt about it. Apache probably was, too. Shalimar and King might turn up on someone's ranch someday, if they got out of the box canyon.

"I think it would just make more hurt," he said carefully.

"You blame me, don't you?"

She looked so small, so defenseless, Jon was reminded of her at six, when she'd been so sick they thought they would lose her. Compassion swept through his body. What a burden she had carried! "No, Mescal, I don't blame you now. You did what you had to, what I couldn't have done. It isn't your fault the odds were too great. If Jim were here, I think he'd thank you for being willing to at least let him stay in the game."

Her enormous eyes devoured him. She gasped, then slipped to her feet, called Patches, and barely touching the stirrup, mounted. "I'll see you back at the house." Before he could reply she was gone.

It was just as well, Jon thought. He'd lived a lifetime in the past hour. The sun was still as brassy; the leaves of the aspens had quivered back to life; the curious cloud had gone on about its business, yet everything had changed. Jon threw himself full-length on the needle-strewn ground. "I suppose I'm still in a shocked state," he told Dark Star, who had come closer. "Part of me is dead. Jim's gone, for keeps. Even when he was fighting Indians, I always knew he would come back. I always felt, if anything happened to him, I'd know it, because I was part of him.

"I still don't feel he can be gone, even though I know he has to be. There was one chance in a thousand, and Mescal was willing to try it. Well, there's maybe one chance in a million that Jim and Apache are holed up somewhere, waiting for the rains. Why not believe it until summer's over and fall comes? Time enough then to say good-bye." He lightly vaulted to Dark Star's back and followed the trail Patches and Mescal had taken toward the ranch.

In the next few weeks, Jon observed Mescal closely. Her confession had freed her. Some of her rosy hue returned to chase the dead white from her face. She smiled more often — and he never saw her look toward the northeast. It was as if, in accepting the worst, healing had begun.

Not so for Jon. Jim's laughing face peered at him from every small pond of water, every deep glade, each place they'd roamed together. Sometimes it was the way Jim had been at six or eight, other times twelve or sixteen —

never the emaciated, drawn countenance of the dying man.

At first Jon started whenever his twin's image rose to his mind. Then he shrugged. With Jim on his brain so much of the time, it was natural. Besides, there was plenty to do. Ranch chores were never done, and this summer they cried for his attention. He took a morbid joy in branding cattle, herding horses, even working in the vegetable garden. While his parents never lost the shadows in their eyes, Jon's natural buoyancy restored some of the happy home they'd known.

"Now it's *you* who looks northeast." Mescal slipped up behind Jon one evening when silver streaked skies and clear lemon clouds trimmed with old rose sent flattering glances at the coquetting aspens.

"Habit, I guess." Jon had decided not to let Mescal know a lingering hope filled his heart. Maybe it was merely stubbornness, yet it remained with him.

"It's too late, you know."

"Too late for what?" Matthew Sutherland stepped out. "You two fighting again? Seems as if you'd make up and settle down. Mother and I'd be mighty proud if Mescal Ames became Mescal Sutherland."

"So would Jon Sutherland," Jon told his father wryly after Mescal fled, her face the color of the sky.

"Is it the memory of Jim standing between you?"

"Partly. There are other things." Jon bit his tongue. It wasn't the time to tell how he wanted to be a minister and that even if Mescal loved him, instead of his twin, it would be a hard life for her. He watched the sky redden even more, then purple into dusk. "Another hot day tomorrow."

"Sure will be." His father heaved himself up from the step. "Reckon it's bedtime soon. Busy days." His face shadowed before he went back inside. "Too bad things didn't work out different. We could have used Jim. Now it's just the Double S."

"Don't ever change it!" Jon's voice rang in the gloom following the spectacular sunset. He laughed to cover the sharp command. "Besides, Mescal makes it Triple S, doesn't she?" He felt the sharp scrutiny in watching gray eyes before his father said, "I hope so, son," and left him alone on the porch.

August died, and September was born. Even Jon's determination shook. The parched land cried for water. His parched heart cried for reassurance. Mescal was the only one he could talk to, and he wouldn't admit to her how he clung to an impossible idea. Yet never did he take time from his work to rest without facing northeast with a prayer in his heart. Not a formal pleading to an Unseen Power, but an unspoken "please, if there's any hope" sustained him through the long, hard days and nights. More than once he stopped what he was doing and listened. But the sound that whispered "Jon" in his ears was merely the chatter of squirrels or a rustling in the grass or the cry of a hawk. He knew Mescal was concerned about

him, and even as she'd avoided him earlier that summer, now he tried to keep away from her.

He did not succeed. She caught him at dawn, saddling up for another hard day. "You've got to stop working this hard," she scolded. Her simple dress showed she was doing inside work, probably helping can the hundreds of quarts of fruits and vegetables and meat they'd need for the winter. The rolled-up sleeves showed the line where tanned hands met smooth, white arms.

"Work never killed anyone." He hadn't meant to sound so abrupt, but he didn't want to talk to her just then. He'd awakened from a dream in which Jim called over and over, but Jon couldn't get his legs to move to go help him.

"I wish I'd never told you the whole truth," she blazed, dark eyes glaring at him. "Ever since then, you've hoped for a miracle."

"Who's to say there won't be one?" He set his lips firmly and led Dark Star away from the house.

"Just because you want to be a minister, you don't have to be an ostrich. It's nearly the end of September. Do you really think, after all these months, they could be alive?" Scorn lashed him, and Mescal rushed on. "Oh, yes, I know what you want. You want Jim to come back and everyone to live happily ever after, the way it is in fairy tales." Some of the rage left her face, and she leaned toward him, sympathy in her eyes. "Jon, it just isn't going to happen that way."

The truth of what she said drove the last bit of hope from Jon. He had to strike out, hurt as he was hurt. "Who do you think you are, God? First you play the all-wise one and arrange all this. Now you insist on destroying even my sanity. Why don't you just leave me alone?" He regretted it the minute the words were out.

Her face turned deathly pale. "I'll never forgive you for that, Jon Sutherland. Never!"

"Mescal, I'm sorry."

"Sorry's too late. I know now you never did accept what I did, even though you said you understood." Her total control frightened him. "Just when I was beginning to think —" her sentence died. She left him without another word.

"Come back, Mescal." He started for her, but she reached the house before he could gain on her swift stride.

Reality had caught up with him. Not only must he acknowledge his clinging to an unbelievable possibility was stupid, now he had treated Mescal abominably. She wouldn't forgive, either, not after the way he had turned on her as a mistreated cur turns on his cruel master. Any hope of her caring for him, when Jim didn't return, was gone, killed by his own hand. He'd be lucky if she spoke to him, other than enough to keep the folks from knowing the bitter chasm between them.

September ended. At last the rains came, healing, drenching. Then came the first frost. Jon could feel it in the air when he wearily dragged in from riding fences one night. He was cold not only outside but inside. The frosty range would be nothing compared with the frost between him and Mescal. If only he could go back a few weeks and hold his temper! "Sons of Thunder" was right. First Jim had followed his wild inclination; now his brother dwelled in a wasteland of misery. He had given up his plans to become a minister. The Triple S needed him, even if Mescal didn't. The Comstocks had hired away most of their hands, at better wages, and sections of ranch were being left unpatrolled. They'd lost stock, a few horses.

One night it snowed. All Jon could see was the heavy way it hung on the evergreens, not the beauty. Snow meant death, a decent burial to all the plants and flowers that died in fall. Spring and resurrection were far away. Somewhere in the blanketed country, Apache and Jim slept. But there was no sleep for Jon. Red-rimmed eyes in the little mirror, the next day, showed what night had done. Specters he thought vanquished had stood in his room, taunting, enticing. Maybe he was going mad. His mind knew things that even yet his heart would not admit.

"Mescal," he told her brusquely at breakfast, "don't ride out today. Radford Comstock's been making threats again." He didn't add he was just about ready to ride into Daybreak and put a stop to them. One more story about the sheriff's comments, and badge or not, he was going to get the beating of his life.

"I ride where I please," Mescal reminded him. Never had she been prettier than in her simple riding outfit, with flags of color flying in her smooth face.

"You'll stay in, or I'll rope you to the bedpost," he warned and saw amazement change to rebellion in her scarlet face.

"Here now, that's no way to talk to Mescal," Matthew Sutherland protested. "Jon, what's got into you? You're touchier than a wolf with a sore paw lately."

"Just see that she stays inside." Jon's measured gaze never left the girl. "There's going to be a kidnapping around here, if you don't." He heard a step behind him and snapped shut his mouth on what he'd been going to add. No need for Mother to know Comstock's threats.

"Shucks, ain't one kidnapping around here enough?"

Jon froze. He saw his father turn white. He watched Mescal's face flame before she hurled herself past him at a snow-covered figure. Still he couldn't believe — until a drawling voice said, "If I'd known my own brother wasn't going to be any more excited about my coming back, Apache and I'd have stayed out a little longer."

Something burst inside him. Jon turned, swept aside a crying Mescal, and felt himself gathered into a snowy, crushing bear hug. Thin, bearded, strange, Jim Sutherland had come home.

6

Mescal was the first to come to her senses. "I have to warn Mother. She's been so frail the shock might be too much." She fled toward the kitchen area and was stopped when the older woman stepped through the doorway.

For a single instant, she put one hand to her heart. Her face blanched. Her lips moved soundlessly. Then she dropped into a pitiful heap on the floor. If Jon lived to be a hundred, he would always associate breaking crockery with this homecoming. He started forward and was brushed aside. Jim flung off his snowy, tattered coat and knelt on the floor. "Get a glass of water," he ordered the confused Mescal. "She'll be all right. See, her eyelids are beginning to quiver."

"My son, my son!" Jon couldn't stand looking into the great gulfs of spilling pools and plunged blindly through the door. He nearly upset Apache. Like Jim, the Indian had leaned to fence-rail proportions. One of the few smiles Jon had ever seen on the rich, brown face curled the thin lips and lightened somber eyes.

If his life had depended on it, Jon couldn't have spoken. He clasped Apache's worn hand in his, acknowledging what lay between them. At last he said, voice husky with both gratitude and joy, "My two brothers have come home — and I am glad."

A lightning ripple crossed Apache's face. His grip tightened until Jon felt he must cry for mercy. Then without a word he motioned to the yard behind him.

A drooping buckskin horse and a weary but proud gray stood with reins hanging. Snow softened their images but didn't hide ribs just below the skin. Yet to Jon, the gaunt shadows of what they had once been were beautiful. He leaped from the porch. "Shalimar!" He threw his arms around the buckskin and was rewarded with a soft nicker. Heart in throat, eyes wet, he turned to King and buried his hot face in the shaggy mane. When he could speak again, he whispered, "Thank God — for you all." He stepped back and examined the horses. "They're thin, but they'll fatten up." His anxious gaze went back to Apache. "How — no, we'll all want to hear the story, but first, let's get these horses cared for. Dad!"

Matthew Sutherland stumbled to the porch. Great drops stood unashamedly on his face and beard. His working face told everything, and

45

wordlessly he held out a crunching hand to Jim's deliverer. Jon felt his own throat muscles tighten in response and covered by saying, "Apache, get inside and into dry clothes. Mother and Mescal will feed you. Come on, Dad, these horses need us."

The practical everydayness of Jon's reminder cleared the air of emotion but not of snowflakes. They melted on Jon's bare head, yet felt strangely warm, a benediction to the return of his twin. He and his father worked in silence, drying, cleaning, currying Shalimar and King, then giving them grain.

"Not too much at first," Matthew warned. "They'll founder."

It took a long time to get morning chores done, when every nerve and cell in Jon's body wanted to be inside. Once Mescal came out, her strange reserve gone. "They're both sleeping. It's the best thing for them. Jim wanted to tell us, but Mother said no, not until they rested. Now it would take cannon fire to awaken either of them." She adjusted the shawl over her head, to ward off the thickening snow. Her face gleamed in the half-light made by the storm. "I was wrong, Jon. There are miracles. One just rode into the Triple S." Her face pearled into wonder. "Can you forgive me?"

"Forgive *you*!" Jon was jolted into amazement. "It's the other way around. You were right, too. But we can be thankful sometimes all the knowing in the world doesn't change how things will be."

Apache woke at sunset, an unreal, red-and-gold hour when the snow stopped and the sun flung a defiant challenge to clouds gathering forces for another attack on the earth. He refused to say anything about the journey. Jon wanted to shake him but respected the Indian's right to be silent. He couldn't keep back one question, however. "Jim's really well? There will be no recurrences?"

"There will be none." Apache looked first at Jon, next at Mescal. "Your brother is well, healed by herbs and the desert and canyons." He fell silent then added, "Perhaps even by the God my people call the Great Spirit." It was the biggest concession Jon had ever heard Apache make, and before he could reply, Apache glided to Jim's room. Jon had already peeped in dozens of times. Jim lay in a stupor, exhausted by his ordeal but sleeping naturally and deeply — a far cry from the tormented, thrashing nights he'd spent months earlier. There wasn't a moan to betray what had passed.

Twenty-four hours later, the entire family gathered in front of a roaring fire banked with half a log that could be pushed in as it burned. Apache sat back in the shadows, part of the group yet aloof. The older Sutherlands occupied handmade chairs away from the blaze. Jim stretched on a couch, with Mescal and Jon close by.

'Now, Son," Matthew prodded. "We want the whole story."

Jon caught the way his twin angled a look at Mescal before his blue eyes caught fire from the flames' reflection. "*All* of it?"

Mescal's face turned scarlet, but her eyes flashed. "Yes. All of it."

A hundred devils danced in Jim's eyes. "All right. Remember, you asked for it. I was cruelly snatched from my bed by a wild Indian, thrown on a horse, forced to ride when I was dying, cut into, starved, forced to submit and —," his clear gaze sought Apache, "and healed because a grand girl and a faithful *man* wouldn't give up on me."

"Is that true?" his mother burst out, veined hands clenched, horror and rejoicing on her face.

"Sure." Jon knew by the careless way Jim replied that's all they'd get as to why he had disappeared. "But let me tell you what happened after that first part." He leaned forward, thin face aglow.

"I will speak first." The voice from the shadows startled them all. Apache never put himself forward. Now there was authority in the deep tones. "If your son had not stopped to save a wounded Apache, he could have been back with you weeks ago." He described the scene when they left the valley in a few words, yet Jon could see it all — the quick fear of the burro, the smashing rock, a crumpled man beside the waterfall.

"By the time I could ride, it was too late to leave what little protection we had in the valley," Apache finished.

Jim looked at him intently, and Jon realized there was more to it than Apache was telling, but Jim shook his head and cut off anything else the Indian might add by asking, "How would you like to eat lizard, Mescal? And fried desert mice? And roots and foliage?"

Disgust left her face wrinkled. "Is that what you did?"

"Sure." It was obvious Jim was enjoying himself. "You can't believe all the stuff you can eat, if you have to, at least until it runs out." His voice faded, and his eyes glazed with memories clearer to the enthralled audience than words could have been. He shrugged it off. "Anyway, when the waterfall dried to a trickle and we polished off the last of the burro meat, we were in bad shape." His face flushed, but he met their anxious looks steadily. "I wanted to butcher one of the horses."

Mescal gasped audibly. Her hands clenched in her lap. Jon could feel her disbelief. The way Jim loved horses — nothing could have told them better how desperate and crazed he had become.

"Apache said no, they were our only salvation. When we got so weak we could barely ride, he bled King, and we drank a little. Shalimar wasn't strong enough to stand it. King carries two scars." Reverence shone on his countenance, and the dying embers cast golden sparks that matched the gleams in his hair. Jon knew with sudden clarity that never again would Jim refer to the hardships of that journey.

"We'd about given it up, although Apache said we weren't quite to the end of our rope, as long as we tied a knot and held on." His voice sank to a whisper. "I got to hate the sun. It was a personal enemy, sneering its way up mornings, gloating during the day, while we lay in what shade we could find, hating to go down at night. Apache made me walk nights, for hours,

at least until my strength failed. That way we could sleep days and eat our scarce meal at night.

"I loved the nights. You know how the stars are. I used to watch them and pretend they'd drip pretty soon, and I'd catch it and get rid of my thirst. It sounds loco, but things out there were crazy."

Jon could bear it no longer. "Tell us how you got out."

"It rained." The simple words rang triumphantly. "I'd been in a drugged sleep. I woke to see Apache standing facing the sky, torrents of water pouring off him. When I could believe what was happening, I went wild. I screamed and shouted and even thanked whatever power there might be for the rain. It meant life."

Jon struggled with the disappointment Jim's words "whatever power might be" brought. Even Apache had recognized the hand of God. Why not Jim?

No longer was Jim the beaten captive of the canyon. He jumped from the couch and threw his arms out to them all. "The next morning we started home. By the time we could get to the first signs of human habitation, we were all in. You think we're thin now, you should have seen us and the horses when we got to a homesteader's little place." A strange humility filled his story. "He didn't have much, but what he had he gave. We stayed there several days. He even asked us to stay on, when the frost came, but we couldn't. We were all right by taking it in easy stages. A lot of the time we walked to spare the horses." He swallowed hard, and Jon caught a quick dash of moisture in his eyes before he finished with, "Someday I'd like to go back."

"What!" his father roared. "After all that, you want to go back?"

"Yes." Jim's chin didn't budge a fraction of an inch. "It was night when we went, or else I was too sick to care. Coming home wasn't much better. Before I die, I'm going back the same way and see what I missed." Jon shuddered at the prophetic tone in his twin's voice. Why should he feel a cold wind blowing down his back, as if the door behind them had suddenly been flung open? Jim's desire might be a little morbid, but it was natural. There wasn't anything in it to bring this premonition of some future terrible event.

"So the prodigal son returned." Jim's eyes danced. "See, I remember some of the Bible stories. This was almost like that one, wasn't it? Return of the prodigal, a great feast —" He motioned toward the remains of their bounteous dinner, where Mescal and his mother had covered things and left the dishes in order to hear his story. "One big difference, though. Seems I remember the brother in that story wasn't as happy as the brother in this one." A poignant light shone from him to Jon, belying the casual way he referred to the episode.

"That's a story to tell your children and grandchildren, huh, Apache?" Matthew chuckled. But the corner where Apache had been stood empty. He'd slipped out, unnoticed, sometime during the end of Jim's story.

Jon found him in the small cabin they'd erected for him when he came to the ranch, since he preferred not to live in the bunkhouse. "Is there anything you want to tell me, Apache? Maybe something Jim forgot?"

Black eyes fixed on him. With an expressive gesture, Apache said, "Your brother knows there is one good Apache."

All the thanks Jon had wanted to express in the earlier handshake dried up. He mumbled something and left the cabin, with Apache standing at the door. A little soreness formed around his heart. Never had there been secrets that he and Jim couldn't share. Now summer days and nights and their anguish lay between Jim and Apache, a bond not to be spoken even to a brother. He felt it again when Jim came to him later that evening. "I was wrong about Apache. He's a white man all through, and I don't mean the color of his skin." Jim didn't elaborate, just yawned and told him, "Good night, Jon. Back to our old room for us and glad to be there." His smile lingered in Jon's mind, long after Jim lay sleeping in the bed across the room, the same way they'd done since childhood.

For days after their return, Jon watched Jim for lasting effects of what Mescal called "the missing months." Early snow melted and changed into a glorious late Indian summer. Thanksgiving brought extra reason for a feast. It had a dual meaning this year. Tragedy had brushed its skirts against their hearth and been vanquished. Jim laughed and teased Mescal as he'd always done. If something new and smoldering had been added to the way he watched her, only Jon noticed. He hadn't dared broach the subject with Jim. The early time after their return found Jim wild to ride, work, and hunt. He seemed obsessed with the idea of making sure there would be plenty, in case of a long winter.

Jon watched and understood. Jim had told him through clenched teeth, "I will never, as long as I live, be hungry again." His lips had curled in an ugly snarl. "No matter what I have to do, me and mine will have food."

"We always have had," Jon reminded him. "Why think we won't now?"

Some of the defiance melted. "If you'd let me go after the Comstocks, we'd have a lot more cattle. Until we take a stand, they're going to hound us."

"Things have slacked off now. Why don't you take some time off, ride into town, and see some of your old friends?"

Jim's eyes lighted. "Good idea. How about coming with me?"

Jon shook his head. "No, I'll stay home. Go on and have a good time." But after a few times Jim was gone overnight to appear loaded with presents for them all, Jon wondered if he'd done the right thing in suggesting it. "Where'd all this truck come from?" he demanded of Jim. "Not that we can't use it." He fingered a new rifle and pointed at a braided rug on the floor and pictures neatly hung on the walls.

"Got lucky at cards." Jim's grin failed to hide satisfaction.

"All this stuff?" Jon eyed him. "Must have been pretty lucky. Who have

you been fleecing?''

Jim leaned his chair back on two legs, until it squawked a protest. His grin widened. "More than one way to get back what the Comstocks have stolen from us, now isn't there? You might say I'm just taking what's rightfully ours."

"Comstocks! Better not get around that outfit." Jon hesitated then plunged ahead. "You hear any more about his being after Mescal?"

Jim's eyes turned to blue metal. "Not from him, but one of these times he's going to leave off that badge, and when he does, I'll be there."

"Get that crazy notion out of your head. If you kill a sheriff, you'll hang." Cold sweat broke out on Jon's neck at the thought. He could see Jim defending Mescal's honor and being lynched by an angry mob of Comstock relatives and friends.

"Let me handle it, little brother," Jim smiled the tormenting smile he always used when he considered a subject closed. He stretched full height, a tawny cougar ready to pounce. "Speaking of Mescal, when are you and she getting hitched?"

If Jon hadn't known him so well, he'd have missed the intensity of the nonchalant question. His face burned. "Me! It's you she'll marry. If I'm a preacher by then, I can even tie the knot." His attempt at laughter sounded good even to himself.

Jim dropped his teasing. "You really think so?" He sank back to the floor with all four legs of the sturdy chair, face eager. "The whole time we were gone, it's what kept me going."

Every word thrust iron pokers into Jon's soul, red-hot, searing.

"Apache said she told him to bring me back — for her." Jim admitted, "I thought he was punishing me, but when I got to know him, I believed him. Now that I'm home, I can't see it. She's with you all the time."

"Of course she is!" Jon rose above his heavy spirit to match Jim's confidence. "Don't you know anything about girls? I'm her brother. She can be more natural around me. You used to be her brother, but once she started thinking of you in a different way, well —" He let his unfinished explanation hide what he felt.

"Yeah, you may be right." Jim scratched his head as if puzzled. "Alice Johnson used to act the same way." He grunted. "Peculiar, ain't it? If Mescal likes me so well, seems as if she'd show it."

"Maybe she's waiting to see if you plan to stay."

It was out, the thing Jon had known would come. The way Jim responded would irrevocably affect three lives. Why didn't he answer, declare his intentions? He'd done his share of work around the place since he'd gotten back, but Jon feared the restlessness in him. Sometimes there was a look of desperation on the handsome features. Maybe, once he knew Mescal cared, it would make the difference.

"I had a lot of time to think this summer," Jim said. The faraway look

Jon had seen in his eyes so many times over the past weeks stole back to their hiding place. "If Mescal really loves me, the way I think I love her —"

"*Think* you love her! Don't you *know*?" Scorn brought Jon from his chair, to glare down at his brother.

"Sure, sure." In spite of his grin, Jon knew Jim meant it, at least as far as his selfishness could love. "Anyway, if she does, we'll be married, and I'll run the Triple S into the biggest ranch in the country." There was no doubt about his enthusiasm now. "We'll take out a loan and stock it and hire riders. We'll hold what's ours and fight anyone who tries to take it away." He sprang up to pace the floor. "You can have everything you want, even be a parson."

Not everything, Jon's aching heart whispered. *Not Mescal.* He forced the thought back, glad for Jim's statement. If he and Mescal could be happy, good for them. Who was he to stand in Jim's way? Yet a rebellious part of him insisted, *Must you always give up your own dreams for him? How far will you sacrifice for your brother?*

The nagging questions haunted him: in velvet-black nights, early gray dawns, slanting sunsets. It didn't make it easier when he saw how Mescal stayed with him. Finally he spit out, "You were so anxious to get Jim back. How come you're never with him?" At the storm warnings in her look, he hastily added, "Not that I don't want you with me. I love it." He tempered his voice to disinterest, aware how hard it was to cover his own feelings. She must never suspect but that he'd accepted and rejoiced over her choice of Jim.

Mescal's dusky head drooped. "I'm not sure he cares — enough."

Jon had started to protest but was stilled by that last word. She had instinctively put her fingers on the exact thing that troubled him. Did Jim care enough, or would time be forced to deal him a second excruciating blow before he changed from light-hearted boy to a responsible, mature man and mate for Mescal Ames?

Gradually Mescal drifted to Jim. He put up a winning campaign for her love. He brought her presents until she protested. He paid her compliments, and she resembled the setting sun's rays. Every day her beauty increased. Jon gloried in it, even while exquisite pain burned within. He could only be glad no one knew. Amused by Jim's pursuit of Mescal, Matthew Sutherland watched and was glad. His wife spent every spare moment making pillowcases and sheets for Mescal's wedding, "Whenever it might be," she said primly. Jim and Mescal appeared too involved with the wonder of dawning love to see Jon's inner troubles.

Only Apache knew. He had come on Jon watching Jim and Mescal starting for a ride one afternoon. She shied away, but laughed as he snatched her and put her on Shalimar. Jon tore his gaze free when Apache said, "My brother's heart is big to give up the white flower."

Jon hadn't pretended. "It isn't easy."

"No." The resonant voice echoed through the now-quiet clearing. "Love is pain. Yet the world could not continue without it. Stags fight to the death. The wild things burrow together. Even the birds must mate. But you and I, Jon Sutherland, know loneliness." He remained etched against the sky, a tragic figure, long after Jon saddled and rode away.

In one way it brought things to a head. The day Jim and Mescal announced they would be married in the spring, Jon gathered courage in both hands and broke the news. "Mother, Dad, since surprises are being given, although this is no surprise —" He glanced at the pair holding hands after their betrothal speech. "I have a surprise, too. Before you speak, let me tell you I've considered this over and over. I want to study for the ministry."

A ricochet of rifle bullets could have produced no more pandemonium than his simple statement. His mother gasped; then a pleased smile wreathed her face. His father looked stricken, clearly amazed at the news. Apache said nothing; Mescal and Jim wished him well.

"But when did this all happen?" Matthew asked helplessly, spreading calloused hands wide. "You never said a word."

Jon leaned toward his father, earnestly pleading for understanding. "Don't you see, Dad, until Jim came back I couldn't have gone? Why waste time over that? If I'd been your only son, I never would have left."

"So I gain one son and lose another." Bitterness corroded the kindly face.

Jon heard Jim's quickened breath. How would he take Dad's reaction? Desperate, wanting to be fair, Jon said, "Jim and Mescal are staying. Some day when I finish my training — a few months, maybe — I'll be back. Not to ranch, but to make better feelings in this place. Haven't you said again and again Daybreak needs a minister, someone who can offer comfort?"

"I never knew I'd have to lose a son to get one." Defeat sagged his great shoulders, but he tried to be a good loser. He rose and towered over his son, an uncertain smile on his bearded lips. "You have my blessing, Jonathan."

He hasn't called me that in years, Jon thought bleakly. *He's already accepted it, although he doesn't fully approve.* "Thanks, Dad. You know, it's your own fault for stuffing Jim's and my head with Bible stories while we were growing up!"

"Lucky it only took on one of us," Jim drawled. "Don't worry, Dad, I'll be a faithful son, and we'll make the Triple S one great ranch."

"I'll help, too," Mescal promised, face alight with happiness.

"Of course you will, and glad I am for it." Matthew got back some of his heartiness. "When Preacher Sutherland comes home for a meal, we'll have something better to offer him than a chicken neck."

In the laughter Jon noticed Apache's eyes on him, and later the Indian came to his room. Jim was still with Mescal. The sound of their low laughter drifted into the twins' room. "What would you have me do?"

Jon jerked himself up from the deep study he'd gone into. "Why,

whatever you choose. You've more than paid your debt."

"There are debts — and debts. Would you have me stay and care for your brother the way you would do?"

Jon faced the enigmatic man. An issue too deep for words lay between them. He must reply, must say what was right. He chose his words carefully. "I would trust my brother — and Mescal's and my parents' lives to you, even as Mescal entrusted Jim to you months ago."

A tiny movement that could have been approval flickered in the watching eyes. "Then I will stay, as long as I am needed." Apache extended his hand and gripped Jon's. In that touch, Jon knew he had transferred his twin into Apache's keeping.

7

The bittersweet winter finally melted into spring. Was it because of the coming separation that everything seemed so intense? The cold snapped trees that had stood for years, guardians of the Triple S. The wolves howled louder and closer. Jon and Jim grew accustomed to finding where a cow had been brought down by the starving predators. Sometimes they saw skulking, gray forms disappear into the woods when they got to a frozen, gnawed carcass.

The pile of household linen steadily grew. Mescal protested, "We won't need all that! We're only going to build on one large room, and heaven knows we've enough quilts and blankets and sheets to furnish a hotel!"

Abigail Sutherland quelled her. "No daughter of mine will start married life, even to my son, without spanking new things of her own."

Happiness mingled with pain when Jon heard Mescal's trill of laughter, saw her ecstatic face over the simple white wedding gown she and her mother made. It took all Jon's control to hide his own emotions. Jim hadn't been allowed to see Mescal in the dress, but Jon was privileged — and regretted it. Her dusky face radiated charm. Her tanned skin contrasted with the froth of lace at the neck, and never had her eyes been more golden. *Portrait of a woman in love,* Jon told himself bitterly, even while he forced himself to cock his head and tell her, "Not bad for a wild Indian rider who usually wears homespun."

For every mountain there was a valley. At least Jon could give profound thanks for the change in Jim. His brother's worshipful eyes never left Mescal if she was in the room or on the trail with them. He slipped back to the good comrade he'd been years ago. He and Jon rode, when the snow's crust would support them, stalked the range and trails for wolves, searched out the weak and helpless of the now-small herd.

"I can't wait for spring," Jim told Jon one snowy day. The two had just returned from feeding the horses in the barn. Jim paused on the wide porch and shook snow from his boots. "Ugh! It's cold." He rubbed mittened hands over his face until it glowed. "Dad's agreeable to getting a loan, so we'll be restocking cattle. We don't really need horses. I'd rather wait and pick up one or two extras that are worth something

54

than get a batch of broomtails. We'll —" His voice died, and his eyes widened. "I keep forgetting you won't be here."

Jon's cold heart warmed to the genuine regret in his brother's face. "At least we will have this winter to remember." He fell silent, thinking of the long days riding, the interminable evenings watching Jim and Mescal dreaming about their future.

"Yeah." Jim's mood lightened. "Besides, it's not as if you're going away forever."

"No." But Jon knew Jim recognized as well as he did the gulf that would soon come between them. With Jim and Mescal married, Jon studying, then preaching, never again could things be the same. He'd be back for visits, but as someone foreign to their way of life, a visitor rather than one of them, except in blood and spirit. Jon could almost feel the doors closing against him, shutting him away from all those he loved most on earth.

He shrugged off the morbid thoughts and kicked off his boots. "Mother'll have a fit if we track in on her clean floor. Can't say as I blame her. Dirty snow's not the easiest thing in the world to mop up." He bent and brushed snow off his pant legs to hide the rush of feeling he couldn't seem to shake.

Christmas came and went; January trailed behind. February opened clear and relapsed into a final frenzy. March first was the date set for the wedding. Jim had ridden down all Mescal's protests that it was too soon and swept aside Jon's objections that he wouldn't be able to marry them by then. "What difference does it make? You'll be my best man." A crooked grin tilted his face, until he looked like some elf in the old fairy-tale book Mescal still kept from childhood. "And I do mean the *best* man. Mescal should have married you, you know. Not that I'd let her," he rattled on, seemingly oblivious to the strained pose Jon assumed. "From the time I came home, I —"

Jon didn't follow the rest of it. He met Mescal's startled gaze, filled with an unasked question. Never since Jim returned had either referred to Jon's earlier attitude. Now her eyes demanded the truth — and in spite of everything Jon could do, got it. Her lips formed in a little O, but Jon shook his head, furious with himself for betrayal, fiercely glad she had learned he cared. It would do no one any harm.

"Don't be stupid," he told Jim, with a wrack between his shoulder blades. "Mescal's my sister."

"We're going to name our first boy *Jonathan*."

Jon could feel his muscles tighten, his throat constrict. Mescal cut in sharply, "Don't be talking about babies when we aren't even married, Jim Sutherland! You better treat me nice, or I may up and decide not to marry you after all," but her curved lips took all the seriousness from her threat, and Jim only laughed.

A few days later, Jon was surprised when Mescal sought him out. Her

troubled eyes went straight to his heart.

"What? No shadow?" he teased, but subsided before the flash of her dark eyes.

"The weather turned so nice, Jim rode to town." Mescal sighed and followed the trail with her glance as if willing him back from whatever might hold him. "He said he thought he'd drop by and see if Radford Comstock would come to our wedding."

A chill coasted down Jon's spine. "That crazy fool!" He threw down the harness he had been mending and started for the barn. "I'll go get him."

"You won't have to. I sent Apache." Mescal came close and looked into his face. "Jon, will he ever really settle down? Or am I tying myself to a whirlwind or tumbleweed?"

Jon fought the longing to catch her close and protect her from all hurt. "I don't know." He could not and would not lie. "Sometimes I think he will. After you're married and I'm gone, he'll have the biggest responsibility of his life. It can make a man of him."

"I really love him," Mescal whispered, her voice carried by the capricious breeze tugging at her hair. "But sometimes I wish — Jon, if only he were more like you!"

"*Mescal!*" Jon seized the slipping reins of manhood that kept him from pleading with her to forget his brother and marry him. "Don't. . . ."

"Don't worry about Jim," an amused voice spun them around. "He's back from Daybreak in one piece with news that Radford Comstock will be happy to attend the marriage of Mescal Ames and James Sutherland." One tawny lock of hair hung over his devil-may-care face.

Had he heard what Mescal said? Jon couldn't tell. The steely glint in the wary blue gaze betrayed nothing. Jon's heart plummeted. Jim would never understand that Mescal could love one twin with all her heart yet long for assurance of a settled future.

Jim gave no sign of anything amiss, just caught Mescal, kissed her soundly, and chuckled as she ran toward the house. "Some little wife she's going to make, huh." He headed after her, whistling a few notes of "Dixie." Yet in the few days remaining before the wedding date, Jon sensed restlessness such as Jim hadn't shown since he and Mescal announced their plans to get married. Was it spring fever, anticipation of the coming event, or something deeper and akin to the wanderlust rooted inside Jim? Jon couldn't tell. Now he concentrated on forever putting aside his own longings and waiting for the wedding. He took care not to see Mescal alone, not trusting himself to get through a final interview. And always he wondered: had Jim overheard?

The night before the wedding, Jim insisted on riding into Daybreak. "Got to tell everyone I'm getting married to the greatest girl in the West," he proclaimed. They tried to talk him out of it. It didn't help.

"A man's got a right to get drunk before he gets hitched," Jim insisted.

Mescal had remained silent, but now her whole body tensed to spring. "You come back drinking, and there won't be a wedding." Indignation etched her into a statue.

"Sure there will, sweetheart." Jon hated the careless way Jim tore down her objections. "You won't give up the second-best catch in Arizona, will you? Especially since the best man's your brother?" He strode off, leaving Jon and Mescal staring after him.

He didn't come back.

Apache rode in before dawn and roused Jon from an uneasy sleep.

"Where's Jim?" Jon demanded, focusing on the erect figure at the side of his bed.

"Gone."

Jon felt he was living a repeat of another scene months before, only that time it had been with Mescal. "Gone where?"

Apache's expressive face turned south and east.

"The canyon country?" Jon shook his head to clear his disbelief. "But why?" The stone serving for his heart moved and settled back in place when Apache said, "Jim told me to give you this. I started to follow, but he cursed and sent me back, then called out he was sorry and had to do it this way."

Jon took the crumpled scrap of paper and read the words. He read them again, although there was no need. They'd already burned into his brain: THE BEST MAN WINS — AGAIN.

He sank his teeth into his lip and tasted blood. "God," it was not a curse but a prayer. "How can I tell Mescal?"

"*I* will tell her." Apache drew himself to full height. "He gave me a message only for her ears." He glided through the door, and although Jon heard no footfalls, his keen ears detected a light tapping at Mescal's door. A little scrape, a muffled cry, then the patter of flying feet.

Mescal burst in, regardless of the restraining hand Apache placed on one shoulder. Her face flamed. Her dressing gown gaped to show a hint of high-necked white gown and bare feet clung to the cold floor. "That — that *brother* of yours has done it now." She glared accusingly at Jon. "Where did he get the idea I was in love with you?"

Jon stiffened under the unspoken accusation. "Not from me. I never even let him know *I* cared." His contempt matched her own. "I believe now he overheard what you said about wishing he could be more like me. Maybe he decided he didn't want to be tied down, after all."

Common sense returned with a flood. Mescal studied her feet. Her shoulders drooped, the heavy hair almost too heavy for her slender neck. "I'm sorry, Jon." She couldn't stop her lips from trembling, Jon saw.

"What did Apache tell you?"

Jon thought of a frightened fawn when she bravely lifted her face. "He said to go ahead with the wedding — the best man had won."

An Indian tomahawk in his vitals couldn't have hurt as much. Blood gushed to Jon's head, leaving him speechless. How long had Jim known? All the time he thought he had fooled his twin, had their special knowledge of each other been working against him? How like Jim to wait until the eleventh hour to spring his trick. Had he figured Jon would marry Mescal rather than see her embarrassed? Who knew what went on inside Jim's wild head?

"I'm going after him." Jon reached for his boots. In the split seconds after Apache went to Mescal's room, he'd jerked on pants and shirt.

"No." Mescal's dead voice stopped him short. Rays of dawn stole softly in the open window and highlighted her troubled face. "He wouldn't come back. If he did, I wouldn't want him."

Jon sucked in a breath of clean, woodsy air.

"I mean it." Her shut lips showed how much, refusing to admit the pain in her eyes. "If he was so eager to hand me over, he couldn't have really cared — enough." She turned, head held proudly, and walked out the door.

"She is wrong, but she must find out for herself." Apache's sonorous words played "Taps" in Jon's spinning brain. "Jim does love her, but he knows his wildness could destroy her."

Jon sank back to his bed in despair. "Why?" he cried. "Everything was going so well for them. What will it take to make Jim into a man?" He balled his hand into a fist and smashed it against his pillow. "I thought his brush with death would do it, but it hasn't."

"Someday he will meet what life has for him. He will not be the same again," Apache prophesied. "Until then, who knows? He rode into the canyons with the Radford Comstock relations."

The fiddle string of Jon's nerves snapped. "What?" His laugh grated. "You didn't say *the Comstocks*!"

"Yes." Apache folded his buckskin-clad arms, face impassive.

"But why? If he had to leave, why join *them*?"

A shade of reluctance reached Apache's eyes. Then he quietly said, "Apaches are good listeners. A deal has been made. The Triple S is not to be harmed so long as one of its owners rides with the Comstocks."

Sheer rage threatened to unbalance Jon's reason. "That means Jim's the same as a rustler already."

"Yes. It also means his brother and family are protected."

Somewhere under the Ice Age covering over his soul, Jon felt a match strike. Lawless, untamable, mocking that he was, Jim Sutherland loved his family — and Mescal. He had done this monstrous thing for them. Jon stumbled to the window and plucked at the sheer curtain with nerveless fingers. Once he had told his brother the greatest thing on earth would be to die for someone. What about living for someone, even though it were in shame and as an outlaw? Hot lava flowed inside his eyelids, forcing its way out. There was good in Jim. Not the kind he'd hoped for, but a mistaken

idea of how to save them all — by sacrificing himself. A lonely grave, this time unmarked forever, awaited Jim. He was bound to know it. Yet he'd chosen the dead-end trail over his dream of a Triple S with great herds, choice horses. Over Mescal and the son he'd never have. Jon knew his brother too well to think there would ever be another woman for him.

"I can't let him do it," Jon groaned.

"You cannot stop him. Only Apache can follow." The tall figure stood out more plainly, now the day had begun.

"Would you do that for me — for him — for Mescal?"

"I only returned to bring the messages." Apache hesitated. "What would you have me tell him?"

"To come home, where he belongs! We'll fight the Comstocks, if we have to, but in our own way." Jon could feel his own dreams die. If sacrifice had to be made, his career must go rather than the terrible thing Jim planned.

"Can you send word you do not love the white flower?"

Sickness spread through Jon, and he slumped against the window frame. "No. But I can send word it is Jim she loves and always has."

Apache moved his head slowly back and forth, inscrutable eyes never leaving Jon's. "It will not be enough, but I will try." For the second time he glided from the room, and a little later Jon saw him emerge from his cabin. Jon headed for the door, but by the time he reached the porch, Mescal had flown to Apache. She was too far away for Jon to hear her speech, but the imploring white face said it all. The poignancy of it struck iron into Jon's heart. Her wedding morning, and Mescal stood pleading with an Apache to find her bridegroom. His lips curled ironically. For one craven moment, he considered offering himself as substitute, the way Jim had suggested.

"Skunk!" he thundered to himself. Mescal had turned back toward the house, clad in her usual worn dress, tears streaking her smooth skin. In her present state she might even accept, clinging to him for strength. No. He couldn't insult her by ever speaking. Let the neighbors come. They'd brave it out, and maybe someday Jim would return.

The older Sutherlands reacted as Jon had known they would. Matthew roared; his wife cried. Jon and Mescal had agreed not to let them know where Jim had gone, just that he had "got a fool notion in his head he wasn't good enough for Mescal and rode off a spell." If Apache did get Jim back, no use folks being any wiser. Jon sent word to the invited guests the wedding was off and gave no reason why. It was none of their business. If they chose to think Mescal had cancelled it, so much the better.

The long day droned and dragged. Nature tried to compensate by sending forth her best green buds, her brightest March sun. Mescal disappeared, riding Patches. Apache had been sent away on Shalimar. At least Jim hadn't torn off on King, but had taken Dark Star. He must have known, when he rode away, he wouldn't be back.

Jon sat before the smoldering fire with his father. For the first time, Matthew looked old. The gray hair and eyes had never aged him before, but now Jon noticed how heavy the lines had grown in his face. Did he suspect more than he'd been told?

As if in answer to his question, his father raised his shaggy head. "Looks like I've lost two sons, instead of one." There was no hint of self-pity in the statement, just fact, but it couldn't hide what Jon had tried to ignore ever since Apache came in at daybreak.

"I won't be going now."

The leonine head raised. "I'm not asking you to stay. It's your life, and you've got to live it as best you see fit." Yet hope underscored every word.

Jon neatly tied the strings around the package of his dream and put it away. "I reckon if I can be as fine a man and as good an example to folks hereabouts as you've been, that'll be enough." He forced a light laugh. "Besides, any reason why a man couldn't study the Bible and learn enough to tell folks what's in it without going away?"

"I don't know why not. Best preacher I ever heard was a circuit rider back in the hills." Eagerness warred with unwillingness to give advice in the older man's face, and Jon saw what it meant.

"Then it's still the Triple S."

"I was wondering if there'd be enough Sutherlands left to keep it that way," Matthew admitted. " 'Course Mother and Mescal and me still makes it triple, but a son's special." He rose and yawned. "Now that's settled, guess I'll wander out and see how the hands are. Gave them all a day off for the wedding and didn't have the heart to order them out when it got cancelled." He surveyed Jon, and Jon caught the twinkle in his eye. "If Apache doesn't get that brother of yours home, you'd better make up to Mescal."

Jon dropped his head and didn't answer. He heard Matthew's heavy tread across the room followed by a "got back, did you, Mescal?" then light breathing at his elbow. Mescal stood motionless. Her hands clasped in front of her scarlet sweater, and she waited. For what? What could he say to her? "Did you have a good ride?"

How dumb could he get! The day she'd set apart and looked forward to for weeks now shook itself once more and hibernated, and all he could ask was what kind of ride she'd had! A picture of the unused wedding gown floated and danced before his eyes, desecrated by Jim's desertion.

"What are you going to do now?" she asked. One grumbling coal flared to light her.

He didn't pretend to misunderstand. "I'm staying."

"You're giving up your dream?"

Both of them. Had he spoken aloud? No — she still waited, clear, dark eyes demanding truth. He leaned back so his face would be in shadow, away from her searching. "There are many dreams. I'll still do what I can. Once I've studied, maybe even preach in Daybreak. Even a cowpuncher

preacher will be better than none."

"I wish he'd never come back."

Jon's anger was no more at her than at the echo of the wish in his own heart. He made a futile gesture and was interrupted by her passionate outcry, "I'd accepted he was gone. I'd even begun to forget and think maybe someday —" She caught her throat. "Then he came. I believed he cared. Can't you see it's better if he'd been lost in the desert? Then the voices would have stopped after a while. Now all I can see is what will happen." Her face turned chalky. "Will it be a bullet or a rope? Better if he'd died in the inferno." Her eyes glowed red, and she pressed one hand to her lips.

Jon was shocked into protest. "You love him that much?" The world stilled for her reply. Even the burning coal stopped snapping.

"Yes."

If she had declared it in fervent tones, it couldn't have been more convincing. Jon felt his face blanch to match hers. That single word killed any hope he might ever have had. "Mescal," he took her cold hands into his warm ones. "Someday, I don't know how or when, but someday I'll bring him back to you."

A drop splashed and glittered on his hand. Her fingers convulsed; her slender body went rigid. "Do you promise?"

"I promise." The vow he made was not the one he'd dreamed of for years, but the reward was great. Mescal threw her arms around him, pressed soft lips to his in gratitude, then fled as if pursued by demons, leaving Jon shaken to the tips of his boots.

8

Waking and sleeping, Jon Sutherland waited for one thing — Apache's return. Never a frosty morning passed that he didn't scan the clearing to see if Shalimar had come in the night. Not a busy moment passed that part of his mind wasn't on his brother. Nightmares of Jim crying for help left Jon drained, thin. Everything hinged on what Apache found out.

It ended one early March afternoon. A mud-stained Shalimar and a set-faced man rode in. Mescal erupted from the house, Matthew and Abigail close behind. Jon laid aside the ax he'd been using to split great chunks of pine.

"Well?" Matthew boomed. "Did you find him?"

Jon saw the longing in his father's face. How terrible to be the father of a prodigal son! He turned his gaze to the splattered Apache. A bloody bandage bound one hand. Circles of fatigue made half-moons under the fine eyes. Jon's hopes sank.

"Did you find him?" Matthew asked again.

"Yes."

"Where?" Jon leaped to help Apache dismount and supported him to a seat on the porch.

"In hell." Apache's ghastly voice rang in the clearing.

"What do you mean?" Mescal snapped out of the frozen state they'd all gone into at Apache's appearance. Her eyes burned. Jon felt his heart turn over with pity for her and for their mother.

"He's gone into the canyon country with the Comstocks. I tracked them. There's a valley hidden between canyons that only the eagles know. It's filled with cattle." Even the anger in the dark face couldn't hide pain. "Some wear the Triple-S brand."

Abigail Sutherland caught at the porch rail for a moment. Her parchment face and twitching fingers showed her agitation. "Jim has gone in with rustlers — of our own stock?"

"Why did you tell her, Apache?" Jon cried. "Why didn't you wait and tell me when I was alone?"

Apache's lips set in a straight line. "My story is not finished. I crawled near and listened. Every Triple-S steer and heifer and calf is to be driven back. In return, your son stays with the Comstock band." He closed his

eyes as if too tired to continue.

"I don't understand." Abigail pressed closer to Apache. "Why has he done such a thing?"

Jon knew it could not be hidden. "Because he'd rather sacrifice himself than see Mescal unhappy."

Matthew wagged his big head. His eyes rolled. "Jim knew Mescal was happy. What changed it?" His heavy breathing set the air quivering with trouble.

"Once Mescal told me that although she loved Jim with all her heart, she wished he could be more like me." Jon knew a dark stain colored his face but kept steadily on. "I know now he overheard, decided in time she'd learn to — to care for me, if he left." He turned unseeing eyes toward the drooping Shalimar, outlined against the swaying aspens. "She never would. But Jim wouldn't see it like that. I sent Apache to tell him."

Every eye swung back to the Indian when Jon asked, "Did you see him at all? Did you give him my message?"

"I did." Apache's form straightened.

"And?" Eternity waited on the answer. Jon felt his heart skip a beat.

"He said to tell you once he rides down a trail, he doesn't ride back."

It was so like Jim, Jon could almost see the bright head toss and the mocking smile on his face when Jim sent the message. Mescal gave a little cry and darted into the woods for refuge. The older Sutherlands turned to each other, seeking comfort. Abigail buried her head on the massive heaving chest and sobbed until Matthew's gruff voice ordered, "Get hot water and medicine, Mother. Apache's hand needs bandaging."

"How did this happen?" Jon wanted to know as his mother dried her tears and expertly tended the wound.

A grim smile heightened rather than lessened the tragedy written in Apache's face. "I slipped away, after finding Jim. No one saw me, but Shalimar snorted when I mounted. Three men ran toward us. One called, 'Hey, that ain't Sutherland's horse,' and reached for his gun. I spurred Shalimar, and we rode straight for them. Two leaped out of the way, the third sprawled on the ground, when Shalimar's shoulder hit him. One shot and it creased me."

"Creased!" Jon looked at the deep groove. "Do you think they recognized Shalimar?"

"No. Radford wasn't one of them. These were others I hadn't seen before. No reason for them to connect me with Jim." Apache took up his story. "I knew some of them followed me from the pounding of hooves and the crash of brush. I lost a lot of blood before I was far enough ahead of them and could cover my trail to stop. I crawled in a rock and slept a few hours, then came on home."

Even through his worry and disillusionment about Jim, Jon couldn't but catch the way Apache referred to the Triple S as "home." At that, it was

probably the only real home he'd known for years. Jon watched Apache walk across the clearing to his own cabin, wondering why it was two men reacted so differently to adverse circumstances. Out of gratitude, Apache chose to become the Sutherland's defender. Jim, who had been raised in a God-fearing home, who knew right from wrong and bad from good — Jon couldn't finish the thought.

If waiting had been hard before, now it was unbearable — not that Jon thought Jim would repent and return. He just waited with heart in mouth every time a neighbor reported a missing cow or a stolen horse. Several times news of petty raids on lone travelers and even one bank robbery reached the Triple S. Once a man was killed in a holdup. Jon didn't breathe easy until he rode to Daybreak and discovered the man was a total stranger who might or might not belong to the Comstock Gang, as he called them in his mind.

Fickle March grew into April. The earth warmed. Birds came back from their winter abodes and filled the quiet air with song. Squirrels scolded, and signs of new life appeared regularly. Yet spring did not come to the Sutherlands' hearts. Always winter's shadow lay long and thick, like the snow blankets that bowed great tree limbs until they touched the ground and sometimes broke from too great a weight. Laughter came on infrequent visits, and personal solitude reigned.

One bittersweet moment came when the ranch hands whooped into the corral one morning yelling, "Cattle are back!"

In spite of knowing what it meant, Jon couldn't help the thrill shooting through him. He cornered one of the men. "What do you mean, *back*?"

"Just what I say." Dusty, exuberant, the bowlegged man's grin split his grimy face with a white flash. "Funniest thing, Slim 'n' Dave 'n' Shorty 'n' me had ridden to the south pasture area." His hands stilled on the saddle he'd ungirthed and started to throw off. He scratched his head with a tobacco-stained forefinger. "Three riders came yellin' behind enough cattle to start a small ranch. We figured they were headin' for the waterhole and didn't pay no partic'lar attention. All of a sudden the cattle were on our range, and the riders headin' back the way they come."

"What did you do?" Excitement ran through Jon like forked lightning.

"Hollered at 'em and asked where they found the stock." The cowhand's face wrinkled into a prune. "They waved and rode out of sight. First off, I thought it was your brother, 'cause one horse looked like Dark Star, but they were too far away to be sure. 'Sides, if it was, he'd a' answered. Then we thought it musta been some of our boys, but none of 'em were down there. Guess some neighbors found where the herd drifted durin' the winter. One thing sure, 'twarn't rustlers."

Jon started at the conviction in his voice. "How come you're so positive?"

The hand stared at him then roared. "Ho, how many times do cow

thieves bring back what they took? An' without ever changin' their brands?" He turned away before Jon could answer. Just as well. His logic would convince the rest of the country there was nothing unusual except the three riders being too busy to stop and pass the time of day.

Jon rode out with Mescal later that day, into a green-and-gold afternoon. Sluggish blood and a stupor of thought that had held Jon prisoner for the weeks since Jim left lifted. "How can a man help having hope on a day like this?" he asked her, guiding King over to one side of the broad trail so Patches could trot alongside. Apache had ridden out again on Shalimar, scouting the area to see if there was any more news of Jim.

Mescal smiled. Jon realized how rare her smiles had become and how he had missed them. How much she'd changed from the active, touchy kid and even the ecstatic engaged girl. A new womanliness rested on her like blooms on a lilac, adding to her natural charm. "If Jim cared enough to send those cattle back, maybe —" Her appealing eyes lifted. "Once you said you'd bring him back, sometime. Would he come home if you went after him?"

She only echoed the same idea that had been playing tag in his brain from the time the cattle reappeared. "I don't know," he told her honestly.

She didn't answer until after they'd come out on a slight rise, and ahead lay the missing herd. "Oh, Jon, look at them! They're beautiful." Awe stood in her voice; her whole body came alive, more alive than Jon had seen her for a long time. "Our cattle and look over there —" She pointed across the tree-dotted meadow. "There are the horses that vanished last fall!"

Jon strained his eyes. Mescal could see things outdoors with an uncanny, farseeing sight. She said Apache had trained her to see, not just to look, as the white people so often did. "Let's ride down there and get them home." He circled to the left, with her close behind. Still it took a good half hour to get to the horses. Not a one that had been gone so long was now missing. Jim had evidently done his work well.

"But at what cost!" Mescal finished his unspoken thought aloud. Jon saw the glitter in her eyes and her white convulsed face as she wheeled Patches and rode the other way to head off one of the horses that didn't appreciate being driven.

"What's this?" Jon's sharp eyes fixed on a tiny white something tangled in the mane of a big bay. "Whoa there, boy." He soothed the skittish stallion with his voice until he could reach the snowflake-sized white patch. "Paper! No bigger than. . . ." He could feel the blood drain from his head, leaving him curiously light-headed.

"A message?" Mescal's breathless voice called. She dug her spurless boot heels into Patches' sides and galloped to Jon. "Is it from Jim?"

He couldn't speak, held it out, watched her congeal at the three words: A WEDDING PRESENT.

"The fiend!" Where Jon had reacted in shocked disbelief, she stormed, "Isn't it bad enough he goes to the devil, breaks your folks' and your hearts?

Must he taunt me with it?'' Magnificent in her blazing response, Mescal leaned low over Patches' neck. "Get going!" The pinto, galvanized into speed, raced back the way they'd come, leaving Jon to start driving in the returned horses.

Halfway home, he met her coming to him. Red spots still rode her cheeks. Her eyes still shot lightning bolts. But her voice was normal pitch. "Sorry I ran out on you. No need disturbing the folks with this, is there?"

"Not the message. Just the return of the horses and herd." Jon crushed the infinitesimal paper to oblivion and tossed it to the range. "He's doing everything he can to make sure we stay in business — and keep away from him." Corroding bitterness ate into Jon's soul.

"I release you from your promise." The red bloom withered and died from her cheeks.

Ten minutes before, Jon would have sworn he was beyond shocking, no matter what happened. He had been wrong. It was the last thing on earth he expected from Mescal. "You mean . . .?"

Her chin lifted, her throat was steady. "I mean you are no longer bound by the promise you made to sometime bring him back." She turned Patches without another word, letting him pick his way home.

A hundred yards behind, Jon followed, stunned by Mescal's final acceptance of what he himself would never accept: that Jim wasn't worth it. Winds of protest blew through his body, chilling the marrow of his bones. If even Mescal gave up on Jim, could keep faith that one day his brother would be free of the life binding him? Depressed, sick, Jon cared for the horses but didn't feel he could face Mescal yet, not as she now was. He walked aimlessly into the woods in back of the ranch house and was stopped by some sound that did not belong to the place. He quietly parted the slender branches of aspens, hiding their contents.

Mescal lay half hidden in a circle of compassionate, shivering leaves, crying her heart out.

For a moment, only Jon watched her, transfixed by her grief so strangely in contrast with her last words to him. Then step by noiseless step, he retreated and went back to the corral. By the time she appeared, he had erased every telltale sign of his private turmoil and was able to greet her naturally. There was no trace of tearstains on the smooth cheeks, but her eyes had been freshly washed. Her determined manner didn't fool Jon a bit. She could battle valiantly and without quarter, but she could not change her feelings for Jim.

"Mescal." He stopped what he was doing. "I want you to listen and not interrupt. Then I'll never bring it up again. I promised you I'd bring him back, and I will." He held up a hand to silence her automatic protest. "If you don't want him, then you can decide and tell him so. But because you release me doesn't mean I won't keep my word. I have to. I promised myself as well as you, and someday, when the time seems right, I'm going after him."

With an inarticulate cry she ran past him and into the house.

May brought fresh news of various crimes committed by an unknown person or persons. Jon took the bull by the horns and buttonholed Radford Comstock on the dusty street of Daybreak. "You're sheriff around here, aren't you? When are you planning to do something about what's happening?"

The lean, dark face never betrayed by a flicker anything other than contempt. "From what I hear, the Triple S ain't suffering, so what's your gripe?"

Jon longed to lash out and strike down the reptile before him. "Plenty of others are wondering the same thing. Enough, in fact, that the next time it comes time to get a sheriff appointed, I reckon I'll be applying for that job."

Hate gleamed in the dark eyes watching him. "Thought you aimed to be a preacher."

"Even preachers have been known to kill rattlesnakes — if they curl too close around their boots." Jon stalked off before he could add more, aware of the hostile look boring holes in his back the way Comstock would probably send bullets flying if he dared.

"He won't forgive me for that," Jon soliloquized on the ride home. "Wonder what he plans to do about it? Sheriff's job doesn't pay much, but Comstock probably thinks it gives him some kind of honor in Daybreak." The threat he'd made popped into his mind. "I might just try for sheriff myself. This'd be a whole lot better place to live."

Comstock's reply to Jon's prodding wasn't long in coming.

Two weeks later Apache rode in on a winded Shalimar. He waited until he got Jon alone and gave him the bad news. "Radford Comstock's got Jim just where he wants him."

Jon mutely stared, heart in his boots.

"He's given out how since the Triple S is the only place not getting raided, stands to mind there's a reason. Since Jim Sutherland 'ain't been heard of' for a time, and rumors have been flying, he's going to get himself a posse and go into the canyon country and 'stop this . . . stealin' for once and all.' "

"So that's his game." Jon dropped heavily to a chair. "I never gave him enough credit for having that much brains. He must have planned it all along." Revenge surged up in a swelling tide. "When do we ride?"

"Tonight. The posse's already getting ready, but it's better for us to go after dark. We'll be between two enemies, remember. The Comstocks aren't going to be any gladder to see us than the posse."

"They'll be even less happy when it's all over," Jon promised through gritted teeth. "Let's see, how many in the Comstock outfit?"

Apache inclined his head. "About a dozen, unless some are on a raid. I wouldn't put it past Radford to set something up to catch Jim red-handed."

Jon fought nausea and checked his rifle. It was against everything in him to go after men with a gun. All his principles said, "Don't kill." Yet what choice had Jim left him? "And in the posse?" he asked.

"Six or eight."

Jon could feel Apache's appraising surveying of him when he laughed harshly. "That makes eighteen or twenty. Odds are about right, I'd say."

"How many of the hands are you asking to ride?"

"None."

Apache grunted, but Jon saw the slight smile that showed he was pleased. "Be ready at nine o'clock."

Eerie clouds covered the moon when Apache, on the big bay, Jon, on a dead black, quietly left the ranch. Shalimar had been ridden too hard to take, and when Jon started to saddle King, Apache stopped him. "Dark horses this night."

Dark horses and dark deeds. Jon had never been torn apart the way he now was. Emotions birthed and died: anger with Jim for getting him into this position; hatred of the Comstocks and the evil they stood for; pity for the folks and Mescal, if his plan didn't work. It was likely neither twin would survive the coming hours, if either the Comstocks or the posse, all cut from the same rotten bolt of cloth, had their way.

Hours in the saddle left him tired and sore. He'd finally given up trying to pray or even considering what lay ahead. What would happen must be allowed to run its course.

An uneasy dawn broke, with rain pouring and a shroudlike gray fog descending, until at times he could no longer see Apache on the unused trail ahead. Once he asked, "Wouldn't it be better for us to get there ahead of the posse?"

Apache only shook his head, ghostly in the misty morning. "No. Let all be together. Surprise is our only real weapon. The posse will have scattered the Comstocks — trust Radford for that. He'll be sure enough noise is made by his hand-picked riders, so his relatives can get away. They've probably been alerted anyway."

The callousness of the sheriff's plan dried Jon's mouth and shut off his inner, insistent voice. What he had to do was wrong. Jim had been right: The only way to kill a snake was to step on it and crush it forever. Jon's throat filled with ashes of fiery dreams to make men listen to a better way of life; when he mounted the black, to save his brother, he destroyed any chance of that.

A lifetime later Apache took yet another of the tortuous turns into what he said was the hideout. How he knew the way, God only knew — and the eagles. "We'll hide the horses here," Apache whispered. "I can see camp-fires ahead. They have one outside the cabin, a big one." He slid forward on wet leaves that camouflaged and deadened his slow movements, Jon at his heels. "Now we wait."

Jon buried his face in his arms, to still the heavy breathing from crawling and from fear of what lay ahead. When he raised his head, only Apache's warning hand over his lips kept him from crying out. A pine tree stood out clearly in the firelight ahead. Over it hung a limp rope, sinister, suggestive.

Jon clenched his teeth to keep from retching. Across the firelit clearing, Jim stood with both hands over his head. A bearded stranger held a gun on him. Jim's defiant voice cut clearly into the falling night. "I tell you, I wasn't in on any bank robbery yesterday. Cookie can vouch for me." His disheveled hair looked gold in the flickering light.

"That's right." A pallid man spoke up. "Sutherland an' me played cards all afternoon."

"Shut up," his captor snarled. "Inside the cabin, Sutherland. I got a hunch the sheriff'll be along soon." His furtive glance toward the darkened rim where the firelight ended gave away knowledge of a well-laid plot, and Jon shuddered in the darkness.

Jim stepped inside the cabin. Jon could hear the creak of leather and the jingle of spurs. Once Jim mumbled something, but the sound of a sharp blow cut off words. Jon's hair rose, along with his temper. "I'm going in after him," he whispered.

"Wait!" Apache's steel fingers bit into his arm. A second later the gun-carrying stranger came back outside. He looked both ways then motioned to the cook and another man to go. Cookie glanced toward the cabin.

"Get out of here, you —" The man and two others who stepped from the shadows herded the two off into the woods. Galloping hooves portrayed their rapid departure.

Jon could see it all clearly. Beard would come back, wait for the posse and "try" Jim. "I can sneak in, get him out, and we'll get away before they come," Jon urgently told Apache. "You stay here and give me all the time you can. If you have to, run off any spare horses or ride away yourself and lead them into thinking Jim got away." Before Apache could argue, Jon slipped to his feet, skirted the fire and slid behind the rude cabin, praying there was a window at the back.

His prayer was answered — a window with a heavy shutter had been carved into the logs of the cabin. Jon slid the blade of his hunting knife up, slit the buckskin thongs that held the shutters in place, and laid them on the ground without a sound. He thrust his head and shoulders inside, ignored Jim's low cry, and stepped through onto the dirt floor.

PART III
Sons of Thunder

9

Jim Sutherland pulled back on King's reins. "Whoa, boy." King slowed and stopped at the edge of the home clearing. Jim opened his mouth to call a greeting to Jon and Mescal ahead. It died on his lips when he heard her troubled whisper carried straight to him by the breeze lifting her hair and playing with her eyelashes.

"I really love him, but sometimes I wish — Jon, if only he were more like you!"

Jim barely heard Jon's stunned reply. The clouds he'd ridden for the weeks since he learned Mescal loved him turned to solid earth. In a moment they'd see him. They must never know he'd overheard.

"Don't worry about Jim." He tried to sound amused. He went on to flippantly tell them Radford Comstock would attend the wedding, kissed Mescal's protest away, and walked after her when she ran, forcing a whistle. He knew Jon watched with tortured eyes, told himself fiercely he didn't care. Mescal had chosen, and she was his, not his brother's. Yet her wistful eyes haunted him, and her wish sank deep in his soul. *More like Jon.* His carved lips whitened. Hadn't it been that way ever since he came back? Better if he'd stayed away. He wasn't Jon and never would be. Spineless, refusing to fight — hot tears crowded his eyelids, and he forced them back. No, Jon was none of those things. It took more courage to do what he believed right than to give in.

So what should he do? Day and night the question mocked him. He'd been so sure Mescal and the challenge of making the Triple S a tremendous ranch would be enough to hold him. Why not do nothing? Jon would be gone soon. He and Mescal could go ahead with their plans. Besides, Mescal didn't love Jon, not in the way needed for marriage.

She might, if you were gone.

Cursing, he plunged into frenzied activity. Anything to drown the nagging reminder. Although he tried to hide his knowledge of the conversation, small taunts escaped him, and the last day of February something dark and undeniable rose in him. "I'm riding to Daybreak for a last fling," he announced. Over Mescal's threats and protests, he slipped to the stable, started to throw a saddle on King, and stopped. No. Dark Star would be better for whatever lay ahead. Everyone in the country knew King, while

70

Dark Star could be mistaken for a dozen other local horses.

The ride to Daybreak cleared his mind. He wouldn't go back. Jon once said doing things for someone else was pretty great; well, he'd make himself scarce. He shut his mind and heart to the dull ache when he thought of Mescal. So what if she cared now? In the long run she'd be better off. Even if Jon went ahead and became a preacher, Mescal would have the best man.

"The best man!" His grating laugh shattered his last dream, along with the silence of the woodsy trail. "I'll go whole hog. Send word the best man wins. That'll turn Mescal away from me, and she'll forget in time." He clamped down hard with his teeth, and blood spurted from a cut lip. The pain released some of the pain inside. He mopped at it with his kerchief and rode on.

By the time he reached town, his mood bordered on the dangerous. First thing he did was ride straight to the jail. "Out." He jerked his thumb over his shoulder at the hangers-on surrounding the sheriff. When they'd gone, surprise showing on their ugly faces, he came straight to the point. "Know anyone around here who needs a good man?"

Radford Comstock's sensual, cruel mouth dropped open. He leaned his dark-clad body back in his chair until his shoulders touched the dirty wall. His wolfish eyes never left Jim's face. "Depends on who that man is — and what he can do."

Jim's reply was to snatch his gun from its holster, flip it toward the sneering sheriff, and put three bullets over his right shoulder, into the wall behind him. A sneaking admiration filled him. Comstock didn't move an inch.

The next moment the room was full of men. "What's going on in here?"

Comstock reached for cigarette makings and drawled, "Sutherland here just killed a spider."

"Three shots in the same hole?" A hawk-eyed man ran his finger in the hole, checked the wall for other holes, and shook his head when he found none. "Musta been *some* spider."

"If you men will get out of here, we'll finish our talk."

Grumbling, the others went back outside. Comstock slowly rolled a cigarette. Jim's sharp eyes noted a slight unsteadiness of the long fingers. The sheriff wasn't as nerveless as he'd thought earlier.

"As we were saying —" Jim paused suggestively.

"So what's wrong with the Triple S that — a man looks for another job?"

A wild idea crossed Jim's mind like a racing mustang. He rejected it, reconsidered. Could he pull it off? His eyes gleamed, and he leaned forward, voice low. "Radford," it was the first time in years he'd called the man anything but *Comstock*. "The Triple S isn't big enough for my brother and me. Besides, some thieving varmints are running off the stock. Not much future there."

A curl of smoke hid Comstock's face, but the razor-keen voice cut

through. "Just maybe both those problems could be solved at once."

He'd swallowed the bait whole. Jim exulted, but carefully hid his excitement. "Which means?"

Comstock's casual tone roused the primitive in Jim. "If a good man chose to work for the right people —" He paused and blew another screen of smoke. "I could just about guarantee no more cattle and horses would disappear from the Triple S."

Jim had never wanted anything in his life so much as to launch himself headlong into the bogus sheriff. He forced a light laugh that set his nerves on edge. "Could you also guarantee the return of stock and horses already gone?"

A long silence ensued. Jim held his breath. Had he gone too far? He could feel sweat trickle down his neck. If he gave up Mescal, but could see the Triple S on its feet again, maybe it would be worth turning outlaw. Nothing else he could ever do would show his twin how much he cared. Jon's eyes rose to accuse him and were forced down. There were many ways to fight the Comstocks. Jon could choose his, Jim would do his own deciding. He knew his reasoning was faulty but refused to admit it. If it came to an all-out fight with the Comstocks, he'd probably be killed anyway. Might just as well get something for the folks out of it. At least when he was dead it would be one decent thing he'd done, even though the way it had to be accomplished might not be square.

Comstock's low voice jerked him back to attention. "I'd say as long as a Sutherland stuck with his new boss, even that might be done. I've heard tell Sutherlands are trackers and know every inch of this country, almost as well as Comstocks."

Jim was tempted to tell the gloating man where to get off, but caught himself up sharply. He laughed instead, then shot across the room at a rustle in the leaves outside the jail window. "What was that?"

Comstock reached the window at the same time. "Don't see anything."

"Something made that noise, and there's no wind." Jim pressed his face to the heavy iron bars. His keen eyes examined the clump of pines, whose swaying branches proclaimed any disturbance to high heaven.

The branches moved again, and Jim drew his gun. Then a squirrel leaped from one branch to another and disappeared into the distance.

"Stupid squirrel." Jim sheathed his gun, and swung back to face Comstock. "Well?" The word cracked like a revolver shot.

"Soon as the range is so cattle and horses can be moved, the Triple S stock will be sure to wander back from where they wandered off."

Jim hated the triumph in the smoky black eyes, but hid it. "I'll be around town, whenever my new boss — whoever that might be — wants me." He eased across the filthy floor and into the street, torn between wanting to go back and force a confession of rustling from the sheriff and determination to follow the course he'd laid out for himself. The second impulse won. He

headed toward the saloon and met Apache halfway down the street. For a quick moment he wondered if the Indian could have been outside the jail window during the conversation. He shook his head impatiently. Impossible. He'd seen the squirrel; besides, in the time it took him to get down the street, Apache wouldn't have been able to get ahead of him. He dismissed the idea and demanded, "Are you following me?"

"Do you need following?" Was it contempt in the bottomless depths of Apache's eyes?

Jim dropped it. "Are you headed back for the Triple S?"

"Yes. Soon." If there was significance to that, Jim failed to catch it.

"Good. Take this to Jon —" He scribbled, THE BEST MAN WINS — AGAIN, on a torn piece of paper he found in the street. "And tell Mescal Jim says to forget him. Jon will make her a better husband." Something in the steady scrutiny made him add, "I'll be riding out. You can tell Mescal it won't be hard for her to love one twin as well as another." He spun around on his boot heel and left Apache in the street.

Weeks later he reined in Dark Star miles away in the canyons. God must have made the place then forgotten it, he thought. Piles of rock crouched like mountain lions on both sides of a perilous trail. Overhangs encroached on the trail, at places, until horses could barely get through. The perfect hideout. And the valley beyond defied description: Long, narrow, yet big enough to hide the stock driven in from the other way, over a bare rock trail that held no tracks, lush and green fields broken with trees contrasted strangely with the outlaw band who inhabited it. What a place to live! Jim rode to the rude cabin ahead. If only he could show Mescal this place.

Reality fell on him, a mountain of depression. Mescal would never see this place. No one else he loved would either. The Comstocks guarded it and jealously protected it, even from other outlaw bands. There probably wasn't one man in Arizona outside those brought in by the gang who knew it.

"Except Apache," Jim mused. "Bet he could find it, if he wanted to." A hard-bitten smile split his grim face. "Wouldn't be surprised to have him ride in sometime. Mescal and Jon won't let me get away so easily. Wonder if they're married by now?" He knew he lied when he said it. Yet in no other way could he keep on with the trail he'd chosen to ride. Only knowledge he was doing it for his family kept him from sloping off in the night, now he knew the ways in and out of the valley. He was tired and sick of the small stuff they'd done — a few cattle here, a good horse there. Once Radford gave the order, and the Triple-S stock was sent home, maybe he'd head for New Mexico or Texas, start over. It wasn't as easy squandering his life as he'd thought it would be, and memories of home lay raw and exposed, unless he guarded against them every minute.

A night or two later, a stealthy step behind him caused Jim to turn toward it, gun in hand. Before he could speak, a sinewy hand covered his mouth, and a voice hissed in his ear, "It's Apache."

Jim relaxed, tore himself free. Gladness filled him, quickly replaced with alarm. "You shouldn't be here!"

"Should you, James Sutherland?"

Jim recoiled from the question and whispered, "What do you want?"

"To give you a message." Apache repeated what he'd been told. "Mescal cares nothing for Jon except as a brother. She loves you. She wants a home and freedom from fear."

"I can never give her that." Jim felt ragged breaths bolt through his lungs. "Tell them — once I take a trail, I don't turn back." He wrenched free of Apache's hand that still lay on his shoulder. "Now get out before you're discovered."

Not even a rustle told of Apache's passing. Jim stood with head bent, ears strained. An oath, then, "Who's that? It ain't Sutherland's horse!" burst into his brain. He leaped forward, ready to defend Apache, if needed. Three of the men Comstock had recently imported raced off in the direction Apache had taken. The next instant Shalimar lunged into view, knocked one man aside, and scattered the other two. One shot ended in a sickening thud. Jim's heart dropped. Was Apache hit?

"After him." Jim leaped astride Dark Star's bare back, senses alert. The others followed, grunting and cursing. He had to be first down the trail, to buy Apache time. He deliberately slowed Dark Star, who must have recognized Shalimar and wanted to run. "This way, you rustlers!" He veered to the left, away from Shalimar's path. The rain had started. By the time morning came, all sign of Apache's trail would be obliterated.

A long time later he gave up in disgust. "No use going on in this downpour!" he told the disgruntled outlaws behind him. "Anyone recognize the horse?"

"Not me."

"Or me."

"Me, neither. We ain't been here long enough," the third new man apologized. "Haw, haw, give us a few weeks an' we'll make a handshakin' acquaintance with every good saddle horse in this country."

They reached the cabin, and the strangers gathered inside, along with some of the regular men, who'd been playing cards, but Jim checked both ways then nonchalantly slipped to the location where that single shot had been fired. A careful search revealed a bullet imbedded in a tree trunk. A slight reddish stain showed where it had gone in. "Must have nicked Apache, but couldn't have done much harm," Jim decided.

The best day of the wilderness sojourn came when Jim and two others drove the Triple S stock home. "Don't anybody get near enough to be recognized," he ordered sharply.

"Don't see how come we steal then take it back," one griped, but Jim's quick gesture toward his gunbelt silenced him. Not a man in camp but what recognized his superior draw and edgy temper. He'd backed off the biggest

bully in the outfit, bearded Nil Hathaway, when he caught Nil cheating at cards, and since then the men steered clear of riling him.

It was a poignant moment for Jim when they left the Triple S to head back into the canyons. Radford Comstock had made good his word, loudly boasting he expected to get a hundred times the price of the stock out of Jim's daring and knowledge of the area. His wicked glee even rubbed off on his men, and raid after raid was planned. Now all Jim wanted to do was join the Triple-S hands. When one of them raised one arm, to wave, Jim's heart lurched. Had he been recognized, or had Dark Star given him away? He deliberately waved back, then with a "Hi-yu!" such as a helpful neighbor would give, rode slowly on.

Never thought I'd miss the place so much, Jim confessed to himself. *April's got to be the best month of all — new leaves on the aspens, flowers thinking about growing, and birds and animals coming back alive.* The familiar ache inside expanded. He might ride away from the ranch, but he couldn't ride away from himself. He'd tried it Indian fighting. It hadn't worked now anymore than then.

"Reckon as soon as I can get away, I'll head off into the lonelies." He gazed south. "Maybe try California then work back to the Tonto." But all his plans were forgotten when he reached camp. "Anything to eat, Cookie?"

"Not much." The disgruntled cook spread wide his hands. "Comstock says he's too busy chasin' outlaws to haul in supplies." He reluctantly checked the chuckwagon and produced a chunk of meat and some cold biscuits. "That'll have to do 'til supper."

"Want me to get you some meat?" Jim patted his rifle.

"You bet." Reluctance died. Jim knew he'd made his first friend among the rustlers. From then on he supplied Cookie with deer, rabbits, and birds. He'd always liked hunting, and it kept him away from camp. Now he'd made up his mind to go, the best way was to allay any suspicions anyone might have, before slipping off.

May scampered by on sunny feet. Jim was almost ready to leave. He'd made an effort to be agreeable lately, and all except Nil Hathaway seemed to relax around him. The bearded giant had never forgiven Jim for showing him up in front of the men, Jim knew. He was careful never to turn his back on the man.

Comstock jerked most of the men from camp for a gigantic raid one night. He'd ordered Jim to stay behind. "You could be too easily recognized," he stated flatly. "This one's near Daybreak — horses." His flushed face showed he'd been drinking hard.

Uneasiness slid through Jim's veins at the strange look on Comstock's face — half triumph, half anger. Jim decided right there he'd ride out when the others had gone. That afternoon he carefully rolled his few belongings together and hid them near the sheltered nook where he kept Dark Star. He'd moved his horse from the corral after seeing the greedy eyes of some

of the men following him, especially Nil's. He spent the afternoon playing cards with Cookie, tossed and turned during a miserable night too black to hazard the trail out, and headed away from camp the next day, in a gray fog. He hadn't gone far when he ran smack into Nil and part of the gang riding in.

"Where you think you're goin'?" Nil challenged, jaw stuck out.

"After meat."

"When all the game's lyin' down under trees?" Nil's scarred face contorted into a knowing smile.

"You calling me a liar?"

· The men on both sides of Nil broke away from him at the menace in Jim's voice and the steadiness of his left hand, holding Dark Star's reins. Jim could see the temptation to draw in the pale blue eyes and the final decision not to push it. "Naw. Just be sure you come back." He laughed coarsely and moved on.

Jim didn't dare try for a break after that. Tension mounted. There had been something strangely triumphant in Nil's face, the same look Radford Comstock had worn when he gave the orders for the last raid. Jim shrugged. Nothing to do but wait. He succeeded in scaring up a deer, killed it, and packed a haunch back to camp. He caught the disbelieving stare Nil bestowed on him and cheerfully told Cookie, "I'll get the rest for you later, unless one of these wild raiders want to pack it in." He rubbed his hands over the fire. "Feels good."

The rain stopped, but the fog remained. Jim brought in the rest of the meat, then ate a silent supper. When darkness fell, he stood and yawned, "Me for the sack." He turned from the giant fire Cookie used outside when he could.

"Hold it, Sutherland." Nil whipped out his Colt. "I been deputized to arrest you for killin' a man in yesterday's bank robbery." He flung back his steaming coat. A silver star bounced firelight beams into Jim's face.

Jim laughed scornfully. "You know better than anyone I wasn't in any bank robbery. Cookie can vouch for me." He ran one hand through his hair, tensed to spring, if there was any opening.

"That's right. Sutherland an' me played cards all afternoon."

"Shut up!" Nil glared at Cookie. "Inside the cabin, Sutherland. I got a hunch the sheriff'll be along soon."

So that was it. Jim hesitated on the doorsill, ready to turn. A harsh jab reminded him of the futility of it. He went on, suffering himself to be securely tied and thrown on a bunk in the corner. Through the open doorway, he could see a long, limp rope dangling from the big pine. He went cold to his toes. Comstock would come, probably with a posse. They'd have trumped-up charges, and hang him. No matter what Cookie said —

"Get out of here, you!" With a mighty effort, Jim raised up in spite of his bound hands and feet. Cookie and Tom were being pushed off to the

woods. The sounds of pounding hooves indicated their escape.

A bitter smile crossed Jim's face. Twice before he'd been on the verge of death. Both times Apache had come. This time would do it. There was no Apache to rescue him. The enormity of what he'd done swept over him. Would any of them ever recover from the shock of learning he had been hung? The damning evidence against him would linger in their memories forever. The one time he'd been innocent, and he was going to hang, be dragged back dead as an example by a sheriff who would loudly proclaim his victory over rustling and robbing!

"God, what have I done?" Jim licked parched lips. "And what will happen to my family and Mescal?" Too-vivid scenes painted themselves on the dimly lit cabin walls: Mother, dying from the shock; Dad, hair turning whiter, shoulders stooped with shame; the Triple S robbed and ruined; Mescal — he shut his eyes but couldn't keep out the images of the future. What a devilish way to get Mescal. Radford Comstock had planned it all along. With him out of the way and Jon disposed of. . . .

A slicing sound interrupted Jim's hell on earth. He peered across the cabin. A shutter disappeared. Another. A man's head and shoulders came through the window.

"Jon!" It rattled in Jim's throat.

The next instant his twin was beside him, cutting his bonds, freeing him, then gathering Jim into an embrace that threatened to choke the breath from him.

"Don't try to talk," Jon whispered. "Comstock and a posse are on their way. Apache's outside, with the trail in blocked. He'll ride off and make them think it's you, if he has to. Come on!"

"Too late!" Jim heard shots and the voices of men. "Go, Jon, save yourself. I'll hold them off." He met his brother's blazing eyes. "I'm guilty of small raids, nothing more. I've not killed, and I wasn't in on the bank robbery yesterday. Radford wouldn't let me go."

"Is that square?" An unearthly light whitened Jon's face.

"God as my witness!" Jim's talonlike fingers gripped Jon's shoulders. "Now that the cattle are back, I was going to ride out. California or somewhere. I'm not good enough for Mescal, never was. Tell her I really loved her — and hope someday you and she . . .," his voice failed.

"Mescal never loved anyone but you, Jim." Jon half dragged him across the floor. A volley of shots and the steady drumbeat of a running horse stopped him cold. "That's Apache and the bay. Come on!" He almost jerked Jim from his feet.

"How could Sutherland get untied?" a new voice roared. Jim recognized Radford Comstock's cry and dug in his heels. "Too late, I tell you. Save yourself." He snatched the revolver from Jon's holster and sprang back to the bunk. "If you're caught, it will mean both of us. Mother couldn't stand that. For God's sake, go!"

"For *God's* sake?"

Jim caught the tone in Jon's voice. Smothering fear, such as not even death could bring, pinioned him to the bunk. From faraway he heard Jon's whisper, "Good-bye, pard."

Something exploded in his head, white-hot, crippling. Through the waves he heard a voice, "Check that cabin and stop whoever's on that horse!"

On the brink of consciousness, Jim felt someone fumbling with his clothes. He couldn't move. He must save Jon. He started to cry out and was vaguely aware of cloth being stuffed in his mouth. He felt misty air, a mighty shove. Jim Sutherland, hung for rustling.

Another explosion inside him. Was it his heart tearing apart from regret? Then — eternal blackness.

10

Thousands of hammers beat in Jim's brain. He moaned and tried to open his eyes. When he succeeded, he thought he'd gone blind. Or was he dead? He remembered that suspension in space. The muffled sound he knew came from his own throat made it hard to breathe. He reached with trembling fingers and tore the gag from his mouth. Forcing himself to close his eyes, then reopen them, he saw nothing but blackness. The only sound was the steady drip, drip, drip of the mist turned to rain.

Where was he?

He tried to sit up, failed, and tried again. His head brushed wet leaves. He rubbed his eyelids clear of rain and finally got to his feet. What was he doing lying in a cluster of wet aspens?

Little by little it came back: the accusation, Jon's arrival — "Jon!" He shook his head violently and cleared the mental fog but not the dull ache. His exploring hand came away wet from the back of his head. What had happened after the explosions in his head? The stains were not water, but sticky ooze he knew had to be blood.

With returning consciousness came caution. Why was camp deathly quiet? He dropped to all fours and inched out of the thicket. His searching fingers touched the rough logs of the cabin. He must be behind it. Jim slid forward, taking care not to rustle. It might be a trap.

He was around the cabin now. The dim glow of a dying cooking fire barely lifted the shadows. It was enough to show his reaching arm. He recoiled violently. Where was his coat? This was Jon's. A premonition of something terrible awaiting him drove him on, more cautious than ever. For minutes he lay still, watching the firelit area. At last he was satisfied it was empty. The gang had gone. Then why did this chill grip him in claws of suspense? Why was he wearing Jon's coat?

Again he slipped forward, eyes straining for he didn't know what. Across the circle of pale light something moved. Jim grabbed for his gun, clawed at emptiness. The revolver he'd taken from Jon was gone.

An ominous sawing sound halted him. He barely breathed. Then when his nerves screamed for release from whatever evil spell lay ahead, the almost-dead fire eagerly pounced on one untouched log. A great flare of flame brightened the camp. Jim could feel blood pounding in his brain.

The next instant, "Apache!" Jim sagged with relief, but only for a heartbeat.

Apache's tragic face accused him from above a long, inert form.

Jim's blood slowly turned to ice. His breath rattled in his throat. "Not . . .?"

"Your brother." Never had Apache been more magnificent than when he strode forward, carrying the lifeless body of Jon Sutherland.

"But, I don't understand!" Jim backed away, unable to tear his fascinated gaze from the gruesome burden, protesting with every cell of his sickening body.

"He took your place!" Apache hissed. "Worthless white man, your brother took your shirt, your coat, *and your punishment*!"

"No!" It echoed through the trees, returned to mock him. Jim could feel terror mount. "It isn't true!" He wildly ran forward, ignoring his spinning head and his churning stomach. With a mighty grasp, he tore back the canvas tarp Apache had mercifully drawn over Jon.

His twin's convulsed face, still strangely radiant, stared up at him.

"No!" Jim shrieked. He dropped the tarp and fell to the dirt. His revolting stomach and breaking heart took control. A long time later, spent, sick, crazed with grief, he sat up and wiped his streaming face. Memory of a year-old conversation taunted him. Jon's voice, *"Suppose saving my life meant taking my place and dying yourself so I could go on living?"* His own, *"Not many men would do that."* Jon saying, *"One did."*

Jim writhed in agony. *"One did. One did. One did."* He hadn't cared about that one. Now his own brother had done the same. He understood Jon's repetition of his own plea, "For God's sake," just before —

"He must have knocked me out and pitched me through the window." Was that his voice, that shaking, pitiful whisper?

"Yes." Apache's inflamed eyes never left him. "While I was leading the gang away, so he could save you, your brother was dying for your crimes."

"I was innocent." Even in his own ears it sounded craven.

"Perhaps this time." Apache gently covered Jon. Without another word he picked him up and walked away. At the edge of the firelight, he stopped. Without turning he asked, "Are you man enough to go home with me and tell your parents and Mescal what happened, or must I protect you again, the way Jon —" He let the sentence hang in the damp air.

I can't go home, ever! Jim's soul burst forth. The words died behind his lips. Despising himself, sick, aching in body and mind and heart, he followed Apache.

Only once on the long, mournful ride home did Jim speak. "Will we be trailed?"

"Why should we be? Radford Comstock and his snakes killed Jim Sutherland, didn't they?"

A new spear impaled Jim. He didn't answer, but his numbed mind turned

it over and over. He was dead. So far as anyone except Apache knew, Jim Sutherland was dead. Better if he had been. Wasn't there someone in a Bible story Dad used to read, some guy who'd been dead and lived again? What had that man done when he found himself alive when he should have been dead? A vista of endless, torturous years lay ahead. What would he do with the life Jon had restored at such a terrible cost?

He couldn't think, couldn't decide. First he must face the family.

It was worse than he expected: the joy on Mescal and his folks' faces turning to white horror, the blank stares as he tried to stammer, "I didn't know. . . . He knocked me cold. . . . I tried to make him go. . .," blended into nothingness. When Jim could stand no more, he wheeled Dark Star and bolted. Anything to get away. He'd brought Jon's body home. Now he would leave them before reproach and hatred could replace their love for him and what he had brought about by his rebellion and pride. He spurred Dark Star to a gallop and didn't stop until he could hear the horse breathing hard. Then throwing the reins over Dark Star's head, Jim sprawled on the ground, clutching handfuls of pine needles and earth. A paroxysm of shock, disbelief, and horror held him until at last sheer despair and fatigue claimed him.

He awoke to Apache's veiled glance. "What are you doing here?"

A contemptuous smile crawled over Apache's face. "I am to go with you."

Jim sprang to his feet, fists clenched. "Just who's idea was that?"

"Mescal's."

It took the fight from Jim. "*Why*?" The world hung on Apache's reply, and Jim felt blood in his mouth from clamping down on his set lips.

"She said I must give you a message and remind you of it every time you forget." Steel underlined every word. "Mescal said, 'Tell Jim he no longer owns himself. He has deprived the world of someone whose living would have made it a better place. And now. . . .' "

Jim's nerves tightened until he thought he'd break the way a guitar string snaps under tension. "Well?"

Apache's inscrutable eyes fixed themselves on Jim's face. " 'Now he must take Jon's place.' "

Jim couldn't grasp what he was hearing. "Take Jon's place! Me?" His harsh laugh ground into the dark gray day.

"I know you cannot do it. Mescal says you must." Apache folded his arms. "White man, I hate what I am to do, but I will do it. She saved my life. I saved yours, then you saved mine. Now your brother chose to give his own life that you might live. I will eat and sleep and stay with you day and night until the debt is paid. Then I will never see you again — and give thanks for it!"

The finality of the sentence Mescal had pronounced made Jim shiver. It was too incredible to believe — that Mescal ordered him to take Jon's place!

"Come." Apache turned. For the first time Jim saw King and Shalimar were saddled and packed.

"Let Dark Star go. He will return home."

Jim found his voice, tried to put scorn in it, failed miserably. "Where are you taking me on Mescal's orders?"

Apache's somber eyes turned north and east. "Once your body was healed by the desert. Now its voices cry out for revenge. We will go back to the valley behind the waterfall. There you can think." He swung his gaze to Jim. "If as Mescal believes, there is any hope for you to become a man, it will be there." He motioned Jim to Shalimar and easily swung astride King.

Jim started to protest, shrugged. What difference did it make? It would be as easy to dispose of himself one place as another. No one who had done what he did had a right to live. Yet through his pain and loathing floated Mescal's face. He could almost see her white lips as she pronounced judgment — to give him a final chance in a trial by fire. Once he had said he would return to the desolation of the canyon country. He'd laughed and joked about it. Now he began the long journey. Would he ever make the even longer journey back?

He closed his eyes to the past, future, and present, lapsed into deliberate blankness, and followed Apache.

In many ways the trip was a repeat of the one before. Then he'd been oblivious to his surroundings because of physical weakness and pain. This time he saw little in the tremendous willpower it took to erase memory of Jon's face as he last saw it. It intruded between him and King ahead, always leading deeper into the wounded land. It crept between him and the nightly campfires. It appeared and vanished in the morning mist and the evening twilight. Something in the apparition's eyes always called, demanding that which Jim couldn't give. Apache spoke little. Was it part of his plan to let Jim go insane, bury him far away from the Triple S, and finally bring peace to the Sutherlands?

Jim shook off the recurring apprehension of the thought. Apache would be true. He would repay Mescal with every fiber of his being. He might secretly despise Jim, but it would not stop him in his pursuit of duty.

At first the landmarks they passed meant little, but gradually Jim began to see the places crying out for his attention. He recognized where Apache left him and went for pack burros. He noticed marks along the trail, telling him they were getting near their destination. The homesteader's cabin was empty. Had he been run out by thieves or given in to the relentless weather? It didn't matter. Jim wouldn't have wanted to see him if he'd still been there. Every unusual noise on his overstrained system brought a whiplike response. It wasn't until after they reached the waterfall curtain hiding the valley that would be stage for whatever lay ahead that Jim lost some of the numbness shielding him.

What the blood-red and crimson cliffs hadn't been able to do, that

glistening waterfall accomplished. Returning life and feeling made his former anguish nothing. When he rode through the waterfall and into the verdant valley, not all the streams on his face were from the fall.

"Look!" he pointed to the closely grouped cottonwoods. "The deer have come back."

"Life goes on." Apache's ponderous statement did nothing to bring light to his eyes. He hadn't smiled once since Jim had discovered him by the cabin, days before.

For one unreal moment it seemed time had turned back almost a year. The same sage smell tantalized Jim. The same wild flowers waved greetings in the gentle breeze. Even the burros and horses rolling in the grass, when they'd been unpacked, were the same sight they'd been there.

Jim did his share of the work setting up camp, then wandered off. He had to be alone. He could never forget or even think when Apache was near, never accusing in words anymore, but a constant reminder of tragedy. Jim aimlessly followed deer trails, noticing wryly how this time the deer were wary. Last summer they'd been unafraid. They'd learned from experience, from seeing many of their number hunted and killed.

Cold sweat formed, although the day had grown scorching. Jim's teeth chattered. Could he ever kill anything again, even to eat, without remembering? He clamped his mouth tight against the familiar gorge rising within him, determined not to give in as he had before. It was useless. Retching, sobbing, he collapsed on the ground until the spell was over. Perhaps in time it would become less violent. All he could presently do was fight it.

Days dragged leaden feet, each hour torment. Unless Jim spoke directly to Apache, the Indian never talked. It was just as well. Jim had nothing to say, no defense against memory. Nights were worse. The voices he'd heard calling intensified to a roar that drowned out even the waterfall's moan. Night after night Jim awakened bolt upright, shivering, clutching his blanket, and dripping sweat. Until he could convince himself it had been an owl or night creature, he never slept. He became gaunt, haggard, and great silver patches tinged the hair at his temples. The face peering back from the stream was years older than it should have been.

Only once did he rail against Apache. It came suddenly. The weight of the days and nights, coupled with regret, burst forth in one mighty demand, "Why don't you go back and tell them I am dead?" He felt foam rise to his lips. "It's true enough, I *am* dead — a walking dead man."

Apache didn't deign to reply, but the next morning, when Jim awoke, something hard and square pressed into his outflung hand. A carefully wrapped package tied with string lay on the edge of his tarp.

"What's this?" He spoke to empty air. Apache was nowhere around.

"Stupid to feel afraid of opening it," Jim muttered. Yet he let the package lie until he had breakfast of bacon and biscuits then shaved a week's growth of beard. His heart thumped when he fumbled with the

string. The brown paper wrapping fell back. Jim scrambled back as if it had contained a rattler.

Jon's well-worn Bible dropped from his helpless hands and fell open before him.

"No!" His cry was a repetition of the one he had uttered when he had seen his lifeless twin. He let the book lie and rushed headlong into the cottonwoods, stumbling over downed branches, slapping leaves out of his way. Their ooze coated his fingers with their sticky substance, the way the blood from his head wound, where Jon hit him, once coated the same hands. Great, tearing sounds issued from his chest. "Why does everything remind me of it?" Bitter laughter grew into maniacal screams. Had Mescal sent that Bible, or was it Apache's idea of a fitting end to his sanity? Either way it had succeeded. Still shrieking, Jim sank into a stupor that at least quieted his torment.

He never mentioned the Bible to Apache. When he returned to camp, with set face, he gingerly moved it aside with the toe of his boot. He carefully saw to it the tarp covered it from rain but refused to pick it up. Yet the next morning he had rolled over and could feel it under his arm. Teeth imbedded in his lower lip, he reached for it. A flood of feeling engulfed him. It was all he had left of Jon, except Jon's shirt and jacket, carefully stuffed in the bottom of his saddlebags. Slowly he drew it out, noting the way it fell open to marked passages he couldn't read for the red haze in his eyes. He closed the cover and put it under his pillow.

Several days later, Jim waited until Apache left camp. Many times the Indian disappeared for hours, leaving Jim in full possession of the camp. It was pleasant: bordered by cottonwoods, a few larger trees, and the greenness of grass still tasty to the animals who grazed nearby. Summer hadn't yet clutched the earth with heat, and the stream chuckled its way by over red stones. The hum of bees and call of birds added to the charm.

Jim lounged on his bedroll and cautiously took out the Bible. Some of the horror of the past faded, and when Jon's face etched itself on his mind, no rush of nausea accompanied it. The same steady look was in Jon's eyes, but the condemnation Jim had read there before seemed strangely missing. Jon looked more the way he had during those early winter days when they planned their futures around the home fires.

Jim scratched his head. "Wonder if I could find in here whatever made Jon the way he was?" He awkwardly turned pages, reading here and there some of the places Jon had marked. They seemed scattered and disjointed. Jim sighed and put the Bible away.

Yet day after day, when Apache restlessly roamed the valley, Jim dug out the Bible. He couldn't say he got that much from laboriously picking out the verses. He'd always hated reading, while Jon loved it.

"Why learn all this stuff?" he'd protested angrily against his mother's teachings. "I can ride and shoot and rope. What else do I need?"

His mother remained firm. "No son of mine will be illiterate. You'll learn

to read and write and figure enough to make sure you aren't cheated in your cattle deals. Now get to it and no more sass out of you, young man!''

"It's not so bad," Jon interspersed. His blue eyes glowed. "Some of those stories are about battles and stuff.''

"Yeah, you read about them, and I'll fight them!" Jim taunted, but Jon only grinned. "I get the best of the bargain.''

Jim snapped his book of memory shut. He'd fought all right, and Jon had lost because of it. He sighed and went back to his reading.

Now the night voices changed. Along with wildlife cries came new voices — Mescal's, charging him with the responsibility of not being his own man but bound to replace Jon in some way; Radford Comstock's, gloating. This brought him out of his reverie in a hurry. With Jon, Apache, and himself gone, what was happening at home? How could he have allowed even his own misery to lure him away? But what if he went back? Comstock would bring charges again and. . . .

Jim felt his heartbeat quicken. Apache had told him, "They've killed Jim Sutherland, haven't they, why should we be trailed?" The rankling memory brought daring back to the battle-torn Jim. Suppose he accepted in life the identity Jon had given by his death?

"Impossible!" Jim grunted and lay back down but the haunting idea refused to budge. Like a squirrel in a cage, it circled, reversed, circled again. From early childhood he and Jon had delighted in fooling everyone except their folks and Mescal. If they chose to dress alike and watch the way they talked and walked, not another soul on earth, except Apache, could have told them apart. What was to prevent him from becoming Jon Sutherland and protecting his family?

All night long he accepted and rejected the plan, weighing the pros and cons, unable to sleep. When dawn broke and Apache's moccasined feet noiselessly stole away for his vigil in some unknown part of the lonely canyon, Jim followed him. "Wait.''

The tall frame hesitated at the brink of the stream.

"Apache," Jim wondered if his pounding heart was loud enough for Apache to hear. "What if I went back — as Jon?''

Apache spun toward him.

Jim could see that for once the Indian had been shocked from his impassive calm. He rushed on, "Only four people know us apart. Everyone else thinks I'm dead and Jon's alive. I can't live wondering what's going on back at the Triple S. Comstock won't let Mescal alone." His fingers clenched and his lip curled. "Neither will he leave the stock on the range. Without a strong hand to protect it, how can the riders stick and fight off the Comstocks? We need to be there.''

Apache's expressive twist of his head followed a grim surveillance of Jim from boot toes to tousled hair. "You think you can be the man your brother was?" He half turned, as if to end the conversation.

"You know how to shove a keen blade in a man," Jim flared.

Satisfaction filled Apache's face. "See? You anger too easily."

Jim's grand plan curled but refused to wither. "I know I can't be Jon, but maybe I can fool others into thinking I am. I'll know myself how poorly I play his part, but does that matter?" He warmed to the idea again. "Look, I'm desperate. I have to do something — not just stay out here and rot inside from the sun and regret." He bent his head. When he raised it again, an odd look rested on Apache's face. Jim tried to interpret it and failed. It couldn't be approval, could it? He shrugged. "Can you burn a tiny scar over my left eye? Jon had one."

"I can. But you forget something." The inexorable Apache gave no quarter.

"What?" Jim rose to the challenge. "With the scar and being on guard all the time, why can't it be done?"

Apache lifted one hand, pointed to the sky. "Your brother planned to preach."

Sickening defeat downed Jim. He'd forgotten how the whole country knew Jon's dream and waited until he was ready to lead them. He turned and bolted from Apache, a wolf fleeing from danger. As he passed his bedroll he snatched Jon's Bible to him and clutched it for a talisman. For hours he walked and ran, pursued by his own soul. Sometimes he tried to read, shook his head, and gave it up. At other times he rested on rock outcroppings, from weariness of body and soul. Even as his original idea had been accepted and rejected a dozen times, a newer, outrageous idea form was squashed and re-formed to entice him.

Could he become the minister Jon had wanted to be?

"Never!" He lifted his face to the sky, almost afraid to look up. Surely a bolt of lightning should strike him for even considering such a thing. "I don't know much about religion, but it would be blasphemy, a man like me daring to. . . ." He couldn't even finish the thought coherently.

It wouldn't be *you*, a small breeze whispered. Jim Sutherland is dead, remember? If you should carry out your plan, it would be the same as if Jon had lived to do it. Remember what Mescal said? *You must take Jon's place.*

"Not literally!" Jim cried. Yet the seed was planted. Despite the burning rays of late afternoon, somehow it sank deeper in his soul and flourished. By the time the distant red rimrock turned purple with evening and a lavender haze filled the valley, it was ready to grow and bloom. Jim started back to camp and met Apache on the way. After long minutes of silent walking, Jim paused near the edge of the stream. "Tomorrow Jon Sutherland goes home." He waited for Apache's protest. It didn't come. "Did you hear me?" Jim demanded, although he knew Apache had.

"I hear, white man." Apache gazed at him through the gloom, "Tomorrow Jon Sutherland returns from the dead."

11

For the fourth time Apache and Jim rode the trail between southeastern Utah and the Triple S. This time Jim's watching eyes missed nothing. Every rabbit or ground squirrel that moved caught his glance. Each tumbling weed and sagebrush clump came in for a share of attention. He couldn't explain, even to himself, yet somehow he was alive. He lifted his face to the southwest. Instantly his elation turned to foreboding. He'd gambled all his life, but never like this. This time he was gambling with his life and for the Triple S.

"I have to win," he whispered passionately to Shalimar. The horse whinnied in response, but Jim had already drifted back into his churning thoughts. First he had to meet his folks and Mescal. Fear that had nothing to do with death gnawed into him. They might turn him out, order him away, as the murderer he was. He set his jaw. He had to meet them truthfully and tell them what he planned to do. First he'd thought he might just go ahead and drop clues along the way through Daybreak but rejected the idea. For once he'd be square and do it right.

His dusty fingers explored the tiny scar Apache had inflicted. He'd known by the Indian's grunt he was pleased, after a few days, when it healed. It had given Jim courage to ask, "Will I pass?"

"Perhaps — on the outside."

Jim hated the note in Apache's voice but knew it was justified. Now it lay in his own hands to change things. It wouldn't be easy. It meant controlling a temper he had never tried to check, acting the way Jon would in like circumstances.

Jim sighed, and Shalimar's ears perked up. It would be so much easier just to blast his way into Daybreak, kill off Radford Comstock and as many of his gang as possible, then ride off, if he were still able. "Can't do it, old boy." He twisted his hand in the tangled mane. "Wonder if I can stand the inaction?"

The same question rode sidesaddle with him through the weary miles and past Daybreak. Try as he would, Jim could not feel prepared for what lay ahead. Uncertainty had always given him the urge to crash ahead against obstacles. This time he didn't even know what they'd be.

Once they left Daybreak, every hoofbeat drummed in Jim's heart. He

relived former scenes: Here was where that miserable borrowed horse had bolted. Over there was where he'd first seen Apache — He rudely came to the present when Apache ordered, "Stop!" The Indian and King turned to statues, and Jim followed suit, peering through the trees to see what had alarmed Apache. Apache's face gleamed, and he slid from the saddle, motioning Jim to do the same. Noiselessly they crept forward, Jim's heart doing double time without knowing why — until a low cry from a clearing ahead chilled the marrow of his bones. Mescal! His muscles tensed to spring and protested when Apache's bearlike grip stopped him. Apache moved a little and urged Jim forward, but dropped his arm only to cover Jim's mouth.

Jim choked against the strong hand. Hatred pounded in his temples. In the center of the clearing Radford Comstock stood, braced on both feet, iron grip holding Dark Star's reins. Mescal glared down at him, anger spilling into her flushed face and dark eyes. "Get your hands off him!" She lifted the riding whip she never used and slashed him across the face. Twin welts followed the second blow; then blood spurted.

Comstock fell back but never loosened his hold.

"Let go, I tell you!" Roused to fury, Mescal hit again and again, until Comstock dropped the reins but grabbed the whip, jerked Mescal off balance, and hauled her off the snorting, terrified animal.

Jim leaped to his feet, but Apache seized him in a grip stronger than Comstock's on Mescal. "Wait!" he warned. "You are Jon — remember?"

Though he was almost berserk, it was the one note that could stop Jim. The entire future hung on the next few moments. He must not fail. Before he moved into the clearing, Comstock bellowed, "You devil! All I wanted to do was talk." He shook her fighting body hard.

"Talk!" Mescal blazed back. "The way you've wanted to talk every time you've waylaid me?" Midnight hair set off her white face.

Dark color rolled through the scarred face. "It's your own fault." His hoarse voice echoed through the still air. "I told you I'd marry you proper, but no, you won't have nothin' to do with decent folk, but throw it in my face you loved Jim Sutherland!" A wicked laugh followed. "That rotten thief was hanged for bein' an outlaw."

Jim's involuntary spurt of joy turned to black despair and madness, but Mescal's retort cut through his passion, "Decent folk? Radford Comstock, you're nothing but a cheap rustler who hanged J-Jim Sutherland on a trumped-up charge!" Her break sent chills through the listening man, pride for her defense of him. "Yes, I loved Jim Sutherland, and I always will. Even if I didn't, do you think I'd wipe the muck of the corral off on you?" She jerked hard and freed herself. In one bound she was after Dark Star who'd shied away from the fracas. Comstock leaped after her, then stopped. His eyes bulged. Mescal had snatched a rifle from Dark Star's saddle, aimed it at his middle, and in one motion, cocked it.

"Hold on! I didn't mean —"

"You've gone too far this time," Mescal spit it through clenched teeth. "When I tell how I shot you in self-defense. . . ." Her eyes turned red.

Comstock's livid face and working mouth were almost ludicrous. "You're not goin' to shoot me!" Disbelief settled over his features.

"Why not?" Her question bounced into the air, echoed and disappeared. "I'd kill any skunk in my way, and you've tried to maul me for the last time — ever." Her finger slowly pressed against the trigger, and Comstock stumbled back, tripped, and fell heavily. Groveling in the needle-strewn earth, he cravenly pleaded, "Maybe Sutherland wasn't in on that robbery. Anyone can make a mistake, an' —"

Jim shook off the mingled desire to shout in glee at Mescal's courage and fear she might really kill Comstock. He had too many relatives who'd come after her. It was time for the resurrection. He took a deep breath and strode forward before he could think anymore.

The reaction was instantaneous. Comstock sagged as if he had been shot through. His mouth dropped, his face turned dirty yellow.

Mescal gave a little cry. The rifle barrel wavered, turned a little aside. Her involuntary tightening of fingers fired the gun, but the bullet whistled harmlessly past the crouching Comstock. "J —"

"Yes, it's *Jon,* home at last." His eyes warned her, and he took the rifle from her hands to train it on Comstock. "What's all this about?"

For all Comstock could get out, he'd become permanently dumb. His protruding eyes still held shock. When he finally mustered words, he said, "You, you ain't been seen since —" He couldn't go on.

"Since you murdered my brother for something he didn't do," Jim told his caustically. Inspiration struck. "Unless you swear before these witnesses that my brother was innocent — *and he was.*" Truth rang in Jim's voice, remembering Jon's sacrifice. "I can't speak for what will happen to you." The rifle never wavered as he ejected the spent shell, and a new bullet dropped in place.

Some of Comstock's natural bravado crept back into his mocking laugh. He stood and dusted himself off. "I reckon no preacher's goin' to shoot me, at least not when there're others around to see, even if they are family and a stinkin' Indian."

Jim's whole plot lay imperiled by the insult. Only Apache's quiet, "That won't hold a 'stinkin' Indian back," saved Jim. He shot a look at Mescal, rigid as a fencepost, then the menacing Apache. "You were saying?"

Apache took one step closer, slid his knife into his palm, and eyed its glitter.

Comstock gave in. He ran his tongue over his lips and muttered, "Like I said, a man can make a mistake." He inched backwards to where a huge bay stood tied to a pine.

"Get out of the country, and take your scum with you," Jim ordered.

"Otherwise I'll turn Apache loose on you."

Comstock's dark face shot lightning bolts, but he didn't answer, just swung up on the horse and spurred him. But before he was out of earshot, he called back, "Next time it won't be two to one."

"Three to one," Jim yelled with a roaring laugh. "Seems to me Mescal was doing fine all alone, outlaw!"

The clattering of hooves and a dying curse dwindled into silence. Jim turned to Mescal. "Are you all right?"

Great gulfs of darkness without their golden specks greeted him. "Why did you come back?" Her terrified whisper cut him to the heart. Even after everything, when he had heard her defend him, Jim hadn't been able to control his leap of hope. Now it snuffed out, leaving him a cardboard character with a part to play.

"I'll tell you at home." He paused in the act of helping her mount. Her burst of defiance had gone; he could see in the way her shoulders sagged. "Will I be welcome?"

"Yes."

It kept him together through the ride home. The scene had left him so numb he could feel nothing. He did notice things were far greener than the previous summer. Evidently there had been rain. A little feeling of relief melted one corner of his frozen state when he saw the tranquility of his home. No signs of strife or war marred its usual peace.

From numbness to burning life, Jim made the jump in one giant leap when his father stepped from the porch. Matthew Sutherland didn't extend his hand, but his voice boomed, "So you've come back." He betrayed neither joy nor surprise, although Jim noted the new lines in the craggy face, the heaviness of his father's carriage.

"If you'll have me, but not Jim." His muddled explanation died in Abigail's arms. "My son, my son!" she cried from the doorway, and he cleared the porch in one bound. Head buried in her apron, the final bitter drop of his deeds reproached him. A long time later he lifted his face to his father. "Dad," a tremor shook him against his best intentions, "I've come home, but with a plan. Let me tell you what it is, and then you can have your say."

To gain time he looked around the small circle. Apache had dropped to the top step, immovable as the big pine in the yard. Mescal showed signs of the trail encounter, and he couldn't read her expression. Mother still kept her hand on his arm, as if afraid he'd vanish. Dad —

He cleared his throat. "It's my fault Jon's dead, sure as if I'd pulled the trigger." The early agony threatened to overcome him, but he fought until his brow turned clammy and raised his hand against whatever his father had been going to say. "Wait. I can't undo anything. But Mescal sent word I didn't belong to me anymore. She's right. I owe it to Jon to pay my debt any way I can. I about went crazy in the desert, trying to shut out its voices calling for me

to do something, anything. I decided I'd come back, as Jon." He ignored the collective gasp from his audience and doggedly went on. "The only thing is, Jon aimed to preach. That means I have to, too, or I'll never get away with it."

"You reckon on saving your skin by playing at preaching?" His father's words slashed as Mescal had slashed Comstock.

"No!" Jim sprang to his feet, horrified. "If it was just me, I'd rather take a beating. It's the only way I can help save the Triple S — and Mescal." He rapidly sketched in the scene in the clearing. "I can't guarantee Comstock will even ride off. He's banking on my being a weakling and you're being so cut up over your son's death you're worthless. It's for you, Dad, and for Mom and Mescal, not for me!" All the weeks of hurt fused into a lump in his throat. If Dad didn't believe him, what was life worth, anyway?

Slowly the hostility for his son left Matthew Sutherland's face. The beginning of a tortured smile fought at the corners of his lips. He asked, "Then it's not being irreverent, what you plan to do?"

"I hope not." Jim forced himself to meet his father's searching stare. "If it is, I'll have to pay the price. I don't know how else I can be worth anything, alive or dead." Bitterness crept in, and he tried to hide it. "It's all I can think of." He saw the disbelieving way his father shook his head then looked at Mother and caught fire.

"Son, Comstock was right. I'd about given up fighting. With you back, and with Apache, maybe the Triple S can still be something." Matthew's eyes turned to the corrals, past them to the clump of aspens with its fresh mound of earth. "It's what he'd have wanted."

Jim bolted from the sound of his father's voice. The faltering hope and acceptance flayed him, poured salt on already aching sores. Even with all his good intentions, could he live up to that hope and make it reality? His steps turned unerringly toward Jon's grave. The simple headstone that read JIM SUTHERLAND stopped him cold. The next moment he laughed, a dreadful sound. Dead and buried.

He knelt by the mound that was already covered with small flowers and tiny green grass blades, making a coverlet. "With God as my witness, Jon, I'll try and take care of the folks and Mescal the way you'd have done." A slight rustle behind him froze him to the spot. Mescal's voice said, "We thought it better to do it this way, in case anyone ever looked at the grave."

Jim slowly turned and met her intent look. "It's a strange feeling, seeing your name on a headstone." His attempt at lightness was a disaster. "Mescal, will you help me?"

He could see her spirit flee before she asked, "How?"

"I don't know much about the Bible. I thought if I give it out I'm spending the next few months getting the place in shape, then plan to study this winter, I can get by until spring before folks pester me to preach. Could you help me study? I hate reading; you know that."

She didn't answer for a full minute. One golden gleam had returned to her eyes, but never had he seen her so subdued. Even the simple blue shirt she wore looked faded and worn. "I'll help you, but can you go through with it? When spring comes, will you really stand before folks and preach?"

"I'll have to." The little grove had turned cold. Jim shivered in the warm day and wondered why life had to be lived at all. Everything preyed on something else. Man on animals. Wolves on rabbits. Mountain lions on deer. Yet only when man preyed on man were the laws of nature broken. Animals killed for food, man for greed or power. Now in order to survive, he was forced to play a different type of game, and one he despised.

Jim played that game all the rest of summer, into the fall. As he feared, Comstock had regained his boldness once away from the Triple S. While not much stock disappeared, and that could be attributed to natural wandering for graze, ugly rumors of persistent attacks on other ranchers and lone riders continued. By the time autumn rode the trails, with its golden showers of colored leaves, everyone for miles around Daybreak was keyed to fever pitch. Men slept with loaded rifles and pistols in easy reach. Those who had anything worth stealing kept it buried or locked up. Herds were moved closer in when possible. Still the outbreak of terror went on, and Mescal never rode alone. Apache faithfully shadowed her if she left the immediate area of ranch buildings.

"Something has to break soon," Jim told Apache one glorious afternoon. They'd ridden out to see where the outfit was in rounding up and tallying strays. "I've let Comstock go his way, hoping he'd get so tangled up in his schemes he'd hang himself, but the whole country's ready to fight at the drop of a hat. I'm not even sure how many of our own hands are loyal."

"Slim, Dave, Shorty, and Red."

"How do you know?" Jim couldn't keep surprise from his voice.

"Apaches have — ways." The slight smile that always accompanied Apache's confessed eavesdropping disappeared. "The others are like the wind in the aspen leaves, tossed about and up for the taking."

Depressed, Jim rode on. "That's four plus you and Dad and me. Not enough if we get a big raid."

"Better to stop the raid before it happens."

Jim's lip curled with some of his old arrogance. "Any ideas?"

"One." Apache shrugged. "You might not want to do it."

"I'm desperate enough to try almost anything." Jim gazed across the land he loved so well, automatically noting the dying of the year. "Shall we round up everything and sell?"

Apache considered a long moment. "That might be good. But it wasn't what I had in mind."

"Well, what was?" Jim's impatience boiled over, a teakettle that had been forced to simmer too long.

"Jon told me once he threatened Radford Comstock with getting himself

appointed as sheriff. Comstock showed it hit him hard.'' Not by an inflection did Apache show it mattered one way or another, but Jim sat up straight from where he'd lounged in the saddle. "You don't mean *me* as sheriff!" He threw back his head, and peal after peal of laughter splintered the autumn air.

Apache didn't even smile. "You asked. I told you.'' He wheeled King and was gone, leaving Jim alone with the echoes of his own mirth and prey to a host of new thoughts. Time after time he rejected the whole thing as even more insane than his idea of becoming a preacher. What a joke it would be on the Comstocks — Jim Sutherland, whom they'd hung for a crime he hadn't committed, thrust into a position of authority that could break the backbone of their evil deeds.

Although Jim continued to laugh down the idea, the more he thought about it, the more it intrigued him with the possibilities. Meanwhile, the roundup went on. Practically all the stock was sold at top dollar and the money carefully hidden on the Sutherland ranch. "Don't trust it in the bank," Matthew announced. "Too many holdups lately." He personally buried it, refusing to tell the others where it was. "Anything you don't know can't be dug out of you," he insisted. "There are those who know we have a tidy little sum and who wouldn't be above relieving us of it.''

Winter swooped with eagle's claws, but the Triple S lay unmolested. With practically all the herd gone and most of the hands off for the winter, an uneasy peace came with the isolation. Jim felt Mescal's eyes on him and wondered. Did she think of the plans and dreams they'd made last winter, before the roaring fire? Or had her show of spunk been for Comstock's benefit only? He couldn't read her eyes, and most of the time she avoided him. Jon's shadow lay between them, ever present, ever real, despite the months since he'd died. When they studied the Bible, there was none of the old teasing that should have gone with it. One late afternoon, when it had grown too dark to study and the older Sutherlands and Apache were in other rooms, Mescal closed the Bible and said, "I don't think you will ever preach, not even one sermon.''

"Why?" Jim noted the drooping curl over her left cheek.

"I don't know." Her pensive face caught the fire's glow, and she let her hands lie still in her lap. "It's just a feeling.''

"Would you care?" Why had he blurted it out, the first hint he'd let escape that what she thought was of supreme importance to him?

She evaded it. "What will you do, instead?''

"I could become sheriff and clean out the Comstocks.''

His random statement turned her face to parchment. "They'd kill you!" She caught the front of his heavy shirt in both hands. Terror shone in her eyes. "Besides, how could Jon Sutherland, learning to be a minister, take the sheriff's job?" She laughed wildly, and her slender body shook. "He couldn't. Daybreak wouldn't stand for it, much as they want and need a

new sheriff. They would never let you go against the Comstocks."

Jim caught both hands in his strong ones and pulled her close to him. He could feel the frightened beat of her heart and longed to wrap his arms around her and protect her from any harm, forever. Realization came like a summer storm, quick, unexpected, violent. Months ago he had held her, thought he loved her, looked forward to their being married. It was nothing compared with the sweep of feeling that now rose within him. In one heartbeat Jim saw his former love for what it was: selfish, demanding, a boy's careless asking for a priceless gift.

He drew a dazed breath. A man loved differently. The desire to protect, give, love overrode carelessness in the age-old way of creation of man seeking his mate.

Mescal's fists pounding against his chest and the realization she had mistaken his silence for argument brought him back to the firelit room. Tears chased each other down her cheeks as she repeated, "Jon Sutherland cannot be sheriff. Don't you understand?"

Light through darkness. Lightning in the fog. A rainbow in the rain. Enlightenment, sacrifice, determination. Jim lifted his head, looked above hers into the future. "No —" His jaw set. Jon had gone the last mile; his twin could do no less. *"But Jim Sutherland can."*

12

Jim had once heard a trapped fawn whimper the way Mescal did now. He had freed the spotted animal from a mucky pool and set it back on dry ground. He washed the scratched leg until the water ran clear, and the fawn limped away. But Mescal was no fawn. She was a living, breathing girl-turning-woman who clung to him. "No! Don't do it, Jim. We'll go away and be married. No one will know or care where we came from. Dad Sutherland will give us some of the cattle money to get started." Her strong arms threatened to destroy him; her pleading undermined his determination.

"I have to do it, Mescal, it's the only way." He inexorably loosened her clinging fingers, led her to a chair, and saw her collapse in its depths. His hands shook when he lit a nearby lamp from a fireplace brand then raised his voice, "Dad, Mom, Apache — will you come in here, please?" Every task he had faced paled into nothingness before the one he now faced: convincing them it was their only chance to survive. He sternly stamped out of his heart Mescal's solution to run away, knowing he might also be killing any chance of her sticking with him.

"What's wrong, Son?" Matthew's keen eyes missed nothing. "Did you make Mescal cry? And why?" He crossed the room and patted the dark head. Abigail and Apache both glanced at them then at Jim.

"I've just been telling Mescal how to get rid of the Comstocks."

Jim's father burst into great laughter. "Wish you'd tell the rest of us."

"I will." Jim fixed his penetrating gaze on Matthew. "Jim Sutherland is going to be resurrected and take the sheriff's job in Daybreak, at least for a time."

"What?" Matthew roared, his face turning beet red. "After all the planning to get the country to believe you were Jon? It doesn't make sense. No wonder Mescal's upset, you young hothead!"

"It makes all the sense in the world." Jim unfolded the plan he'd been making ever since Apache mentioned Jon's threat. "Once folks around here know their crooked sheriff hung *the wrong man* in his little game of covering his own tracks, they'll want something done about it."

"But what about your being in the gang? You think they're just going to overlook that? Or do you think Comstock'll keep his mouth shut?" Matthew pounded a big fist against the arm of Mescal's chair.

Jim hesitated a moment to find words that could cross the throbbing barrier of his heart. Every day of his life had aimed toward this minute. He must make them accept it. "I intend to tell them myself." For the first time he tore himself free from the locked gaze with his father and shifted so he faced them all. As long as he lived he'd remember Mescal's contorted face, his mother's eyes, Apache's suddenly glowing countenance.

"When the snow lifts, we'll ask all the ranchers here for a secret meeting. We'll invite a few of those from Daybreak we know we can trust. I intend to make a clean breast of it and ask for a second chance so I can do something with the Comstocks and make this a fit place for women and children." His soul flamed into his speech. "I tried being Jon, and it didn't work. One thing good came from it. When Jon took my place, I realized Jesus had done the same thing a long time ago. I decided if He — and Jon — cared that much, I had to accept it."

He saw gladness fill his mother's face. "But in spite of all that, I can't take Jon's place, and I don't think he'd want me to. Did you know he was ready to give up everything and fight, if he had to?" Needles poked into Jim's eyelids, and he found he was having trouble breathing.

"There is another way." Apache's voice intruded into Jim's ringing ears. "I can sneak in at night and kill Radford Comstock and maybe some of his relatives. The rest might take warning."

"You'd do that for us?" Jim choked, suddenly feeling Apache had grown to giant proportions.

"Apache pays his debts." The troubled months since Jon's death faded. Jim knew he was again the comrade he'd become after he and Apache shared the burning hell of imprisonment long ago. He gripped Apache's hand but shook his head.

"No. It would only bring the others forward, or worse, put them into hiding. They'd kill from cover. Don't you see?" he appealed to the others, who silently stood a little apart. "It's the only way."

"I can forbid it." The patriarch of the clan's deep voice rolled into the stillness.

"Don't do it, Dad!" Jim dropped Apache's hand and spread his own wide. "I hoped never again to go against you, but even if you order me out of your house, I have to do this last thing I know is right." He threw out the challenge with sinking heart. What lay ahead would be rough. Without his father's backing, it would be worse.

"Stubborn mule! Son of Thunder! How could I have raised such a one?" Matthew Sutherland foamed at the mouth.

Deep insight crept into Jim's feverish brain. He seized his father's mighty arm. "Dad, if it were you in the same place, *wouldn't you do the same thing*?"

Appalled by his daring, but unwilling to take back the cry, Jim watched the storm rise, break, and rage until his father thundered, "Yes! You know I

don't hold with killing, but God forgive me, *yes!*" His big eyes rolled. "If it hadn't been for Mother and Mescal and Jon holding me back, I'd probably be out there with him now." He motioned through the snow-draped window to the lonely mound.

Jim knew he had won, but at what cost! Never had his father turned his heart inside out before. Jim instinctively knew he never would again, but for this moment the naked truth shimmered and danced in the room, a fragile but unbreakable strand that bound them together.

"It's settled, then." Matthew's great gulps of air sounded loud. Mescal and Abigail had turned to each other, silently crying. Apache remained where he stood during the conversation, a softness in his look Jim had not seen before.

There was nothing of softness in any of them, weeks later, when the snow began to melt and trails became passable. Matthew and Jim made quiet visits to selected neighbors and ranchers, setting a time for their secret meeting. A full score arrived one afternoon, ate heartily of the excellent supper served, and crowded around the fireplace.

"Some of you are wondering why you're here," Matthew boomed. "No use stalling. It's time the Comstocks were run out of the country."

"Agreed," a lanky rancher cut through the low rumble of assent. "But how're we goin' to do it? Any one of us leaves our place, it gets robbed."

"If we had a new sheriff, things could be mighty different," Matthew cautiously suggested. Jim noticed the way the visitors' faces lighted.

"Shore, but who's goin' to be fool enough to take it away from Radford and get killed for his trouble?" the same rancher inquired.

"My son."

In the quivering stillness Jim heard the hiss of indrawn breath, followed by uneasy shifting of men's bodies. Neither drowned the music in his father's words. They would sing in Jim's ears all through the messy business that lay ahead.

Before anyone could ask the question hovering on everyone's lips, Matthew said, "I've got a story to tell. I ask you to listen without interrupting; then you can have your say."

"Fair enough," several mumbled.

"You all know the Comstocks hanged a son of mine last year." Matthew's voice hardened. "Since then Radford confessed to my other son, Mescal, and Apache, who's been the best friend we could ask for, he made a mistake and that Jim Sutherland wasn't even in on the raid. It came out Jim joined up with the Comstocks in the mistaken idea he'd be helping us. He did succeed in getting our stock and horses back. It doesn't excuse him riding with the gang, but he was wild, you all know that."

"Too bad he got hanged — we could use him right now," someone called.

Matthew's face shone. "Carter, do you mean that?"

Jim could feel his nails digging into his palms and sweat start under his shirt collar. Everything depended on Carter's answer — and the way the others replied.

"Yeah." Beefy, belligerent, Carter leaned forward. "Long's he hadn't killed anybody an' was willin' to help get back what I lost, it'd tickle my funny bone to have Jim Sutherland walk in."

"That goes for me, too," someone else called, but a third said, "What's the use us talkin' about a dead man? He ain't here, is he? He's out there right now." Silence fell as the man beckoned outside.

It was time. The hands of life's clock had ticked off the past, and the present demanded action. Jim stepped forward from the back of the room, where he'd been a silent bystander. "Men, Jim Sutherland isn't dead. *Comstock's outfit hanged the wrong twin!*"

The scrape of someone's boot sounded like an explosion. Taking advantage of the stunned condition of the crowd, Jim said, "I was trussed up, ready to be hanged. My brother Jon came. Knocked me out cold and pitched me through a window. I woke up wearing Jon's shirt and jacket." He felt a pulse beat hard in his temple. "Jon was dead; he'd passed himself off as me so I could go on living." He tried to clear the obstruction in his throat, forced himself to go on. "I went crazy, decided to kill myself. Apache and Mescal saved me — again — him by despising me and calling me a coward, Mescal by believing in me.

"Out in a God-forsaken canyon, I decided to square things to Jon by taking his place, becoming a preacher the way he wanted to do. I can't. I'd be a hypocrite. But I can be a new *Jim* Sutherland." He noted the paralyzed state of his audience. "Apache told me Jon once threatened to run Comstock out of office and take the job himself. At first it seemed insane. Then I saw it was the only thing to do. If you'll give me a second chance, let me do what Carter said and repay you for what I helped take, as soon as I can get the money, just maybe we can get rid of the Comstocks — for good." He could feel his knees start to buckle and grabbed the mantel for support. "I never was in on the killing."

"No one'll have to wait for money, either," Matthew promised. "I can settle up right now, with the roundup money."

Carter finally stood, looming large in the crowd. "Reckon we'd like to talk it over without you here, Matthew. Take Jim outside and wait."

Jim stumbled through the door and into the kitchen. Mescal met him with outstretched hands, a terrible question on her lips. "At least they're talking about it," he told her and his mother.

"Thank God for that." Abigail pushed her hair back with a soapy hand, from behind the mountain of dishes she and Mescal had been doing. They lapsed into waiting. One minute. Two. Five. Ten. Then, "Come in here," Carter ordered them curtly. Jim swept the room with a lightning glance. His heart dropped at the expressionless faces, but

rested on Apache's. Was that a slight smile?

"Jim Sutherland, are you willin' to uphold law an' order, even if it means bein' killed in doin' it?" Carter demanded.

"I am." A world in a whisper, a second chance.

"Then you're our new sheriff, on one condition — you go after Radford Comstock now, an' we all go with you, every last man of us. We figure he an' his outfit may take a mite of convincin'." Carter's ruddy face split into a broad grin. "I ain't never ridden with an Apache before, but I'm aimin' to now, if he's willin'."

Jim saw the quickly concealed look of amazement in Apache's face as he said, "I will ride." Moments later Matthew Sutherland burst into the room, a heavy sack dangling from one hand. "Before we go, I'll just settle up."

"Nothin' to settle," Carter announced. "That's how come we took so long. You've done given one son an' may have to give another. None've us as what's done that much." He brushed aside Matthew's protests and shoved open the door. "All right, men, ride!"

Jim ran for Shalimar, Apache for King. Matthew saddled Dark Star. A few minutes later the new sheriff and his deputized posse gathered by the front porch.

"I'll be waiting, Jim." Mescal's low voice carried to the mounted men.

Carter said, "Reckon that's enough to get him through!" And the others laughed. One called, "If he don't come back, I will," but there was no insult in the sally, and Mescal smiled tremulously, then slipped back inside. In a body the men rode down the trail and headed for Daybreak, Jim at their head.

"Apache," he turned to his comrade riding abreast of him. "What's the best way to handle things?"

Apache never hesitated. His hands spread in an expansive gesture. "Have some slip in unseen. Let the town people go in naturally. Give the order to wait five minutes until you, your father, and I get to the saloon or sheriff's office — Radford'll probably be at the saloon. When we meet him," a cold smile twisted the thin lips, "you'll know what to do."

Jim gave the orders as stated. It was just before midnight when they reached town, a black, cheerless night well-suited to their errand. Men would die; how many they didn't know. Some of them, some Comstocks. "God," Jim prayed. "If only the wholesale massacre can be avoided." A deep ache inside made him wonder — was the sickness threatening to overwhelm him the same thing Jon experienced that other night?

"Apache, is there any chance we can keep it from being a slaughter?"

Only the voice in the darkness proclaimed Apache still rode near. Vicious clouds had totally obscured the moon and stars, and a dark velvet blanket muffled even the sounds of the posse.

"Perhaps. It all depends on Comstock."

And then they were there, in place. Matthew, Apache and Jim

dismounted behind an empty building and dropped their reins. Step by careful step they went until Apache stopped them. "Wait here!" He was gone no more than a minute. "Sheriff's office is empty. They're in the saloon." When they reached the crouching building, Apache grunted. "Good — not many horses." Again he left them, scouted, returned. "Radford Comstock, six of his gang, a bartender, two town drunks off to one side."

Jim's heart leaped. Chances were slim the Comstocks would surrender without a fight, but it was not impossible.

"Stay outside the window until your eyes can stand the light," Apache cautioned. Jim blessed him for the thought. The moment he changed from dark night to brightly lighted room his eyes betrayed him. He blinked several times, and his vision cleared.

"Now!" Apache whispered in his ear.

A board creaked under Jim's foot as he crossed the rude porch floor. There must be no time for warning. He burst through the doors, revolvers in both hands. "Up with them!" He could hear his father's breathing over his shoulder, feel Apache's arm graze his as he pushed to one side.

Radford Comstock leaned his chair back, a sardonic smile on his face. "Well, if it ain't the preacher!"

"Not the preacher." Jim flipped one revolver the way he'd done in camp and was rewarded by Comstock's scrambling to his feet, craven face etched in horror.

"I hanged you!" The damning confession bounced off bottles and tables, and the men around Comstock leaped to one side, leaving him alone to face his ghost.

"You hanged my brother." Jim's strident voice turned Comstock's face even more ashen. "For a crime not even I was in on."

"Yes, yes." Comstock was beyond reason. "But there were other times. . . ."

"We know all about them, an' about you." Carter's authoritative voice came from the door at the back. He and a half-dozen other heavily armed ranchers pushed their way in. "Now we've decided we're goin' to have a new sheriff."

Jim saw the moment knowledge he was finished sank into Radford Comstock's brain. He raised his shaking hands. "I'll leave, get out of the country. My men'll go with me." His dirty-gray face shook.

"Better make it a long way out," Jim suggested in a soft, chilling voice. "We could hang you right here and be perfectly legal."

Comstock shot him a venom-drenched look but said nothing.

"We'd just as soon not have your dirty blood on this town's conscience. Get out!" Jim threw wide the doors and waited until the last of the men were outside. Under close guard they were hustled onto their horses and driven down the inky street, cursing all the way. They headed out, and Jim

felt his screaming muscles unknot. "Not a shot fired!"

He spoke too soon. From the pitch darkness a single explosion came. Jim was half lifted from his saddle, spun around and fell.

"Son!" Matthew was beside him. "You all right?"

Fire ran down Jim's left shoulderblade. He reached toward it. "It's high."

"Thank God!" Matthew caught his son in his arms and took long strides toward the doctor's home. "Apache, run ahead and tell Doc I'm —" but Apache had disappeared. "Gone after them," Matthew muttered.

"Not alone!" Jim cried. "They're seven to one!"

"Naw, the rest of the posse's followed them." Matthew stayed with Jim while Doc removed a bullet, poured whiskey in the wound until Jim thought he'd shriek, and bandaged it tightly.

"Don't s'pose there's any use tellin' you to take it easy," Doc said sourly, and Jim laughed. "What good's a brand-new sheriff who lets his posse go after a gang of outlaws without him?" He swung his feet to the floor, clutched his spinning head with his right arm, and fell back.

"Told you so." Doc seemed to get a grim satisfaction from his awkwardness and shoved him back down on the table. A little later he helped Jim to a narrow cot but wouldn't let him get up. "What's left of tonight will at least give you a head start on healin'," he said. But neither Matthew nor Jim got any sleep. Somewhere out in the night men battled not only for life, but for the right to live free of fear. With all their hearts they longed to be there.

A disturbed dawn broke, and Jim could be restrained no longer. He struggled into his boots and with his father made his way outside. The slow steps of tired horses nailed him to the ground. The posse had returned. Haggard faces and a significant shape on one of the horses' backs told the story. Jim searched the group. "Apache?"

Carter, all red gone from his heavy face, stepped forward. "Gone. We caught up with them and were all for hangin' them. Apache said no. He said you didn't want killin'. We covered him, an' he checked the guns to see which had been fired. When he got to Radford, the fool grabbed for his gun and shot Apache." Carter's mouth twisted. "Rest of us were so stupid we couldn't move. Apache jerked Comstock off his horse, fightin' every inch, an' headed for a tree. I flipped my rope over a limb, an' Comstock went loco. Never saw anyone so strong." Carter wiped his sweaty face, and Jim's nerves shrilled. "Turned his own gun on himself."

"But Apache!" Jim cried.

"Said to tell you the debt was paid, whatever that means, an' he reckoned you wouldn't care if he took King. He rode off, saggin' in the saddle, spite of all we could do."

Matthew leaped for Dark Star, patiently standing near. "We'll go after him. Bring him back. He can't die out there alone."

Out there. Jim bit back a sob. Sullen red walls. Parched earth. Barren miles. A waterfall. Desert voices, whispering, echoing with final understanding. "It's what he wants. He'll die alone or maybe heal as I did." Love for the tragic mixture of white and red blood filled his farseeing eyes with sand. "Maybe, someday. . . ." A vision of a plodding figure on a powerful gray horse crossed his vision and disappeared.

Carter and the posse fell back. Matthew didn't speak for a long time. Tragedy hovered too near, too real. When he did, it was gruff. "Can you ride? Mother and Mescal will be waiting."

Jim looked north and east once more. "I can ride." He wet dry lips and called Shalimar. The debt *had* been paid — in full.